A CHILD SHALL LEAD THEM

A CHILD SHALL LEAD THEM

A JOE BURGESS MYSTERY, BOOK 6

KATE FLORA

ePublishingWorks!
love what you read.

Book and cover design by eBook Prep
www.ebookprep.com

June, 2019
ISBN: 978-1-64457-044-9

ePublishing Works!
644 Shrewsbury Commons Ave
Ste 249
Shrewsbury PA 17361
United States of America

www.epublishingworks.com
Phone: 866-846-5123

To all the generous cops who've helped me along this writing journey, with special thanks to:

Chief Carl Johnson (ret.)
Commander Hugh Holton, Chicago PD, deceased
Assistant Chief Joseph K. Loughlin, Portland PD
And
Deputy Chief Brian Cummings, Miramichi Police

PROLOGUE

Veteran police officers often say they've seen everything. It's a reasonable assumption. After the decades on the job Burgess had, the accumulated experience of inhumanity, filth, and horrific crime scenes had dulled his ability to be shocked. He'd seen the disemboweled, the beheaded, the decomposed. He'd dealt with victims where justice had failed, and the memories of those cases never left him. More recently, though, his solitary obsession with victims and crime solving had been derailed by the acquisition of a family. Having people in his life whom he loved and needed to keep safe changed him. They pulled him in a new direction and divided his loyalties between work and home. Still, when faced with the mutilated body of a brutally abused young girl, the pull of work became paramount.

Until he got the phone call that almost stopped his heart.

The two a.m. call from his sister Sandy came during those hours when calls seem most urgent—when people only disturb each other's sleep when the matter can't wait.

Not that he was sleeping. Burgess was up to his ears in the search for the killers of a young girl. He was at their third crime scene in as many days, waiting for an ambulance to arrive, his focus on a missing man, a drugged woman, and a mystery man. But his sister wouldn't call this late at night if it wasn't important. As the roar of an arriving ambulance filled his ears, he reached for the phone, mumbled "Burgess," and Sandy's terror poured into his ear.

"Cherry is missing, Joe. She didn't come home." A gasp for breath, and then she said, "She wanted to help you with your investigation. She said she had an idea about someone who might be involved. I told her to call you and let you follow up. But dammit, Joe! She wants to be a cop like you, and insisted she had to investigate it herself. She wanted to show you how clever she is. And now she hasn't come home. She always obeys her curfew or she calls. But she didn't and she's not answering her phone. It's going straight to voice mail."

Burgess stepped away from the ambulance's engine roar and began the litany of questions that might help locate his missing niece, cursing himself for the foolish enthusiasm he'd displayed when he told Cherry about his work. He should have told her horror stories instead. Now, given what he'd learned about the people he was dealing with, he was really worried that a sweet sixteen-year-old girl he loved might have set herself up to become his next horror story.

ONE

The call from dispatch came in the middle of a Fourth of July picnic. In Burgess's experience, callouts to a crime scene often came when they could cause the most disruption. They were having the picnic in his sister Sandy's big back yard, and the kids—his three, Sandy's two, and Moira's one—were excited at having a big gathering and the prospect of a family softball game after the cookout.

Burgess and Sandy didn't always get along. Despite his role as the big brother who'd kept the family together during their father's descent into alcoholism, as adults they'd drifted apart. She had been scornful of his dedication to his job, accusing him of using it as an excuse to avoid commitment and family. She'd softened since his precipitous acquisition of a family—his partner Chris and three children in only a couple of years. Now his kids were getting to know their cousins, Cherry and Maddie, and, for the next generation at least, things were without stress or acrimony.

His other sister, Moira, was there with her second husband, Patrick, and their twelve year old son Jared. His investigative team, Terry Kyle and Stan Perry, were there with their families. Terry with Michelle and his two daughters, Lexi and Anna, and Stan with his quite pregnant girlfriend Lily. There was betting at the department about whether Stan would marry her before the baby came. So far, even those closest to Stan had no clue, unless his girlfriend's smiling demeanor was a clue. Chris, who was a nurse, and had a low opinion of Stan in the commitment department, thought it was pregnancy hormones. Stan was silent on the subject. Burgess figured discretion was the better part of valor, and Terry, who was under increasing pressure about marriage from Michelle, gave the subject of matrimony a wide berth.

Plunked down in a lawn chair and surveying things with a benign smile was Chris's mother, Dorothy, or Doro, whose presence in their lives gave the kids a loving and doting grandmother. The weather was warm and perfect, though the temperature was forecast to drop later, with clouds and wind coming in. The wind and clouds were going to blow out to sea in time for the evening fireworks.

It was a classic moment of the job jangling its way into his personal life. Burgess, having courteously waited until the kids and the ladies had been served, was just biting into a hot-from-the-grill burger when the phone in his pocket vibrated. He let it go a moment while he savored that first bite. He'd been a detective long enough to know it wasn't going to be good news, and he hated to spoil a perfect July day. He took a second bite, knowing he was going to answer, and Dispatch was going to get an earful of Detective Joe Burgess chewing. Then he drew out the phone like a reluctant gunslinger, and mumbled "Burgess."

The calm, efficient voice on the other end said, "Jogger reported a body on the Stroudwater Trail. Patrol is on scene." As she reeled off directions that he really didn't need, he was already picturing the spot, a parking lot and running trail along the Stroudwater River, out past the airport.

"Has Lt. Melia been notified?" Melia was his boss, the head of Portland's CID.

"He's not answering. We've left messages for him."

"Kyle and Perry are with me. We'll respond," he said, and shoved the offending device that had ruined so many of his days back into his pocket. Knowing the body would wait another thirty seconds, he took one more bite

Across the yard, Chris had interrupted her conversation with Michelle and was watching him. He saw her face fall as he headed toward Kyle. She had been looking forward to a family day. Now this one, like so many others they planned, was going to be a Chris and the kids day instead. He hated to do this to her. True, she'd known about the demands of his job when they met, and she was the one who wanted kids, but despite her best efforts, she didn't always roll smoothly with the punches his life served up. In fairness, neither did he. Transitioning from someone answerable only to himself to someone who answered to four other people was an ongoing challenge.

Kyle was watching his daughter Lexi teach Neddy, Jared, and her younger sister, Anna, some soccer moves, while the teenagers, Burgess's son Dylan and daughter Nina were hanging out in a corner with Cherry, the three of them laughing about something. He loved watching Nina and Neddy, the foster children they were adopting, recovering from a life that had dished up unimaginable trauma, and his son Dylan turning into a protective big brother, just like he had been.

Kyle shifted his gaze as Burgess approached, and knew without a word what was happening. "Damn, Joe. Not today," he said. "We need this break. You know we do."

"I can call in the B team, Terry, if you want to stay."

Kyle's fierce gaze turned toward him, blue eyes lasering Burgess's face, looking for information. "Like you'd ever do that. Unless this is one the B team can't screw up?"

In reality, there was no B team, just one of the three of them and some other detectives from personal crimes that Burgess had trained enough to trust them to help investigate a homicide. But Kyle knew, just as Burgess did, that if it was a tricky scene or a case that was going to draw the press and the public's gaze, their bosses would want the three musketeers to handle it. Assuming they were upright and taking nourishment.

"Jogger found a body out on the Stroudwater trail," he said. "No details, but dispatch said it was a bad one. So I'm thinking this is one for the A team."

"I'll tell Michelle. She's going to be pissed. She's been looking forward to this. She made a point of saying she didn't want to be doing this picnic by herself."

He gazed heavenward. "Things are getting tense in the Kyle household. It's three women against one now. The girls are lobbying for me to marry Michelle. Don't know how much longer I can hold out."

"So don't hold out," Burgess said. "She's great. You love her. You guys are happy."

"She wants a baby," Kyle said.

"I've got three kids," Burgess said. "It's not so bad."

"Except you missed the sleepless nights, diapers, and potty training."

It hadn't been a choice. Burgess didn't even know he had a son until the boy was fifteen. "I'm just one clever guy," Burgess said. "You talk to Michelle. I'll grab Stan."

He grabbed Stan, got another version of "what the hell!" and went to update Chris and the kids. By the time he'd done that, apologized to Sandy, and said a quick goodbye to Moira, Kyle and Perry were ready to roll. Sandy, after complaining about what she was going to do with so much left-over food, said she'd give Chris and the kids a ride home, so they took his truck.

"Maybe they can bring some food home with them," he suggested. "I'm so frustrated to be missing all this."

"And there's strawberry shortcake," Sandy said.

"Don't rub it in."

That made Sandy grin, and for a second, they were kids again, teasing each other like siblings do.

When they were belted and rolling, he shared the other details he'd gotten from Dispatch. "Looks like a young woman. ID's going to be tough, though. She's got no head and no hands."

TWO

The two patrol officers protecting the scene had their hands full with complaining runners and walkers venting their displeasure at being unable to use their favorite trail. That was the nature of the business. Cops were the bad guys, and patrol took a lot of the heat from a public unwilling to have their lives disrupted in any way just because some poor unfortunate had been murdered.

En route, Burgess had made the phone calls necessary to bring their crime scene techs and the Medical Examiner to the site. Since the trail ran along a river and through some dense woods, he grabbed insect repellent along with the rest of his crime scene gear. They took a moment to spray themselves before heading down the trail. He was glad he hadn't worn shorts to the cookout, as Stan had. He and Kyle both wore jeans and polo shirts.

Stan wore a tee shirt for a music group Burgess had never heard of, and those shiny, baggy athletic shorts all the kids wore. He studied his costume ruefully, shook his head, and said, "At least it's not as bad as at the Timmy Watts scene." After dressing while still half asleep, Perry had appeared at that scene on a blistering hot summer day wearing a tee-shirt that read: **Homicide - Our day begins when your day ends**. Burgess had loaned him a jacket and he'd nearly died of heat, but it was better than letting the press photograph him in that shirt at the scene of a small boy's murder.

Before they started down the trail, Burgess spoke to the officer controlling the scene. "The guy who found the body. Where's he?"

The officer pointed to a man in running shorts about fifty yards away, pacing nervously back and forth at the far end of the parking lot.

"Can you call someone to take him downtown? I don't want him talking to anyone before we interview him, especially not the press, and they are bound to be showing up soon."

"I'm on it, sir."

"Who's at the scene?"

"Aucoin and Simmons, sir."

"Any joggers come through since you set up and started taking names?"

"Just one, sir." He pointed to a name on the sheet.

Burgess copied the information. One of them would need to talk to the man later. He might have seen someone on the trail or in the lot before he started his run. Might even be the perpetrator. Burgess had no idea yet how big a net he'd have to spread.

As they headed down the trail, he was already running questions in his head. How long had the body been here? Why here? Why choose this spot, which was remote for the city of Portland, but used by enough joggers so the body was likely to be found quickly. Was this what the killer wanted? Was the body displayed for the shock value? For some message it might send? When would this place be deserted enough for someone to dispose of a body unobserved? He figured Perry and Kyle were running similar questions. Maybe what they found at the scene would answer some of them.

Because of what Dispatch had said, he expected to find the body right on the trail. Instead, after walking about five minutes, he came to crime scene tape stretched across the trail, but no sign of officers or a body. They ducked under the tape, then stood there, taking their bearings, looking for tracks or something that would tell them where the body actually was. Rather than waste time, he yelled, "Aucoin!"

A voice came from the woods to his left. "Over here, Sergeant. Follow that line of tape I've laid down."

Burgess looked down. About five feet to his left, a stripe of muddy yellow crime scene tape lay on the ground, snaking between two trees and disappearing into the brush. *Smart,* he thought. One essential element of preserving crime scenes was identifying a single route in and out for everyone to use. In thick woods like these, and with a scene some distance off the trail, that was harder. He'd ask, but he assumed Aucoin had chosen this route to protect what might have been the one the killer used. He took an almost paternal pride in watching Remy Aucoin become a good police officer.

They followed Aucoin's yellow tape for fifty feet or so, and came to another circle of crime scene tape. Aucoin and Simmons were waiting for them at the edge of it.

"She's over here," Aucoin said. "I probably don't need to say this, but brace yourselves. This is pretty ugly."

Before they moved, Burgess said, "How the heck did that jogger find her? She's not visible from the road."

"Two things," Aucoin said. "He had a dog with him. And says he stepped off the trail to take a leak."

"I didn't see a dog," Kyle said.

"Guy had his wife come and pick it up."

"Did it disturb anything?"

"Can't say. Nothing seemed disturbed, but you'll have to ask him. He'd already gone out to the trail and made some phone calls by the time I got here. I guess he didn't call us until he was back out to the parking lot."

"That a guess or something he told you?" Kyle asked.

"What he said."

Burgess studied Aucoin. Not because he didn't believe what the young officer was saying. He just wanted to see how Aucoin was. Aucoin had been one of the Portland officers shot by an angry sniper who had lured three officers into a trap at an abandoned warehouse. He'd only recently come back to work. The kid looked good, though a little pale and thin.

Aucoin caught the scrutiny. "I'm doing great, Sergeant," he said. "Getting married soon. I hope you all will come."

"I hope so, too, Remy," he said. "Unless I'm called out like this. We were all at a picnic."

"Well, this is going to be no picnic."

Abruptly, Aucoin turned and walked away. The three of them followed while Officer Simmons, a rookie who was looking slightly green, stayed back by the tape, ready to repel anyone who found their way past the officers out in the parking lot.

The three of them studied the naked white body laid out on last year's damp brown leaves. The jagged red tangle of skin, veins, tendons and bone where her neck ended, the abrupt ends of both arms where her hands should have been. It was ugly and disturbing. It was also disturbing—and telling—that no effort had been made to cover the body. It had been arranged there, legs spread, the girl's private parts waxed free of any signs of a mature woman's body hair. One arm was heavily decorated with a sleeve of elaborate body art.

She was a small girl, thin arms and legs, but with full breasts. Where her skin was visible, on her stomach and legs, and on the untattooed arm, there were numerous large, dark bruises.

"She was just like this when you found her?" Kyle asked.

The flash of anger Burgess saw on Kyle's face wasn't about Aucoin. He was thinking of Lexi just as Burgess was thinking of Nina. Of young girls and how vulnerable they could be. How much evil there was in the world. Cops absolutely believed in evil.

"Well, you can be sure I didn't have to disturb this body checking for signs of life," Aucoin said gruffly.

"It's okay, Remy," Burgess said. "It's all right to be disturbed. We're not supposed to get used to scenes like this."

He looked at Kyle and Perry, who had moved to his right and his left and were making their own assessments of what they were seeing.

"Somebody beat the hell out of her," Perry said. "ME will have to tell us whether the amputations are premortem…" He hesitated. "The hands, I mean. Obviously. She wasn't killed here." He looked around at the trees, the tangle of vegetation, and back toward the now invisible trail. "This is one sick fuck, Joe. Ballsy, too. Takes something to kill a girl, chop off her hands and head and then carry her from the parking lot down the trail and out into the woods. Too many chances to be seen. Unless he did it at night?"

He continued, wondering aloud. "Why put her here, far from the trail, then display her like this? And unless he wrapped her in something to transport her, guy must have gotten covered with blood. Maybe even if he did. It's awkward, transporting a body"

"So you think it was a guy?" Burgess said.

"Can you see a woman doing this?"

Burgess agreed, but said, "I've been surprised before."

"Joe Burgess always says 'Don't let your speculations get ahead of the evidence,'" Kyle intoned. "And Burgess is always right."

"Could be a first time," Perry said. He swung toward Burgess. "It could."

Despite the time they'd worked together, there was often still something of the defiant child about Stan Perry, though he had a great facility for pulling rabbits out of hats just as Burgess was getting ready to kick him off the team. So Burgess let it go. Perry had been seriously stressed about Lily's pregnancy, and that had been affecting his mood, but it was time for him snap out of it and settle back down. Burgess was just about out of forgiveness.

"Right now, we don't know a damned thing, except this poor girl has been butchered," Burgess said. "This is only where it begins."

"Hello? Is there anybody out there?"

Burgess recognized the voice of their chief evidence tech, Wink Devlin. "We're over here, Wink. Follow Remy's yellow line."

There were muffled voices and then Wink and Dani Letorneau, Wink's right hand woman, appeared.

"We followed the yellow road," Wink said, "but I am quite sure this isn't Oz. Where is our client?"

Burgess and his team stepped aside so they could see the body.

Their reactions were immediate, and different. Wink said, "Oh, shit!" and Dani said, "Oh the poor girl."

"I was at a family baby shower," Wink said. "Mrs. Wink wasn't pleased when I got the call, but I'd had enough of silly games and women squealing with delight. I got to miss decorating a onesie."

"I had a hot date," Dani said. "Luckily, he's a cop, so he understood." She gave them all a cryptic smile, leaving them to speculate about who the lucky guy was.

Without further comment, Wink and Dani went to work, taking pictures and measurements and all the details that went into making a thorough record of the crime scene.

THREE

The day of the Fourth had dawned soft and sunny, perfect for enticing people out for ball games and outings and family picnics. Now, as the afternoon wore on, the morning's lovely blue sky had turned a clotted gray, the thickening layers of clouds beginning to look like a dirty down comforter. A wind had come up and it carried the suggestion of rain to come. While Wink and Dani worked, Burgess, Kyle, and Perry spread out and began to search the crime scene. There would be more searching after the body was removed, but for now, they searched the surroundings as they waited for Dr. Lee, the medical examiner, to arrive.

The department's call to the ME's office had probably found Lee on the golf course. It was where he could usually be found on a lovely day. There was a Mrs. Lee, and some little Lees as well, but the ME rarely mentioned them, and Burgess didn't know what they did while the Doc decompressed from his day job by hitting a small white ball around.

They were also waiting for Vince Melia. He'd been called, but Burgess didn't know whether Melia had been reached or whether he was out of touch. Melia was still recovering from a gunshot wound that had nearly taken his life. He was supposed to be driving a desk and avoiding crime scenes, but he wouldn't miss a bad one like this. Still, the clock was ticking. There was no sign of him. And Burgess and his team weren't waiting. The last thing any of them wanted was to lose some potentially useful piece of evidence because they stood around and waited for the rain to start.

He also realized it was probably a waste of manpower for all three of them to hang around here. One of them, probably Kyle, should go back to headquarters and interview the jogger who'd found the body. Kyle was an intense and skilled interviewer. Something about those cold blue eyes made bad guys want to give it up. Burgess was very curious about how he'd describe finding the body. No one needed to go this far off the path to take a leak. He wanted to know whether it had been the dog and not the man who'd found it, and what kind of dog it was. Was it looking for food or did the dog have some search and rescue expertise?

He smiled at the thought of sending Kyle back to police headquarters at 109 Middle Street, known to all of them simply as 109, to interview a dog. Even though he was the sergeant and they theoretically worked for him, that would not go over well.

He'd given Stan Perry the trail of broken and disturbed branches that was likely the killer's mode of entry when bringing in the body. It was worn enough that he suspected this was not the first time it had been used. Perry was still a kid, with sharp young eyes and endless energy, while Burgess was a slow moving old dinosaur, and Kyle wasn't so far behind him. It was tiring work, demanding painstaking concentration and close attention, and he'd sent Remy to ask Simmons to get them some bottled water. Burgess was a big guy. He'd skipped breakfast in anticipation of the picnic, and three bites of a burger and a forkful of Chris's delicious potato salad weren't enough. He wished he could send for food, but seasoned though they were, none of them could eat at a scene like this. Even if they could, the optics of a cop carrying takeout to a crime scene would be terrible. He knew it was the one photo that would make the front page.

He had cleared his area, then searched beyond the body, thinking the killer might have overconfidently discarded something in that direction, assuming the cops would stop at the body. So far, he'd found nothing, not even the usual litter of cans, bottles, tissues, and food wrappers that followed humans wherever they went. Now he was waiting for Dr. Lee and using these few quiet moments to study the scene. The vegetation, the size of clearing, the placement of the body. Anything could be information about the perpetrator's experience, mindset, attitude.

He'd long believed that if he stayed still and listened, crime scenes would tell him things. This place was just beginning to speak. It told him that this wasn't the first time the killer had been off the trail in these woods. It was too obscure a spot, and too far down the trail. He didn't yet know why. He was wondering what a search dog might tell them, what it would scent that they wouldn't see. The scene was also telling him that the killer was a cold, manipulative bastard. He didn't yet know whether the display was meant to manipulate them, or someone else. Perhaps another young girl. The perpetrator's colleague. Or to shock someone into keeping quiet.

As he stood waiting, he began the list of questions to be asked once they were done here. The investigative avenues they would pursue and what priority they'd be given.

Perry and Kyle were still snuffling through the bushes. He could hear the occasional snort, or exclamation, but so far, neither man had summoned Wink or Dani to record any evidence. Burgess was surprised. Criminals almost always left something behind, even the most devious and careful ones. The removal of identifying body parts and the time taken to display the body suggested confidence and preparation, but still, he expected something. Organized killers like this were often overconfident. There was something to be found here. He was sure of it. If they didn't find it today, he'd come back.

He'd have to come back anyway, once the body had gone to the Medical Examiner's facility. It was something he always did—taking a photo of the crime scene without the body in it. That empty space represented the problem he needed to solve. It was his job to fill it with answers.

They were all thoroughly frustrated, worn out, and unpleasantly cooled by the chill in the rising wind, when there was the rustling of feet and Simmons appeared, leading Dr. Lee.

Dr. Lee was sharp as a tack, Asian, and moved faster than other humans. His crisp, efficient method of working was so different from the ME Burgess had worked with for years, a man who approached the dead with deep reverence, that it had taken Burgess a while to develop a relationship with Lee. The two of them still did a cautious dance around one another. But Lee often spotted things another ME might miss, and those findings had proved invaluable in sending overconfident killers to prison.

"I was golfing," Lee announced. "First a family picnic with Mrs. Lee and three small Lee children. Very pleasant if you like sandwiches and don't mind bugs. Only then could I escape to the golf course." He eyed Burgess. "I know you don't 'get' golf, Detective, but I find it a very soothing activity. Then I get a call that there's a body, and my assistant is on a boat somewhere on Moosehead Lake."

He produced one of his rare smiles. "I did those last four holes at lightning speed. It was almost amusing to ask other golfers to let me play through because I had a murder victim waiting. They seemed not to know what to make of it."

He stared at Burgess uncertainly. "I do have a murder victim waiting, right?"

"Well, Dr. Lee," Burgess said. "She certainly didn't do this to herself."

Realizing his bulk was keeping the smaller man from seeing the victim, he stepped aside to let the ME get a look at the body. "She's all yours."

Dr. Lee stared silently at the body, seeing, Burgess knew, beyond the breasts and the tattoos. Finally, he spoke. "Don't let things fool you, Detective. Those breasts are fake. They're implants. See how they stay upright and perky, even though she's lying on her back? I'll know more when I have her on the table, but I can tell you this—she's hardly more than a child. A child someone has used as a sex toy or has pimped out. Someone victimized in life and then victimized again in death."

The smiling golfer was gone, and the man Burgess knew was back. A man who, like himself, was especially committed to bringing to justice people who hurt children.

Burgess flashed on Nina again. And on his niece, Cherry, with a woman's curvy body and an innocent, almost childlike world view. Cherry, who wanted to work for the FBI. Both were hardly more than children, with their mature appearances thrusting them into a world of men's advances, catcalls, and risks that they didn't deserve.

This wasn't the time to be thinking about other kids. He brushed his thoughts away like annoying cobwebs and followed Lee closer to the body.

As he watched Lee kneel to examine the girl, Stan Perry's muffled yell came from ground level behind some bushes. "I've got something!"

Watching Dani Letorneau headed off to document Perry's find, Burgess almost missed hearing Lee say, "Something else I can tell you. This was not done by a professional. It's a total hack job. Literally. See how the skin is shredded? Looks like the killer used a saw."

FOUR

Total hack job didn't sound like something Dr. Lee would say, but that's what Burgess heard. Then Dr. Lee repeated his earlier statement. "I'll know more when I get her on the table."

"What's your schedule like?" Burgess asked, knowing he would have to be at the autopsy, and not wanting to be there. He figured he might as well get it settled now, before he went back to 109 and immersed himself in the details of the investigation.

"Pretty open. Barring catastrophes overnight. How does ten a.m. sound?"

It sounded too early and too soon, but experience had taught him that if he questioned the good doc, resentment might cause the autopsy to be scheduled at seven a.m. or not for days, and he needed the information they'd learn there. "Sounds fine," he said—as if there was anything fine about this situation.

He might hope they'd get back to 109 and learn that a frantic parent had filed a missing person report, giving them the girl's name and people to interview about her. Hope springs eternal in a homicide detective's heart, but he already knew that wasn't going to happen. The kind of parents who'd file a missing person report weren't the kind to allow a child this young to get all those tattoos or breast implants. More likely, no one would claim her and they'd have to knock on doors, scour DHS and school records, and see how they could find a way into Portland's dark underground of those who trafficked young girls and boys.

The killer had been clever. He'd taken away three primary sources of identification: fingerprints, facial recognition, and the possibility of leads from names or labels in the clothes. What he hadn't taken, and what might give them a good chance for an ID, if Dr. Lee was right, was the implants in her breasts. Implants had numbers, and those numbers led to records. Even if those records were falsified as to the identity of the patient, with luck, and good old detective work, they could lead to the surgeon who'd done the implants. Even a reluctant surgeon might have some useful information, and Burgess and a search warrant could be very persuasive.

They also had that tattoo sleeve. It was still a work-in-progress, with much of the picture yet to be filled in. Much like this case. If the tats were local, which seemed likely, they might find the artist, which might also lead to further information, like a name or description of the girl, whether she'd come alone, and whether she, or someone else, had paid for the work. That would be a job for Super Stan, who had a few tats of his own.

"Any idea how long she's been dead?" Burgess asked. He knew Dr. Lee wasn't one of those TV cowboys who gave exact times or very narrow windows. He thought this body was very fresh, and was curious about what the ME would say.

"It's July," Dr. Lee said, "and despite this afternoon's cooler air, it's been hot. If she'd been here long, decomp would be rapid, and it's barely begun." He lifted an arm, then slowly lowered it. "Rigor is dissipating. So a twenty-four to thirty-six hour window, perhaps. And she hasn't been here long, or she'd be crawling with maggots and flies."

Burgess nodded. Made a note. Everything was ballpark, but it gave them something to work with. Unless she'd been in someone's freezer. He wondered what the killer had done with the head and hands. Put them in a dumpster somewhere? Buried them in the garden or in a compost pile? Or was there another clearing somewhere along this trail, and the rest of the body was there?

"She can go now," Dr. Lee said.

For a moment, lost in speculation and list-making, Burgess didn't understand what the ME meant. How could she leave without her head and hands? He rubbed his forehead, trying to clear the fog, then told Aucoin to go out to the end of the trail and tell the Medical Examiner's van to drive down the trail so they could load the body away from the prying eyes of what was likely a pretty big crowd in the parking lot by now.

The three of them watched her body zipped in a body bag, then carried down the trail to the van. Then, like three scavengers, they knelt beside the patch of earth where she had lain, and carefully scrutinized the dirt for anything that might have been left behind.

Nothing could be discounted at this point. They collected a balled up tissue, a nondescript brown button, the bottle cap from an obscure brand of beer, and several used condoms. All carefully photographed in place, then put in evidence envelopes and labeled.

"What did you find over there, Stan?" Kyle asked.

"It's probably nothing. A pink barrette. Well, a broken pink barrette. But since our girl has no head, and therefore no hair, it's not likely to be hers."

"This is so revolting," Kyle said. He looked at Burgess. "What now?"

They'd been at this for hours, and it was starting to get dark. "Back to 109 to start developing a strategy, and to interview the man who found the body, then home to sleep."

"Wink, Dani, let's call it a day," Burgess said.

They packed up their stuff, and were heading back toward the trail, when Dani said, "Wait."

Everyone stopped, frozen in place. She bent down, crouching low, staring at something. "Take a look at this, Wink," she said. "This is a really unusual footprint."

It was an unusual footprint. Definitely not from any of their shoes, as the sole was almost entirely smooth, like an ancient, well-worn pair of sneakers, except for a strange round spot on the heel.

"Worn out old sneakers with a thumb tack stuck to the sole," Burgess said.

Perry touched his forehead. "The great Carnac has spoken."

"I don't care who has spoken, long as we catch the fucker who did this," Kyle said.

Normally, Kyle didn't swear, but kids brutalized and discarded like trash always pushed his buttons. Burgess was the same. He had sworn he'd never work another kid, and yet they kept showing up, needing him to do something. It wasn't easy to avoid cases where children were the victims. The problem was, cops usually didn't know what they had until they answered the call and were at the scene. Then it was too late to say no.

Vince Melia never appeared.

FIVE

Ignoring the news trucks and the throng of reporters and cameramen who swarmed them as they came out of the woods, the three musketeers headed for Burgess's truck and climbed in. They watched Aucoin and Simmons clear a path for Wink and Dani and the crime scene van, then followed the lumbering van out of the lot and onto the road.

"I know it's unseemly," Kyle said, "but can we grab some sandwiches on the way in?"

It amused Burgess that Kyle really did use words like "unseemly." He also knew that if he didn't keep Kyle fed, his friend might fall by the wayside before the investigation was even underway. Kyle was whippet thin and ran at such high revs he burned through food before others had even finished eating. Michelle joked that her life's work had become feeding Kyle, but it wasn't entirely a joke.

"Melina's meatloaf okay?"

There was a murmur of agreement. Then Perry said, "If they're open on a holiday."

Sometimes having Stan Perry around was like having a teenager in the house.

"We can hope," Burgess said.

Melina and her husband ran a deli where the food was great, and she loved to feed cops, calling them "her boys." If they were lucky, she'd also have fresh baked chocolate chip cookies.

They were in luck. The deli was open. Burgess wondered if she and her husband ever took any time off. He'd never seen them anything but cheerful, though. When he'd asked, Melina insisted that they loved the work, loved feeding people, and couldn't complain. He wished he could bottle that attitude and hand the bottles to some of the more disagreeable people he worked with, in and out of 109.

Melina smiled when they came through the door. "Joseph!" she said, nodding at the others. "I hope you all are very hungry, because I have had this meatloaf just sitting here, waiting for the right person to come along."

"I hope we're the right people," Kyle said. "We're starving and there's nothing in Portland better than your meatloaf."

She made a swatting gesture, but her smile grew.

Perry, who had hung back, now stepped forward and held up his hands in a pleading gesture. "Melina, do you have cookies for some cold, hungry cops?"

She looked at Joe. "Has this boy been good? Should we give him cookies?"

Kyle said, "You should give me and Joe cookies and Stan a lump of coal."

The cheerful woman studied Perry. "No, Terry, I think you are being unkind. Anyway, I am saving the coal for Christmas, and you will all get it if you are not nice to each other."

"Yes, ma'am," Kyle said. "You can keep the coal. We will be nice."

"So, it is a holiday today, yes? Why are you not with your families? Has some poor soul been killed?"

As she spoke, her hands were moving, cutting and slicing and spreading, and a pile of sandwiches was growing.

She knew them so well, Burgess thought. "Yes, Melina. A poor little girl."

"This is horrible," she said, "but you will find out who did it, won't you?"

"We will try," Kyle said. "We always try."

"I am sad about the girl," she said. "I think you may need extra cookies today."

Which they did.

They paid for their sandwiches, despite Melina's protests that they were a gift, and headed back to 109. Burgess's phone rang as they were turning on Franklin. He expected Vince Melia, looking for an update, or, worse, Captain Cote, who always wanted an update, but it was Chris.

When he answered, she said, "I don't care who has been killed or how critical the first twenty-four hours are. You promised to take the kids to fireworks and you are going to keep that promise."

"Yes, ma'am," he said.

"Don't you 'yes, ma'am' me," she said. "Just show up."

He suppressed a sigh. "What time to they start?

"Be home by eight-thirty," she said. "Or else."

He couldn't resist. "Or else what?"

"You know what else."

"Does it involve the presence or absence of a silky blue nightgown?"

"Joe Burgess, are you alone?"

"Nope."

"I will see you later." Chris hung up on him.

"Uh oh," Perry said. "She's going to cut you off."

"She won't," Burgess said. "Because I am going to be home by eight-thirty to take the kids to fireworks."

"Me, too," Kyle said. "Guess you'll have to solve this one by yourself, Stan."

They had two hours before they had to show up for family obligations, and they all knew that Burgess and Kyle would be back afterwards. As Chris had pointed out, the first twenty-four hours were critical.

Vince Melia was waiting for them at 109, looking dapper as always, and abashed that he had just learned about the crime. "We all went sailing," he said. "It was great. The boys loved it. Gina got seasick. And there was no cell phone service."

He looked at his shoes, then back at them. "It was deliberate. We needed a nice, normal family day. And it was great."

"We were at a picnic at my sister's," Burgess said. "Where unfortunately there *was* cell phone service. Now we've got at least three women and a lot of children who are mad at us."

"The policeman's lot is not a happy one," Melia said. "Speaking of not happy. One of you better get in there and interview the man who found that body. He is seriously unhappy with us for keeping him waiting all this time."

"Kyle, he's yours," Burgess said. "Stan, you watch, okay?"

As the two of them turned to go, he said, "Wait," and held out the bag of sandwiches. "Terry, eat something first. He's waited this long, he can wait another five minutes. Stan can eat while he monitors the interview."

Melia was looking longingly at the bag. "From Melina's?"

"Of course," Burgess said.

"I don't suppose you have…"

"Of course," he said again. "Serve and protect. That's what we do."

He handed Melia a sandwich.

Kyle had seated himself at the nearest desk and was devouring his sandwich like a hungry wolf. Perry grabbed one for himself and handed another to Burgess. Then they went off to get the story from the man who'd found the body, and Burgess went into Melia's office to update him on the case. He didn't like to delegate. He wanted to be the one in that room watching the man's reactions and listening to his voice. But Kyle was good, Perry would spot anything that needed to be followed up, and Melia needed to be brought into the loop.

Melia was right. A policeman's lot was often not a happy one. There was nothing pleasant about describing what they'd found out in those woods.

They both ate as he told the story. He'd barely started describing the scene—the distance from the parking lot and the distance from the trail—when Perry appeared in the doorway. "Joe, you've got come see this."

He and Melia followed Perry into the room where he was watching the interview on a monitor.

Detectives get used to working with people who are offended by being asked to cooperate in criminal investigations, even when they are critical witnesses. The overreaching sense of entitlement many people carried around these days made their jobs very difficult. Yes, the man Kyle was interviewing had had a terrible experience, finding that body and then being forced to cool his heels in a police department interview room for several hours. Still, Kyle would have apologized to him and explained the reasons for the delay. He would have acknowledged the traumatic nature of the experience. He would have emphasized the critical importance of his questions and the man's information. He would have made the man understand that he was an important witness and his information was essential to the investigation.

None of that seemed to have worked. What they were seeing on the monitor was a large, red-faced adult male behaving like a toddler having a meltdown. He was storming around the room, kicking the walls and furniture, and demanding to have his phone back and to be allowed to leave. Despite the tee shirt, running shorts, and pristine white running shoes, he didn't look much like a runner. Maybe an athlete once, he now had the look of strength gone to seed. He didn't look like he spent much time outside, either, despite owning a dog that needed to be walked. One thing

Burgess knew right away—those shoes were too new to have made Dani's print.

"It's the goddamned phone," Burgess said. "Probably wanted to call up all his friends and spew about his terrible adventure and we didn't let him do that. Kyle did explain why we didn't want him discussing this with anyone until we'd had a chance to talk with him, didn't he?"

"Of course," Perry said.

This was Kyle. Of course he had. Burgess should have sent him back hours ago to do this interview. Then maybe this mess could have been avoided.

In the midst of this over-the-top adult tantrum, Kyle sat still as a sphinx, watching the man like he might have watched a cat chasing a catnip mouse. After the man had raged a few more minutes, Kyle said, "Are you done yet, or do you need a few more minutes?"

"I want my phone!" the man yelled. "I want my phone."

"You'll get it," Kyle said soothingly, "Just as soon as we finish this interview."

"I want it now!"

"We need to finish this interview first. It shouldn't take long," Kyle said, pushing back his chair. "Why don't I give you a few minutes to compose yourself."

He stood and headed for the door.

The man threw himself before the door, blocking Kyle's way. "You have no right…"

"Sit down, Mr. McCann," Kyle said in a voice that made it clear it was not a request. "Sit down now."

The time for politeness and consideration was over. "You saw that poor girl out there in the woods. Our job is to find the person who did that horrific thing. At this point, every bit of information is critical. You found that body. Now we need to know everything you saw, everyone you saw, everything you did, and everything your dog did. That victim doesn't need, and we don't need, your tantrums and acting out. We need your cooperation. When we are done, you'll get your phone back and someone will drive you back to pick up your car. The longer you rant and rave and refuse to cooperate, the longer this will take."

McCann folded his arms and stared stubbornly at the wall.

Kyle made a show of looking at this watch. "I have an appointment at eight that will take a few hours. It would be nice if we could be done here before that. Otherwise, you'll have to wait a little longer. That would be unfortunate for both of us. But I have demands on my time. Perhaps you do, too. So…"

The man threw himself sullenly into a seat, while Kyle remained standing, towering over him like a hungry raptor eyeing a tasty morsel. "Shall we get started?"

McCann muttered a grudging, "Okay."

Kyle looked at the camera and rolled his eyes, then started asking questions.

McCann's belligerence had set off alarm bells. Maybe he was just an asshole, one of those people who believed refusing to cooperate with the police was their job. But maybe he was somehow involved and had something to hide. It was unusual that he hadn't expressed any concern for the girl who was killed, nor any curiosity about her identity or what the police had learned. It didn't take three detectives to do an interview, and Burgess had things to do, but he really needed to hear this.

SIX

"Vince, what do we know about Cary McCann?" he asked.

"Not a lot, Joe. I had Prentiss pull together what he could. It's on your desk. Guy's married, no kids. Works at an insurance company. Has a condo out in North Deering. One speeding ticket. Got caught up once in a prostitution sweep. Judge dismissed it. That's about all."

Prostitution sweep? That was interesting. He'd have to look at the date. Have a chat with Vice. See what other info might be in the file—like whether when he was caught the guy had been with a younger girl. He wanted someone to take a look at McCann's car before they drove the man back to it. They couldn't search it without a warrant, and they didn't have the grounds for that. He just wanted it eyeballed to see what might be in plain sight.

They hadn't released the scene yet, thinking maybe they'd need to go back again in the morning, so he was sure patrol was securing it. Remy was likely long gone. He could ask any officer to take a look at the car, but Remy was already in this and Burgess trusted him. When he called, he got Remy right away.

"Aucoin."

"It's Burgess. Any chance you're still at the scene?"

"No sir. Sorry. I'm on my way back to 109. What can I do for you?"

Because Burgess didn't call to chat, or check in, Remy knew that when he called it was because he needed something and could be pretty fierce about what he wanted. Behavior that had gotten Burgess labeled as the meanest cop in Portland. It was an old label. By now, he was sure, another stickler for the rules had taken his place. But his reputation persisted.

"I was hoping you could take a look at McCann's vehicle. He's the guy who found the body."

"I'm only five minutes away, sir. I'll just turn around. Anything particular you wanted me to look for?"

If he'd been there, this would have been a teaching moment. But time was short. Remy would be tired and even if he might want to act tough, he was still getting back on his feet after being shot. Feet he'd now been on for hours. "Just what's in plain sight. Anything you notice about the inside—spare clothes, shoes, just note whatever you see. And check the area around the car."

"I got you," Aucoin said, and Burgess was pretty sure he did.

The many other people who'd been in the lot had probably wiped out any footprints that might have been there. But Aucoin had been at the scene when Dani found that footprint. It was distinctive enough for Aucoin to know what to look for.

He left that in Aucoin's capable hands and shifted his attention back to the monitor. Kyle was leading McCann through his timeline, and McCann was as vague as it was possible to be. He wasn't sure when he'd arrived at the lot. He wasn't actually a jogger, though he was planning to change that, thus the new shoes. He was really out there to take his dog for a long walk. It was a high energy animal and needed a lot of exercise.

Stan Perry, who couldn't stay still for long, and who liked to be doing something, said, "Joe, if you've got this, I think I'll check with missing persons, see if the girl's been reported, then get on to Vice and get them working on what they might have for us."

Burgess nodded. Stan left, and he pulled his attention back to the monitor.

Kyle picked up that thread and went with it. What kind of a dog was it? A mostly lab mix. How long had they had the animal? A year. Where had they gotten it? At a shelter. His wife had wanted a dog, something to make her feel safer when he traveled for work. To the best of his knowledge, had the dog had any search and rescue training? None that he knew of. All he knew was it was very stubborn about following its nose, practically pulling him off his feet when it wanted to follow a scent. Was that what had happened this morning?

McCann went silent.

"Let's back up," Kyle said. "Take me through things, step by step, after you arrived at the parking lot."

"I parked the car, got Fideau out…"

"F. I. D. O.?" Kyle asked.

"No. It's Fideau, like French or something. Pretty dumb, you ask me, but that's what he was called by his prior owner. He came with the name and Annie, my wife, didn't want to change it. She figured it was bad enough that he'd ended up in a shelter."

"Ok, let's move on. You got your dog out of the car and then?"

"Then we started down the path."

"Do you and Fideau often walk the Stroudwater trail?"

"Not often. We usually stay closer to home."

"You picked this place today because?"

"Because I picked it. What difference does it make? I wanted to take the dog for a walk and this is where I decided to walk."

Burgess looked at Vince and quirked an eyebrow.

"Was Fideau on a leash?"

"You're investigating a murder and you care whether my dog was on a leash?"

"We try to be meticulous about details," Kyle said.

Burgess was amazed he could keep a straight face.

"He wasn't on leash."

"Let's back up a sec," Kyle said. "When you arrived at the parking lot, did you notice other cars there?"

"Not really."

"See any other people heading for the trail?"

"Nope."

"What about people on the trail? Did you meet anyone on the trail?"

"Nope." McCann seemed pleased with himself for his noncooperation.

"How far along the trail were you when you stepped off to relieve yourself?"

Instead of answering, McCann got belligerent. "When a man's gotta go, he's gotta go. You have a problem with that?"

There might be a problem called indecent exposure, but Kyle wouldn't raise that yet. "Just tell me what you did, Mr. McCann."

"I got off the path, pulled out my dick, and relieved myself."

Kyle didn't take the bait. "How far off the path?"

"I don't know. Maybe ten feet."

The body had been about fifty feet off the trail.

"At what point did you find the body?"

"Didn't find it," McCann said. "Wouldn't have. It wasn't anywhere near the trail. That damned dog did. He ran off. Then he started barking. I called him but he didn't come, he's like that when he's caught a scent, so I followed the noise and I found her and he was…uh…licking…"

He put his hand over his face and turned away, still talking, "and I grabbed Fideau by the collar and dragged him back to the parking lot and called you guys."

As Burgess made a note about the licking, McCann shoved back his chair and stood. "And now you guys have had enough of my time and I would like my phone, right now, and a ride back to my car."

The fact that they were police had kept him here, sort of cooperative, this long. But he wasn't under arrest. If he wanted to go, they had to let him go. Given his attitude, it was surprising he hadn't made this demand sooner. Maybe there hadn't been anyone in authority to make the demand to?

There were a lot of things about his story that raised flags. They would definitely be digging in deeper, and likely talking to him again, but for now, Cary McCann was free to go. Burgess called patrol to give him a ride, and Kyle walked him out.

When Kyle came back, he was shaking his head. "This guy is wrong, Joe. I don't know how, but he's got something to do with this."

Burgess agreed.

They made a plan to meet in the morning and lay out the next steps in the investigation. Melia still didn't look great, and Burgess was glad everyone was going home so their boss didn't feel like he had to stay all night, supervising these all-important first hours. Melia probably knew his team would be coming back later, even though they'd agreed on morning, but Burgess thought he'd have sense enough to get some rest so he'd be ready in the morning when all hell broke loose with the press clamoring for details and Captain Cote sniffing around for the juicy details for his press conference. Sadly, this case had just the kind of details Cote loved.

SEVEN

Burgess called Chris to say he was on his way home. She sounded pleased, and surprised, when she said they'd wait for him. She said the kids were very excited. He took the guilt he felt at not spending these hours looking for answers for that poor murdered girl and tucked it away. It was a good trade-off. Spending this time with his family now would ease the guilt as he became immersed over the next few days.

When he pulled up out front, they were waiting in the driveway, Chris smiling, Nina and Dylan bantering, and Neddy cavorting with excitement. As they climbed in, he was overwhelmed by their noise and sheer physical presence. As Kyle noted, he hadn't raised them from babies, and was still getting used to having a family. He drove them to his favorite spot to watch the fireworks, a place known only to a select few, and parked. They all got out and stood in a row, leaning against the SUV, Burgess on one end, Dylan on the other, two big Burgess males bracketing the others. It was eerie how much his son resembled him, so much so he might have been cloned. It gave him shivers to think that if the boy's mother hadn't contacted him when Dylan became a curious—and surly—teenager, he might never have known he had a son. That his doppelgänger would have grown up in an entirely separate world.

His timing was perfect. They'd barely gotten out when the sky exploded with the first burst of color.

Chris moved closer to him and wiggled into her favorite spot, tucked right under his arm. As he watched their delighted faces, illuminated by the fireworks, he felt a stab of sadness that was almost physical, thinking about the happy childhood that girl out in Stroudwater Park had likely missed, and the fact that she would never see another Fourth of July. The rule cops were taught was to keep things at a distance and not get emotionally involved. But if you were human some cases got to you.

Chris, who had an uncanny, and sometimes disturbing, ability to read his mind, said softly, "You're thinking about your victim, aren't you."

Could she really sense him drifting away? He pulled her closer. "I was watching all of your faces and thinking how great it is to have this family." And that was the truth, too. She didn't need to know about the ugliness out there this afternoon. It would hit the news soon enough. There were always leaks, no matter how careful they were. Kyle would have cautioned McCann not to discuss what he'd seen, but Burgess doubted that the man had much concern for anyone but himself. They'd also cautioned the man against sharing any photos he might have taken. As phones were becoming more ubiquitous, and people less inhibited, the photos people shared were increasingly having a negative impact on their investigations.

He pushed the case away and lost himself in the magic of the night.

Afterward, the kids clamored for ice cream, and he saw no reason to say no. They chose the place where he had first spoken with Neddy and Nina, back when they were foster kids out searching for returnable bottles. They had found some clothes in a trash can relevant to an investigation he was working and had the wisdom and decency to call it in. He wondered if they remembered. Whether, as they ordered and then waited at a table for their treats to be delivered, Nina remembered the boy who served them staring at her budding breasts, or Neddy recalled insisting on a double cone and then spilling much of it on himself despite his sister's and Burgess's efforts.

That was the trouble with this city. Or with him. He'd been a cop here for so long there weren't many places he could go that didn't have some memory attached, and few of them were good. The streets were like a Monopoly board of crime, though the game pieces wouldn't be houses and hotels, but knives and guns and drugs and tiny people beating on each other. He pushed those thoughts away and tried to enjoy his chocolate cone. Though he kept himself too buttoned up to enjoy many sweets, he loved an ice cream cone on a warm summer night.

"Did you get any dinner?" Chris asked. "We brought home some food from Sandy's. The kids ate a lot of it, but I saved you a couple burgers and dogs and some potato salad. I think she was glad you came even if you did have to leave early. Family is funny like that. Sometimes it seems like the most important thing is to lay eyes on you. Conversation is barely necessary."

"I'll get it later," he said, deciding not to mention Melina's sandwiches. "I love your potato salad almost as much as I love you."

"Don't get all mushy on me, Burgess," she said, swiping at a drip of ice cream on his chin just like he was one of the kids. Her gestures still surprised him. He wasn't used to being cared for. His job, and his life, had always been about caring for others.

"Are you going back in after the kids go to bed?" she asked, still keeping her voice low so the kids wouldn't hear. They were two teens and a tween, not small children, but they had challenges, especially Nina and Neddy, and she was still working on providing stability in their lives.

"I have to," he said. "I owe it to her."

"Was it very bad?" She leaned in and rested her head on his shoulder.

"Very. I don't want to tell you about it. Not yet."

"That's okay. I'm sure we'll hear about it on the news soon enough."

"You will. They're going to love this one. It has a high gruesome factor."

"Oh no," she said, and he knew she was thinking of his demons. The cases that haunted him. The dreams that wouldn't stop coming. That sometimes pulled him awake from nightmare sleep, yelling and soaked with sweat.

"I don't think this is going to be one of those," he said.

After spending so many years holding back from relationships because of demons, his father's and his own, he kept being surprised by how much of their relationship was unspoken. They read each other in the same compatible way that they slept together. In life, their minds were spooned, in sleep, their bodies.

Burgess sometimes forgot to be grateful for the good things in life, but for this he never forgot. He might be a weary old flatfoot burdened by the most awful cases, but he came home to a good woman and happy chaos.

So far. He knew what could happen to cop marriages.

As they finished their ice cream and headed back to the car, Dylan said, "Dad, can I drive?"

Dylan was taking driver's ed, and was a careful and responsible driver, but the prospect of the day he'd climb into a car alone and drive away terrified Burgess. He'd seen too many bad results of that. But he couldn't keep his son from growing up. He wanted to say "sure" and hand over the keys. If it had been Chris's car, the answer would have been yes. but this vehicle belonged to city. It was probably time to get another car. A nice, safe boring car that Dylan could drive to school.

"Wish I could say yes," he said, "but this is not my car. We should look for a second car pretty soon. You'll want one to drive to school."

"Cool," Dylan said. "Thanks, Dad."

So Burgess dropped them off and headed back toward 109. He realized he'd never heard back from Remy Aucoin, and when he checked his phone, he found he'd turned it off during family time. That was a new one. His phone was so much an essential element of his life he was surprised it hadn't grown attached, like a new body part. He pulled it to his ear and listened to Remy's message.

"Here's the list, Sarge. Pile of rumpled dark clothes on the back seat floor behind the passenger seat, including what might be a raincoat. What looks like a dirty brown blanket with a lot of dog hair covering the seat. A pair of worn old sneakers. A box of plastic trash bags. Umbrella. A Sea Dogs baseball cap. An empty plastic water bottle and a metal dish, maybe to give the dog water. What looks like some magazines under the clothes, but I couldn't see the titles. That's about it."

Burgess wanted those clothes. The blanket. Those sneakers. But he had nothing that would justify a warrant. You can't go after someone just because he's an asshole. Not even if he has a bust for solicitation. He'd have to dig in deeper and see what he could learn about the man. It wasn't uncommon for a perp to call in his own crime, just like it was common for fire setters to call in their fires or offer to help put them out. For now, he had the name of McCann's employer, and the car's make and model, a blue Toyota Prius, and the plate number. He could swing by the employer's lot in the morning and see if those items were still in the car. If not? There was always McCann's trash. Not so easy, maybe, if the condo dwellers dumped all their stuff in a communal dumpster.

He hoped his days as a dumpster diver were over. There were youngsters for that. It was one reason God made rookies.

He cruised by 109 and checked the parking lot. Kyle's car was there. No surprise. They might have agreed to meet in the morning, but none of them would want to let another six or eight hours pass without digging into the case. The naked vulnerability of that girl, and the outrage done to her body, would have made it impossible to sleep anyway.

He was just getting out of the truck when Stan Perry pulled in beside him. Perry bounced out of his ride with the youthful enthusiasm Burgess both admired and resented, and fell into step beside him. "Got something to ask you, Joe," he said, and then fell silent.

Burgess had no idea what was coming, so he stayed silent, too, waiting for Perry to cough it up.

"It's…uh…well, Lily wants to get married, see, and so I guess we are and…"

"If she wants you to take some leave Stan, this is not the time. You know that." He bit his tongue and didn't add that they'd had months to get around to this, so a sudden decision didn't make it an emergency.

"It's not that. Time off, I mean. It's…we're doing it a week from Saturday, and I was hoping you'd be my best man."

Burgess was speechless. Despite working closely together, he and Stan were at odds as often as they were at evens. Before he could stop himself, he said, "Why me?"

Perry was silent again. They walked toward the building, the only sounds their footsteps on the concrete and the background hum of the city. Finally he said, "If I pick my dad, my brother will be jealous. If I pick my brother, my cousin will be pissed. If I pick any of them, my best friend will have his nose out of joint. You're the perfect solution."

"The guy no one can be jealous of 'cuz I'm your boss?"

"Kind of."

"But not because I've been your firm but caring mentor all these years?"

Perry burst out laughing. "That's exactly why, Joe. Because you represent the man I'm trying to be."

Now it was Burgess laughing. "Grouchy. Perpetually irritated. Impatient. A man who doesn't suffer fools or bad guys gladly. A lonely old bachelor still floored by the acquisition of a family. This is what you want to be?"

Perry grinned. "Definitely floored by the acquisition of a family."

"Are you sure I'm the man for the job?"

"Lily wants it, too," Perry said.

"Thought Lily didn't like me. Doesn't she believe I'm your mean boss who is always coming between the two of you and forcing you to cancel your plans? Aren't I the guy who applies too much pressure and is too demanding and just generally a mean-spirited jerk of a boss?"

"She does think all that. She also thinks you're a good role model for me. And…uh…there's also this. She thinks if you're standing up with me, I won't bolt and run."

"Best man *and* jailer? I'm so flattered."

They reached the door and Burgess punched in the code.

As they started up the stairs, Perry said, "So, will you do it?"

"How can I refuse such an appealing offer?"

"So say yes. Then I can call her and tell her it's all set."

"Yes."

They joined Kyle in the conference room that had now become their work room. Kyle was already pinning the first round of Dani's pictures to a board. Evidently, like the rest of them, Dani couldn't go home to Fourth of July festivities and leave it until morning.

In the center was an enlarged map of Stroudwater Park showing the trails, with the site where the body had been marked in red, with the distances from the parking lot to the spot where whoever dumped the body had left the trail, and from the trail to the dump site recorded. There was another parking lot farther along. That distance hadn't been measured. Burgess assumed that there were officers sealing that end as well.

"It doesn't make sense," Kyle said.

"What doesn't make sense?" Burgess asked.

"To take the body so far from the trail. Most perps would just go a little way into the woods and dump it. You've read the literature. At night, people always think they've gone farther than they really have."

"She wasn't dumped," Burgess reminded him.

"Displayed. But who was the display for? For us or for someone else? Was it an 'in your face gotcha' to the cops or a warning to someone?" Kyle said. "And if it was for someone else, why choose that spot? Did those woods have some particular significance or was it just the killer knowing that the story, with all its ugly details, would be heard by someone else who would understand what it meant?"

He stared at the map. "Maybe there are other girls who are being turned out by the same person? Maybe it's a warning about what happens if they get defiant?"

"Or a warning to customers who've use that spot to keep away," Burgess said. "We need to go back and look again. Learn more about that site. See if there are trails leading into that clearing that we missed. If we missed something obvious about the site because we were so focused on finding evidence. Same with the path Remy marked out with his tape. Did he create a new path or follow an old one? I'll do that. I'm going back out there as soon as it gets light."

As usual, the more they talked, the longer the list got. "We need to talk to Remy about what he saw when he first got there. Can you do that, Terry? And we're only assuming it was done at night. Someone's going to have to be out there to interview regulars, to get a sense of the flow of people and when they tend to appear. We don't have time to do that ourselves, so Stan, maybe you can talk to patrol?"

He told them what Remy had seen in McCann's car. "Might be nothing. Might be something. I could swing by there on my way to Augusta. Dr. Lee wants to do the autopsy at ten."

"I can check McCann's car," Kyle said. "You want one of us with you in Augusta?"

"I'll grab Sage Prentiss. I need you two working on things here. Terry, follow up with Remy, get background on McCann, then call the middle and high schools and see if they're missing a student who fits our girl's description."

Kyle shot him a look.

"The sleeve, Terry," Burgess said. "I don't imagine they know of any students who are normally missing their heads. Actually missing their heads."

One of Kyle's rare smiles came and went. *If you didn't know the man, you'd never see those,* Burgess thought. Kyle wasn't humorless, just very contained.

"Stan, you see if any tattoo artists in the city recognize that sleeve. We've got to ID this girl. Then get on to Vice, see if they have anything."

Perry focused on a blow-up of the girl's tattoo sleeve. "Can I take this?"

Burgess nodded, and Perry unpinned the picture and put it in a folder.

The unfinished tat reminded Burgess of his crime scene photos—that blank space waiting to be filled in. He hoped he'd be luckier than this girl. She'd died before she had a chance to finish.

"We need to give her a working name until we find out who she is," Burgess said, peering at the tattoos in another photo. "I hate to keep calling her 'the girl.' Got any ideas?"

He could tell Perry was suppressing a smartass remark. Maybe the kid was finally learning some self-control.

Kyle was looking at the pictures, too, muttering, "Headless, vacant, missing." He leaned in closer to the photo and pointed to the central figure in the sleeve. "Mermaid," he said. "She's our mermaid."

They headed home to grab a little sleep. Tomorrow would be here soon enough, and it would be all about a mermaid.

Burgess, unable to help himself, took a detour.

EIGHT

It was just after midnight as Burgess drove out Congress Street, heading for Stroudwater Park. With the clouds gone, and only a sliver of moon overhead, the sky was a deep blue-black and the stars were brilliant. Burgess liked the night. Lots of people were scared of it. Lots of cops, even. It brought back memories of monsters hiding in the closet and under the bed. Scary stories by the campfire. And for cops, bad guys suddenly popping out of the darkness, with fists or knives or guns. Bad things happened at night.

But for Burgess, it also meant peace and quiet. He liked to drive past houses where people were sleeping and recall nights on patrol, eager and vigilant, knowing it was his job to keep them safe, to let them sleep undisturbed by the dangerous things that happened in the dark. These days, with his small house full of noisy kids, often kids fighting over a computer, or TV, or who got to eat the last cookie, night was a refuge. It was the place where he could be alone with his thoughts.

He was driving on autopilot, radio chatter turned down low, running those endless lists of questions to be answered that were the beginning of any investigation, when there was a blur of motion and a deer leapt into the road. He jammed on the brakes, the Explorer bucking and sliding as he brought it to a stop just inches from the animal. With a bound, the creature leapt into the bushes and was gone.

Clutching the wheel, bathed in the intense adrenaline of a close encounter, he waited for his breathing to settle. Experience said wait for something else, and he sat patiently while two small spotted fawns emerged from the shrubbery and followed their mother across the road. Raising children was so fraught with danger.

He wanted to think somewhere in this city, or elsewhere, someone was missing a child and worrying about her. So many years dealing with bad stuff—coupled with what he'd seen today—told him that was likely wishful thinking. Sometimes, sad as it was, cops were often the only mourners.

He waited until the little white flags of their tails had disappeared, then drove on. Wildlife sightings were also part of nights in his city. The more common raccoons, bunnies, owls, possums, skunks, and rats—the good citizens of his city would be shocked at how often he saw rats—but also deer, foxes, coyotes, once or twice a fierce and terrible fisher, and, more rarely, a moose or a bear. His mother had been a keen-eyed observer, and she had taught him to be one as well. Things other people never saw, Burgess did. That childhood training in being observant had been useful in his chosen profession.

There were two Portland police cars in the lot. Otherwise, it was deserted. He didn't immediately get out. Instead, he sat and took in the environment, just as he'd observed the streets driving in.

One of the patrol officers strolled over and knocked on his window. "Anything we can do for you, Sarge?"

"Just getting a feel for things without the Lookie Loos and the press," he said. "Things been quiet?"

The officer shrugged. "Mostly. There was one odd thing," he said. "Guy who found the body? McCann? He was out here about an hour ago. Said he'd dropped something. Wanted us to let him go back out there and look for it."

The officer snorted. "No way that was happening."

"He give you any trouble?"

"Got kinda mouthy, said he'd had enough of cops today, he just wanted to get his stuff, what the hell was the problem."

The officer leaned away from the car and adjusted his duty belt, just like Burgess figured he'd done for McCann. "I said it was a crime scene was the problem. Investigators would likely be out to search again in the morning. If he wanted to tell me what it was, I could pass it on, maybe the investigators would find it for him." The officer grinned. "He didn't seem to like that much. Man said a few bad words and then he drove away."

"This was about an hour ago?"

"Right around eleven, Sarge."

So not when they'd dropped McCann off to pick up his car. Burgess wondered whether McCann really was looking for something, or just setting up an explanation in case the cops had found, or would find, something connecting him to the crime? One more reason to come back in daylight and have another look around. Early daylight, since he was due in Augusta at ten.

Now that they'd made a concrete plan for the morning, and he'd gotten a feel for this place, he was ready for bed. He'd already put the truck in gear when he thought of something else. Trash cans. He could do them in the morning, but what if trash pickup was early? What if some of those nocturnal animals he'd been reminiscing about came looking for goodies and dragged something important away?

Was it only a few hours ago that he'd decided his dumpster diving days were over? Probably. But he wasn't about to call some poor guy or gal from patrol out here at this hour so they could check the trash. He sighed, shut off his engine, and walked around to the back. He grabbed a flashlight, a tarp, and his search gloves. Then he headed for the can nearest to where McCann's car had been parked. He carried the contents over to the base of a light illuminating the parking lot, spread out his tarp, pulled on his gloves, and poured out the whole disgusting contents.

His periodic forays into people's trash convinced him of several things. First, that he'd never make it as a garbage man. Second, that people discarded an astounding amount of uneaten food. Third, that there is little in the world more repulsive than a dirty diaper. Except, possibly, old, half-eaten steak.

Luckily, this mess had no steak or diapers. He had learned to be grateful for small things.

He found a sturdy stick, which he used to distribute the contents, studying them each time he shifted them around. He was about to pack it all up when he found a glittery pink barrette. He could be wrong. It could be just coincidence, but it looked like the mate to the one Perry had found in the woods. If it was evidence, it was weird evidence, since the victim had no head, and therefore no hair. But if she'd been in the killer's car before the mutilations, she might have had barrettes, and might have lost them there. One of them might have hitched a ride on whatever the body was wrapped in, and dropped off as she was carried through the brush.

He carefully collected and bagged it, then returned the rest of the stuff to the bin. There was another trash container at the other end of the lot, so he checked that one, too. He wasn't expecting anything, and got no further reward for his troubles, but it was always better to be thorough.

Then, with something to show for his efforts, and a long day ahead of him tomorrow, he drove home, showered the garbage smell off, and climbed into bed.

Someone in the bed was wearing that silky blue thing he liked so much, the item of clothing that more enticed than covered, and as was often the case when the blue thing appeared, his day ended on a very fine note.

NINE

Morning, as was its wont, came too early, bringing with it familial commotion. Today's commotion was Dylan getting ready to go to his job as a life guard, Nina heading out to be mother's helper to a mom overwhelmed by the arrival of twins, and Neddy getting ready for day camp and unable to find his bathing suit. Through it all, Chris was calm and cheerful. Sometimes, he wondered how he got so lucky.

His feeling of being lucky lasted less than five minutes. That's when the phone rang and Captain Cote, his nemesis, called with his predictable complaint about not having their reports. To his credit, after making Burgess's life hell for years, Cote had mellowed since Burgess saved his life. But it is hard to teach an old dog new tricks, and without frequent reminders, Cote reverted to his numbskull and abusive ways. One of those was to call up his exhausted detectives after a day, or often a day and a night, of working a crime scene, disturbing their sleep to demand reports about the details. Reports his detective hadn't yet had time to write. Details they liked to bury, given his predilection for carelessly disclosing important details to the press.

But Cote was not calling a solitary Burgess desperately trying to get some sleep anymore. He was calling the Burgess household, where the Burgess kids actually vied for the chance to speak with Cote and keep him from reaching their dad. Today it was Neddy's turn. Burgess heard him take the phone, say very politely, "I'm sorry sir, but my dad's still asleep."

Then say, "Sorry, I gotta go. I'm late for camp. Call back later." And that was that.

Burgess had learned to find joy in small things. He rolled over and was about to snatch a few more minutes of sleep when the words "crime scene" flew into his mind, and he flew out of bed.

He needed to go back out there, take a close look at the scene and its surroundings, and make the call whether they should get a group of officers out there to do a more detailed grid search. Allowing himself a moment of regret for his lost sleep, he got up.

"Bright-eyed and bushy-tailed?" Chris asked as he came into the kitchen.

"Not very."

She leaned against the counter, an impish smile on her face. "Think how much more sleep you'd get if you gave up sex."

"Give it up? Ma'am, I am just getting started."

She laughed and went to dress for work.

"Hey," he called after her. "Guess what? Stan and Lily are getting married a week from Saturday, and I'm going to be best man."

"So you can keep him from running away?"

"How did you know that?"

"Just a good guess. You'd better take your suit to the cleaners. Or are you supposed to wear your dress uniform?"

"Guess I'll have to check."

"Where are you off to today?"

"Back to Stroudwater Park, then on to Augusta for the autopsy."

"I guess I won't say 'have fun' will I?"

Burgess had been a slave to his work for so long he should have been heading out the door. Instead, he went to the bedroom and watched Chris dress.

"Mister," she said, "there is nothing sexy about scrubs."

"I think sexy is in the eye of the beholder," he said. "And I am beholding you. Speaking of sexy, do some people find tattoos sexy?"

"Maybe. But if you're thinking of getting one, be warned that I am not one of those people. Young people don't think about this, but as we age, the skin stretches. Never mind what happens when people put on weight. There's not much sexy about a stretched out dragonfly being swallowed up in rolls of fat."

She wiggled her feet into her clogs. "What makes you think about tattoos?"

"My victim," he said. "Kyle's calling her The Mermaid, because of her tattoos."

"Body art," she said.

"That's what it's called now?"

"Called lots of things, but that's what I recently heard. It beats tramp stamp." She checked herself in the mirror and picked up her purse. "Call me if you won't be home for dinner."

"Will do. But you know…"

"How you get? I sure do. And speaking of how you get, did you remember your knee brace?"

She was only nagging him for his own good, as she often reminded him, so even though he hated how it reminded him that he was a creaky old gimp, he put it on.

He walked down to the cars with her, watched her drive away, then climbed into the Explorer and headed out. Between getting extra sleep and then taking those moments with Chris, he really hadn't given himself enough time to get out to Stroudwater before the autopsy. Now the roads were filling up with people on their way to work. People who seemed not yet fully awake. People who were giving more attention to their phones than their driving. People who were finishing their personal grooming in their cars. His mother would have been scandalized, and frankly, he wasn't far behind.

If he weren't in a hurry, he would have pulled a few of them over and delivered a lecture on inattentive driving. Until, Holy Fuck! The woman who was eating cereal—spoon in one hand, bowl in the other, veered into his lane and missed him by a whisker, then overcorrected and rolled up onto the sidewalk, heading right at a woman with a stroller. The woman screamed and jerked the stroller aside.

He couldn't let it go. He pulled a U-turn, flipped on his siren and his blues, and pulled her over.

He wasn't sure how she managed to pull over, because when he walked up to her window, she was still eating. He had to bang on it before she rolled it down.

"License and registration, please, ma'am."

She tossed her hair, shook her head, and went on eating.

He reached in, took the bowl and spoon, and set them on the ground. "License and registration, ma'am."

"That was my breakfast," she whined. She was a cute girl, with fluffy blonde hair and wide brown eyes, her lashes stiff with mascara. She wore a flowered minidress—he could tell it was mini because it barely covered her crotch—and had a daisy inked on one arm. Nothing else resembled his dead girl, though. This one was driving a blue BMW and reeked of privilege. She still had a head, though she wasn't using it.

"License and registration," he said. Maybe he roared. He wasn't sure. The clock was running and she was being an idiot. He didn't have time for this.

"I'm in a hurry," she said. "I'm late for work."

"That makes two of us," Burgess said, "and if I don't see your license and registration right now, you are going to be later for work because you are going to be in jail."

She batted the big brown eyes. "You don't mean that."

"Ma'am, will you step out of the car, please?"

"Can't," she said brightly. "I'm not wearing shoes."

He couldn't help himself. "You're going to work barefoot?"

Another bat of her eyes. "I think I've got some shoes in the trunk."

He made one more request for her license and registration, then got his phone out and called Dispatch, asked them to have patrol come and pick up a driver who refused to produce her license and registration and who had been stopped for inattentive driving and a marked lane violation. He gave the make of her car and her plate number and described what she'd been doing. Before he went back to his car, he reached in and snagged her keys. She was exactly the type to drive away.

Back in his car, he asked Dispatch for a check on the plate and got back a Thomas Bailey, who was clearly not her. He was in the middle of that when there was a tap on his passenger window. He was expecting the girl from the car, but it was the woman with the stroller.

He rolled down the window. "Ma'am," he said, "are you and your child all right."

The woman had been crying, and she was clutching a small baby protectively in her arms. "Not really," she said. "She came so close. Actually, she brushed the stroller. Thank goodness I had Emilie in her baby carrier. She was fussy, so I picked her up, and then that woman. That girl. She…"

"It must have been very frightening," he said, which was an understatement. The baby could have been killed.

"You are arresting her, right? Promise me that you're arresting her!"

"Yes, ma'am. I am. But it would help to keep her from doing something like that again if I could get a statement from you. It doesn't have to be right now. Just give me your contact information, and I'll check in with you later."

"Gladly," she said. "Gladly. That little bitch skates on everything. It's about time something sticks."

Obviously, this wasn't the first time the girl's driving had caught this woman's attention. Probably not the first time the girl had been stopped. He was intrigued, but he didn't have time to follow up. He needed to hand this off to patrol and head up to Augusta. He got her information and would have asked a few more questions about her previous experience with the subject, but the baby was wailing.

"I've got to get her home," the woman said, and hurried away.

He'd asked for patrol, got Remy Aucoin, and that gave him an idea.

First, though, he had to hand off this dangerous woman. In his mind, he said, "Dangerous dame." He liked the alliteration, but that wouldn't play in the 21st century. Neither would airhead, bimbo, or twit, however apt they were.

"I need you on my homicide, Remy," he said, "Can you get someone else to take this woman back and book her?"

Remy didn't quite suppress an exuberant grin as he slipped back in his cruiser and got on the radio.

Before the rest of his life had passed, and before he was infuriatingly late heading north for the autopsy, a twenty-year-old woman named Bambi Bailey was on her way to jail, and Burgess and Remy had their heads together in the Explorer.

Burgess got permission from the patrol supervisor to borrow Remy for the day, shared his team's questions about the spot chosen to dump the body, and then described the kind of search he wanted Remy to make. Remy was a hundred percent on board.

He was almost out of time, but Burgess had one more idea. He told Remy about Cary McCann's desire to go back onto the trail to recover his "missing property." "Tell the officers who are securing the scene that if he turns up while you're out there searching, it's okay for him to look for his property as long as you accompany him. If he agrees, that should give us a read on what he's up to and what he's looking for. If he refuses? That's information, too."

"I'm on it, Sarge," Aucoin said. "If I find something, or I need help, do I call you?"

"I'll be at the autopsy. Call Kyle or Perry. I'll check in with you when I'm done, though. Got some follow-up questions about yesterday."

"Yes, sir."

Aucoin continued on to Stroudwater Park while Burgess headed north to Augusta, where Sage Prentiss would meet him. As he drove, he made quick calls, leaving messages for Kyle and Perry about the task he'd delegated to Remy Aucoin, and that he'd follow up with Remy later, taking that task off Kyle's list. He was just flying past Brunswick when his phone rang. Expecting Kyle or Perry, he answered without looking, and had the pleasure of Captain Cote's voice exploding in his ear.

"What the heck were you thinking, Burgess?"

There were so many possibilities. He was thinking about crude amputations and what instrument might have been used. Where they might look for the missing body parts. What kind of killers posed their victims, and why. Whether the ME would find something they could use. Whether Remy would find anything. And a critical, maybe existential question: how comfortable was he about delegating what might be important tasks to anyone outside his team? It was hard to teach an old dinosaur new tricks.

"About what, sir?"

"That girl you arrested. Do you have any idea who she is?"

"Other than a danger to herself and others, sir? No. I do not. Did you read the report?" Burgess had never been interested in curtsying to the self-important, something Cote excelled at and frequently berated Burgess about.

"She's Senator Bailey's niece."

Now he understood the source of her careless indifference. She thought she was untouchable. "And?"

"And now we have a public relations mess on our hands."

"All I have on *my* hands is a legitimate traffic stop, an infant that was nearly killed by a driver who drove onto the sidewalk while eating with both hands, and a distraught mother. Oh, and a savagely mutilated body, Paul. If you want to let Bambi go, despite her outrageous behavior, feel free. Now excuse me, but I'm late for an autopsy."

Cote began to sputter. Cote spent his life demanding reports. In this case, so patrol would know what to charge, he'd done a quick write-up of the girl's erratic driving and the offenses she'd committed, so Cote had a report. "Paul," Burgess interrupted, "she's a dangerous driver. You let her go and she kills herself or someone else instead of learning a lesson, it's on you."

It was insubordination, for sure, but he disconnected and went back to driving and thinking about his case. Let Cote sort this one out. That's why he got the gold bars and the big bucks.

Burgess took a moment to savor the phrase "let Bambi go," thinking "Catch and Release Bambi" sounded like a movie title, and then went back to thinking about his case and to exceeding the speed limit, because catching Bambi had really taken a bite out of his morning.

Wink was there without Dani, processing the body and taking his pictures and shaking his head at all the things he'd normally do that he couldn't do here. No fingernail scrapings. No head and pubic hair combing. No fingerprinting. He did take a footprint, just in case there was a birth certificate somewhere with an infant's footprint on it, and lots of close-ups of the bruises and the unfinished tattoo sleeve. Unless they found the missing body parts, or someone came forward, those tattoos were one of their best shots at identification. If the tattoos were local. People who trafficked young girls often sold them, traded them, moved them around so she might not be local.

Sage Prentiss looked as pale and stiff as a man going to his own execution. Burgess took a moment with him before they went in. "It's ugly," he said, "so brace yourself. But it's still our job to find out who she is, and find her killer, and we may miss something important if we're thinking of our own discomfort instead of focusing on what we can learn. If you feel sick, go outside and get some air. There's no shame in that."

He wouldn't tell Prentiss this, but he had to brace himself as well. Maybe he was getting soft in his old age. Maybe things like this just got harder when you had a daughter.

Before Dr. Lee could begin, Burgess had a request. "Could we put something, a towel, or a cloth, over her…" He fumbled for a word, then came up with an ugly one. "Stumps."

The ME gave him a puzzled look, but signaled to his assistant to find something.

"Leaving her in the woods like that…it was bad enough. Being laid out on a stainless steel table depersonalizes her even more. I want a moment when I'm just looking at her body, not distracted by the amputations, to see her."

He wasn't explaining this very well but he didn't have better words. The assistant covered her neck, a white cloth where her head would have been, two more covering the ends of her arms. Everyone was silent as Burgess studied the form on the table. He felt, at last, like he was speaking to her, to a person rather than a mutilated body, as he quietly made the promise he made to all his victims. "I will get you justice."

He nodded to Dr. Lee. "Sorry for the delay." And the autopsy began.

Lee began at the neck, describing what he was seeing, amplifying what he'd said at the scene about the crude method used to sever the head, pointing out the torn flesh and muscle, the scrapes and nicks on the spine, leaning in closely to examine the neck.

Burgess and Prentiss were in wait and watch mode, listening, but settling in for a long process, when Lee reached for some tweezers, poked into the wound, and pulled out a small piece of metal.

"Here's something for you, gentlemen. Looks like this broke off a hand saw."

The small piece of metal clanged into a dish, and Wink moved in to photograph it while Lee dictated the details of his find.

It was a piece of evidence, certainly, but one that only amped up his frustration. He couldn't find the saw because he couldn't find the owner of the saw because he didn't know who the victim was and so he didn't know where to look. If only this were television. Then they'd stick this piece of metal into some machine and magically know the brand of the saw. Then another machine could quickly trace it to the store that had sold it. Which store would, of course, have a clear video of the purchaser and a sales slip with the man's name and address. Oh, to live in a CSI world. He suppressed a sigh. Dr. Lee didn't like sighs in his autopsy room.

"For what it's worth," Lee said, as if he'd read Burgess's mind, "it looks like a new saw. And it has deeper gullets between the teeth than many."

Lee knew the most amazing things. Burgess got out his phone and snapped a picture of the broken saw tooth. In his business, you never knew what might be important.

So it went. By the end, Burgess had the serial numbers for both breast implants, while Wink had the implants themselves, Dr. Lee's opinion that the girl wasn't older than fifteen and might be younger, and that, for a girl so young, she had had a lot of sex. The ME had confirmed the presence of semen in both anus and vagina, which would be sent to the lab for testing. The bruises were premortem, but recent, and her body showed evidence of previous beatings and old breaks in her bones, some of which likely hadn't had medical care. They would check for drugs in her system, but there were no needle marks or other obvious signs of drug use.

"That break in her ulna," Lee said, "is recent. And it was treated. You get a name, you might find x-rays."

The body can tell a lot about how it has been treated, and this girl had been someone's punching bag since she was very young. Someone's punching bag and someone's sex slave. Just one person using her for sex, or was someone pimping her out?

Now, with those two attributes humans used most to connect with the world—head and hands—removed, she had been thrown away. Dehumanized. Just a thing. A girl no one seemed to have missed.

"You'll find him, Joe. Him or them," Lee said. "She's counting on you." The ME let that hang in the air a moment, then he added, "I'm counting on you."

Burgess was surprised. Normally, Dr. Lee was clinical and efficient. The only thing that got to him was kids. Which, Burgess supposed, this girl was. "One of these days I'm going to let you down," he said.

"How about not this time?"

Burgess felt the weight of Dr. Lee's expectations join his own. The girl was slight but the weight was not.

TEN

As they walked out to their cars, Wink lugging his cameras and workbag, and Burgess carrying the bits of evidence they'd collected, Sage Prentiss said, "That was a good suggestion, Sarge, covering her neck and arms like that. It sounds weird, but it made her come alive…I mean, more real, more human somehow."

"That was the idea," Burgess said.

Prentiss ducked his head like he was being reprimanded.

"No," Burgess said. "I mean I'm glad it worked."

Wink shot him a look, probably wondering if mean Joe Burgess was a thing of the past. He was beginning to wonder about that himself.

"Got something you want me working on?" Prentiss asked. He was young and eager, still excited to be on the detective's squad, still learning the ropes. The task Burgess had in mind was boring and a real long shot, but it needed to be done. "See what you can dig up about people who've recently bought hand saws," he said. "Especially ones with deep…what did Dr. Lee call them? Gullets. And maybe check reviews, see if some are more prone to breakage?"

"I'll give it my best shot, sir."

Prentiss might like the job, Burgess thought. *Going to big box stores and hardware stores, flashing his badge, and looking for answers.*

"Hold on," he said, pulling out his phone and showing Prentiss the close-up of the piece Lee had pulled from Mermaid's neck. "Teeth like this," he said. He shared the photo to Prentiss's phone.

He sat in his car and watched them drive away, glad he would be driving back alone. He used his patches of alone time to think about his cases and plan what avenues to pursue next. He always hoped that he'd get back to 109 and something would have broken or some essential piece of evidence discovered. He didn't dawdle, exactly. But back at 109, a prune-faced Cote was waiting for his not yet written reports, and to complain about Burgess's treatment of Bambi. Who would hurry toward that?

He would be writing reports, and nagging his team to write reports, though there was little to put in them at this point beyond the initial information from the scene. He understood reports were important. But in these very early stages, particularly when confronted with a puzzle like this one, investigative time was better spent investigating.

Cote was always looking for a quick solution, which, in this case, was even more unlikely than in most. Even though Kyle and Perry were good, cases took time. Long, slow, slogs of time as they explored and collected and built their case. It was a lot harder when the opponent took essential pieces off the board. But hope sprang eternal. Hope and determination. They would identify their Jane Doe, their mermaid. It might just take a long time.

Now that he wasn't immersed in the autopsy, Burgess realized he was hungry. He'd lost some weight over the past year, and was trying to keep it off for the benefit of his bad knee, and his good partner, but healthy eating could be incompatible with his irregular work schedule. When he was rushing from point A to point B, and fielding questions along the way, salads didn't work. Trying to eat a salad while driving was a recipe for disaster. Dressing would drip, those slimy little tomatoes would escape into his lap, and recalcitrant bits of lettuce would go everywhere. He'd be as bad a driver as Bambi. And salads, like cereal, took two hands.

He compromised on a chicken sandwich from his friends at the Golden Arches. That he could eat with one hand. He even skipped the fries, though hot, salty fries often had a positive effect on his disposition.

Back at 109, he braced himself for the message that Cote wanted to see him as soon as he came in, but there was no such message. Either Cote was also mellowing, or he was tied up practicing his curtsy. *Better him than me,* Burgess thought. It was hard to curtsy with a bum knee.

He dropped into his chair and picked up the stack of waiting messages. Given the effect of cop cuisine on their digestive systems, Pepto-Bismol pink was a poor choice for the pieces of paper thrust in their faces every day, but he couldn't remember a time when message slips weren't that color.

Nothing that couldn't wait. No one had called and confessed. No anxious parent had left an urgent message.

Continuing to procrastinate, he checked his phone in case there was a message from Kyle or Perry. Nothing.

Dammit. There had to be something. Somewhere. Growling with frustration, he pulled up the report template and went to work.

He'd just hit "save" on the last report when he saw Janice, the new CID assistant, approaching his desk, followed by a man he didn't recognize. The man was dressed like an office worker—khaki pants, blue shirt and tie but no jacket—tall and well-made and looked to be in his forties. "Joe, this is Mr. Hooper. He's a foster parent. He read about that poor murdered girl in the paper, and his foster daughter is missing, and well…" She stammered to a stop, blushing. "I'll just let him tell you."

She waved vaguely at the chair beside Burgess's desk and fled. Once Burgess had yelled at her when some important papers had gotten misfiled. He'd apologized and tried to be extra nice ever since, but she still acted like he'd probably bite her if she got too close, and likely was rabid as well. His life never stopped teaching him lessons about his temper, though he thought he lost it more rarely than most people.

"Mr. Hooper," he said, thrusting out a hand. "Detective Sergeant Burgess. How can I help?"

Despite his vigorous appearance, Hooper's handshake was a limp, slimy press. Then he drew his hand back and parked it under his buttock, like he needed to protect it or was about to use it to vault from the chair. Cops made people nervous. Some more than others.

"I don't know if you…I just read in the paper that…I mean, maybe I should just file a missing person report? Because my daughter. Our daughter. Our foster daughter. She's missing. Run away again, I guess?"

It was the first time he'd heard an adult male use what Nina told him was called "upspeak", a form of talking where everything was posed as a question and the speaker ended everything on a high note. She'd made him watch a YouTube video that explained it. He hadn't noticed it in the real world before now.

He got Mr. Hooper's first name, address, date of birth, and phone number—the usual information police collected. Checked the license to confirm it, and wrote down the driver's license number. It took some time and Burgess was already frustrated before he asked his first real question.

He collected the missing daughter's name, Alicia Johnson. How long she'd been with the Hoopers. Three years. Alicia's age. Sixteen. How long she'd been missing. He wasn't sure.

"Are we talking a day? A week? She lives with you. You must have some idea."

Alicia, it seemed, ran away a lot. She always returned home after a few days. Once after a week. But when his wife had read about the girl in the paper, she'd been concerned that it might be Alicia, and sent him to inquire.

"What does your foster daughter look like?" he asked. It was the all-important question. He already believed this wasn't on the up and up. There was something off about this guy.

Hooper hesitated for a while, and Burgess forced himself not to drum his fingers on the desk. If this wasn't going to be productive, he had better uses for his time.

"She's maybe 5' 5", slightly built. Pretty. Very pretty."

"Hair color?"

Hooper shrugged. "It changes all the time. Last week it was kind of a mahogany red with a few pink streaks. Curly. Long."

"And before that?"

"Black."

Burgess's sense was that their girl was a brunette, but he had no basis for that beyond gut.

"Eye color?"

"Hazel. I think."

Right. She's lived with you for three years. There's no reason you should have noticed. "Distinguishing marks?"

"What does that mean?"

"Moles. Scars. Birthmarks. Short leg. Missing digits. Piercings. Anything personal that could be used to identify her." He wasn't going to mention tattoos. If Mermaid was Hooper's daughter, that was the first thing he'd mention.

But Hooper shook his head. "I can't think of anything."

"When did you last see Alicia?" Another version of the question he'd asked earlier.

Hooper shrugged. "I don't know. My wife might remember."

This was the situation the state was putting foster kids into? No wonder the girl ran away, if that was in fact the case. If anything this man was saying was true.

"Does Alicia have a cell phone?"

Hooper shook his head.

"What about friends? Who could we contact who might have an idea where she is?"

"My wife might know."

What was this guy doing here? Why hadn't his wife come instead if she was the person who might know something about the girl?

"What about school? Which school does she attend? Who was her last homeroom teacher?"

Hooper didn't know.

"How is she spending the summer? Does she have a job?"

Hooper looked confused. "I didn't realize this was going to be so hard," he said.

Burgess didn't think it had been hard at all. Nor did he believe Hooper was confused. The man was here for a reason. Possibly not one involving a missing child, or at least, wanting to locate a missing child. Maybe his goal had been to get Burgess to describe the murder victim? Or was he here to suss out the detectives?

"Can you excuse me for a second, Mr. Hooper? I have to grab a form."

In the assistant's office, he asked to Janice to arrange for someone to follow Hooper when he left. Get his plate number and record where he went. "Unmarked," he said, though Janice probably knew that. It wouldn't be the first time someone involved in a case came in "innocently" looking to file a report. Kyle had once spotted a guy in the lobby who was there to report his wife missing. The officer taking the report had missed the fact that the guy had blood on his clothes. The man's wife wasn't dead yet, but she would have been if Kyle hadn't acted.

In this case, Burgess was wondering whether Hooper was hiding his hands because they had blood on them. It could be darned hard to get it all off. Then he grabbed a form and went back to his desk, making a pretense of transferring his notes to the form.

"Do you think your wife might be able to provide more information about Alicia?"

Hooper shrugged. "She might."

"When would be a good time to contact her?"

Hooper wasn't sure.

"Does Alicia work?" Burgess asked again.

"She's got a job somewhere. Ice cream place, I think."

"Have they contacted you wondering why she hasn't come to work?"

"Nope. Maybe she's going to work but staying with a friend. I just wanted to know, you know, if something had happened to her. If she'd gotten herself killed. Because of the crowd she hangs out with."

"Who's in that crowd, Mr. Hooper? Where do they hang out?"

He shrugged.

"Did you happen to bring a picture of Alicia, something we could use to help us find her?"

"I did," Hooper said, sounding proud of himself. He pulled out a photo and handed it to Burgess, quickly tucking his hands away again. The girl in the picture was about ten years old. According to Hooper, Alicia hadn't lived with them when she was ten.

"This is the girl who is missing?"

"Yup."

"Does she still look like this?"

"Nope."

"Do you have a more current photo at home?"

"My wife might."

The girl in the photo had brown eyes. He turned it over. Someone had written Shelley, 2006. It was 2009, so even if this was his foster daughter, she wasn't sixteen or named Alicia.

Burgess flashed on the bar scene in Star Wars. There's nothing to see here. He didn't know if the child in the picture was the droid he was looking for. It was time to move along.

"Why are you here, Mr. Hooper?"

The man shifted in his chair and gave Burgess an innocent look. "To see if Alicia's been murdered."

"Without a photograph, information about her friends or employment, or even the date she went missing?"

Hooper failed to suppress a smirk. "You're the cops. I thought you could figure that out. About this murdered girl. What did she look like?"

Burgess thought he understood why the man was here.

"I'm afraid we're not releasing any information about the victim yet, Mr. Hooper. I'm sorry. When we do, it will all be in the papers."

Anger flashed across the man's face, and he tensed, like he was about to start yelling. Then it faded, and he used the hands under his buttocks to push himself up. "I expected you to be more help," he said, and headed for the door.

Burgess picked up the phone and called down to the reception area. "The man I want followed is just leaving. Forties, sandy hair, white shirt and tan pants."

Then he turned to his computer and typed in Hooper's name, address, and date of birth. Despite the fact that he'd checked Hooper's license, there was no such person. The number on Hooper's license belonged to an elderly lady named Ida Mae Wilson. Burgess wrote down her information. He'd have to check it out. He glared at the screen, hoping Kyle and Perry were having better days.

ELEVEN

Sighing for his wasted time, he opened the notebook where he had recorded the serial numbers for Mermaid's implants. After five minutes online it was clear to him that making the calls to track their manufacturer wasn't a job he had time to do. It required someone with the patience to spend hours at a desk and on the phone, and to find that kind of sleuthing interesting. While he could do it if he had to, he wasn't the best man for the job. He called Rocky Jordan, their computer whiz, and asked if he had some time. Rocky usually had time for him and he liked solving the puzzles Burgess's cases presented. Burgess gave him the serial numbers, explained what they were, and asked him to track down the manufacturer and get the name of the surgeon who'd installed them.

Rocky said it sounded like fun, and he carried off the numbers. Burgess was reaching for his phone to check in with Kyle and Perry when it rang. Remy Aucoin said, "Got a minute?"

Burgess had a minute. "What's up?"

"I think I've found something. A black plastic trash bag. A buried bag. It was farther into the woods, but in the same area as the body. I started to uncover it, then I thought someone should be with me. Or maybe Wink or Dani should collect it. From the shape, it doesn't look like it's the missing body parts. It's too flat. It may not even be related."

"Flag it," he said, "and meet me out on the path. I'll grab Wink or Dani, and meet you there."

Nearly six hours since he'd sent Remy out to recheck the site. A long time to make the kid crawl through the woods. Between the mosquitoes and the ticks, it would be a lucky thing if Burgess's assignment didn't kill him. Remy's fiancée would not be pleased by that. Kid survives a sniper attack and Burgess kills him with an evidence search?

"Remy, have you been working all this time? Have you taken any breaks? Did you get lunch?"

Misunderstanding the question as meaning he wasn't working hard enough, Aucoin said, "My supervisor, Sarge. He said I had to take a break, hydrate, and get some lunch. It's not me, sir. Honest. I would have worked right through. But my uncles are on my case to take it easy."

His damned reputation again. Invaluable for getting officers to take him seriously and to do the job well. Difficult when it put pressure on the wrong people. "I wasn't criticizing you, Remy. I'll see you soon."

Aucoin had two uncles, Guy and Steven, both Portland cops. They'd raised him from a pup and were always there to look out for him, sometimes to the detriment of his career. But when Aucoin was shot, Burgess was glad he had his uncles, and a lovely young woman who said she was his fiancée, pulling for him. He might not be a religious man himself, but he believed that having people praying for you, and surrounding you with love, could make a difference in your recovery. It was between him and God, but maybe, when Aucoin and Melia were shot, he'd added a little prayer of his own.

In any case, he was glad Aucoin's supervisor was looking after him. Looking after your people was important. Speaking of people, he needed to check in with his. He popped down to the lab, didn't find Wink, but grabbed Dani to come back with him to Stroudwater Park. She said she'd drive herself because she had an errand to do on the way home, so he agreed to meet her there.

In the truck, he called Kyle, and got a brisk, "Terry Kyle."

"Burgess," he said. "Getting anywhere?"

"I checked McCann's car. It's been cleaned out. There's nothing in it. Not even a water bottle or the dog's water dish or that blanket Remy described covering the back seat. Schools are a bust, too. It's summertime, so there's no one to miss her if she doesn't show up. They're pretty short staffed, and no one who was around, which is just the office staff, remembered a student with a heavily tattooed arm. You get anything?"

"Not much. Remy just called and said maybe he had a find, so Dani and I are going to check it out."

"Out at Stroudwater Park?"

Burgess made an affirmative sound.

"What about Stan? Anything?"

"Haven't caught up with him yet."

"I can't ever remember a more unproductive first twenty-four. We meeting later?"

"Can you?" A question the old Burgess, the one who didn't understand about families, wouldn't have asked.

"After dinner, if that's okay."

Part of the deal when Kyle got custody of his daughters from the ex-wife from hell was that he'd be available to take care of them. The PMS Queen, as they called Kyle's ex, liked to drop around from time to time, just to see if she could catch him out. It had always been ugly, and was ugly still. Kyle had Michelle, and she was wonderful, but it wasn't her job to raise his kids. Or rather, it was fine with her to raise his kids so long as she would eventually get a kid of her own. Kyle loved her, but he was scared of another failure. Of marriage. It was not easy times at the Kyle household.

"After is fine. I'll let Stan know."

His call to Stan Perry went to voicemail. Probably Perry was talking to someone and didn't want to break it off to talk. Burgess hoped that was the case. Someone had to have something. He just prayed this wasn't going to be one of those cases where they hit nothing but brick walls. It happened sometimes. No matter how hard you worked, how many people you interviewed, how many angles you tried, you couldn't solve it.

It worried him that he wasn't feeling the obsessive thrill of the chase that usually enveloped him at this stage in a case. Did his cop gut know something his body didn't? Was this one going to drag them through everything, wring them out, and then leave them without a resolution for that butchered girl? It would be an albatross they'd carry all their lives if they couldn't get this victim justice.

He was hitting the beginning of the end of the day rush hour this time and there was plenty of traffic. At least there was no BMW Bimbo eating breakfast. Ah, he thought. Alliteration again. Maybe he should chuck it in, take retirement, and become a poet of the mean streets.

The two officers who were guarding the scene and still blocking access to the path looked like they'd had a hard day. It was a rotten job dealing with a public unused to having anyone say no, and they'd just had a whole shift of saying no to walkers, bikers, joggers, and to dog owners who believed their pets were their children, and that their children should be denied nothing. The same dog owners who didn't clean up after their pets, or left bags of poo on the ground like there was a designated poo collector who would come and pick it up. Kyle sometimes expressed a desire to become the poo police. He'd be dynamite, and Portland's poo problem would vanish. But Burgess needed Kyle for more important work.

He got his search gloves, some evidence bags, and a shovel out of the truck, and paused to ask whether they'd seen anything suspicious. No. They hadn't. Unless raging entitlement was suspicious. Well, there was a guy who drove in, circled the lot slowly as though looking for a way around them, but that was all.

Could they describe the man or the car?

Both, it appeared. The man sounded suspiciously like the one who'd presented himself as Charlie Hooper. The car was one of those ubiquitous Priuses that were so quiet they could sneak up on people. They had the plate number for him.

Aha. Some small corner of the plot thickened, Burgess just had no idea how. He wrote down the number, told them to send Dani in when she arrived, and headed down the path.

He'd revisited crime scenes countless times over the years, and never quite got over that eerie sense of menace when he did. Today was no exception. He wondered if it spooked Dani as well, and decided to wait for her and walk her out to the scene. No matter how often he thought he was done with monsters in the closet or under the bed, not even now that he chased them away for Neddy, they could still haunt him. He couldn't shake the sensation that something was lurking just beyond the tree line. That maybe a gun was pointed at him even now. Someone with a crossbow crouched in the undergrowth. A thug with a knife waited in the clearing. Not so long ago, someone with a gun had been waiting. He had the scar to prove it.

He shook his head to clear it. He was being ridiculous. There was no reason to think there was any danger lurking in these woods. He faded back against a tree and waited.

Dani wasn't far behind, striking him, as she always did, to be too small a woman to carry such a big job. The equipment was heavy and the hours were long. And he was a chauvinist dinosaur. She spotted him instantly and swung the heavy bag off her shoulder. "You can carry it, Joe, since you think it's too heavy for little me."

"Am I so obvious?"

"Afraid so. I find it sort of charming, partly because I know the next thing you'll do is *not* hit on me. I don't go for the 'let me carry that big old bag for you, honey, so I can get close enough to cop a feel.' You and Wink are just paternalistic representatives of a bygone era."

"In my day, we called them 'gentlemen,' Dani. Do people still say 'cop a feel' these days?"

"Don't know. It's not like they announce it. They just do it. Anyway, in my case, wouldn't it be to feel a cop?"

But Burgess was being paternalistic again. "Police officers? In our department?"

"You bet your ass," she said.

"I never bet my ass."

"I've heard. So why are we here?" She burst out laughing. "That sequence didn't sound quite right, did it?"

"Remy says he may have found something."

"I hope so. We find who did this to that poor child, and I want to chop off a few body parts myself."

Strong words from Dani, who was usually so quiet and reserved.

"It's just, Joe, you know, that I'm kind of sick of seeing young girls victimized."

He knew the case she was thinking of, and he agreed. "As a paternalistic dinosaur, I wish you didn't have to see these things. But you are critical to getting them justice. You know that."

"Thanks, Joe. I appreciate that. Wink and I often feel like we toil in obscurity."

"Don't we all."

Aucoin was waiting where his yellow tape led the way off the trail. They followed him to the clearing where the body had been, and beyond it through thicker brush until he came to an abrupt halt. "It's right here."

Even though Aucoin said he had partially excavated it, when Burgess looked down, he couldn't see a buried object. Obligingly, the young cop got out his flashlight and illuminated an area of disturbed leaf mold and branches. "Right here. I kinda put it back together."

"Wow," Dani said. "How on earth did you ever see it in the first place?"

Her gaze fell to the muddy knees of his uniform pants. "Have you been crawling through these woods all day?"

Aucoin looked away, embarrassed. "Not all day. When I came back after lunch, I was trying to think like a tracker would, and I noticed some kicked rocks and sticks and some broken branches. I got down on my knees to follow the trail, and found this."

"Let's see what we've got," Burgess said, sincerely hoping what they were unearthing was not someone's dead cat.

Dani took her pictures, and then Burgess used his shovel to carefully remove the layer of old leaves and earth until they could see a black plastic trash bag. Dani took pictures again. Burgess was about to pull out the bag and open it when he thought of Remy Aucoin crawling through the woods on his knees.

"You want to do the honors, Remy?"

Aucoin's grin was huge as he reached out with gloved hands and gently extricated the bag from its burial site. He gave the bag to Burgess, who undid the plastic ties and peered inside. The others leaned in for a look, then pulled back with disappointed faces when they saw the bag held a handsaw.

Trying to keep his hands in one spot, to avoid smudging any prints that might be on the bag, Burgess peeled it open more so he could look at the blade of the saw, his eyes slowly running down the row of teeth until he saw it. A place where some teeth had been snapped off.

He'd been holding his breath as he examined it. Now he could breathe again.

"Dani. This picture," he said, tilting slightly so she could get the saw and the bag. "This is fantastic. Remy, without you crawling around, we never would have found this."

Remy still looked puzzled. "Why would someone come all the way out here to bury a saw?"

"Because it's what they used to cut her head off."

Dani flinched. Aucoin stared. And Burgess wished he'd tempered his words and avoided such a brutal statement. He wasn't with the musketeers right now. They'd understand, but showing enthusiasm about the instrument of someone's beheading generally wasn't cool. "I should explain. This morning, during the autopsy, Dr. Lee found a piece of broken metal in the victim's neck. He said it was some teeth from a saw. Now you've found a saw with missing teeth. We can't be sure the two are related, but circumstances suggest that they are. Remy, this could be huge."

He was good at finding evidence, but would he ever have found this? His knee wouldn't have let him do what Aucoin had done.

Maybe it was time to get a dog out here to see if anything else related to their case was hidden in these woods.

As Dani collected the saw, still in its bag, Burgess took a step backward, watching her work, trying to keep his enthusiasm in check, but hoping this meant they weren't going to be totally empty-handed in their first twenty-four.

TWELVE

Back in the parking lot, he thanked them both for their good work and saw them both react with pleasure. He told Dani that as soon as she'd determined the make of the saw, she should let Sage Prentiss know. Then he watched them drive away. They'd done good work out there. Now he had to curb his impatient desire to know what that saw could tell them. Would the section of broken teeth match? Would there be blood on the saw that could be matched their victim? Could Wink and Dani find fingerprints on the saw or the bag? So many possibilities. It would be hard to wait for the answers.

He sat in the truck, debating whether to get the dog out here now, or keep the path closed for another day. The expense of another day of patrol's time, plus the complaints they could expect from frustrated walkers and joggers brought him down on the side of now. Assuming, of course, that their K9 handler was available. He made the calls to get that underway, confirmed the dog, and called Kyle and Perry to update them.

This time, Perry answered. "Got anything?" Burgess asked.

"Maybe. It's the usual, 'I think I remember her, but the person you really need to talk to isn't in today' thing. And I can't reach the person I really need to talk to, so I'm in 'come back tomorrow' mode. How about Terry?"

"He's drawing blanks. But I may have something." He told Perry about the saw.

"Cool. People have no idea how weird these cases can be. I couldn't even tell Lily about the crime scene. She just patted her belly and said she didn't want to hear it."

He battled the urge to ask Perry whether he was comfortable with a lifetime of not being able to discuss his cases. Some cop marriages worked like that. Perry was in a bind. He loved Lily and she was pregnant with his child. Burgess didn't see how he could have had a relationship with someone who never wanted to hear about his cases. He was lucky Chris was a nurse. She didn't flinch at things, frequently reminding him that nurses saw a lot of ugly and troubling stuff as well.

"They're bringing the dog over to see if there's anything else out there we might have missed. Remy spent hours crawling around on his hands and knees, but he's done, and the dog will be more efficient. Maybe you want to come out, we can have our meet here, then go home and have a quiet evening."

Stan Perry laughed. "In your dreams. The night Joe Burgess goes home and has a quiet evening with an unsolved homicide going? Not possible. But sure. Meeting now would be good. Then I can go home and listen to Lily fuss about how impossible it is to find a dress when she's big as a house, and what color the linens should be. I am really looking forward to that. See you in ten."

"Before I forget," Burgess said, "The best man thing. Suit? Tux? Dress uniform?"

"I don't even know what I'm wearing," Perry said. "I'll check with Lily. She's going nuts. I think the invites will be e-mailed. They should be going out tonight."

"So what happened? You finally propose?"

"I was getting around to it. Before I got there, she proposed to me and I could hardly say no."

Musing on how that proposal went—had Lily gotten down on one knee? Had she had a ring in her pocket?—Burgess called Kyle and updated him. Kyle was good with meeting now. Said he might need twenty minutes, he had to pick Anna up at day camp and bring her home. It was just weird, according to the rest of the world's norms, to go from a horrific crime scene to taking the family for fireworks and ice cream. To go from trying to identify a murdered girl to picking your own girl up at day camp. How did they all manage to sit at their dinner tables, chatting about everyday stuff, when the insides of their heads were papered with horror?

In cop world, of course, nothing ever goes as planned. The dog had to be postponed because they had a missing three-year-old. Kyle had to pick up Anna and then Lexi and drive both girls to their mother's house and Stan was needed at home to consult about the flowers.

So, despite the strain it put on the department's budget, Burgess left patrol in the lot for another night. They'd release it in the morning after they brought in the dog, but if there was more to be found, he didn't want to make it easy for the bad guys to sneak in and get it. It frankly didn't make sense to him for the killer to leave something like that saw near the body site. Nor, for that matter, to have left the body there. But killers were sometimes stupid, or had their own kinds of logic. Often part of his challenge was understanding that logic.

He called Chris, said he'd be home for dinner after all, and headed back to 109.

There was a message on his computer from the officer who'd followed Hooper. He'd run the plate number. Car belonged to an eighty-five-year-old woman named Ida Mae Wilson who lived out in the Deering Flats. They had followed the car to that address, where Hooper had parked and gone inside.

Who was Hooper and what was his relationship to Ida Mae Wilson? Another question for Burgess's growing list. He'd get Dani to grab a shot of Hooper from their surveillance tape, see if anyone recognized the man. Get Rocky to do a search, learn everything he could about Charlie, or Charles, Hooper. If that was even his name. Despite the sins parents committed in naming their children, Burgess was pretty sure the man's name wasn't Ida Mae Wilson. Probably good to do a search on Ida Mae Wilson as well.

He ran his own quick search to establish that she wasn't dead. Then, because he still had some time before dinner and it was too soon to expect anything from Dani and Wink. He decided to pay a visit to Hooper to see if Mrs. Hooper was at home. His desk was covered with messages, but a quick review said none of them were urgent.

On the drive to Hooper's house—if it *was* Hooper's house—Burgess puzzled over Captain Cote's uncommon silence. He couldn't recall a newsworthy homicide in the past where Cote wasn't breathing down his neck immediately, demanding updates and reports. Was the man unwell? Up to his ears in the challenges of handling the business with Bambi Bailey? Afraid to put his usual pressure on Burgess because he owed Burgess his life? That would be a surprise. A leopard doesn't change its spots, and when he and Kyle had rescued Cote, they'd never for a moment expected Cote to return to work as anything but his usual aggravating and insensitive self.

Figuring he should be grateful for small favors, he shelved Cote and thought about what approach he should take when he got to Hooper's house.

As it turned out, he didn't get to take any approach, because Hooper's —or Ida Mae's—car wasn't there, and no one answered the door.

Deciding to come back later, he headed for home. His family wasn't back yet, so he grabbed his good suit, his dress uniform, and Chris's favorite dress, and drove them to the cleaner's.

Windows down, enjoying the salt-tinged, soft summer air, he was cruising back home, thinking of summers in his childhood, when his cell phone rang. Cote, at last? But it was Stan Perry.

"I'm back at the tattoo parlor, Joe. The guy who may have done Mermaid's tattoos just came in, and they had him call me. I think you should hear this."

He reeled off the name of the place, Sweety's Tattoos, and an address.

So much for family dinner. He was almost home, so he stopped and dropped off the flowers he'd gotten for Chris, left a quick note of apology, and got back in the truck.

This wasn't the first time he'd used a tattoo to help ID somebody, just the first under these circumstances. He didn't understand the desire for tattoos. His concern was keeping his skin intact, not decorating it. His decorations were the scars from crossing paths with bad guys during thirty years on the job.

He found the place, parked, and found Stan inside, deep in conversation with a guy the size of a refrigerator, with a braided red beard and a ponytail. Perry introduced him as Levon "Call me Vonnie" DeSpain.

DeSpain offered him a beer, which he refused, and pointed to a chair. "Take a load off, Sarge. Me and Stan here are hoping maybe you've found your girl."

THIRTEEN

"I wouldn't normally discuss one of my clients," DeSpain said, in a voice so deep it sounded like the rumble of a Harley, "but Stan here tells me that the girl you're looking for is dead, so I guess talking about her can't do her any harm."

He flicked a glance at Perry, looking for confirmation.

"If it's our girl,' Perry said. "Tell Joe what you just told me."

"She was just a kid," DeSpain said. "I'd guess not more'n fourteen, if that, except she looked older 'cuz of the boobs, you know. Kids don't have boobs like that. At least not skinny little kids like her. But she was very poised. Very sure of herself. She knew what she wanted and she had the money to pay for it."

"When was this?" Burgess asked.

"Back in the winter. January, I think. Business was kinda slow after Christmas. People were kinda tapped out, so I had the time. Come spring, summer, I have people booked maybe two, three months out."

"Did she come alone?"

"Nope. Had some guy with her. First I thought maybe her daddy, but she didn't act like he was her daddy. Then I thought maybe he was her sugar daddy, but there wasn't nothin' sweet about him. He didn't say much, but he just acted indifferent, maybe, and kind of irritated, like he'd let her come get a tattoo, but he was pissed about it. Except when I balked at her age, which she lied about anyway, he said 'we're paying you, okay, so just give her the goddamned tat that she wants.'"

"What did she look like?"

"She was pretty. Very pretty. Maybe 5'5". Long dark hair, a brown that was almost black. Big brown eyes with a ton of eye makeup. Had one of them…what are they called? Heart-shaped faces. I think that's what they're called. She was a sweet little thing."

A big guy himself, Burgess figured everyone was little to DeSpain. "She tell you her name?"

DeSpain tugged on his beard. "She was a little hinky about that. She started off okay, said her name was Shelley. Then the guy said something, or maybe it was just he made a sound, you know. And she kinda gasped, like she was scared. I was fillin' out the card, see. I keep cards on people, you know, so I can keep track of appointments, and what work I've done for 'em. Sometimes, you know, person'll come in complaining about some work I did, only it worn't work that I did. It was someone else screwed up and they're trying to put it on me. Anyways, she stops and won't give me her last name. She says just Shelley will do."

"Do you take pictures, too, so you can keep track of the work you do?" Burgess asked.

"I do. Lotta times, it's not of people's faces, you know. Just of my work." He smiled proudly. "It's art, you know. We don't always get credit for that, but it's art."

Burgess looked at Perry. "Is there a card? You've seen it?"

"There is. It's definitely the same tattoo. But it's just the arm. There's not much more to see."

Burgess was disappointed, of course. But still, they were getting closer. "Do you mind if we take the card and photos, Mr. DeSpain? So we can match it to our victim?"

"I got no problem with that."

There was a curtain behind DeSpain, and behind the curtain, a tool was buzzing and someone was moaning softly, a steady, sotto voce litany of oh my God, oh my God, oh my God.

"How many times was Shelley here?"

"Three, I think."

"And did the man always come with her?"

"Two times it was that same one. The light haired, indifferent one. One time, it was another guy. Looked like a businessman. He was meaner to her.

But that girl, someone was using her as a punching bag. She was always bruised."

"Can you describe the men?"

"The first one, he was in his forties, maybe, with light hair. He used something on his hair, what my teenage kid calls 'product' to keep it in place. Kind of a narrow face without enough chin, if you know what I mean. He looked weak. Like a wimp. His body, it looked strong and fit. It was just his face, you know. It was weak and what my grandma woulda called peevish. Like he was not a happy guy and liked to take his problems out on others."

Hooper, Burgess wondered? When he got a picture, he'd bring it back and see if DeSpain recognized the guy.

"Tell us about the second guy."

"He looked, I don't know, kind of like an insurance salesman. He was wearing pants and a vest that matched, like somewhere there was a coat to make it a suit. Shirt and tie. Nice if you don't mind guys wearing lavender. The shirt, I mean. The tie had purple and pale yellow stripes. Kinda bright. 'Course, I don't know what he does, so maybe where he works they're okay with lavender shirts and purple ties. World is changing, ya know?"

He got kind of a gleam in his eye. "You'd never guess I used to work in insurance, would you? I was shaving one morning, getting ready for work, and suddenly I thought, *this sucks. I'm not happy, why am I doing this?* So I studied the art of the ink, as I like to call it, and when I was ready, I gave my notice, started growing my beard, and quit."

He waved an arm to indicate the room. "Been doing this twelve years and I've never been happier."

"Anything distinctive about either man? Anything that might help us locate them?"

"Not really. We didn't chat or anything." DeSpain shook his head, then said, "Well, the meaner one, and he was older, too, like fifties, not forties, he drove something like a town car. You know, those black cars that pick up VIPs at the airport. Like one of them. I kinda wondered if he was a limo driver. They dress nice, too. I didn't ask him, though. He was a snob and made it clear he wasn't interested in talking to someone like me. That time, it was maybe February, the girl, Shelley, seemed real down, so I was paying attention to her."

"Did you notice bruises on her that time, too?"

DeSpain nodded. "That time was when I called DHHS, hoping maybe they could do something for her. Kid like that should have a better life."

He stopped, remembering why they were there. "'Course, I don't know whether they even would have been able to find her, when all I had to give them was a first name, Shelley, and a phone number. That number could have been fake. Her name coulda been fake, but I thought it was real from the way the guy acted when she said it. I never called her or nothin'. I decided the next time she came, I was going to get more information from her and really do something. We had another time scheduled, to put some more flowers around that mermaid, but she never came back. And I forgot about calling that number."

He looked at them, like he wasn't sure, after what he'd said, that they'd believe him. "I've got a kid of my own. She's sixteen. I worry all the time." He grabbed his head in two big hands. "And now you're telling me this girl Shelley is dead."

"If that's your work in the picture Perry showed you, then yes," Burgess said, "she is dead. We appreciate your help. We'd also appreciate it if you didn't speak of this to anyone. We're trying to keep the details about her tattoo out of the press. We don't plan to use it unless we can't identify her any other way.

"No problem there," DeSpain said. "I've got no love for…what's it called? The Fourth Estate."

Burgess and Perry didn't either.

He thought of something else. "This girl, did she ever touch them, the card or the pictures?" He was thinking about fingerprints.

"Not that I recall."

It was a long shot. Not likely that girl that young was in the system anyway.

"Thank you for your time," Perry said, and they left.

Perry had the card, and DeSpain's pictures of the girl's tattoo as it progressed. They'd go over them with a magnifying glass, but it didn't look like the pictures were going to give them much.

"Good work, Stan," Burgess said. "Got time for a drink or are bridal flowers and table linens calling?"

"When you put it that way, I've got time for several drinks. Guess I should be grateful we're planning this in two weeks instead of two years. Oh, and I spoke with Lily. She says your dress uniform."

Burgess didn't drink that often. Alcohol represented his best friend, temptation, and nemesis. He sometimes needed the comfort it brought.

Always feared that he'd find he was turning into his father. But tonight he wasn't ready to go home. It looked like Stan wasn't, either.

"I think we should call Terry, too."

They'd be getting together anyway. Why not now? So Burgess called him.

Kyle rarely came out to drink either. But sitting around relaxing and batting ideas around had proven to be a good way to give nebulous investigations some structure. So far, this felt like trying to reassemble a broken vase from tiny pieces without knowing what it had looked like before it was broken.

Kyle said yes.

FOURTEEN

Burgess and Perry hadn't eaten yet, and Kyle was always hungry, so drinks became dinner at the steakhouse where Kyle had met Michelle. It was quiet, affordable, and a place where they weren't likely to run into anyone they knew. They didn't need the romantic, candlelit ambiance, or the soft jazz, but it was soothing. Even hardboiled homicide guys sometimes needed to be soothed.

Burgess waited until their drinks arrived to bring up business. Before that, it was family stuff and cop shop gossip—who'd had what crazy cases, who was sleeping with someone other than their spouse, who was in trouble with the brass.

"Speaking of trouble," Burgess said. "Has anyone heard from Captain Cote?"

"Not me," Kyle said.

"I did," Perry said, and the other two leaned in, astonished. "He asked me for an update. Asked where were my reports. Wanted to know all about the crime scene." He grinned at his colleagues. "Don't know how I got anointed. Maybe he's afraid of you two now."

"What did you tell him?"

"What could I tell him? That we were working on our reports but everyone was out in the field, first twenty-four and all that, and I'd pass his questions along to Joe. Did I do okay? Because I really do not want to become his go-to guy."

"You did great, Stan," Burgess said. "It's going to be hard to bury the missing head and hands, but we want to keep the tattoos out of the press as long as possible. True, they may be how we have to identify her in the end, but I'd like to exhaust other avenues first."

He sipped his drink. An old fashioned. The bartender here was topnotch. He could almost feel the bourbon's heat rolling through him. "I got tied up today with a traffic stop," he said, "so I sent Remy out to do some more searching. The kid crawled around on his hands and knees and found something."

He filled them in on the piece of metal with teeth that Dr. Lee had found in the wound, and how it looked like it matched up with the saw Remy found. Then he told them about Charlie Hooper, and the faked driver's license number belonging to Ida Mae Wilson. "Maybe when we're done here, we can take a ride out and see if the Hoopers are home."

"Sounds like a plan," Perry said, and filled Kyle in on the info he'd gotten from DeSpain at Sweety's Tattoos.

Kyle looked unhappy. They tried not to be competitive, but when the prize was solving a young girl's murder, it was hard not to be, and he hadn't had a productive day.

"The description of the man who was with her the first two times sounds an awful lot like the man calling himself Charles Hooper who paid me a visit today," Burgess said. "Allegedly looking for his missing daughter. The one who gave me his license, the number of which turned out to belong to Ida Mae Wilson. Wilson's address is the same one Hooper gave, and he's driving a car registered to Wilson."

"Stranger and stranger," Kyle said. "I wonder if Wilson is his mom or his granny. If she's buried in the back yard or the cellar?"

"Perhaps we'll learn more if we pay them a visit."

"Hey," Perry said. "Maybe those missing body parts are buried in the yard."

He said it just as their waitress delivered their dinners, and she gave him a quizzical look.

"It's a scavenger hunt," he said. "They're not real."

"Oh." She smiled at him, as women always did with Perry. "You had me worried." It took a special type to love Kyle's intensity, and Burgess, having become a graying older man, was invisible despite his height and his bulk.

When she was gone, Stan Perry sighed. "To think that my days of flirting with waitresses are over."

"Doesn't it get old?" Kyle asked.

"Guess I'll never have a chance to find out." He stared down at his plate. "I don't know. Seems like this is all happening too fast. I mean, I can still flirt, can't I?"

Burgess and Kyle treated it like a rhetorical question and didn't answer.

When their steaks were reduced to a pile of blood and bones—a visual that wasn't lost on any of them—Kyle said, "So, Hooper. Are we really going out there?"

"I'm torn," Burgess said, "between waiting for DeSpain to ID him as the man who was with our girl, or just dropping in to see if his wife is home. And someone needs to talk to the neighbors, to see whether they know what's up with Ida Mae Wilson."

"And whether there really is a wife," Kyle said.

They sat for a while, considering. Their sense of urgency made them want to rush it. Their desire to maximize the value of any visit to the investigation as a whole cautioned them to wait.

"I'll call over to 109 and see if that picture is ready," Perry said, taking out his phone. The photo was ready. He arranged for patrol to run it over to Sweety's, and called DeSpain, who'd said he was working late, to tell him it was coming.

"Why don't I call the number Hooper gave you, Joe, and see if anyone answers," Kyle said. "On my burner, of course."

"You carry a burner? Really?" Perry asked. "Why?"

Burgess thought it was obvious, but waited to see what Kyle would say.

"So I can call my mistress without leaving footprints in the department's records."

"You have a . . ?" Perry grinned. "Like you'd have time for that."

"A motivated man makes time," Kyle said with a straight face. Even Burgess, who'd known him many years, sometimes got caught by that.

"Like hell," Perry said. Then he switched gears. "Hooper's number," he said. "Is it different from the one the girl called Shelley gave DeSpain?"

Burgess checked his notebook, while Perry got out the card. The numbers were different.

"So let's call the girl's number," Kyle said.

Perry read off the number. Kyle dialed it. Listened. Shook his head. "No longer in service. But we can get the records." He looked at Burgess. "Now the number that this Hooper guy gave you."

Burgess read it off and Kyle dialed. It rang and rang, but no person, and no answering machine, picked up.

"Something about this Hooper guy feels very wrong," Kyle said, and the others agreed.

What Hooper was up to was a puzzle. First the mysterious visit to 109, then leading the police to Ida Mae Wilson's house in Wilson's car. Had Hooper not known he was being followed or had he led them to the house for a reason? Was he just playing games with them? If he was somehow involved, wouldn't he want to stay under their radar? Criminals played all sorts of games, and often believed they were smarter than the police. But this was flat-out strange. Could it be a strategy to distract them while something else was happening?

"If we're going at all, we're wearing vests and expecting trouble," Burgess said. "But first, let's get that photo over to DeSpain."

They had coffee while they waited for a response from DeSpain. Fifteen minutes later they had confirmation that the man who had been with Shelley at Sweety's was the same man claiming to be Charlie Hooper.

"Let's take a look at this," Burgess said. "At where we should be focusing tomorrow. The implants, and Lee's statement that for her age, the girl had had a lot of sex, and recent sex, suggests someone was prostituting her. Stan, what does Vice say. Are there known traffickers we should be looking at? What about girls who've recently been arrested. Young girls. Very young girls. Would they know something? Who's dealing with trafficking victims at the Preble? Maybe we can come at this from that angle. Has someone seen her? Does someone know her? Her tattoos are pretty distinctive."

"Does this mean we're not checking out Hooper tonight?" Stan said.

Burgess understood everyone's frustration. They liked to move on things. Move fast. What had been done to their victim amped that up. It was hard to reign in their impatience, but slow and steady was more likely to get them results.

Kyle was staring at the candle on their table, watching it flicker, like he was being hypnotized. Someone who didn't know him might have thought he wasn't present, until he said, "What about McCann?"

"The guy who found her?" Perry said.

"And the guy who wanted to get back out there and look for his 'missing' property. The guy whose car was a jumble of clothes, old shoes, dog's dish, a blanket to protect his seat, all that crap yesterday and today it's neat as a pin. Could be coincidence, or weekend vs weekday behavior, but I'm not buying it. I would be very interested in seeing Mr. McCann's trash."

Too often, as in this case, they were working on two fronts: both to identify their victim, so they could do victimology, learn about her life, answer the "whys" of her murder; on the other front, there was the search for her killer, a search hampered by their lack of answers about their victim. Someone killing a prostitute was, sadly, not uncommon. Subsequently mutilating the body wasn't rare, either. It was the lengths the killer or killers had gone to, the choice of where to dump the body, the killer taking the time to pose the body, and then burying the saw not far from the dump site instead of pitching it into a dumpster somewhere. It all made the case unusual. Unusual being a euphemism for damned hard to solve.

"Tomorrow, Stan, you check in with Vice, recent soliciting busts, and the Preble center. Who's the new guy on sex trafficking? He should be in the loop." Burgess shrugged. "Who knows. Maybe you show him those tats and he's got a name."

"On it, boss. Keep me busy as hell. Otherwise, it's wedding central." Perry narrowed his eyes. "How come you guys get to live with your women and I've got to marry mine?"

"I tried to marry mine," Burgess said. "She's waiting for me to settle down. Or refuses to marry a cop because our lives are too dangerous."

"Been there. Done that," Kyle said. "Marriage, I mean. Probably going there and doing it again. I'm just waiting for the Xanax to kick in."

"You're no help," Perry complained.

"Sure we are," Burgess said. "I'm getting my uniform cleaned and Terry is going to sprinkle rose petals. And we'll still be here to listen to you bitch, won't we, Ter? Besides, Stan, you're having a baby. It's exciting. Terry can help you with that. My kid arrived at age fifteen, so I'm useless unless you want to hear about how terrifying it is to have a kid about to drive away in the family car."

This was a moment, that lull in the investigation when they all relaxed, connected, remembered what their team was all about.

"Hey, Joe," Perry said. "We've both got our assignments. What are *you* doing tomorrow?"

"Seeking advice from a former lady of the night."

Perry fanned himself and rolled his eyes. "Maybe you need some Xanax, too. What do you think, Terry?"

"I think it's an inspired idea. I think he's a lucky dog. But she'll only to talk to Joe anyway, so there's no sense in being jealous. Even though she's out of the game, she may have some ideas. Some connections."

Burgess hoped so. It was an imposition to go talk to Alana Black, undoubtedly the sexiest woman he'd ever known, about prostitution in

Portland. With his help and support, and after some backsliding and causing him and his sister Sandy endless frustration, she'd left that life behind and trained as a massage therapist. She'd gotten her GED, gone to school, and was developing a successful practice. He'd even, with great trepidation, introduced her to his family. That had been Chris's idea. She was the most generous woman he'd ever known.

The kids loved Alana. It wasn't unusual for him to come home to find the four of them in the living room, watching some dumb movie, Neddy snuggled up next to her, while Chris beamed at the scene like exotic, voluptuous Alana was a fourth child. Burgess supposed she sorta was. Ever since the night he'd found sixteen-year-old Alana beaten and bloody in a Portland park on a freezing night, and saved her life, she'd belong to him. Chris called them his "waifs," the kids he'd rescued over the years.

The ones who'd lived.

FIFTEEN

Burgess paid the bill and they walked out into a soft July night, the kind of night that reminded him of summer nights growing up and the excitement of being out after dark. Now when he was out after dark, it was usually because something bad had happened. Last night's fireworks had been nice, and a change from bad things. They already seemed far away.

As they headed for their cars, Perry said, "Before we call it a night and retire to get our beauty sleep, can we check out Hooper's place? Just do a knock and talk?"

"I think it's Ida Mae Wilson's place," Burgess said. "Sure. Vests."

Moments like this, he still felt like the dad Perry sometimes called him. His kids impulsive and eager to make something happen, him acting as the sea anchor, responsible for keeping them as safe as he could. The possibility that Hooper had led police to the house deliberately made him nervous. It wasn't so long ago that he'd been led to a house that was booby trapped. Waiting for the bomb squad to defuse it had been the longest hours of his life.

First they'd drive the streets around the house, getting a feel for the neighborhood. Then Burgess would take the door, with Kyle as backup, and Perry would take the back, in case anyone ran that way.

On TV it looks easy, but knocking on a strange door, not knowing what's on the other side, was one of the most dangerous parts of policing. Right up there with traffic stops. You didn't just walk up to the door and knock. Unless you've gotten lazy or careless about training, you placed yourself strategically to the right or left, depending on whether the door opened in or out. In case the answer was gunfire, those behind you arranged themselves so if you were shot they wouldn't be next.

Ida Mae Wilson's house was a cape with an attached two-car garage, perched on a steep knoll, set well back from the street on a large lot. A curving driveway lead down to the street, the curves masked by large clumps of yew bushes. It was surrounded by something police officers hated—bushy, overgrown shrubs that partially blocked the windows and made access to them difficult. There were privacy hedges along both lot lines, one of cedar and the other scraggly ten-foot lilacs. A very desirable property for someone who liked privacy. He was reminded of Captain Cote's house. And how easy it had been for bad guys to get at him unobserved.

The lot was deep and backed up to another deep property. The houses on either side were also shrouded in bushes. There were no lights on in the house or the neighboring houses. They parked a few houses away, geared up, and headed up the drive. Perry headed toward the rear of the house, swinging wide in case there were motion sensor lights. Burgess headed for the door, Kyle behind him and to his left.

A moment's pause. He rang the bell, then knocked, announcing "Police, Mrs. Wilson. Please answer the door."

He waited, heart pounding.

No one responded. No lights came on.

He waited. Vigilant. Listening.

He heard Kyle slip through the shrubs and up to the windows, cautiously shining his light in, moving methodically from window to window. "Looks empty, Joe," Kyle whispered before he moved around the corner of the house.

He heard the muffled voices when Kyle met Perry in the back. Then nothing for so long he went to see what had happened to them, moving quietly and without lights around the side of the house opposite to where Perry had gone. Apparently empty house or not, there was still a chance this was a trap.

At the back of the house he found Perry crouched in a window well, Kyle standing over him and leaning down, both of them fixed on something inside as Perry played his lights around.

"What?" he said.

"The house is empty, except for this. But it's a big this," Kyle said, stepping back. "See for yourself."

Burgess peered through the dirty window into a basement laundry room. Half the room was a normal room—washer, dryer, shelf for folding laundry, and a laundry cart. The other half was partitioned into a crude wooden box. Though the interior of the box was dark, they could see the end of a cot and a bucket. There was a pool of blood on the floor and broad streaks leading toward a closed door. A lot of blood.

He'd seen plenty, over the years. Now that plenty was supplying possible narratives. He tried to not rush to conclusions, to let the scenes speak to him, but he couldn't block the image of a helpless girl being butchered here. His stomach clenched and he regretted his heavy meal. Scenes like the blood promised this might be went down better on an empty stomach.

"Exigent circumstances, Joe?" Perry said. "Can I kick the door?" There was a vibe in his voice, a Holy Fuck vibe, a regretful, 'I know I wanted something to happen tonight but I didn't mean this' vibe.

"You bet."

All three pulled on gloves before Perry mule-kicked the back door. It burst open, slamming with a crash into a wall. Burgess searched for a light switch. He found it and flipped it on, illuminating a dated kitchen with beige walls stained by decades of tobacco smoke and dirty beige linoleum. There were blood smears across the floor leading to a closed door that likely led to the garage.

Kyle and Perry fanned out to search the house, reassembling in minutes in the kitchen, where Burgess waited beside a second door he'd opened to reveal basement stairs.

"Empty," Kyle said, "except for two filthy mattresses on the floor in a back room."

So much for calling it a night and getting some sleep. Already weary in anticipation of the hours to come, Burgess pulled out his phone and called for their crime scene team, then Vince Melia.

"Happy fifth of July," he said when Vince answered. "We may have found the murder scene."

"Catch me up."

He told Melia about Charlie Hooper's peculiar visit. The fake license with this address. Hooper, if that was his real name, driving a car registered to Ida Mae Wilson, the record owner of the property. How officers had followed Hooper to this house. How Stan's interviews had put Hooper at the tattoo shop with the victim. Their decision to do a knock and talk, and what they'd found.

"We haven't entered the basement yet. Waiting for Wink and Dani."

"One of these days, Wink's gonna retire. Especially if you Crips keep calling him out at night. Mrs. Wink grows weary."

The Crips was the name Burgess had given their team when they were all injured in one way or another and still limping their way through, solving crimes. The name had stuck. Now even their colleagues called them Crips. Still, he always hoped they'd get through an investigation with nothing worse than his bad knee. He figured he'd hurt enough and limped enough. If there was getting shot to be done, someone else could do it.

"The Crips are weary, too, Vince. We can't help if it bad guys don't work nine to five. My cop gut tells me this is going to be a long, bad night. One of those nights when taking my pension and taking up golf looks appealing."

"You can't quit on me, Joe."

"Wasn't planning to."

"You'd hate golf," Melia said.

"You coming out?"

Melia sighed. "I'm coming out."

"You don't have to, you know. We've got this."

"Right. See you soon."

Just thinking about limping made his knee hurt. If he'd known he was coming to a crime scene, he would have worn his knee brace. He wasn't about to go home for it, though. He should get a spare one and keep it in the truck.

"Vince coming?" Kyle asked.

Perry had wandered off, doing another tour through the house, looking for small things they might have missed.

Burgess nodded.

"I know the kid was hoping something would happen tonight. Not me. I was hoping for a quiet night."

"Me, too. A nice steak, a drink with friends, a quiet evening with my family."

Kyle's eyes follow the smeared blood trail across the dingy floor. "Not likely. Think this is where she was killed?"

Burgess shrugged. "Something bad happened here. Think that's why Hooper led us here? Why would he do that?"

"Guilty conscience?" Kyle suggested.

"Pretty damned weird way of getting our attention. Why not just make an anonymous call?"

"Maybe he underestimated us," Kyle said.

Stan Perry was back, rocking impatiently from one foot to the other. "What are we waiting for? I'm going down."

Knowing he didn't have to give the warning, Burgess said, "Stay to one side and try not to muck things up."

"Right, Joe. Like I'm a rookie and this is my first crime scene."

"Despite appearances, Stan," Kyle said, "we don't even know if this *is* a crime scene. Yet."

"You think maybe someone was using tools in the basement, got injured and dragged off to the hospital?" Perry said. "In an empty house? Shitload of blood for something like that."

"Just go," Burgess said, "and leave us old farts in peace."

"I am not an old fart," Kyle said. "I am in the prime of life. You are the old fart."

Burgess didn't argue. He was thinking about what they'd all seen through the window, and wondering how their reactions differed. Whether they saw things he wasn't seeing, or drawing different conclusions.

"What were you thinking when you looked through the window, Ter?"

"That we're looking at a place where someone was held prisoner. And most likely a place where someone was killed. Wondering whether just Mermaid, or many girls, were held in that cell. How scared they were. Did they lie there on that cot and hope for someone to rescue them? Did they scream for help, not knowing how isolated this house is? I'm wondering who would do this. Who *did* do this? What kind of a person can mistreat another human being like our girl was. What were you wondering?"

"Whether that volume of blood meant the victim was likely dead. I see something like that, I start thinking evidence. What the scene is going to tell us. Whether we'll read it right. I worry that we'll miss something. Thinking about the victim? Often I do that once preservation of the scene is underway. Or driving home. I'm like a cow chewing a cud. I keep pulling things up and chewing them over. Sometimes, when it's hard to go home after something especially bad, I'll just go park somewhere, watch the city, and process for a while."

He looked at the blood smears on the kitchen floor and thought he saw a faint footprint. As he knelt to inspect it, he said, "It was easier when I was a solitary curmudgeon. I love them and I'm grateful to have a family to come home to, but I still get these fears that the pressure to get home and be a good dad means I'm rushing things. Distracted by my kid's issues. That I'll miss things. That I'm not the detective our victims deserve. I don't know how you've done it. With the girls. The PMS queen.

All that weighing on you. Distracting you. And you're still such a good detective."

Kyle swept off an imaginary hat and bowed. "My thanks, kind sir."

From below, Stan Perry yelled, "Oh Jesus. Holy fuck! Get down here, you guys. Call Medcu. Call Medcu!"

There was the distinct sound of gagging and he pounded up the stairs, staggered across the kitchen, and vomited in the sink. He stared at them, white faced. "Get some fucking ambulances over here. Maybe some of them are still alive."

"Them?"

Burgess headed for the stairs while Kyle got on the phone. "Brace yourself, Joe," Perry gasped between gags. "It's a fucking horror show. Better call the fire department, too. Tell 'em to bring tools to cut the chains."

SIXTEEN

It *was* a fucking horror show. What they couldn't see from the window was the rest of the cell. In the bright light from his flashlight he saw a decomposing head resting on the far end of the cot, facing the inside wall. On the floor, displayed as though they were reaching for something, were two severed hands. Chained to the wall were four naked girls. *Hispanic,* Burgess thought. *Probably teenagers, but small as children.* Two of them lay on the floor, unmoving. He couldn't tell if they were breathing. Two others huddled together, staring at him with dull, glazed eyes. The airless box reeked of fear, unwashed bodies, feces, decomp, and blood.

In the hot July damp the stench was overwhelming. His stomach flipped. He stepped out of the box, zigzagged across the room, trying not to step on the blood, and tried to open the windows.

They were nailed stuck.

He grabbed a big jug of detergent and swung it until he'd knocked out the glass.

Then he stepped back into the cell, checking the two unmoving girls for pulses. With the first, he couldn't tell. In the second he found a faint pulse. The other two stared at him, not making a sound. Horrified past fear? Brutalized past protest? Starved into submission? His anger swelled at whoever had done this. He tried to recall the Spanish words for friend and safe. Amigo? Seguro? He tried them a few times in a soft voice but got no reaction.

He tested the chains, but they were sturdy. There wasn't much he could do until the fire department got there with tools to cut them loose. He went back upstairs, found two plastic cups in the cupboard, filled them with water, and took them downstairs. He offered them to the girls, but they only stared. He mimicked drinking. Neither one moved. Finally, he put a cup against one girl's lips and tilted it, wetting her lips. Slowly, a tentative hand came up and took the cup.

He moved to the second girl. Offered her a cup. Pointed to the girl who was drinking, and said very softly, "It's okay." Slowly a dirty, shaking hand came out and took the cup, crouching over it protectively. She would take a sip, check to see if he was going to take it from her, then sip again.

"Sweet Jesus," he whispered. This fucking job broke your heart. His heart. Dammit. He'd said no more kids. He briefly closed his eyes, summoning the strength to get through this. Then he opened them and went to work.

Help would come. Pouring into the cell. His scene would necessarily be disrupted. He hated to do this, invading their dignity like this, but no one would believe what they'd seen unless he took some pictures. He swallowed, feeling like a rat, and photographed everything. The severed head. The posed hands. The small girls chained to the wall. The pool of blood. The marks where something had been dragged. The foul bucket that had served the girls as a toilet.

He wished he could photograph the smells. There was really no way for anyone who wasn't here to understand it without the smells. The horrific, gag-inducing, stomach-turning smells. Bad enough for someone who could leave periodically to gulp some fresh air. Hell on earth for someone chained to a wall.

He didn't want to leave them, but there was a footprint upstairs that was about to get trampled and he didn't want to lose anything that might help get the filthy bastards who'd done this. All of this.

He dashed upstairs, phone in hand, and knelt to photograph it. He looked around for something to cover it. Found a dry plastic dishpan and placed it, upside down, over the print. Placed a chair over that. Chances were small it would survive the onslaught that was coming at them—preservation of life was paramount—but he had to try.

Kyle was still on the phone, asking for patrol to help control the scene.

"Nothing Bothers Me" Perry was still clinging to the edge of the sink, gagging and green. Burgess waved a hand to get his attention. "Go outside. Take your flashlight. See if you can find a bulkhead door, so everyone doesn't have to come through here. Then, if you've got any blankets in your car, we could use them."

Perry waved a hand, picked up his flashlight, and wobbled toward the back door. It wasn't weakness to be shocked by a horrible scene. You could have seen it all a dozen times and then one day, one scene, one smell, one awful thing too many, it hit you. You still had to do the job, but you were allowed to be human. Most of them had days when they had puked into the bushes and gone back to work.

Burgess called Vince and told him what they'd found. Vince was four minutes out. Burgess told him to brace himself for a horror show.

A commotion of sirens and lights said help was arriving. Soon they'd be overrun with cops, medical personnel, and if they were unlucky, the news.

First through the door were fire fighters. Burgess explained what they needed. Two returned to the truck for tools, a third said he'd walk around the house, find Perry, and see if they could find and open a bulkhead door.

Before they piled down the stairs with their bolt cutters, Burgess cautioned them they were walking into something unusually ugly. He got a "we've seen it all, Sarge," look from the older guy, and nothing from the younger, so he shrugged. He was just trying to prepare them. If they wanted to be jerks, he could be one, too.

"The severed head and hands," he said, "try to work around them if you can because our crime scene team hasn't got their photos yet."

"Yeah, right," the world weary one said. Maybe thinking this was part of the friendly rivalry between police and fire and Burgess was jerking their chains. Like Burgess ever went out of his way to be friendly. Or to jerk someone's chain.

The young guy shot him a look and slowed his pace.

"I'm not kidding," Burgess said, following them down.

The arrival of the two big men carrying tools terrified the two girls who were conscious. They crouched together in a tight ball, pressing small hands over their eyes.

The firemen were pretty terrified themselves. The cocky one paused and looked at Burgess. "What the fuck?" he said.

Burgess shrugged. "I got no answers. We found them like this. Don't know much more than you do at this point. Just cut those damned chains, if you can, so we can get these poor kids to a hospital."

"You gotta get these freakin' hands out of the way so we can work."

Getting the girls to a hospital was paramount, so he carefully lifted the posed hands and set them on the cot by the head.

"Fuckin' freak show," the man said, barking some instructions to his sidekick as he moved into the small space and started cutting chains. "When I cut her free, you lift her out of the way so I can get to the next one."

"Where am I supposed to put her?" the sidekick said.

"Medcu's on the way," Burgess said. "I'll see if I've got some blankets in my truck."

There were footsteps on the stairs. Kyle coming down. He was carrying a couple of blankets, and clearly was bracing himself for what he was going to see. Even warned, it rocked him.

"Jesus, Joe!"

A silence. He heard Kyle swallow.

"What if we'd decided to call it a night and put this off until tomorrow?" Kyle said.

As the second firefighter lifted the first girl, Kyle passed a blanket to Burgess and opened the other one to receive the first girl. He wrapped her tight, holding her against his shoulder like an infant, murmuring soothing sounds to her as he carried her up the stairs.

Burgess opened his blanket for the second girl. Someone better get here soon. The other two were in worse shape. He was really afraid one of them was dead.

Imitating Kyle, he wrapped this girl tightly and held her against his shoulder. As he turned toward the stairs, there was the sound of hammering and splintering boards, and Stan and a couple firefighters broke through the wall beside the washer. Stan was holding a blanket.

"Medcu here yet, Stan?"

"Just pulling in." He held out the blanket. "Let's swap. I'll take her out."

Burgess handed the silent girl to Perry and opened another blanket. This girl, when they passed her to him, was limp and unresponsive. He was afraid maybe they were too late. Leaving them to deal with the fourth, he followed Perry through the broken wall and around the house to the waiting ambulances.

"There's one more coming," he said as he handed his girl over. "She's in the worst shape."

"I'll come with you," said his favorite EMT, a woman named Mary, who had an ocean full of patience and compassion. He led her around the house and into the basement.

The younger firefighter had spread his jacket on the floor, laid the girl on it, and was giving her CPR. He looked up with relief when he saw Mary, and stepped back. "She's all yours."

"Thanks, Jed," she said. "I really need to lose another child."

She looked at Burgess. They'd been together through enough losses to have become fatalistic, but she never did, and he tried not to. Especially when the victims were kids. She knelt beside the girl who looked horribly dead. Then she started giving Jed orders about what to go and get her, and started CPR.

"Anything you need me to do?" Burgess asked.

"What I always ask you to do. Find the bastard who did this." She worked on the child, her face set. "Come on, sweetie. Come back to us. Come on."

She shook her head and looked up at him. "I know I sent Jed for stuff, but I don't want to wait. If you could carry her out. There are things I can try here, but we've really got no time to lose."

He scooped up the girl, and the fireman's coat, and followed her out. Wishing there were a way to infuse the small body with some of his life force. Out in the driveway, he gratefully delivered her to Mary and her colleagues, saw her swept inside, and surrounded by hands and equipment. He recalled another child, an infant, and how hard they'd worked, and prayed, for his survival. They couldn't always win, but did their best. The doors swung shut. He watched as the first ambulance, then the second, backed down the drive and headed off into the night, the screaming sirens echoing through the quiet neighborhood.

The crime scene van and Melia's truck moved into the spaces where the ambulances had been. Burgess directed Wink and his team around the house to the bulkhead, then took a moment to breathe, wishing he could clear the stench from his lungs. It would linger there, clinging to his clothes. Travel home with him. Live in the Explorer for days, if not weeks. Tonight he'd be undressing outside the door and stumbling to the shower in the robe he kept on a hook out there. He felt a thousand dark ugly years old.

Kyle and Perry were standing in the darkness with him, each in his own private space, illuminated by strobe-light flashes of red and blue. Taking a moment before heading back inside. Tucking that initial horror on a shelf, hoping it would stay there and, please God, let them work. As though more bad stuff wasn't waiting for them.

There was a sudden, startling flash off to his left. The news was here. Before he could move toward it, a large uniformed officer appeared, fierce-faced and black as the night that surrounded them, moving toward the offender with the inexorable force of a bulldozer. Pinning the man and his camera in the beam of his flashlight, he barked a command in a loud, resonant voice, "Back to the street. Behind that line. Now!" and kept moving. Another time, different circumstances, the way the photographer turned and fled from the force of Officer Gabriel Delinsky would have been amusing. Tonight nothing could be amusing. Burgess was glad to see Delinsky, though. While his own job was to keep people safe, having Delinsky there made *him* feel safer. Gabe was the soul of decency and this was so indecent.

His protective instincts, though, made him glad Delinsky hadn't been in that basement. They'd worked a small, murdered boy a while back, a child in Delinsky's neighborhood. The officer had beaten himself up for his failure to save the child from toxic family circumstances. Not that Delinsky hadn't tried. He'd done all the right things, but bureaucracy can be an ass.

Burgess pulled himself back from another summer, from a steamy morning in a city park, bending over a beautiful murdered child, to find Vince Melia was standing beside him, already embarked on a litany of questions Burgess hadn't heard.

He held up a hand. "Missed all that, Vince. Start again."

Instead, Melia put a hand on his shoulder. "Take your time, Joe."

Burgess brought up the pictures and handed Melia his phone. "This will tell it better than I can. I'll be along in a minute."

Melia took his phone and carried it into the light.

Burgess went on standing in the dark. So did Kyle and Perry. Their crime scene wasn't going anywhere, and Dani and Wink knew what to do.

He should call Chris and tell her wasn't going to be home any time soon, but when he reached for his phone, he remembered he'd given it to Melia. He headed for Kyle, his body moving reluctantly, as if while he was standing there, putting himself back together, someone had coated him in lead. Kyle was staring into the night, his whippet body trembling. As he got closer, Burgess heard a sound, not a hum but a growl.

Kyle jumped when Burgess got close. "Sorry," he said. "I can't..."

"Take your time."

Kyle had gone back to staring. Burgess was worried. Kyle was his rock. His attack dog. Kyle didn't let things get to him. He just plodded on, doing the job, a silent, insanely competent, deeply insightful detective. Perry was the volatile one. But Kyle had daughters. Carrying out that emaciated, terrified waif would have hit him hard.

He headed toward Perry. When he got close enough, he could see the strobes from light bars coloring Perry's silver tears garish red and blue.

Fuck it. They could take as long as they needed.

He went to the house to find Melia.

Melia was bent over Burgess's phone, scrolling through the pictures. Scrolling through. Finishing. Going back through them again. Without a word, he handed the phone back, and Burgess, equally wordless, stepped outside to make his call.

"Hey, Joe," Chris said.

"I love you," he said.

"It's a bad one, isn't it."

He couldn't find the words. "Talk to me," he said. "Tell me about your day. The kids' days. I need something normal and decent."

Guys were always calling their wives and girlfriends angels. But Burgess meant it. Sometimes tough guys need saving. Chris saved him. Over and over.

"Sure," she said, and started talking.

He leaned against the door frame and listened, eyes closed, the music of her voice soothing him as much as her words.

"I won't ask about your day," she said.

"No. I just …I just called to say I'd be late. Don't wait up for me."

"Take care," she said. "The kids will make you a sandwich. I'll keep the home lights burning."

Burgess went to attend to his crime scene.

SEVENTEEN

Their companionable steak dinner might have happened in another decade. By the time they finished, he and Kyle and Perry staggered out into a dawning day so utterly done in they could barely make it to their cars. As if it were part of routine police procedure, they each did the same thing—got in their cars, started them, and then just sat there, staring out through their windshields.

Their conversation about next steps had been nearly monosyllabic. Kyle said, "When?" Perry said, "Yeah?" and Burgess had said, "Noon." Now, sitting in his car, he remembered the dog. He had a date with a dog well before noon. He could have wept.

Burgess moved first, heading not for home but for the hospital to see how the girls were doing. He'd gone to the hospital to check on someone or to get patched up so often there ought to be a Joe Burgess room, if not a whole Joe Burgess wing. A place where a bed waited for him, whether he was a patient or just a tired guy who wasn't sure he could put one more foot in front of the other.

There was no designated Burgess bed, but there was a kind nurse named Susan, a friend of Chris's, who ordered him to sit down, brought him coffee and a muffin, and gave him an update on the girls. Two were being treated for exhaustion, starvation, and dehydration. The other two were in in the ICU. One would likely make it. The other? Only time would tell.

"That poor little evidence tech you sent over to take their pictures? She was crying the whole time." The woman smiled. "Not like Wink, huh?"

"No," Burgess agreed. "Not like Wink." Poor Dani. Devlin was a rock and she tried so hard to be like him.

Before he left, he stopped by each bed, as though a tired old cop standing at their bedside could make any difference. Then he went down to the ER, hoping Dr. Sarita Cohen might be around. They had kind of an entangled history. Burgess had once saved her from a scissors-wielding thug, and she'd stitched him up the last time he got shot. He got lucky. For Burgess getting lucky didn't mean what it meant to most men. It meant getting information. Finding the witness. Having the fingerprints, ballistics, or DNA match. Finding Dr. Cohen in the ER.

Like the nurse before her, Dr. Cohen insisted he sit down before she'd talk to him.

"I'm fine, Doctor, really I am," he insisted.

She gave him the smile he remembered from before. Despite her crisp professional demeanor, it was both warm and impish. "You're too tall for me to talk to when you're standing up, Detective."

She was a very small woman, so he sat.

"I assume you're here about those girls."

He nodded.

"Physically, I believe that three of them will recover. Emotionally, I cannot say. It will depend on what kind of services they get and how resilient they are. The fourth is still a question mark. She is younger, with less to draw on, and she is in very bad shape. I wish I could give you better news."

Burgess wasn't about to accept "three out of four ain't bad." Not that it was in his power to do anything for the poor child. All he could do ensure that whoever killed Mermaid and horribly abused these girls paid the highest price possible.

He didn't realize he'd dozed off until he felt her hand on his shoulder, gently shaking him. "Detective. Joe." She had a musical lilt to her voice. "Go home. Get some sleep. You can't do good work in this state."

He'd never fallen asleep during an interview no matter how tired he was. Was he past his sell-by date?

"I'm sorry. I've never…"

There was that smile again. "You don't owe anyone an apology, Joe. Another day for those girls and it might have been a different story. Go home. Burn those clothes. And get some rest."

He thanked her and gimped out to his truck. His knee was a fireball and Chris was going be on his case because he hadn't worn his brace. At least he had someone to go home to, even if she would yell at him. He rolled down the window, hoping wind blowing in his face would help keep him awake. It was after five a.m. when he climbed the steps, shucked off his clothes, put on his ratty old robe, and let himself in. The house was quiet as he tiptoed to the bathroom. Clean underwear was laid out on top of the hamper with a note: We missed you.

Smiling, he crumpled it up and stepped into the shower. Sometimes, after working a scene outside on a cold night, it would take a long, hot shower to begin to warm him up. This morning, the long shower was to rinse off the crime scene stench mixed with the sweat of working in that humid basement. To steam clean his lungs so every breath wasn't blood and decomp.

Then he slipped on the underwear, hung up his robe, plugged in his phone, and went to bed.

When they weren't spooned together, Chris slept on her back, one arm flung up beside her head, the hair that had escaped from her braid forming a golden brown halo around her head. He could watch her for hours. He didn't have hours, though. He had a little over three hours before his date with Kiki.

Kiki was beautiful, but nothing for Chris to get jealous about, since she was a German shepherd.

He set his alarm and climbed into bed. Chris turned and he wrapped himself around her, asleep in an instant.

Long before he was ready, his alarm roused him, catapulting him into his family's morning chaos. He lay a moment, eavesdropping as Nina and Dylan questioned Chris about last night. Heard her saying, "I don't know. He said it was so bad he didn't want to talk about it. Now, he's still very tired and he has to go out again soon, so no questions, okay? We can talk about it when he's ready."

Then Neddy's voice, "Can I take some coffee to my Joe?"

That was what Neddy called him. Burgess had no idea why, but there was something special about having a kid who'd say, "My Joe, can we go to the park?" His Joe did what he could. When he could. He never forgot what Nina and Neddy had been through.

He dragged himself out of bed, and it felt like dragging, and over to the pile of clothes Chris had put out. Right on top was her wordless admonition—his knee brace. Burgess had never asked Chris to do this for him. Not this. Not his laundry. Not help him raise his son. He'd been a bachelor for a long time. He could take care of himself. Still, he was grateful for the way her caretaking made his life better.

He was buttoning his shirt when the door opened and Neddy came in carrying a cup of coffee. The boy presented it like a gift for a king. "For my Joe."

"Thank you, Neddy. I really need this."

"Chris says you had a bad night last night but we're not supposed to ask you about it. Are you okay?" The boy's anxious eyes roved over him, making sure he wasn't shot or cut or otherwise damaged. Already a cop's kid, though Neddy wanted to be a fireman when he grew up.

"I'm fine. Except for being tired. And…" He raised the cup, "… needing this. This morning I'm going to be doing a search with a really smart K9 named Kiki. Someday, maybe I can take you to meet her. Would you like that?"

"Yes, my Joe. Are you going to find a lost person?"

"More likely a lost button. It depends on what Kiki's nose locates. Dogs have amazing noses, you know. Thousands of times better than ours. That's why the police have dogs. To help us find lost things and lost people."

Neddy grinned. "Do you ever find money?"

"Not very often." He finished the coffee and bent to put on his shoes. "It would be nice to find money. But I couldn't keep it anyway."

"Peter's dad has one of those magnetic things. You know, the ones people use to find things that are buried in the ground. I'd like to have one of those."

Chris stuck her head in. "Neddy. Time for camp. Morning, Joe." She crossed the room and kissed him. He was such a sucker for this woman. She kisses him good morning and he's ready to blow off Kiki and his whole schedule. It was probably a good thing she had to go to work. "Here," she said, holding out her hand, two painkillers in her palm. "And here." A glass of water. "Susan says you were dead on your feet when she saw you this morning."

"I think…" He kissed her again. "I think I'm still alive."

He hugged Neddy. "Have fun at camp." Headed for the kitchen. He felt like Methuselah's grandfather. Dylan and Nina were waiting, shoulder to shoulder, waiting to give him the family body scan before they departed for their respective days.

"I'm fine," he said.

"Toast," said Nina, pointing to a plate.

"I don't have…"

"Toast, Dad," Dylan said. "Or we don't let you leave."

Burgess looked at Chris. "This is what it means to have a family? I'm being bullied by people who aren't old enough to vote?"

"Think of yourself as a lucky man, and eat the toast." Chris smiled, one of her slow growing ones that was like the sun coming up.

Burgess was no fool. He ate his toast.

Then he took a trash bag, went to the entry, and bagged up yesterday's clothes. He tied off the bag and left it there. These clothes were not coming into his house. He should have cleaned his gun. His holster. His badge holder. A stink like last night's clings to everything. There was no time.

As he climbed in the truck and headed out to Stroudwater Park for his date with Kiki, and for what he hoped was the last time, he wondered if Kyle and Perry were able to get some sleep.

EIGHTEEN

Kiki and her handler were waiting. The handler was in neutral mode. Kiki, ears up, was ready to take on the world. The officer whose job it was to ruin the local runners' day once again looked like a man who'd been gnawed on by rats.

"I hope to heck this is thing is done now, Sarge," he said. "I don't think I can keep the ravening hordes out much longer."

Burgess liked the phrase "ravening hordes." Used to refer to walkers and runners, it conjured up quite the image of those half-naked runners with their bright clothes and shoes also carrying maces and swords, perhaps even carrying flaming torches and wearing those dumb horned Viking hats. Picturing it made his morning.

After an hour of Kiki's enthusiastic sniffing around the dump site, Burgess was ready to call it a day, but just as he was about to suggest to the handler that it was likely there wasn't anything to be found, she gave an "I've got it!" bark and lay down.

The handler looked at him and shrugged. "She doesn't like to give up." He reached down with a gloved hand and felt around in the old brown leaves. Burgess, watching, thought he was going to come up empty-handed. Instead he held out a small object to Burgess, then praised the dog and gave her a treat.

Burgess dug out his reading glasses—a new and detested addition to his life—and squinted down at it. It was a pin, the kind organizations handed out as a marker of years of service or to mark a promotion. It was a simple thing, white enamel, with the number fifteen in red. There was something on the back, but it would take a magnifying glass to read it.

"Well. Something," he said. "Some genius back at 109 is bound to tell us what it means."

He bagged the pin, thanked Kiki and her handler, released the weary cop who was protecting the spot from the public, and heaved himself into the Explorer. As he headed back to his desk, stopping to arm himself with a large black coffee, he was aware, once again, what was missing in this case—Captain Paul Cote. No Cote at the scene last night. No wake-up call this morning. It was too good to be true. Maybe Cote had permanently switched his focus to Stan Perry and Perry had gotten that wake-up call. Cote wouldn't call Kyle. Kyle had been with Burgess when they dragged him off to the hospital.

He hoped Kyle and Perry were getting some sleep. Hoped they'd show up around noon rested and with clear heads. His felt like someone had stuffed his with cotton.

Thinking of Cote reminded him of Bambi Bailey. He wondered what Cote had done about that. He was sure she'd been bailed out immediately. What he wasn't so sure of was whether someone with authority had taken away her car keys for the benefit of the traveling—and walking—public. Pretty, spoiled young girls like that always thought they were untouchable.

He was gulping lukewarm coffee and waiting for it to kick in, trying in a fuzzy-minded way to prioritize the direction of today's investigative efforts when he came around a curve and almost drove right into a white pickup stopped in the middle of the road. A man was standing in the road beside it, head in his hands, staring at what was left of a blue BMW that was mostly wrapped around a tree.

Burgess stood on the brakes, and swerved, missing the truck by inches. Then he backed up, flipped on his lights, and called dispatch to send officers, an ambulance, all the personnel needed for a bad accident.

"Police officer," he said to the stunned man, who was bleeding from a bad cut on his head. "What happened here?"

The man pointed with his bloody hand to a side road about two hundred yards away. "She came flying out of there, going about fifty. She was all over the road. She swerved into my lane. I braked and swung to the left but there wasn't time." He grabbed a breath. Staring at the crumpled blue car. At the blood on his hand. He was shaking. "Oh my god! There was nothing I…I don't think she even saw me. She was looking down at her phone. She slid along my truck and swung right into that tree. Never tried to brake or anything. Honest, officer. I didn't do anything wrong."

The man was practically in tears. "It just…I just got out of my truck. I haven't…I don't think I can look…Can you see if she's okay?"

Burgess patted the man on the shoulder, gave him one of the white cotton handkerchiefs he always carried, and pointed to a patch of grass beyond the sidewalk. "There's help coming. Why don't you sit down over there while I check things out."

Handkerchief pressed against his bleeding face, the man stumbled out of the road and sat on the grass. Burgess walked to the BMW. It was a mangled mess. He bent and peered in, trying to get a visual on the driver. He already knew who it was. He'd done his best to keep this from happening, but the world has a soft spot for pretty girls. Especially pretty, rich and well-connected girls.

The airbag had done its best, but things didn't look good. He reached in. Checked for a pulse. The faint, thready response was too much like another neck he'd recently checked. Against his will, the judgmental side of his nature was comparing this girl, who had everything and carelessly threw it away, with those small girls last night, who had had no hand in their fate.

"Get a grip, Burgess," he told himself.

"Help is on the way, Bambi. Just sit tight and we'll get you out of there." He pulled out another handkerchief and pressed it gently against her bleeding face. He stayed crouched by the car, talking to her, hoping she could hear, hoping it might keep her with them, ignoring the angry horns of commuters and the commotion of the curious who had gathered on the sidewalk, until patrol arrived to manage the scene.

The supervisor, Jeff Russell, who took charge and began directing things, just gave him a look. "You doing traffic now, too, Burgess?"

"Just driving by," he said. "It's all yours, and you're welcome to it. Her name's Bambi Bailey, by the way. I stopped her yesterday in this same spot after she nearly ran me off the road and then swerved on the sidewalk and hit a stroller. Seems she was eating cereal and needed two hands for that. I arrested her for inattentive driving and a marked lane violation, as well as refusing to provide her license and registration. She should have been off the road today."

Russell barked some instructions to his guys, and more into his phone. "Connections?"

"Senator's niece."

"Thanks a hell of a lot, Burgess."

Burgess shrugged. "We do our jobs, Jeff. Then people who think they know better or care more about ass kissing screw it up. I hope she makes it."

Free to go, he turned toward the Explorer.

"Yeah," Russell said, "If you believe in miracles."

"The miracle I'm hoping for is already over at the hospital."

"Yeah." Russell spat out some more instructions. "Heard about that. Every time you think you've seen it all."

It was dangerous to think you'd seen it all, Burgess thought, as he got in the truck. *It tempted fate to throw something worse in your face.*

He drove the rest of the way in a meditative silence, the background of the radio's call and response the soundtrack of his life. He was almost back at 109 before he noticed that it was a beautiful July morning.

He needed to stop drifting and get his head back in the game. The coffee hadn't done a thing and his stomach said he'd better not drink any more. It was lucky he'd been doing this so long he could work on autopilot. On autopilot he took the pin that Kiki had found to the evidence room and logged it in. Asked Rocky Jordan to grab the records on the two phone numbers they'd gotten yesterday—the one that Shelley had given DeSpain, and the one that the man who called himself Hooper had given Burgess. He also asked Rocky to find out what he could about Ida Mae Wilson and the property they'd been in last night.

He left a message for Wink to check out the pin when he had a chance. The way things were going, Wink would get to it by Christmas.

When Kyle and Perry got in, they'd organize a visit to Ida Mae Wilson's neighbors. He could have patrol do a canvass, but he thought they needed to see people's faces and reactions, press them for more information if necessary. How could those girls be held prisoner, and another likely murdered there, without someone noticing something?

His voicemail was jammed with question from reporters, messages he barely listened to before deleting them. Vince Melia or Captain Cote, more likely Cote, who loved the press, would do the press conference about last night's horror show.

He sorted through his messages, hoping there might be something that would give them a lead about Shelley's identity. It was a whole lot of nothing. The crazies had come out and not much else. He was listening to voicemail as he sorted the Pepto-Bismol colored slips, an activity so rote he almost missed a message from DeSpain. It was brief and to the point.

"This is DeSpain. There's something I need to tell you. Call me." And a number.

Burgess didn't know whether DeSpain was nocturnal, as his late arrival at Sweety's suggested. Nor did he care. So far, DeSpain was the closest thing they had to a witness.

Before he could return that call, he got a summons to the chief's office. He hoped he didn't look as dissolute as he felt. He hadn't looked in a mirror since he left home, but that one had given him nothing but bad news. He'd rushed out without shaving. His shoes were muddy from tromping through the woods. There was blood on his shirt cuffs from his two accident victims. His shoulders were hunched with weariness and the dark circles beneath his eyes looked like holdovers from his football days. He believed in matching his appearance to the dignity of the job and hated to present like this. Nothing he could do about it now. He had clothes in his locker but he wasn't about to keep the chief waiting while he mowed his face and improved his sartorial splendor.

He assumed the chief was looking for an update about last night's activities, but the chief was focused on something else. There was a man he didn't know waiting with the chief, a man the chief introduced as "Robert Bailey, Senator Bailey's brother," adding, "Mr. Bailey has some concerns about yesterday's traffic stop."

Bailey was exactly what he would have expected. Impeccably dressed in gray slacks, a silky navy polo under a navy blazer with about a hundred gold buttons. Boat shoes without socks. Thick silver hair moussed into place. Pointy nose and pointy chin. The beginnings of broken veins on his nose and cheeks from too many cocktail hours.

Bailey didn't offer to shake a mere peon's hand and Burgess didn't take the offered seat. Instead, he said, "I don't want to be rude, Mr. Bailey, why are you here?"

"Joe," the chief said in his 'let's sooth the raging beast' voice, "I know you think Captain Cote was wrong to…"

"Chief. Mr. Bailey. I have no idea what Captain Cote did or did not do with respect to the arrest of Mr. Bailey's daughter I made yesterday. I've been tied up on a homicide and an incident involving a severed head and hands and four brutalized children who were chained up in a basement."

Yes. Okay. He said it because it was true *and* to make Bailey flinch. Remind the man—and the chief—that police did serious work here. That his workday wasn't about stopping pretty girls and giving them a hard time. The chief had picked a damned poor time to chastise him about a traffic stop, when he had to get through his messages, write reports about last night, and get back out there to look for a killer. Burgess really didn't care how out of line he was. He couldn't be more out of line than a parent, and a department, who allowed that girl to get back behind the wheel today. He was wearing himself and his crew out, dealing with horrific things and neglecting his family, to keep people safe, while *this* is what the chief was concerned about? Bambi might well have killed herself. She could easily have killed that man in the truck as well.

"Now look, Joe," the chief began. "I know you're wrapped up in this homicide, but…"

Burgess held up a hand. "Hold on."

Bailey gave the chief a "do something with your underling" look, and the chief frowned.

Burgess said, "I'm not being insubordinate, sir. I'm asking because on my way back from searching a crime scene this morning with a K9, I came upon a serious vehicle crash involving Mr. Bailey's daughter. Mr. Bailey, are you unaware that your daughter, while looking at her phone instead of the road, drove into another vehicle this morning and then crashed her car into a tree?"

He gave the location and Sergeant Russell's number. "She was still alive when I handed the scene over to patrol, with the fire department and medcu en route. I am very sorry to be the one who brings you this news, Mr. Bailey."

The chief managed a "You can go, Burgess," as he and Bailey dove for their phones.

Burgess went.

He got no pleasure from encounters like this. He wasn't on a crusade to reform policing in his city. He didn't long to work his way up the food chain. He didn't care about bars on his collar or fancy clusters on his hat. He cared about justice, and got annoyed when suck-up bullshit wasted his time and got in the way of that.

By the time he was back at his desk, he'd recognized his bad mood for what it was. He needed rest and food. If he couldn't have that, he needed to be making progress in his investigation. Also, despite his frustration with indulgent parents like Bailey, he was also the parent of two teens and a man who'd seen the tragic results of adolescents' belief in their immortality over and over again. He hadn't knelt by that crashed car, holding his handkerchief against Bambi's face and talking to her purely out of duty. She was someone's child and she was hurt.

Okay. Bambi had occupied real estate in his head long enough. He had other things to worry about.

First, he was going to do something about his appearance so the public didn't see a disheveled bum when they looked at him. If they were going to canvass Ida Mae Wilson's neighborhood, he didn't want to scare off anyone who answered their door. He'd never be slim and dapper like Bailey, and the day he moussed his hair would be a cold one in hell, but he could look better than this. He got clean clothes and shoes from his locker. Peering into the mirror as he mowed his face, he saw a man with gray streaked dark hair that badly needed cutting and a scar that made him look scarier than he was. He dressed, tossed his old clothes back in his locker, and put two more white cotton handkerchiefs in his pocket. He's been stanching the wounds of this city for decades with these. He hoped this case wasn't the time he finally had to wave one in surrender.

He went back to his desk, found the message from DeSpain, and called him back.

He got a sleepy, "Hey?"

"Detective Burgess, Mr. DeSpain. You left me a message?"

DeSpain groaned. "Oh, God. I am so sorry, Detective. I didn't quite tell you the truth yesterday."

Burgess waited.

"I wasn't the one who did Shelley's work. It was Kit, she's a girl I'm training. I didn't mention her because she's not licensed yet. After you left I got to thinking that you probably really didn't care about that. So I spoke to her, and she'll be glad to tell you anything she knows. I can't say it's more than I know, but girls, you know. They talk."

The guy could have told them this last night. But better late than never. There had been no time to follow up yet anyway. Burgess got her name and contact information and thanked DeSpain for his honesty and concern.

"Sure, sure. Better if I'd told you right away, huh? But hey. It's something. I think maybe she knows Shelley's last name."

NINETEEN

As he was setting down the phone, Janice approached his desk, holding a message slip. She halted a few feet away, as if afraid to come any closer. "I don't bite," he said, holding out his hand for the slip. "Really, Janice. I wish you'd stop treating me like I might."

"Sorry," she said. "Sorry." She hurried away.

"You're not winning that one," Kyle said, suddenly appearing in his quiet way.

"Least of my battles," Burgess said. "You get some rest?"

"More than you, I'll bet."

Burgess nodded. "Forgot I had a date with Kiki this morning. And things have gone downhill from there. Except maybe not."

He told Kyle about the little pin Kiki had found, Bambi's accident, and his pleasant visit with Bambi's father and the chief.

"So where's the good news in all that?"

"DeSpain called, plagued by a guilty conscience."

"We could use more of those."

"Agreed. Seems he wasn't quite truthful about who did Shelley's artwork. His apprentice, or whatever they're called, did it. He thinks she may know more about Shelley. Like her last name. I was about to call her when Janice appeared. And you."

"I don't bite," Kyle said. "So what are we doing today?"

Burgess glanced down at the note. "One of us is going to Augusta."

"I nominate Stan."

"Me, too. Seen him around yet?"

"Seen who?" Perry said, appearing behind Kyle.

"Whom," Burgess said.

"You can be a real pain sometimes, you know that, Joe?"

"I've been told. So Stan, you up for a trip to Augusta?"

Perry made a face. "Do I have to, Dad?"

"Yes, Son. You have to."

"It's just a head. Why can't he send a report? Why does someone have to be there?"

"Because that's what we do, Stan," Kyle said. "Look on the bright side. You get a road trip. A nice drive on a beautiful summer day. The company of the lovely Dani. Several hours without Joe telling you what to do."

"When you put it that way, how can I say no?" Perry held his hand out for the note Burgess was offering, saying when the ME was going to deal with Mermaid, or Shelley's, head.

"How are the girls doing?" Kyle asked.

"When I swung by this morning, two were doing okay, two in ICU. The ER doc, Dr. Cohen says she's optimistic about one of them. Other is touch and go. I'll swing back later, see if they able to talk to us, and what language they speak so we can get a translator."

"So how do we catch this fucker?"

"One step at a time?" Burgess said.

"Christ!" Perry said, finally reading the note. "Lee wants us there in an hour. In summer traffic. Nothing like giving us notice or anything. Catch you old farts later." He sketched a wave and was gone.

Kyle looked at Burgess. "I am *not* an old fart."

"No, Terry, you are not. Kid's just trying to piss you off. Looks like it's working, too."

Kyle threw himself into a chair. "Okay, Fearless Leader. Where do we start?"

"I'm going to call this woman. Kit. The one DeSpain was training. Go talk to her. See if she has anything for us. Then we're going to go back out to Ida Mae Wilson's neighborhood and knock on some doors."

Burgess made the call. Kit was working, so, trying not to get their hopes up and failing miserably, they headed back to Sweety's. He'd planning on spending a quiet hour writing reports, but this felt urgent. Who knew when they'd have another chance to talk to her?

Burgess was driving. Kyle was tipped back in his seat with his eyes closed. Without opening his eyes, Kyle said, "Why did Hooper lead us to that house? You believe he didn't know he was being followed?"

"Maybe he was in over his head and didn't know what else to do? Because he's definitely in over his head."

"Speaking of heads, are you really comfortable sending Stan to Augusta?"

"I'm training him to take your place when you take mine."

"And you retire? Don't even joke about it."

"Not sure I am joking. I couldn't get moving this morning. We're all tired, but it feels like more than that. There's no second wind and I'm not thinking clearly. I'm sure there are things we should be doing. Things I'm forgetting. I'm used to having Vince as a sounding board and…well, I'm not sure how to put it. It's like he's absent. I think he came back too soon and he doesn't have the stamina yet. It feels like no one is running interference for us. And like the brass isn't being kept up on what's going on. The thing with the chief this morning is a good example."

Burgess braked for a man in a wheelchair who was crossing the street. The man waved and blew Burgess a kiss. His city, his characters.

"The thing with the chief this morning?" Kyle prompted.

"We're up all night with that scene. Then, when he calls me in, I think he's looking for a firsthand update, right? But no. He's got Robert Bailey with him. The Senator's brother? And what they want to do is rip me a new one because I had the guy's daughter arrested. Never mind that she was eating cereal with both hands, almost hit me head-on, then rolled up on the sidewalk and hit a stroller. Luckily the mom had just picked up the baby."

He was venting. He knew that. But Kyle was the best person to vent to. Kyle would listen, affirm, question, or tell Burgess he was full of it. They did that for each other.

"Not a word about last night's horror show, or how those girls are doing. This is national news stuff and what does he say? Nothing. The ironic thing is that somehow things got fixed with Bambi Bailey's arrest, something Cote did, I guess. So Bailey's daughter was driving again this morning. Today she was speeding while looking at her phone, sideswiped a truck, and drove full tilt into a tree. And I was the first one on scene. The chief and Bailey are trying to take me to task for getting her arrested yesterday and neither one of them knew she'd been in an accident today. I don't even know if she survived. She was alive when I left, but it was bad, Ter. Very bad. So, yeah, I lost it."

He stopped at a light, seething. Someone knocked on his window. He looked sideways and saw a kid named Jason, a foster-care waif he'd been watching for years, who was really coming along now that he was in a stable and loving foster family.

Burgess drove through the light and pulled over, rolling down his window. "Hey, Jase. How are things?"

Jason had been a scrawny, asthmatic kid when Burgess last saw him, when Jason was an invaluable witness in a difficult case. Now Jason was filling out and looked great. "Things are good, Sergeant Burgess. Our baby is walking, and we're maybe going to move to a house."

Burgess loved hearing "our baby," and the way it meant Jason was so much a part of his family. "Still in Portland?" he said.

"My parents are still looking." The boy looked down at his shoes and then straight at Burgess, his smile huge. "I'm being adopted."

Burgess reached out and dragged the boy into a hug. "What great news, Jase. So glad you told me."

"Gotta go," the boy said. "My mom gets worried if I don't come home on time." He sketched a wave and headed off on his scooter.

"There's a Joe Burgess success story," Kyle said. "Two years ago he was headed for Juvie."

Burgess knew Jason's turnaround wasn't due to him, but seeing the boy reminded him how connected to this city he was. "Okay," he said. "So maybe I won't retire this week."

"That's good news for my blood pressure."

"You may have to be the brains of the operation."

"Thought I already was."

Much of the time these streets were a map of the crimes they'd investigated, the people they passed a familiar roster of bad guys. But there were also moments like this one with Jason Stetson. Or yesterday at Melina's deli. They were the good people who reminded them why they did this job.

Kit, the tattoo apprentice, was a small, wiry woman. Her cropped black hair was streaked with electric blue and green, and her arms were a swarm of sea creatures and roses. She was willing to share what she knew, she said, if they assured her that DeSpain wouldn't get into trouble, but she was in the middle of a complicated design. She stepped away from her client, and motioned for them to come outside. "Sorry to drag you out here like this. I thought I'd be done, but he changed his mind. Now I'm going to be at least another hour. Can I call you when I'm done?"

Some days were like this. They could have pressured her, but it was always better to have willing witnesses. Burgess pushed his frustration away and gave her his card. "It's important," he said. "Call us as soon as you're available, okay?"

As they climbed back in the truck, Kyle said, "I'm hungry. Can we go somewhere and eat. Please?"

His toast was somewhere in the distant past, before K9 Kiki and Bambi and the chief and Robert Bailey. Besides, he had to keep Kyle fed. Someone in this operation had to some wits about him. It was a good way to kill the hour until Kit was done. An hour wasn't enough time to start their door-to-door. "Sure. Where do you want to go?"

Kyle chose Italian, and Burgess was reminded how much he loved a big, oily sub full of cheese and cold cuts. It had been ages since he'd had one. Chris was watching his diet and feeding him a lot of vegetables. Kyle ate spaghetti and meatballs. A giant plate of spaghetti and meat balls. Burgess surrounded himself with napkins and bit into his sub. It was just as good as he remembered. The place was dark and restful, despite being crowded, providing a nice normal interval between where they'd been and where they were going. Cops learned to take advantage of those down times.

He was finishing his coffee when Kyle said, "I have a bad feeling about this woman. Kit. I think we'd better not wait for her to call."

Burgess trusted Kyle's instincts. They paid and hurried to the truck. It had only been forty-five minutes, but Burgess had caught Kyle's sense of urgency. He pushed his way through traffic, doing a ten minute trip in five. He rocked to a stop at the curb and Kyle jumped out. He ducked inside, and was out a minute later. "She's gone," he said. "Guy inside says she took off just as soon as we left. Says he's got no address and he doesn't think DeSpain does either."

"So much for a cooperative witness. Let's see if they know her schedule. If this is how she earns her living, she's got to turn up sometime."

Burgess got out and followed Kyle inside. Being jerked around by someone who allegedly possessed critical information about a murder victim did nothing for a temper that had already been tested once today.

He decided they'd play good cop, bad cop. Burgess didn't care which role he played, but big and fierce as he was, it was Kyle who could turn mere mortals to ice.

"Look," he said to the guy who seemed to be in charge, who seemed to be slightly stoned, "Kit said she had another hour with her client and then she'd call us. She's jerking our chain and we're not happy about it. We don't want to get anyone in trouble here, but we need to talk to her." He spread his hands. "Can't you help us out here?"

The guy shrugged. "Kit's kinda like that. She doesn't like to be pressured, and I guess Vonnie put some pressure on her. She gets kinda squirrely when people pressure her."

"So you've got no address for her?"

The guy shrugged again. "Nope."

"You know when she's got her next appointment scheduled?"

"Nope."

"Got any idea how we can find her?"

This time the guy actually grinned when he said, "Nope."

Really bad idea to play stupid games with a pair of cops looking for a killer. People would do it, though. Human nature could be downright perverse.

"Hey," Kyle said, leaned down until he was literally breathing in the guy's face. "I'm sorry you feel this way. See, nope's not good enough. Not half good enough. You've got a gal working here who isn't licensed. You've admitted that. DeSpain's admitted that. So…" He let the word hang a moment. "So since you seem to like messing with a couple of tired cops who are just trying to find out who killed a girl who got her tats here and then chopped her up, I'll tell you what these tired cops are gonna do for you."

The guy was eyeing the door in the far wall, like he was planning to make a run for it.

Burgess moved in closer. Between the wall behind and Kyle and Burgess on each side, he was going to stay and listen.

"First," Kyle said, "there are all the basic things like reporting you to the licensing board, for letting Kit work here and for putting tats on underage kids."

The guy shook his head. "Look, I know what you fuckers are trying to do. Forget it. I'm not giving up a friend."

Kyle shrugged, like the guy had done. Casual. Indifferent. "Really? You know what we're trying to do? So you know that that kid, the one Kit did the work on, she got beaten to death and the killer cut her head off? And since you know so goddamned much, you probably know what he did with her head after he cut it off?"

The guy gave Kyle another smirk.

Big mistake.

"So here's what he did," Kyle said, all casual and conversational, like he was describing someone picking up take-out. "He had these four young girls, Central American, we think, that he was keeping as sex slaves. So he chains 'em up in a basement. No food. No water. Bucket for a toilet. He sets up the head facing them. Oh. Did I mention that he also cut off this girl's hands, the girl Kit did the work on. So he leaves these girls chained up in an airless box with this rotting head and hands while they slowly die of starvation and dehydration."

Kyle's voice had changed as he described the scene until he was at a trembling, barely under control shout. "Really. You knew all this and can't be bothered to help us?"

The man had lost his smirk and was staring at Kyle in disbelief.

"At least one of those girls will probably die. Maybe the rest can be saved. And that doesn't bother you? I guess protecting a friend, which also means helping to protect the person who did this shit, is okay with you? You're the kind of guy who thinks this stuff is okay, long as it doesn't happen to you or your friends??"

Kyle stepped back. Without taking his eyes off the man, he said, "So yeah. You know what we're trying to do. We're trying to stop a monster. We're hoping those girls we pulled out of a cage are gonna make it. And we're trying to protect people so he can't do it again. So if that doesn't move you, think about this, okay, since Kit is your friend. What if that killer decides Kit knows too much? What then? We can't find her so we can't help her."

Kyle gave the man a twisted smile. "By all means, pride yourself on being defiant. On how you stood up to them and wouldn't help the police. In return, since we are about helping and protecting the public, we'll take steps about your license. The licenses of everyone who works here. We'll also make sure that everyone who parks here for a second more than two hours gets towed. We'll drop tickets on any vehicle with faulty equipment. We'll drop in regularly to check that everyone working is licensed. Maybe sit across the street with a video camera, just to make sure your clientele is legit and you don't have any more kids coming in."

A slow, stylish shrug. "Lotta competition for you here in Portland. I wouldn't think you'd want to get on the wrong side of the department, make life hard for your artists. Folks who are just trying to make a living." He leaned right into the man's face. "Why the fuck would you want to do that to yourself just because some girl decides to be difficult?"

He stepped back, surveying the man like a bird looks at a worm, his eyes cold and predatory. Letting the silence grow.

Burgess saw the guy shoot a glance at his phone. Maybe because he had Kit's information there? Maybe because his first reaction to being bullied was to call the cops?

He and Kyle didn't move. Two big determined men who would wait as long as they had to.

The guy caved. "Fuck it," he said. "She's not worth all that." He reached for the phone and gave them her full name, address, and a different phone number.

"She got a car?" Kyle said.

"Old junk heap. Toyota, I think. Silver. Held together with duct tape."

"In case you're thinking that as soon as we leave, you're going to call and tell her we're coming?" Burgess said. "Don't."

The guy's guilty shift was confirmation that's just what he was thinking.

"Thank you for assisting your local police department," Kyle said. "You have yourself a nice day now."

They left.

"You were good in there," Burgess said.

"Had a good teacher."

When they got in the truck, Kyle was trembling. It hadn't been an act. Between them, they had almost five decades of dealing with a public like the guy at Sweety's. Sometimes Burgess thought it would be good to paper a room at 109 with photos from the worst crime scenes they'd worked over the years, blown up in their full color, grisly worst. Blood pooled. Splattered. Staining sheets and rugs. People stabbed so many times they looked like hamburger. Bodies in all the colors of the rainbow. Swollen with decomp. Crawling with maggots. Maybe a special room for murdered children. Just bring people like this guy in, put them in a chair, and leave them for an hour. If it wasn't cruel and unusual for cops, why should it be cruel and unusual for the public they served?

"We know that dismemberment is not nice," Burgess said. "But I was considering it. Except I have faith in your powers of persuasion, Terry."

"Bigger than a mustard seed?"

Burgess nodded. "Much."

Burgess started the truck and Kyle gave directions. What a fucking waste of time. They could have gotten what they needed from a computer if they'd only had Kit's last name.

TWENTY

They caught up with her as she was about to get to her car. Another minute and she would have been gone again. Maybe it was chance. Maybe the guy made that call anyway. People were a perverse bunch.

Burgess got between her and her door, lounging against it like a man with all the time in the world. Kyle stationed himself on the other side of her. Together, they made a Kit sandwich. She looked from one to the other, set her chin truculently.

"You were going to call us," Burgess said.

"Yeah? Guess I forgot."

"So it's a good thing we happened to be driving by, isn't it?"

"I have to go."

"This won't take long," Burgess said. "We just had some questions about Shelley."

"I don't know anything."

"That's not what Vonnie said."

"Oh. Vonnie. He's such a bleeding heart."

A woman passing by was getting out her phone. Maybe to call the cops. More likely to make a video she could post on the internet. If they were bad guys and Kit was in trouble, this woman wouldn't be coming to her rescue. These days, people don't help, they just record. Mothers passed out from drugs on store floors. Kids bullying another kid. Burgess jerked his chin and Kyle turned toward her.

"Police officers, ma'am. Just asking Kit a few questions. There's nothing to see here."

Perfectly calm and straightforward. But Kyle's voice was no nonsense and Burgess knew he wore his "don't mess with this" face.

Flustered, the woman tucked her phone back in her purse and hurried away. Maybe she should have stayed. Maybe seen some police brutality. Burgess's patience was wearing thin. He said, "We're not going to keep chasing you, Kit. We can do this here, or we can arrest you as a material witness and do this back at 109. Your choice."

"I don't have to …"

"Oh, for Christ's sake, Kit. Shelley got beaten to death and someone cut her head off and used it to terrorize other girls. Why on earth would you protect a person like that?"

"I'm not…"

"Fuck yes. You are," Kyle said.

Melia was always on them about language. Usually they curbed their tongues with civilians, but enough was enough.

Burgess got out his phone, scrolled through to a picture of the severed head. "By not helping us, you're helping the person who did this."

Definitely police brutality.

She stared at the picture. Then at him. Then at the picture. "Is that Shelley? I mean, that looks like her hair, but…"

"Come sit in the truck," Kyle said, taking her arm. "It's hot out here. We can turn on the air."

She let him lead her to the Explorer. Burgess started the air.

She was still stunned. "We need her last name, if you know it," Burgess said. "Anything she may have said to you about her home life. Details about the two men who brought her to her appointments."

"All right. Whatever. I'll answer your questions. Just don't show me any more pictures, okay?"

"Okay," Burgess said. "Let's start with her name."

"At first, she only wanted to be listed as Shelley. But when the guy who brought her, the first guy, had stepped outside to smoke, she told me that she did that because of him. She said he was her foster dad and didn't want her foster mom to know that he'd brought her in for this. Her foster mom and Human Services. So he didn't want any record that she'd been here. She said her foster mom already hated her and getting this work done would probably get her thrown out for good. But she didn't care. She didn't like either one of them, but her foster dad was nicer to her. She did things for him so he was doing this for her."

"That mean what I think it means?" Burgess said.

"That's how I took it."

"She tell you her last name?"

"Her name was Miner. Michele Miner."

"Thank you," Burgess said. "What about the second man. The one who brought her to her last session?"

"I can't tell much about him. She didn't talk much that time. I didn't speak to him, Vonnie did. Vonnie said he was an asshole. All I know and it's not from anything she said, but just how she was. The poor kid was scared to death of him. He was an older guy. Better dressed than her foster father. Acted like he was slumming, bringing her. He didn't wait for her. He went out and sat in his car and waited for her. Most of the time he was on the phone."

"You notice what he was driving?"

"Something big and black. That's all I noticed. Sedan, not a SUV."

"What about her implants? Did she have them when she first came?"

"Implants? Like her teeth?"

"Like her breasts?"

"She had 'em. They might have been fairly new, though, 'cuz she made some remark about how weird it was to lie on her stomach. And how they hurt."

"Did you talk about her bruises? Someone was beating her and it had been going on for a long time."

"I asked. It was hard for her lie there, when she was hurt like that. She said they hit her when she didn't do what they said. I said why didn't she go to the police. Call her social worker. Get sent to a different family. She said she'd tried that and it hadn't worked and she'd gotten beat worse than before. So, you guys come here, all muscle and threat, but when that poor kid came to you for help, you sent her back to them. And this is how it ended up."

Maybe she had meant that she went to her social worker for help. He couldn't believe the police had ignored those bruises. Burgess had seen the state fail kids before. Seen another child die because of bureaucratic indifference, despite multiple efforts to get them to act. But if the Portland police had failed her, too? That would be hard to live with. He hated to be on the cleanup crew because agencies, including his own, whose job was to protect and care for people, had failed. It was sometimes the darkest part of his job. It was also when retirement seemed most appealing. He could separate from those who were responsible for screw-ups like this. For letting down the most vulnerable.

He couldn't quit in the middle of this, though.

At least Kit had given them some leads. He hoped the name was real. Otherwise, they were left to search through endless DHHS records, looking for a child named Michele or Shelley. In his experience, DHHS was an extremely uncooperative agency to deal with.

"Can I go now?" she demanded. Trying for bravado, but Burgess's picture had deflated her.

"You have my card?" Burgess said.

A nod.

"You'll call if you remember anything else?"

Another nod.

"We appreciate your help," Kyle said. "We know people don't trust us sometimes. It makes our job harder. But we know you don't want this girl's killer to get away with it."

"I don't. I just…"

"We know," Kyle said.

She slid out and hurried to her car. She jumped in and pulled out from the curb, nearly hitting a cyclist.

"We could stop her," Burgess said.

"Yeah. But we've got places to go and people to see. Maybe, while we've been out having fun with the obliging public, Rocky or Wink have come up with something."

Burgess started back toward 109, brooding on what Kit had told them.

He was deep into brooding when, out of the blue, Kyle said, "Are we supposed to give Stan a bachelor party?"

Crap. He was best man. He was supposed to have thought of this. Maybe Perry didn't want one? He'd ask. He feared Perry would say "yes."

This was more of the peculiar way that their lives ran on two different tracks. On one track there were pitiful, trafficked children and grotesque crime scenes. On the other were life's normal events. Family dinners. Children squabbling. Marriage. Birth. And places where the two tracks intersected. Where families failed their children. Foster fathers had sex with the girls in their care. Wayward daughters wrapped their cars around trees.

"Penny for your thoughts?" Kyle said.

"Wishing something about this would be easy."

"Know what I'm wondering about?"

"What?"

"Why Captain Cote isn't breathing down our necks?"

"I almost miss it. His pressure and interference was so much part of the rhythm of our investigations."

"Well, I don't miss him at all."

"I just wonder if he's okay."

"You're such a masochist. It's a gift, Joe. Enjoy it while you can. And anyway, he did call Stan. So maybe it's just a different form of business as usual. I'm just glad he didn't call me."

Silence returned as they drove past throngs of tourists enjoying Maine's largest city on this beautiful summer day. Cases like theirs could swallow up whole chunks of summer. A detective gets immersed in a case, works it, and him, or herself, to death, and suddenly notices that weeks have passed. Maybe the season is changing. Or the detective only notices the change because people seen through the window are dressed differently. Tee shirts have morphed into hoodies, sandals have become boots.

"How about that?" Kyle said.

Burgess slowed. In Monument Square, two young women, a blonde and brunette, wearing cowboy boots, denim cut-offs, and no tops, their breasts painted red, white, and blue, were handing out flyers to people passing by. Nice breasts. Pretty women. They looked happy. The people—mostly male—receiving the flyers looked happy.

Burgess shrugged and drove on. If someone was bothered by it, they'd call the police and some poor officer would be sent to deal with it.

"I love patriotism, don't you?" Kyle said. "Where were they when I was young?"

"You have gotta stop with this being old business. Don't let Stan get to you. He's just being a jerk because of the pressure of this wedding."

"Joe, in case you haven't noticed, Stan is usually a jerk. He's just our jerk."

"Anyway, Ter. You aren't old. You're in the prime of life. Because if you're old, what does that make me as I creep toward sixty?"

"You mean limp toward sixty? A dinosaur."

"That's what I thought. Fossil, maybe. Relic."

They almost made it back. They were waiting to turn onto Federal Street when a woman came running at them, waving her arms. "Help," she said. "I don't have a phone and someone needs to call the police."

"We're police, ma'am," Kyle said. "What's your emergency?"

"That girl over there," she said, pointing to a bench in the park. "I think she's dead."

TWENTY-ONE

Burgess pulled over and got on the phone to dispatch while Kyle followed the woman. Then he joined them. The girl on the bench was unconscious, not dead. Likely an overdose. He called dispatch back and asked for medcu. The woman hovered nearby as patrol arrived to take charge, and Burgess and Kyle got back in the truck. They drove the two blocks to the garage and went upstairs.

"All of this makes you want to lock girl children in a tower guarded by dragons," Burgess said.

"Roger that."

Burgess's faith in humanity, in all its permutations, was restored when he found a message to call Captain Cote on his desk. Ignoring Cote's peremptory summonses had always punctuated his investigations. Rather than respond, despite his curiosity, he took a few quick minutes to type up what they'd learned from Kit. He still needed to write his reports for last night. Then he went to find Rocky Jordan.

Rocky didn't look pleased to see him. "I'm working as fast as I can, Sarge. This stuff takes time." He picked up a folder. "Here's what I've got so far.'

Burgess surprised him by smiling. Usually, he didn't smile. "I've got something else I need you to look at. Shelley or Michele Minor. Foster kid. See if you can dig up anything about her."

"DHHS records…"

"Just anything. Arrests. New stories. It's a long shot, I know."

"I'll put it on the list."

"Anything on Ida Mae Wilson?"

"It's in the file, Sarge."

"Thanks." He headed back to his desk, thumbing through the papers as he walked, so focused he almost walked straight into Captain Paul Cote.

"Burgess!"

"Paul? You wanted to see me?"

"My office," Cote said, and stalked away.

It looked like the old Cote was back. And Burgess couldn't pretend not to have seen him. He followed the captain down the hall and sat in one of Cote's comfortable visitor's chairs, waiting to hear what the man wanted.

"Your reports," Cote said.

"You should have them, sir. Except for last night. We haven't had time to…"

"Make time, Sergeant. Your team is involved in a major operation involving human trafficking, and I don't have anything to tell the press."

"Terry Kyle and I are canvassing that neighborhood. When we get back, I'll do those."

"Reports first."

Burgess studied his nemesis. Like many of them, Cote hadn't escaped the attempted assassination of their officers unscathed. He was looking better, though. He'd lost some weight and seemed to have spent some time outside.

"Okay. Reports first. How's the puppy doing?"

Cote got a photo from his desk drawer and showed Burgess a tiny animal playing with a tiny chew toy. 'She's great."

The pictures Burgess had to share weren't so cute. He stood up. "I'll go do those reports. Sir."

There was a moment when it looked like Cote was going to say something else, but it passed.

Burgess left.

Irritation made his fingers fly as he and Kyle, at their respective desks, worked on the reports Cote had demanded. Burgess didn't mind that much. Report writing was an essential part of the job. Recording things as they'd happened created the story that prosecutors would use down the road to shape the case for trial. He'd just always been impatient with the process. He needed to be going and doing. Shaking witnesses and chasing leads until it all led him to the bad guy. Or guys.

As he finished and hit save, then print, he looked at Kyle, still a one-fingered typist after all these years. It was the one thing Kyle couldn't rush through with his intense, vibrating sense of urgency.

"Shouldn't Stan be back by now?"

Kyle grinned. "Maybe he ran away. Kid must be scared to death about all the adult responsibilities about to descend on him."

"Mine came more like an avalanche," Burgess said.

"Roger that," Kyle said. "Maybe he just moved on to the next task on his list. What would that be, exactly?"

Burgess was in charge of steering this damned thing, and he couldn't remember. This was where being a compulsive note taker was helpful. "Schools?" he said. "But he doesn't know her name."

He called. Got a slightly slurred, "Stan Perry."

"Fuck no, Stan! Where are you?"

"Lost Moose. S'okay. Dani's looking…after me."

It was three in the afternoon on a work day, and one of the detectives working a front page homicide and human trafficking case was drunk, tying up an evidence tech to babysit him. "Stay there. Terry and I are coming to get you."

"S'okay, Dad. I got Dani."

"Stay." Like Stan Perry was a naughty dog. Which it sounded like he was.

He got up, checking his gear and grabbing his jacket. "Terry, we gotta go. Stan's in trouble."

"I called it, didn't I?"

"That's not a good thing, Ter, being able to predict when our third musketeer goes off the rails."

"My motto is 'Be prepared, and expect the worst,'" Kyle said. "Besides, Stan's predictable. Half the time when we can't find him he's in trouble. Other half he's following hunches and pulling rabbits out of hats."

"I'd be happier with a seventy-five/twenty-five ratio," Burgess said. "Kid's getting married in less than a week. He can't be like this."

"He *is* like this. You think words from a minister and a golden ring are gonna change that?"

Treating it like the emergency it was, they used lights and sirens to clear the ambling summer traffic blocking their path. Clearly breaking the rules and not giving a tinker's dam. To avoid thinking about what they'd do when they got there, Burgess mused on whether people understood the meaning of a tinker's dam.

They went silent before they pulled into the Moose's small parking lot. No sense in calling attention to the situation.

Dani and Stan were sitting at a table in a front alcove. She jumped up when they got there and threw herself into Burgess's arms. "He didn't have that much to drink and suddenly he was like this. I didn't know what to do, so I just stayed with him. It had just…he'd just gotten like this. I was about to call you when you called."

She shifted nervously from one foot to the other. "I don't know if this means anything, but he said he had a headache. He took a couple pills on the way up and then again just before we ate."

As Burgess consoled her, Kyle was getting Stan to his feet.

"Have you paid?" Burgess asked.

She nodded.

"Okay. Let's get him outside." They half-led, half-carried their third musketeer outside. "Dani, go back to 109, and don't mention this to anyone, okay?"

She nodded. "But I was riding with Stan. My camera, evidence, it's all in his car."

Kyle fished in Perry's pocket, and handed her his keys. Along with the keys came a handful of pills. Kyle examined one and shook his head. "Stan's not drunk. He's drugged. Gone overboard dealing with premarital jitters."

They put Perry in the back seat, Kyle got in with him, Burgess behind the wheel, and headed for the hospital. In the interest of Perry's career and reputation, they might have taken him home and stayed with him, hoping he could walk it off or sleep it off. But it had happened so suddenly. They had no idea how much he'd taken. And drug overdoses were nothing to take lightly.

They handed him off to Dr. Sarita Cohen, who seemed to work 24/7 in the Emergency Room. Burgess described Dani's observations, the suddenness of the symptoms, and gave her one of the pills they'd found in Perry's pocket.

"This is helpful information," she said. "I'll take good care of him." She gave quiet orders to the nurses, who began to treat Perry.

"While you are here, Joe and …" She looked up at Kyle. "It's Terry, right? And I am Sarita. Maybe you want to look in on your girls? Two of them are doing very well. We've had a Spanish language translator in to help us communicate. The third has been moved out of the ICU. The fourth?" Her face was sad. "As I told you. It is not looking promising. We are a good hospital, but we can't always make miracles."

"We'll be back," Burgess said.

"I'm afraid this is always true," she said. "Only please. No more stitches, Joe, okay?'

"That's what my partner always says, too."

"You, too, Terry."

They were already at the hospital, so it made sense to look in on the girls. He also wanted the name of the interpreter, and their doctor's opinion about whether it would be all right to interview them. Usually Burgess bulled his way into any hospital room he wanted to be in, but these girls were fragile. He didn't want to inflict any more brutality on them, even in the interest of catching whoever had done this to them.

"I hate this place," Kyle said.

"Not as much as I do. I'm the one with more stitches than a football."

"Yeah, and I'm the one who has had to drag you in here to get those stitches."

"Friends forever," Burgess said.

In an act of kindness unexpected in a bureaucratic medical facility, they had put all three girls in a room. Cleaned up, hydrated and fed, they were a stunning contrast to the filthy, dull-eyed girls his team had pulled out of that fetid basement. A woman was sitting beside the first bed, talking to the girl in language Burgess recognized as Spanish. She turned and smiled as they came in, said, "You are the officers who rescued these girls, aren't you?"

They admitted they were. Burgess said, "There were three of us," giving Perry credit since he was the one who would carry the horror of that initial discovery with him forever.

She introduced herself as Clara Sanchez, then said something to the girls, and the one she sat beside held out a hand to Burgess.

He approached the bed carefully, knowing how big he must seem, how scary his scar could be, and took her hand. It disappeared in his, making him feel like an awkward giant.

"This is Sofia," the translator said. Burgess didn't speak Spanish, but he tried "Hola" and the girl in the bed giggled.

The translator smiled and indicated the next girl. "This is Magaly."

Another small hand came out, this time indicating Kyle. Kyle took it between two of his. "Hello," he said. "I'm Terry."

"Magaly," the girl said.

The girl in the third bed was sleeping. "I don't want to disturb her," the translator said. "But that is Gabriela. Gabriela and Magaly are sisters. Sofia is their cousin. Sofia's sister Maria is still in intensive care. May we step outside?"

They found a small private room to talk. "We need their information about who did this to them if we're going to find the person and arrest him," Burgess said.

"I think you are looking for more than one person," the translator said. "There were two men who were directly involved, I believe. And others who came and went. I know this information is important to you. I am trying to ask them slowly because when these men are mentioned, they get very upset. They cry and go silent."

"Can you tell us anything?" Burgess asked.

"Did they see the other girl killed?" Kyle asked.

She looked from one of them to the other. "To your question, Detective Burgess, the answer is not very much. Yet. I take the questions in small bits, as I'm sure you can understand. One man was younger than the other, with lighter hair, and he was kinder to them. Not kind, just kinder. I think his wife was there as well, but they do not speak about her. The other one, he was, according to Sofia, a better dresser. He wore, as she put it, "shirts in colors." I don't think she has the words to give the kind of description you want. American men, how they look, talk, act, dress, this is all foreign to them."

She shifted her attention to Kyle. "Sofia…she is the oldest and she speaks for them…says the door was shut, but they heard terrible sounds and screams. Then it all was quiet for a long time. Then the men came back, and they made a lot of noise. When the door was opened, there was blood everywhere, and the girl's head and hands were lying on the floor. Sofia says the girl looked after them. She was nice and gentle. Sofia says the girl was trying to find a way to get them some help or let them escape, and that is why the men killed her."

TWENTY-TWO

"I have a photo of a man I'd like to show them," he said. "But I don't want…" He wasn't sure how to put it. Getting answers was critical, but not doing these girls further harm mattered, too. "Maybe I can have it brought to you, and you can show them, or show Sofia, when you think she's ready?"

"That would be a good approach, Detective," the translator said. "I should probably introduce myself. As I said, my name is Clara Sanchez. Many years ago, when I was a small girl, you were very kind to my family, when we were being threatened by some boys in the neighborhood. You made it stop. My family still speaks of it."

Burgess remembered a small girl peering at him from between her parents' legs. "You were a very curious little girl," he said.

"I still am."

Burgess thought that was all, and was about to hand the translator his card, with the usual request to call them with any further information, when the translator added, "Sofia said there was also a woman. Sometimes she would bring the men. And she would beat them if they didn't cooperate."

"It would be helpful if you could get a description of the woman." He wrote his cell number on it and gave her his card. "I'll send you the photo. And please, if any of them tell you something you think I should know, call me."

He and Kyle left. She returned to the girls.

They stopped back in the ER to check on Stan. He was hooked up to an IV and appeared to be asleep.

"We've given him an antidote and some IV fluids. He should be okay in a few hours." She hesitated. "I mean okay to go home and rest, not okay to join to two of you on your next adventure."

"Can someone call when he's ready to be released?" Kyle said. "We'll come and get him."

"Promise you won't put him right back to work? Joe? Terry?"

"Sarita, we promise," Kyle said.

"Then we will call you. Now get out of my ER, and don't come back except to pick up your friend."

"Hey," Burgess said, "This is practically the Joseph Burgess memorial emergency room."

"I think," she said, with that same grin he'd seen before, "that for it to be a memorial, you have to be dead. You do not look dead to me. Now scoot. Both of you. I have work to do."

Before they left the hospital, Burgess asked about Bambi and was relieved to hear she'd survived that accident.

As they came through the doors into the parking lot, Kyle said, "Are you in love with Dr. Cohen? I am."

"Sure," Burgess said. "You know she's had her hands on my bare body."

"Not touching that with a barge pole. So what now, Fearless Leader? Head out to Ida Mae Wilson's neighborhood?"

"That's the plan. Let's see what Rocky put together for us."

He opened for folder Jordan had given him hours before. Ida Mae Wilson, the record owner of the property, was eighty-five. She still had an active Maine driver's license and was the registered owner of a Toyota Prius. Her license number matched the one on the license the man who called himself Charles Hooper had given Burgess, and the plate on the car matched the car patrol had followed to Ida Mae Wilson's house.

"He's probably ditched it by now, but let's put out a BOLO on the car."

"On it, Fearless Leader."

"Terry, you're starting to sound like Stan."

"So you won't miss him. I guess we don't let Lily know what happened?"

"No. We'll just yell at Stan when he's back on his feet."

"What about Dani? Should we tell her what the problem really was so she won't think Stan drinks on the job?"

"Or can't handle his liquor. Sure. Make those calls."

While Kyle was doing that, Burgess's own phone rang. Sage Prentiss. Burgess forgot he'd given Prentiss the job of trying to track down that saw. "Hey, Sarge. Just a quick update. Dani gave me the brand of that saw Aucoin found. I've been to every big box and mom and pop hardware store around. There are only two that carry it. One has no record of a recent sale. The other is still checking. They're going to get back to me but the only person who understands their computer system, who might be able to pull up the records, is off today. They're supposed to call me when she comes in tomorrow."

"Great job, Sage. Let me know when you hear back from them."

"Got anything else you need me to do?" Prentiss asked.

"Check with Rocky. He's got a list. I'm sure he'd appreciate the help."

"Whatever you need, Sarge." Prentiss had the grace not to sound disappointed.

"One other thing. Stan was checking with the schools to see if we could identify our victim. Now we may have a name. Be great if you could check in again, see if any middle or high schools around have any record of a student named Michele Minor."

There was more enthusiasm in Prentiss's voice when he said, "Will do, Sarge."

"Stan's gonna be pissed. That was his job," Kyle said.

"I have something else in mind for young Stanley."

"Part of his training to become mini me?"

"Maybe."

"Don't be coy, Joe. We're both feeling the weight of this. I feel like it takes two steps forward and at least one backward to get a bit of information in this thing."

"Not being coy. The truth is that I don't know what I'm going to do with him yet. Okay? So can we go knock on some doors now?"

"Sure, Joe."

They rode in silence a while. Then Kyle said, "Is it just me or does this day feel endless?"

"Not just you."

They parked in front of Ida Mae Wilson's house, which was still surrounded by yellow crime scene tape. They would keep the house and grounds sealed until they were sure they'd learned everything the site had to tell them. They might walk the yard when they were done knocking on doors. Burgess entertained a secret horror that there might be bodies buried in the back yard. So far, it had been that kind of case.

They crossed the street. He went right and Kyle went left. They'd hit four or five houses, then cross back to Ida Mae Wilson's side and work their way back to the truck.

The first door Burgess knocked on was answered by a small woman whose gray curls were as big as she was, a woman slightly bent over with age. She peered at him through thick glasses as he introduced himself, "Detective Sergeant Burgess, ma'am, Portland police," and held out his badge so she could see it. "I'd like to ask you some questions about the house across the street and your neighbor Ida Mae Wilson. May I come in?"

She stepped back so he could enter, and he followed her shuffling feet into an overcrowded living room. She seated herself in a recliner lined with a layer of afghans. He seated himself on the sofa across from her and got out his notebook.

"May I have your name, ma'am."

"Rose Samson."

"Miss or Mrs.?"

"Mrs. My husband Oliver passed last year."

"How long have you lived here, Mrs. Samson?"

"Forty-seven years next month."

"Are you acquainted with Ida Mae Wilson?"

"We were good neighbors for many years."

"Ms. Wilson's house is empty. Do you know where she's gone?"

"Last I heard, she was in one of those retirement places. The ones where old people go from independent living to assisted living to being warehoused in a nursing home." Rose Samson fumbled with some papers on a nearby shelf and pulled out an address book. "I've got it written down in here somewhere."

She read off the name of the place and its address. "I've got her phone number, too. Don't know if it is still good. I went there to see her once or twice. It was too depressing. Detective, the place was full of old people. Looked nice, you know, but when we were in the dining room, there were all these old, old people in wheelchairs, dribbling their dinners down their fronts and smelling like pee. Ida Mae didn't seem to mind. I'd rather die than live in a place like that."

He couldn't help smiling. "How long ago did she move away?"

She gazed down at her lap, then back at him. "Let's see. This is July, right? So it was about two years ago April, after that awful winter we'd had. She said keeping up the house was too much for her, and that going up and down that steep driveway in the winter made her nervous. She said she wasn't going to sell the house, though, just in case she didn't like where she was. She hadn't moved back and she hasn't sold it. I think maybe she's forgotten about it."

She fixed what Burgess realized were bright and curious eyes on him. "You were part of that commotion over there last night?"

He nodded.

"I heard on the news that there were young girls being held prisoner in the basement."

Fuck Cote, he thought, trying to keep his face blank. "That's why I'm here ma'am. Trying to learn what's been going on at that house. Hoping you can help me with that. But first, let's back up. Do you know whether Mrs. Wilson still drives?"

"It has been awhile since I've seen her, as I said. But she came to a library friends meeting a few months ago, and I believe she drove herself."

"Do you know what kind of car she drives?"

"One of those newfangled quiet things. The kind you can't hear coming?"

"A Prius?"

"That's it."

"Have you seen her Prius at the house since she moved?"

"Oh, sure. See it pretty often, or one a lot like it, coming and going."

"Have you seen the driver, if it's not Mrs. Wilson?"

"I haven't seen him. He usually drives right into the garage. But I know who it is."

She paused for dramatic effect. Burgess thought she was looking forward to tossing him this nugget.

"Who is it, Mrs. Samson?"

"It's her nephew, Charlie. He's kind of a reprobate, but Ida Mae has always doted on him."

"Mrs. Samson, do you know Charlie's last name? Is it Wilson?"

"Why do you know, Detective, I have listened to her talking endlessly about Charlie and the scrapes he got into, but I have no idea whether he's a Wilson or something else."

She tapped her forehead with a wrinkled finger. "Wilson is her married name, of course. I think Charlie is her brother's boy. Ida Mae and Fred never had any children. So sad. Children are such a comfort in your old age. Do you have children, Detective?"

"Three. Two boys and girl."

"And do they give you pleasure?"

It was a question he'd never been asked, and one he'd never asked himself. "Yes, Mrs. Samson, they do."

But he was here to get information, not give it. "Is there anyone you can think of who might know Charlie's last name?"

"Shirley might. She's right next door. I think she and Ida Mae played bridge together. But why don't you just ask Ida Mae?"

She considered, finger to forehead again. "Only doing that might upset Ida Mae, and her heart's not that strong. That's another reason she went to that place. Because she was afraid one day she'd end up on her kitchen floor and no one would notice. You can't be unnoticed in a place like that, even if you want to be."

"I'll be gentle with her, Mrs. Samson. I wouldn't want to do her harm. May I ask you another question? I'm not keeping you from something?"

She consulted a slender gold wristwatch. "Nope. We've got time. My program isn't on for another fifteen minutes. What else did you want to know?"

"Have you seen other cars parking in Mrs. Wilson's driveway, besides her nephew driving her car?"

"A couple weeks back there was a van. Charlie was there and he opened the garage and the van drove in."

"Anything about the van that caught your eye? A business name, anything like that?"

She looked off into space, and he assumed that she was trying to recall what she'd seen. "I didn't get a good look at it. It just whipped up that driveway. The garage was already open, which I thought was odd. It went in and the door closed."

"What about when it left?"

"I didn't see it leave."

"Do you recall what time of day this was?"

"After seven-thirty in the evening, that's all I can tell you. I have a program I watch at eight, which is why I didn't see it leave. But at seven-thirty it's still light out."

Burgess took out a card. He was about to thank her and leave. It was almost time for her program, but he had one last question. "What about other vehicles, besides the Prius and the van?"

"There was one other. A black town car, like I take to the airport when I go to see my daughter in Pennsylvania. I thought it was odd, because Ida Mae isn't there and Charlie already has the Prius."

"Did you get a look at the driver?"

"Beyond noticing that it was a man, Detective, and not Charlie, because his hair wasn't light, I'm afraid I didn't. My eyes aren't what they used to be. Maybe Shirley can tell you more. Shirley's the kind of person who can tell you every piece of clothing a person has on and whether their shoes are worn down at the heels. It would be unkind to suggest this, but sometimes I wonder if she's not looking out with binoculars. She's another widow, like Ida Mae and me. You could pretty much call this 'widow's row,' there's so many of us."

He stood and held out his card. "Thank you for your time, Mrs. Samson. You've been very helpful."

"You're welcome, Detective. You don't mind seeing yourself out, do you? My program's just coming on now."

He stepped out of the dark, musty house into a bright July afternoon, taking a minute to be present before moving on to Shirley's house. In two weeks, he and Chris were taking the kids to a rented cottage on a lake. He'd been fantasizing about sitting in a lawn chair and staring out at the water. Maybe reading a book. No phones. No scanner. He didn't care who got killed, he was going. It kept the pressure on to solve this.

A civilian, hearing him say this, would be aghast that he thought it would take two more weeks. That was because the public's ideas about crime solving came from TV. Crimes had to be wrapped up in less than forty-five minutes. He'd had cases go months, even years. As he often said, investigations took as long as they took. But if this ran long, he'd be handing it off to Kyle and Perry. And if Stan Perry thought he was taking off on a honeymoon during the week Burgess had set aside for his vacation? If this case hadn't been put to bed, young Stanley was in for a big disappointment.

He tucked away his fantasies about leisure and headed next door to Shirley's house. It was a small cape like Rose Samson's, but this one had a wheelchair ramp leading to the front door. Maybe erected for her late husband? Rose Samson had said that Shirley was a widow.

He climbed the steps and knocked.

TWENTY-THREE

Rose Samson's neighbor answered her door so quickly Burgess wondered if she'd been waiting for him. She led him to a screened porch looking into a pretty, private back yard with lovely gardens. She offered lemonade and he didn't refuse. Only when he was settled with a glass in his hand did she ask the reason for his visit. "Are you here about that business across the street at Ida Mae's last night?"

"Yes, ma'am, I am." He got her full name, Shirley Evans, and her phone number, then asked, "As part of our investigation, we're interested in the comings and goings at Mrs. Wilson's house. I understand that she no longer lives there?"

"Please. Call me Shirley. Ma'am makes me feel ancient."

She wasn't ancient. She might have been in her early fifties and looked great for her age. He wondered why she stayed here watching the neighborhood instead of getting out and having a life. "Shirley, what can you tell me about people or vehicles visiting Ida Mae's house?"

She answered with a question of her own. "Is it true that you rescued four little girls who were chained up in that basement?"

Cote's damn press conferences. Burgess cursed the man again, questioning why he and Kyle had saved the man. With respect to information that should have been confidential, Paul Cote was like a sieve. Anything he thought would bring him press attention poured right out.

"I'm afraid that yes, that is true. We're trying to find out who put them there."

She looked at him like he was stupid. "Rose didn't tell you? Of course it was Charlie. Charlie and that horrible man."

"Tell me about Charlie. Do you know his last name?"

"Well, it used to be Dornan, that's Ida Mae's maiden name. Charlie is her brother Parker's child. I don't know if it's true, but I heard that he changed it to Wilson, because he wanted to butter-up Ida Mae so she'd leave her money to him. He has two sisters, but Charlie has always been Ida Mae's favorite. She never made any secret about it. I always felt so for those poor girls. Especially since Charlie is such a rotten person."

"In what way is Charlie a rotten person?"

She poured him more lemonade. "Is what ways is he not rotten? He's always taken Ida Mae for everything he can get. He has an equally rotten wife who works for some charity that helps refugees but likely doesn't have a charitable bone in her body, and then they took in that sweet little girl, and I never saw the little darlin' when she wasn't bruised and cringing. I never saw anyone hit her, but it had to be him. He's always been a rat. Or them. I called the state about that child, but you know how they are. They don't do a thing until the child is dead and then they say they're sorry and will review their procedures."

This was pretty much what Burgess thought.

"So you've seen Charlie's foster daughter?"

"Shelley? Oh sure. She used to come with them when they visited Ida Mae. She'd come over and play with my Anita. Anita was older, of course, but she was kind and felt sorry for Shelley, who was such a timid little thing.

Burgess was struggling to tamp down his anger, because there was more to be learned here. But this was the second person who'd told him that they'd notified DHHS, yet Shelley hadn't been rescued and now she'd been murdered and mutilated, her body dumped in the woods.

"Did Shelley use Dornan as her surname?"

"I don't think so. She wasn't adopted, something they never let her forget. She had a different name. I can't remember what it was. Maybe something beginning with an M."

"Minor?"

She nodded. "That's it."

"Tell me about people and vehicles coming and going across the street." He added, "If you can," because he didn't want her knowing that Rose said she watched the street with binoculars.

"Well, there was Charlie, of course, driving Ida Mae's Prius. There was the man I called, to myself, the Limo guy, because he drove a black town car."

"Can you describe Limo Guy?"

"He was about my age, early to mid-fifties. He was taller than Charlie, and had graying dark hair, worn longer than it should have been. It was nice hair, wavy, and I think he wore it longer because he was vain about it. There was a van that came and went sometimes. I think it was one of those 'rent by the hour' vans, like you could rent at a store like Lowes or Home Depot, or one of those moving places. I can't recall what the writing was."

"Did you see the driver of the van?"

"It was the same man each time. He looked Hispanic. Well, maybe I watch too much television, because he looked like a Miami gangster. His arms were all tattooed and he had his hair in a ponytail. He never looked anything but angry. He'd just drive into the garage and not long after, he'd leave. I wondered what he was doing there. He'd always come when Charlie or Charlie's wife or Limo Guy was there."

"Do you have any idea how often the van has come?"

"I'm afraid I don't. I've seen it maybe three times this year, at three or four month intervals."

"When is the most recent time you noticed it?"

"Last week. I can't remember whether it was before, or after, the moving van took Ida Mae's things away."

Despite Rose's disparaging tone, he was finding Shirley a goldmine. Still, he wondered about a such an attractive person confining herself to her house all day. What was up with that? His answer arrived just at that moment. There was the sound of a motor and a man in a large wheelchair entered the room. To Burgess, he looked to be late teens or early twenties. He was directing the chair with one hand, expertly steering it into a place by the window. He smiled at Burgess and said, "Hello. I'm Deane."

"Joe Burgess."

"My son," Shirley said. "And to answer the question you've politely refrained from asking, why a woman like me shuts herself up in a house and watches her neighbors?" She hesitated, looking at her son, then said, "Rose probably told you I'm a widow like the rest of them. It's a misunderstanding. I let them believe it because it's easier than explaining that my husband, Deane's father, decided that having a handicapped son was too big a burden and left us. Bought us this nice little house, had the ramp installed for Deane's chair, and then moved into a condo and moved on."

The boy in the chair ducked his head and said, "Bye bye, Dad." He grinned at Burgess. "Because of the chair, people assume I'm also feeble-minded. I'm used to it."

Shirley smiled at her son. "Deane has his own web development business. He's quite successful. He employs one full time and two part-time people. And I am insanely proud of him."

"You should be," Burgess said.

"Also contrary to what Rose probably told you, I don't spend my whole day in the window. I have a part-time job. But Rose pretty much does, and she feels guilty about that, so she's made up a fantasy about all of us 'widows' sitting around all day watching the street."

"Getting back to the comings and goings at Ida Mae's house," Burgess said. "You say you recently saw a moving van picking up Ida Mae's things?"

"Sometime last week. I can't be more precise. I'm sorry. But last week, Deane had a health crisis, and we were both focused on that. Maybe someone else on the street can tell you what moving company it was."

Burgess nodded and looked at Deane. "You're okay now?"

The young man smiled. "As okay as a guy who has to spend his life in this chair can be."

Burgess brought his focus back to Shirley Evans. "You referred to the other man you've seen with Charlie as 'that horrible man.' Why?"

"Just being a protective mother, I guess. A few times he's blocked our driveway so the van that takes Deane to work couldn't get in. I had to go over there and ask him to move his car and he was extremely uncooperative. And unpleasant."

"Meaning," Deane said, "that he told her to go fuck herself, he'd move the car when he was good and ready. I had to call the police…uh, you guys…and they got him to move it. I think he figured we were too pathetic to assert our rights. To some people, wheelchairs automatically mean feeble or vulnerable."

At the same time that Burgess was thinking there would be a record of her calls, she said, "I imagine your department will have a record of that. It happened twice."

"When?" Burgess asked.

"Once in June and once in …Deane, when was the first time?"

"The beginning of April. When we had that freak snow and he didn't want to use that steep driveway. It hadn't been plowed."

It was a long shot, but Burgess had to ask. "Any chance you noted the license number of that car?"

Shirley smiled. "I wrote it down when I called the police. I have it somewhere. Probably I stuck it in my junk drawer. It may take me a few minutes to find it."

She left to look and Deane said, "What my mom's not saying, because she prides herself on being fearless, and because she's been such a fighter for me, is that he frightened her badly. I don't think it was only an exchange of expletives, I think he threatened her with harm to me."

A horrible man indeed.

She came back, smiling at her success, and handed him a sticky note with a number scribbled on it. He checked it to be sure he could read the scribbles. "May I keep this?"

"Of course. I hope it helps you catch these people. Deane and I are looking forward to the day when we have new neighbors to watch. Real neighbors."

"Mom, I don't watch the neighbors. Well, except to keep you company."

"Not now that you're a serious grown-up business man."

"Did the man in the town car come often?" Burgess asked.

She looked at her son. "I'd say a few times a week. Weekends. Late afternoons. He may also have come at night, but then I'm not paying attention. Deane, is that right?" She looked at Burgess. "Deane's bedroom is at the front, so he's more likely to know."

"He came pretty often at night. Him or Charlie. Or at least Charlie's car. Which is really Ida Mae's car. I've seen Charlie's wife drive it, too. They'd always drive into the garage when they came at night. Mom won't say this. She's too proper, but we both think that they were running some kind of prostitution ring."

"Because?"

"Because often, when the car came at night, there would be a man sitting in the back, like a limo passenger."

"There would be lights on in the house?" Burgess said.

"Yes," Deane said. "When the black car came, there were be lights on inside."

That was bold, right here in a residential neighborhood. But he couldn't imagine bringing customers to a house where there was no furniture, just a couple of filthy mattresses. So what did it mean that last week the furniture had been removed?

"But you didn't call us about that."

"It was speculation," she said. "And given how responsive bureaucracy was about my call regarding Shelley, I couldn't take the chance that cops would check it out, decide things were okay, and then Charlie or his associate would retaliate against us. We're pretty vulnerable."

Burgess was frustrated on their behalf. They were exactly who the department was supposed to protect. He also hated being tarred with the same brush as DHHS, though he kept his thoughts about that to himself.

"I'm sorry you didn't feel we could protect you," he said.

"We're realists, Deane, aren't we? You can't always be here."

The world was full of quiet heroes. He saw them all the time in his work. There were the people who refused to step up, like Kit, and the people like this, who carefully navigated a dangerous world. Who sacrificed for each other.

"You've said that you saw the van come two or three times. Did it ever come at night, Deane, as well as during the day?"

"It came at night, too. I couldn't see the driver then, of course."

"The house is unfurnished now," Burgess said. "If Charlie was, as you speculate, bringing men to the house for sex, I would assume that there would have to be some furnishings?"

He was thinking of those filthy mattresses. Even the most undiscerning would be unlikely to pay to have sex on them. Well. Pay very much. Pay what one would assume would be involved with an arrangement that involved town cars and drivers and pretty young girls with enhanced breasts. He certainly had seen some sordid conditions where people did have sex.

He wondered about the Guatemalan girls. If men had been brought to have sex with them, wouldn't that have involved a lot more traffic to the house? Enough, he'd think, to trigger someone's calls to the police. Maybe they took girls someplace else. He wondered what Kyle was learning.

"Like I said, a moving van came recently." Shirley said. "They moved all of Ida Mae's things out. I wondered if that meant she'd died and her family was cleaning out the house, but I haven't seen an obituary."

Something else to track down. It seemed odd. It sounded like they'd run this thing here for months, why change now? Was this before or after Shelley was killed? Had they had the balls to empty out the house with those girls chained in the basement and Shelley's blood all over the floor? Had something happened to spook them? Had they moved the operation somewhere else?

"Have you seen Charlie or his associate or Ida Mae's car here since the furniture was removed?"

"A few days ago, both of their cars were here for a longer time than usual."

"And the van? When is the last time you saw it?"

"The day after the movers took Ida Mae's things away."

Was the van bringing the girls? Had there been other girls? Was this a regular thing? The feds might have a better read on this.

In his simple conversations with two of Ida Mae Wilson's neighbors, his to-do list had grown immensely. He was ready to end this, grab Kyle and head back to 109 to put some things in motion, but before he left, he asked the open-ended question that sometimes brought surprising results.

"Is there anything else I should be asking about? Something I've missed?"

Shirley and her son exchanged looks. He nodded and she said, "You should talk with Charlie's wife. Charlie might be tough to get cooperation from. He's always been all about Charlie and doesn't much care about anyone else or what people might think of him. She's a cold fish, but she's a professional in a job that involves working with children. That might give you some leverage."

"Does she use Charlie's last name, whichever one he's using these days?"

Shirley shrugged. "I have no idea. She was Marilyn Dornan. She goes by Lynn. Last I knew, she was working with refugee resettlement."

A woman who worked for a charity that resettled the world's most vulnerable refugees whose husband ran prostitutes, possibly even prostituted, and murdered, their foster daughter? He hoped his incredulity didn't show on his face.

"I know," Shirley said. "It beggars belief, doesn't it. But Lynn is likely the brains in that family. They're like birds. He's all swagger and plumage. She's managing the nest. She also affirmatively practices being ignorant about who her husband truly is. Or she seems to."

"Seems to?" Burgess said.

"I've always wondered whether Lynn has hidden depths. She was never affectionate toward little Shelley, which made me wonder how she treated the people she was supposed to be helping. And she's been in and out of the house, with and without Charlie. How could she miss what was going on?"

He stood. "You've been amazingly helpful. Both of you. Thank you for your time, and the lemonade."

They followed him to the door. "I hope you catch them," she said. "It would make the world a better place."

"I'm trying."

"I'll bet you're always trying, Detective."

In more ways than one, he thought, as the door closed behind him.

TWENTY-FOUR

Kyle reached the sidewalk about the same time, and signaled for Burgess to come back to the truck. The day had gotten hot, and Kyle was looking drained. "Air," he said. "Freaking cats." So Burgess started the air conditioning. Kyle reclined his seat and closed his eyes. "I think I'm done with this, Joe."

"Talk to me," Burgess said. He was the one who was supposed to be done with this, but Kyle was vibrating, and that was a sign something had seriously disturbed him. Or that he was extremely angry. In this case, Burgess was voting for both.

"People who know what's going on and don't do a damned thing about it. And cats. I am so done with batty old ladies whose houses reek of cats. I think there should be hazardous duty pay for anyone who has to go into a cat lady's house."

"Indifference and cats. Are those in the same house?" Burgess asked.

"Indifference in the first. Cats in the second. Just drive, okay. I'll catch you up on the way in. I need a shower. How'd you do?"

Burgess drove and Kyle talked. "She's freakin' seen it, Joe. The woman in that blue house. She saw two men dragging a girl who fits Shelley's description up the driveway and into the house and they were beating on her the whole time. Who doesn't call the police about that? Who lets a child be abused like that and goes back to watching TV?"

"When did she see this?"

"Three, four days ago. She's not sure. She's not sure about much of anything. She's not sure what day, or month, or year, she saw a small naked girl running down the street and a man grabbing her and throwing her into his car and driving back to the house with her. She's not sure when it was that she heard awful screams coming from Ida Mae Wilson's house, but she sure was annoyed that they woke her up."

The tremble in his voice nearly choked him. "Why the fuck do we bother, Joe?" They drove in silence a while, then Kyle said, "And those fucking cats."

Another silence. Over the air conditioning, Burgess could literally hear him grinding his teeth. Then the grinding stopped and Kyle asked, "You get anything?"

"Comings and goings of Charlie Dornan, or Charlie Wilson, whatever he calls himself these days, who is Ida Mae's nephew. The name of the retirement community where Ida Mae is living. Some details about Shelley's life as the Dornan's foster child. Cowed, timid, and always bruised. She called social services but no one came to interview her and nothing changed."

Kyle muttered an obscenity.

"I learned about the comings and goings of the second man, the one in the black town car, and his plate number. Witness says he would arrive both day and night with a man in the back seat. They speculated that prostitution was involved, but they didn't call us because they'd been threatened by the man with the black car. They're a vulnerable family. The son is severely disabled and in a wheelchair."

"I hate this," Kyle said.

"I know. But we can't keep everyone in the city safe. Maybe if one of the neighbors had called us, we could have stopped this before…" But he couldn't blame Shirley and Deane for their choices. Other neighbors had less reason to be cautious, yet as far as he knew, they hadn't reported the situation either. He'd have to have the records searched, and check with patrol about whether they'd observed anything.

"Periodically, a van driven by a man who, in the words of my informant 'looked like a Miami drug dealer' would arrive, drive into the garage, and then leave a few minutes later. Makes me wonder if he was delivering girls like the ones we found in the basement. One witness says that a moving van came for the contents of the house three or four days ago. So what spooked them? Have they moved on to another location? And…" This information made him want to grind his own teeth. "The fact that Dornan's wife works for an agency that helps refugees."

"Oh fuck that's ugly. Her foster daughter is trafficked, murdered, and cut up and she's getting paid to do good works."

"What else is ugly is that second report to DHHS that the girl was being abused. I think we may need to pay them a visit. And let's take a subpoena this time. We waited for frigging ever last time we needed information from them."

"Who's the AAG on this?" Kyle asked.

"I don't know. Melia should be on top of this, but so far he's MIA. Oh, and while we were immersing ourselves in neighborhood gossip and cat stink, guess who held a press conference and tried to give away the farm?"

"Fuck."

Kyle had pretty much become monosyllabic. He never swore like this. But cases with kids, particularly girls around the age of his own, pierced him.

"I wonder if they're ready to spring Stan yet?" Burgess said.

He called the hospital, worked his way through the usual know nothings and bureaucratic tangles until he found someone who knew something. Whenever they wanted to collect him, Perry was all theirs.

"I'll drop you back at 109, then go spring Stan," he said.

Kyle made a sound that might have been agreement. Burgess wasn't sure and didn't push it.

He asked dispatch to run the plate number that Shirley Evans had given him. To see what they had on Charlie or Charles Dornan, Charlie or Charles Wilson, and Marilyn Dornan. He called Melia, got voice mail, said he needed to know who their AAG was, described the subpoena he needed and asked Melia to take care of it. "By need it," he added, "I mean by tomorrow morning, not when it might be convenient for someone. Last time we asked for DHHS records in a homicide, it was like pulling teeth. Cooperation isn't their strong suit."

Burgess was beat, but they had a lot of things to move on, things that shouldn't wait. He just wasn't sure where he was going to summon the energy.

"Soon as you can," he told Kyle, "can you write up what you learned. For my eyes only. I do not want Cote sharing it with the whole world."

"Roger that, Joe. Shoulda left him hanging. We can be too tender-hearted."

Burgess agreed. "Not feeling tenderhearted anymore."

"I thought you missed him."

"Even I can be a fool sometimes."

"Roger that."

He dropped Kyle off at 109 and watched him stalk inside, heading for the shower to wash off the cat stink. When Kyle was in this state, he was an effective attack dog and a dangerous weapon. Maybe the shower would bring him down a few notches.

He looked at the clock. Chris would be picking up Neddy about now. Dylan would be in the driver's ed car, inching closer to sixteen and his license. Nina was staying late so the parents of the twins could grab a quick dinner out. She was good, responsible girl, his Nina, but he couldn't imagine how she could handle twins. Still, she'd been babysitting since she was twelve, and had been in foster care in a house with a baby. She had more experience than that poor frazzled new mother.

Knowing it would put something positive in his ugly day, he called Chris. "Hey, Joe," she said. "I'm in the carpool line waiting for Neddy. How's your day going?"

"It's been amping up my cynicism about human nature. How about yours?"

Chris worked as an office nurse in a group practice. "Kind of the same. Dr. Curtis was in a snit about something and snapped at me all day, and Dr. Reardon, who is just learning the ropes, got almost an hour behind, so all afternoon we were dealing with cranky patients. I'm tempted to go back to working in the hospital, except there they'd always be trying to get me to work double shifts, which, with the kids, is impossible. I don't know how people with kids do it. They must have flexible husbands."

"I wish I were a flexible husband. This bum knee really slows me down."

"Oh, Joe. How is your knee?"

"Not as bad as the rest of my day. The brace helps a lot."

"Coming home for dinner?"

"What time are you eating?"

"Maybe an hour, hour and a half. That's when Dylan is home and he and Neddy are always starving. We're making pizzas. I've got the crusts and a whole bunch of toppings. It's going to be fun. I think Sandy and Cherry and Maddie might come over, too."

That was a lot of people to deal with when he wasn't at his best, but it was still tempting. "I hope so," he said. "Things are breaking fast today, so I may get pulled back in, but family dinner would be fun."

"If you are coming home, can you grab some Coke and Diet Coke. We'll be fine without it, but you know how kids are."

"Roger that," he said.

Chris laughed. "Oh, the carpool is moving. Hope we see you."

He pulled into his usual spot outside the ER and stepped back out into the heat. He never crossed this parking lot without a sense of trepidation. Not so long ago a bullet had found him here.

He went through the doors and into a room full of people in various states of misery. His motto was never to come to the ER, but if he had to come, to enter unconscious. Although, to their credit, this place was very good about accommodating cops.

He found Stan Perry in a cubicle, lying down instead of his usual agitated pacing. He looked deflated and disgruntled. His first words were, "You didn't tell Lily, did you?"

"Of course not, Stan. Why would we?"

"Because she's been calling a lot and I haven't picked up because I didn't want to get into this right now. We're fighting enough about the wedding."

Burgess shook his head. "Stan, how far along is she?"

That brought Perry off the bed in a hurry. He scrambled for his phone and checked it for messages. Then he looked at Burgess, his eyes wide with panic.

"She's here, Joe. She's in labor."

"Then you'd better get your ass up to maternity, don't you think?"

Burgess's plan had been to pick Perry up, take him home, and tuck him into bed, where he could finish recovering and be useful again in the morning. Now he figured he'd better walk Perry to maternity so he could assess how the kid was doing. And to keep him from fleeing. Until now, the baby had been something on the horizon. Now it was in his immediate future.

He delivered a slightly shaky Perry to the desk and passed him over to a nurse who took him in hand and led him off to Lily's room. When she came back, he quietly told her that Perry had been in the ER earlier and asked her keep an eye on him.

She'd swept him from head to toe, and said, "Detective, my job is to keep an on eye on laboring mothers." Then she smiled and patted his arm. "I'll take care of him. That poor sweet girl has been in such a state, wondering if he was going to show up."

"My fault," Burgess lied. "We took his phone away. He just got the messages."

"It shouldn't be too long now. She's doing great."

As he climbed back in the Explorer, Burgess was wondering how anyone could willingly bring a child into this screwed up world. Then reminded himself that "willingly" implied far more awareness and responsibility than many of the people he dealt with were capable of. That he'd brought a child into the world and never knew.

He stopped at 109, found Kyle, and told him to go home and have dinner with his family. Some time sitting at his desk seemed to have brought him down a notch.

"How's Stan?"

"Lily's in labor and he's with her. I hope he holds it together. She'll never forgive him if he can't see this through."

"Wow," Kyle said. "Big changes ahead. So, when do you want me back?"

"What's good for you?"

"Eight?"

Kyle smiled. "You're getting soft, Joe."

"I'm getting old, Ter. Can't run forever on three hours sleep anymore."

"You planning to sleep through family dinner?"

"Wouldn't that be a feat."

His kitchen was an orderly chaos, as an assembly line of pizzas were dressed and popped in the oven. Neddy and a friend had piled hamburger and pepperoni and cheese on a pizza and now were using pepper strips and olives to make face. Cherry and Maddie were going strictly vegetarian. Chris and Sandy had glasses of red wine and were leaning against the counter, watching.

He set the bag with the Coke and Diet Coke on the counter, not missing Chris's smile because he'd remembered.

Chris set her glass down and hugged him. His sister hugged him and then gave him a sisterly assessment. "You look like hell," she declared. "When are you going to start taking care of yourself?"

"Just as soon as people stop doing inhuman things to each other, Sandy." It was the same conversation they'd had as long as he'd been a cop. It had long ago grown old.

"My Joe," Neddy said, "look what we made."

He admired the pizza, hugged his nieces, and settled into a chair to watch. It felt so good to be in a chair, in a house, and not in the truck or at his desk. He didn't remember this chair being so comfortable.

"Wine, Joe?" Chris asked.

In a case like this, "Whine Joe" would be more apt. He and Kyle both got bummed when people who could have prevented bad things from happening sat on their hands. "Love to, but I have to go back in."

"How is it going?"

"We really moved ahead today. I think we're getting closer, but now everything has to be followed up."

She nodded. "How are those poor girls doing?"

"I saw them a few hours ago. Three of them are doing well. I tried out my Spanish, all one word of it, and one of them laughed at me."

She didn't ask about the fourth. He'd told her enough.

"Oh, and Lily's in labor. Stan's with her at the hospital. The nurse said it shouldn't be long now."

Chris shook her head. "How's he taking it?"

"He's in shock. I walked him right to maternity and handed him over to a no-nonsense nurse just to be sure he didn't bolt and run."

He thought about Stan's day, how the young detective had gone from a gruesome autopsy to an accidental overdose to the labor room. Stan was young and tough, but it was a lot for anyone.

"That poor girl," Chris said. "I know she wanted to be married before the baby came. Still, it's exciting news. She's been getting ready for a wedding. I wonder if she's ready for a baby. Do you think they have a crib and a car seat and stuff?"

Burgess had no idea. Cribs and car seats had never come up in Stan Perry's conversation. "I wonder if they'll still go ahead with the wedding." he said.

"Women like weddings," Chris said. "Do they know if it's a boy or girl?"

"I don't think they wanted to know."

"I'd want the surprise, too," she said.

"I think we got plenty surprised," he said. "And they're all perfect bundles of joy."

Chris came and kissed him, resting her cheek against his for a minute. She had longed for a family and had been unable to have children of her own. Adopting Nina and Neddy had been important—and life altering—for her, and had forced both of them to deal with whether their still new relationship could handle becoming a family of four. Then Dylan had arrived. They now lived in a state of constant chaos. Luckily, it was often enough happy chaos.

When she moved away, he felt momentarily bereft. Then she and Sandy went back to drinking wine and supervising the kids. He rested his head against the back of his chair and fell asleep.

He woke to a crash and a voice saying, "Oh my God!"

The crash was his briefcase being knocked over. The "oh my God" was from his niece, Cherry, who was staring at the photo of Shelley Minor's tattoo. "Oh, Uncle Joe. Is this the girl who got killed? I know that girl."

TWENTY-FIVE

"I'm sorry you had to see that," he said. He crossed the room, still groggy from sleep, and fumbled the papers back into his briefcase, glad she hadn't seen some of the more graphic pictures. "How do you know her?"

"From school. She's two years behind me. She's a freshman. But those tattoos were hard to miss. That and how there's a long weekend and when she comes back to school, she's got these great big breasts. She was really shy and quiet, Uncle Joe. She didn't seem like the type to do that. To want big breasts. She wasn't just shy and quiet. She was like a beaten dog. I talked to my teacher about it and she told me they were taking care of it, the assistant principal was going to speak to her parents, and I shouldn't worry. But it never looked like it got taken care of."

He wanted to say "you should have called me," but it was too late for that. No sense in making her feel guilty. Besides, she'd stepped up when the adults evidently hadn't.

"When was this?" he asked.

Cherry considered. Though it horrified her mother, she was planning a career in public safety, aiming for the FBI, and she liked to be precise. It was either the FBI or becoming a singer. She had an amazing voice. "The tattoos appeared in late fall or early winter, like November, December or January. The breasts, I think, were in February. Shelley, that's her name, I think, was a very pretty girl. Dark curly hair and bright brown eyes. Guys were all over her, especially after she got the breasts. She never looked happy, though."

He thanked her. Got out his notebook, wrote down the name of Cherry's school, of the teacher Cherry had spoken to, and of the assistant principal. Took a moment to say, "Now don't go all Nancy Drew on me, okay?" and waited for her to agree. It was almost eight. He'd come home for family dinner and slept right through it. He looked guiltily at Chris. "Sorry. I didn't mean to."

"We thought it was sweet," she said.

Oh Christ. Sweet? This was the second time he'd fallen asleep today. Maybe it was time for a checkup. He'd resisted this as long as he could, but maybe it was time to admit that he wasn't a kid anymore, and start taking better care of himself. Taking care of himself meant rest, exercise, and healthy eating. He resisted because he believed indulging himself meant depriving victims of his full energy and attention. He couldn't figure out how anyone did healthy eating, exercise, and yoga or meditation when the demands of the job were so great. People always said getting old was not for the weak. Neither was working homicides.

"Here." She shoved a mug of coffee in his hand, coffee that smelled infinitely better than the stuff they had at work. Then she pointed to a plate on the counter. "Pizza. Neddy and Alex fixed it for you. I think it has every possible topping on it and maybe a few Legos and marbles. Eat it."

When most people said "Eat it," that got his dander up. People said a lot of bad things to cops that cops were expected to suck it up and ignore. When Chris said "eat it," he did what he was told. Burgess was trying to do a better job on the domestic front. Besides, it would make her smile, and Chris's smile was worth it. Never mind that lunch was a long time ago, and the cop's rule was "eat when you can."

He ate the pizza, and didn't find any marbles or Legos. He was grateful for that. He didn't have time for a trip to the dentist. Then he hugged everyone in sight and headed out.

The unintended nap had left him feeling surprisingly good, and the pleasant summer night helped. It also helped that he got back to 109 without a single idiotic or aggravating encounter with pedestrians or other motorists. Kyle was at this desk, worrying something on the computer. He sorted through his messages. Nothing significant. Rocky Jordan had left him a folder. Depending on what Rocky had found, that might determine their evening's activities and tomorrow's agenda.

"Any word on Stan's baby?" he asked Kyle.

"Nothing yet. But babies take time. You eat?"

"I'm consummate family man, Ter. I walked in, sat down, and fell asleep while they made pizzas." He stretched. "Chris didn't mind, and I feel so much better. Want to sit in the conference room and talk about this?

Rocky's file was a potential gold mine, assuming there was pleasure in the endless labor of mining. He had a license number, photo, home address, and employment information for Marilyn Dornan. She drove a three year old Toyota Corolla. License photos are always awful, but from hers he thought he was seeing something Shirley Evans hadn't mentioned —that Marilyn Dornan was quite attractive. He had Charlie Dornan's driving record, which should have kept him from ever getting behind the wheel. His license was currently suspended. The license he'd shown Burgess was a good fake, but if he ever handed that license over to an officer at a traffic stop, the number would bring up Ida Mae Wilson, and he'd be toast. Rocky had also run Charles Hooper, and there things got even more convoluted. There were several Charles Hoopers, two of whom had Ida Mae's address. One address was Dornan's. The other had a photo of a man Burgess had never seen.

Rocky had run the plates on the black town car numerous witnesses reported seeing. The plates came back to a 2003 Pathfinder that had been totaled in 2008. The registered owner of that vehicle was a John Delude. Records showed that Mr. Delude was deceased. A woman named Nancy Delude, perhaps a widow, was still shown as living at that address. It had probably been burned by now, or gone for a swim, but Burgess put out a BOLO on the town car. Men arrogant enough to run prostitutes in a residential neighborhood might have developed a sense of immunity.

He had enough messages to paper a room, if there was a soul in the world who might want to live with infinite repetitions of black lined Pepto-Bismol pink. As always, there was nothing urgent or even interesting, until he got to the last message. One that made his heart sink. It was from the translator at the hospital. One of the girls, the one named Sofia who spoke for them, had asked if the police knew where her littlest sister Bella was.

Another missing child and Burgess had no idea where to look.

He looked at his watch. It was eight-thirty. Not too late to pay a visit to Charlie Hooper, or Charlie Dornan, or Charlie Wilson. Whatever he was calling himself today. Maybe he had another batch of girls stashed somewhere at his house. Burgess would have preferred to prep for the visit by first calling on Ida Mae Wilson, but it was too late in the evening for that. Those senior residence communities buttoned up early.

"If they were servicing Johns out of that house, Wink and Dani must have found dozens of fingerprints," Burgess said.

"But all the furniture is gone. Oh. Yeah. And I forgot to tell you," Kyle said. "Wink says they only got through the basement and the kitchen. They were going back out today, but Dani had to go to Augusta, and Wink's wife had a medical incident and he had to take her to the doctor. They'll go back out tomorrow."

Burgess had an uneasy feeling about that. Their suspects couldn't know how much had, or hadn't, been processed, but the crime scene tape was still up and the house was sealed. No one had processed the garage yet. Who knew what they might still find? What he did know was that suspects had an annoying habit of covering their tracks by burning buildings and cars. He was surprised someone hadn't reported a burned out town car yet.

"If that house isn't processed yet, I'd like to have patrol sitting on it."

"Shift commander will be pissed."

"Yup," Burgess said. "And keeping patrol happy is my first consideration in life. If I were Dornan and his buddy, I'd have burned it by now."

"I'll make the call," Kyle said.

Burgess stared gloomily at the notebook of reports that represented their investigation. Everything they'd learned so far seemed to confirm that their victim was Shelley Minor, but the best proof would be DNA or dental records. Those most likely to know who her dentist was were her social worker at DHHS or her foster parents. They were waiting on the search warrant, the presentation of which would royally piss off the local DHHS branch. Not that Burgess cared. He wanted to move now, but that would have to wait for tomorrow. He felt like they were circling around two men, Charlie Dornan and another, who were at the center of this thing.

At least now they had an address for Dornan. If it wasn't another fake.

"Want to take a ride with me, Terry, or do you want to go home and we'll pick this up in the morning?" Burgess asked.

"Ride," Kyle said. "I need to move on this. I feel like we're spinning our wheels. Or playing Whack a Mole."

"Let's drop Stan's car back at the hospital. He may need it," Burgess said. "Dani left the keys on Stan's desk."

They dropped the car and texted Perry about where to find it. Then they headed to Dornan's.

Ida Mae Wilson's Prius was parked beside a white Corolla in a driveway to the left of a small, one-story cape. The yard and house were plain and neat. No gardens. Flowering shrubs. Lawn ornaments. There were lights on inside, and the busy blue light and muffled sounds of a TV. Though they were ostensibly calling on a couple seeking information about their foster daughter, Burgess approached the door the way he'd do any potentially dangerous knock and talk, while Kyle slipped around the house to the rear in case someone decided to slip out.

Burgess rang the bell. Waited, and when there was no response, he knocked loudly. The lights stayed on. The TV stayed on. But no one came to the door. He knocked again. Sometimes TVs were so loud people didn't hear. Sometimes they fell asleep in front of the TV. Sometimes they didn't answer their doors because bad things had happened. When nothing brought a response, he moved to the right, over to the picture window, and peered through a gap in the curtains into the room where the loud TV was playing.

There were two people sitting on a deep sofa facing the TV. They sat at opposite ends, like they didn't want to get too close to one another. The sofa was white. The man was on the left side, his head was tipped back like he was sleeping, but blood had splattered the white upholstery. The woman was on the right, her head slumped sideways in what should have been an uncomfortable position. There, too, the upholstery was stained red. With the delicious sickness of cop humor, the dark stuff that kept them sane in the face of horror, Burgess thought they'd made a decorating mistake in choosing white upholstery.

Burgess called for to Kyle to join him, then got out his phone and called Dispatch to send patrol, Medcu, the crime scene van and evidence techs. He called Vince Melia, who wasn't on a boat out of cell phone range this time, brought him up to speed on the situation, and asked him to call the medical examiner.

He told Melia what it looked like. "But Vince, we're not jumping to conclusions. We don't know what we have yet, but it is going to be a long night."

Then he pulled on gloves and tried the door.

It wasn't locked.

He turned the knob and stepped into a narrow carpeted hall. The kitchen was straight ahead, the bedrooms on his left, and the living room on his right.

Kyle went to clear the house while Burgess walked a narrow path close to the wall, avoiding as much of the carpet as possible in case there were footprints or other evidence, until he stood beside the loud TV surveying the couple on the couch. Despite the blood and the damage, he recognized the man who had called himself Charlie Hooper. Now that he was this close, he knew he didn't need to cross the room and check for pulses. The woman had shoulder-length wavy brown hair, pink lipstick, and two bullet holes in her forehead. The back of the man's head was blown off, blood and brains spattering the wall behind him. A gun lay on the sofa near his hand.

Burgess focused on that initial analysis, the time when he surveyed the crime scene. The positions of their bodies. The spatter patterns behind the man's head and on the sofa. Where the blood had oozed from hers. What they wore. Were they dressed for work or leisure? Were they wearing shoes? Was any clothing disarranged, possibly indicating a struggle. Where the gun was. The position of the man's hands. The condition of the carpet—freshly vacuumed. The slightly dirty shoeprints in the thick, light carpet pile. The Dornans left their shoes by the door. The volume of the TV. Where the remote was.

Was there anything on the coffee table? What was the condition of the room? Were there signs of a struggle?

Taking it all in and getting his first gut reactions.

Kyle joined him, following the same careful route along the wall, silently doing his own analysis. "It's recent," Kyle said. "Look at the blood." He pointed to the screen, where CSI was playing. "They can do this in less than forty-five minutes."

"Get lab results instantly, too. Well, they can have this one," Burgess said. "I've seen enough homicide and other brutality this week. Besides, I might have a hot date."

Still without a word, they retraced their route and stepped outside.

Burgess called Dispatch and canceled the ambulance. No reason to have EMTs tromping through the scene so they could declare the obvious fact that this couple was dead.

"Melia coming out?" Kyle asked.

"Time will tell."

"Stan?"

"I left a message. He's probably tied up."

"Maybe you should call Sage."

"Good idea. We're going to need all hands on deck."

The truth, of course, was that they didn't want *all* hands on deck. Didn't want all the department's own Lookie Loos traipsing through the scene, which could happen, and be immensely destructive, if scene security wasn't good. The rule for successful crime scene investigation was to keep it small. A tight, effective team who could cover the ground and communicate well. Who were each meticulous about evidence collection. Who were observant and didn't miss things. Who wouldn't walk into that room and immediately think murder suicide instead of letting the facts tell them what it was. But they couldn't do it without enough hands, either, and Stan had already had a physically and emotionally overwhelming day. If he was going anywhere after assisting with the birth of his child, it should be home.

They stood in silence, in that moment where they could think before the onslaught of personnel necessary at a death scene. It was the moment when someone would smoke if they smoked. The moment for bracing themselves for the hours ahead. For accepting the necessity to be diligent about their observations, about recording everything that needed to be preserved. For accepting that the scene would take as long as it took, and couldn't be rushed because someone was tired, or, like Burgess, might have a hot date.

As the first sirens were heard in the distance, Kyle said, "So is this how we're supposed to read this? Our man Charlie Hooper Dornan Wilson begins to regret his life of crime. Troubled by prostituting and murdering his foster daughter and by the children he's imprisoned and quite likely sold for sex as well, he leads police to Ida Mae's house. As the law—that's us—closes in, and faced with the enormity of what he's done and challenged by his wife about the disappearance of their foster daughter, he sees only one way out. To silence her, he shoots his wife. Then, recognizing the inevitability of discovery and arrest, he chooses to take his life rather than spending it in prison."

After a very still day, a wind had come up. Burgess closed his eyes as it cooled his face. It felt almost silky, like the air was a caress. Overhead, a nearly full moon illuminated the scudding clouds and bathed the world in its eerie, blue-white light. It would have been a lovely night except for this. He inhaled the salt-tinged air, longing to stay out here in the moonlight, just breathing. Just being. Letting someone else handle the mess inside.

"You believe that's what happened?" he said.

"What do you think I am, a rookie?" Kyle said. "Her blouse is misbuttoned. Her slippers are on the wrong feet. There are drag marks on the carpet. I don't think that's where she was shot." Kyle hesitated. "I suppose he could have shot her somewhere else in the house, dragged her to the couch, arranged her, and then shot himself. But why bother?"

"We know what we're supposed to think," Burgess said. "We need to see the rest of the house. We'll listen carefully and it will speak to us. We'll analyze the blood spatter. Check his hands for GSR. Look at where the gun fell."

"Or was placed," Kyle said.

Listening to the scene wasn't New Age twaddle. Long-time detectives knew that the cop gut was a powerful guide in assessing what was what. It was the thing that told them someone was wrong, a suspect was about to explode, a dark room or a traffic stop was dangerous. The innocent-seeming person was about to produce a gun or a knife. The timid housewife was lying. The menacing thug was innocent. They were like crime scene dowsers, carrying their predictive guts into the situation and finding not water but information.

Before chaos descended he stepped away and called Chris. "Got another homicide," he said. "I don't know when I'll be home."

"People have got to stop killing each other, Joe," she said. She dropped her voice into a lower register, the one that had captured him when he first met her. "I had big plans for tonight. Did you see the moon?"

"Leave a light on for me," he said.

"And little else," she said.

"Thinking of that will get me through this."

Kyle was making his own phone call to Michelle. This was going to be another long night.

Burgess called Sage in. As he was putting his phone away, Stan Perry called.

"Joe. Consider this a virtual cigar, okay. Autumn Angela Perry arrived an hour ago. She is petite and beautiful like her mother, and busy and restless like her father."

"Congratulations," Burgess said. "How is Lily doing?"

"She's great," Perry said. "I thought she was going to be mad because Autumn came before the wedding, but she's over the moon." He gave it a minute, reluctant to say what Burgess already knew he was going to say. "I know you need me out there, but Joe, I'm beat, and Lily will kill me if I leave her right now."

"Stan, of course you need to be there. Don't worry about it. We'll be fine. Sage is coming out to help us. Stay with Lily and your daughter."

Perry was silent for a minute. He was, after all, letting down his boss *and* the meanest cop in Portland. And he wasn't keen on letting Sage take his place. Finally common sense prevailed, and there was a very uncertain, "Are you sure?"

"Very sure. Autumn's birth is a once in a lifetime event. Haven't I taught you that people—live people—come first?"

"Yes, but…"

"Why is there a but? Do you want to leave Lily and Autumn?"

Burgess was quite sure he heard tears behind Perry's answer. "God no, Joe. This is the most amazing fricking thing that's ever happened in my life."

"Text me a picture. Now go, before I change my mind."

Burgess disconnected and went to tell Kyle.

"That was Stan. It's a girl. Autumn Angela. Stan's afraid if he doesn't show up here, Sage will replace him. He's afraid if he leaves Lily she'll never forgive him."

"The homicide detective's rock and a hard place," Kyle said. "Kid lacks perspective. There's always another homicide. The day your first child is born is once in a lifetime."

"That's what I told him."

They stepped out to the street to meet the incoming cars.

TWENTY-SIX

The first officer on scene was Gabe Delinsky, so he got the job of Log Officer. Remy Aucoin was next. Burgess told him to string up crime scene tape. In less than five minutes, the crime scene van was there. Wink was complaining, and Rudy Carr, their photographer, and Dani had gone quietly to work.

Before he and Kyle left them to record and measure in the living room, he said, "We have one piece of good news tonight. Stan and Lily are parents of a girl. Autumn Angela."

"Autumn," Dani said as she placed a box of shoe covers by the front door. "I love it." Then, "Gabe, no one comes in without these, okay. Not even the Chief, or Captain Cote."

"Ma'am," Delinsky said, "Nobody is getting past me."

"No, I don't suppose they will." Delinsky was as big as Burgess, but twenty years younger and fast on his feet.

Burgess and Kyle put on their shoe protectors and started their review of the rest of the house. Straight ahead was the kitchen. The room was immaculate. No dishes in the sink. Nothing on the counters except a toaster, a coffee maker, and a small metal dish with two sets of keys. No flyers, photos, clippings or magnets on the refrigerator. Burgess opened the fridge warily. Once you've found a human head in there, you open them carefully for the rest of your life. Even in your own house.

The refrigerator was like the rest of the kitchen. Spotless. Orderly.

There was nothing fun to eat in there. Everything was packaged and labeled. He checked the freezer. It was the same way. While there were packages labeled "Lynn" and "Charlie" there were none labeled "Shelley." Had they cleaned the refrigerator after Shelley was killed, or had this household never included food for Shelley? He couldn't ask Charlie or Marilyn now, but there might be neighbors, friends, or co-workers who could shed some light on the domestic arrangements.

The cupboards were as sterile as the fridge. Even the area under the sink, which became a catch-all for cleaning supplies, plant food, and oversized pots and pans in most kitchens, was orderly and immaculate.

"Remind me that we want to see their trash," he told Kyle.

"It must have been awful to be a child in this house," Kyle said.

They moved back past the small half bath and down the corridor that led to the bedrooms, hugging the wall to avoid stepping where the nap showed someone, or something, had been dragged. Where small dark spots on the clean beige carpet suggested there might be drops of blood.

The first bedroom was evidently used as an office. There was a desk and filing drawers, a calculator and a jar of pens and pencils. Some reference books on the shelves. A small stack of manila file folders on the corner of the desk. The drawers held neatly labeled files. Mortgage. Insurance. Cars. Taxes. Investments. They would need to go through these files at some point, but that could wait.

The second bedroom was tiny, with a single bed, a small desk and desk chair, and nothing else. The desk didn't have any drawers, not even a pencil drawer. There was a faded tan spread on the bed. Nothing on the walls and nothing on the desk. No pictures on the walls, and none of the tape marks, empty nails, or faded spots to indicate there ever had been. There was a small closet but the closet was so empty there wasn't even dust. Kyle got down on the floor and lifted the bedspread. The space under the bed, like the rest of the room, was empty. He flattened himself on his stomach and reached in, feeling around. He got up, shaking his head, and moved the bed away from the wall. At the back, caught between the carpet and the baseboard, was a glittery pink barrette.

"Looks like they tried to eliminate all traces of her," he said. "But somehow missed this."

"So painful to think the child is murdered and they eliminate any trace of her. It's like she never existed in the world," Burgess said. "But we've got the mate to this. And the broken one at the crime scene."

He held the barrette up to the light. "There are some hairs trapped here."

So far, except for the barrette, there was no evidence a foster child named Shelley Minor had ever lived in the house.

The medicine cabinet in the bathroom continued the theme of stark organization. Everything was arranged by size and use. The shelves were perfectly clean. There was no makeup and few grooming products. Just cough medicine, peroxide, mouthwash, Band-Aids, aspirin. No prescription medicines.

The only clutter they'd seen in the entire house was in the second drawer of the vanity. There a collection of make-up, skin products, nail polish, and some scrunchies and elastics were jumbled together like they'd escaped a control freak's notice and gone to frolic in the drawer.

"Maybe he shot her because he couldn't stand being yelled at for getting things out of order?" Kyle said.

"If," Burgess said.

"Yeah. If."

They moved on to the bedroom. Here, at least, there was a story about something other than compulsive neatness.

They stood together in the doorway, staring into the room. The signs of a struggle were small. But small displacements in a neatnik's house stand out. The bedspread was slightly askew. The clock on one of the bedside tables had been knocked over. The lampshade was tilted. There was a minute streak of what might be blood on the wall beside the closet. The pillows were misaligned. Dents in the carpet where the legs of the bedside table had been showed it had been moved. There was a scrape on the wall where one of the bedposts had banged it. All little things, but in a house where nothing was cracked, chipped, dented or dirty, they stood out from the obsessive cleanliness and order.

Burgess checked the closet. Very clearly his and hers sides, with everything arranged by length. There was nothing in any of the pockets. Shoes on the closet floor were lined up neatly. There was no dust. On the shelf above the clothes, more shoes were stored in plastic boxes. Extra bedding was zipped into a plastic bag. A few clear plastic bins held belts, scarves, and sweaters. None of the bins held anything except belts, scarves, and sweaters.

"I wouldn't last a day here," Burgess said.

Kyle was down on the floor again, peering under the bed. "Balled up cloth here, Joe," he said. "We'll want them to photograph it before we drag it out to see what it is."

Burgess checked the tall dresser drawers while Kyle checked the low dresser. He worked his way down through drawers that were the same as the rest of the house. Perfectly neat and orderly. There was nothing hidden under, or behind the clothes. No small slips of paper, or mismatched socks, or random dollar bills or change. He'd almost reached the bottom when Kyle said, "Wow. Here's a surprise. Look at this, Joe!"

He stepped carefully over to where Kyle was standing. Kyle had a large, deep drawer open. Burgess looked at the contents. The entire drawer was filled with sexy women's lingerie in all the colors of the rainbow. Carefully folded. Push-up bras and balconettes and strapless bras, with matching panties, mostly thongs, all carefully organized into sets. Only one bra was out of order. A black lacy one tossed carelessly on top. Kyle left that one there—something else for the techs to photograph—and took another one out and checked the size. 34E. Mousy little do-gooder indeed.

Burgess wondered whether Marilyn Dornan, like her foster daughter, might have had implants. He also wondered where the money for all this came from. Unless they were top management, people working for nonprofits didn't make that much, and Shirley Evans had suggested Charlie Dornan didn't work, except to work scams. Maybe those scams were lucrative?

Kyle went back to searching through women's clothes while Burgess went back to Charlie Dornan's dresser. The bottom drawer, which held a man's carefully folded polo shirts, didn't move as easily as the others.

Burgess wrestled it out, removed the contents, and turned it upside down.

Fastened to the bottom of the drawer with duct tape were two thick manila envelopes.

Before he detached them, he wanted pictures with the envelopes in place.

"Got something here, Ter. Can you get Rudy?"

Rudy Carr was up to his ears in the process of carefully recording every angle and detail of the living room from a distance and close up, so Burgess got Dani instead.

"You guys doing okay?" he asked.

"Be better if we could open a window and turn off that damned TV, but rules are rules, and textbook Crime Scene 101 is do not disturb anything. By the way, Joe, I am so grateful you broke that rule the other night in that laundry room. The stench was horrible enough with the windows open. Here's how we're doing. Rudy's in his element, the Annie

Leibovitz of crime scenes. He's loving the subtlety of it—the way in a house this impeccable the small nuances stand out. Wink is just happy to be away from Mrs. Wink, who seems to always be developing ailments lately so he'll have to stay home and take care of her. He's also getting into the small details. I'm getting good at this, but Wink is a master. By the way, he wants to know if you're going to do the cars and the trash."

When she said "cars," it reminded him that the car that Dornan had been driving, the one that was parked out in the driveway, didn't belong to Dornan. In the "better safe than sorry" world of crime scene investigation, he figured they'd better get a warrant for it. They'd want the records for any cell phones they found, too, if there were any cell phones, but the AAG could take care of that.

He said, "Excuse me," and stepped into the kitchen. Sage Prentiss hadn't shown up yet. Now he could make himself most useful getting a warrant to search the car. He figured he'd put both cars on the warrant, just in case there was something hinky about the ownership of hers, too. And any outbuildings and the trash.

Sage started to apologize, but Burgess cut him off. "You still at 109?"

"Uh. I can be."

"Good. I need a search warrant." He gave Prentiss the particulars. "As quick as you can, please."

"Yes, sir."

"Bring it here as soon as the judge signs it."

"Yes, sir."

Burgess disconnected. Something had held Prentiss up. He didn't care what it was. He just wanted the man to jump now. It made him miss Stan, though. Stan Perry could be a pain in the ass, and he'd come perilously close to getting fired more than once, but Burgess appreciated the way Perry could follow his instincts and suddenly pull some case-changing rabbit out of his hat. And Perry knew the job, so he didn't need much direction.

He and Kyle waited while Dani took her photographs, and since she was there, figured she should finish photographing the room, getting the displaced furniture and other things they'd spotted. While she was doing that, they carried the drawer with the mysterious envelopes into the small barren room that they presumed had been Shelley's. They set the drawer on the bed and Burgess pulled the tape loose. He kept one envelope. Handed the other to Kyle. He dumped his out on the desk, fishing out his glasses.

Once his glasses were on and he stared at the photographs, he wished he could unsee what he was seeing.

Kyle didn't say anything for a long time. There was only the sound of his breathing. Then he said, "They're children, Joe. How can anyone?"

It was the question they came back to again and again in their work. They saw horrific violence and profound evil, yet things still had the capacity to disturb them. Burgess wouldn't have it any other way. No one *should* get used to this.

Another long silence, while Burgess wished he hadn't eaten any dinner. While he wished Charlie Hooper Dornan Wilson or whatever his real name was wasn't dead so Burgess could kill him in some drawn-out, painful way. While he imagined these photos on the internet, and the vile men who traded them. Got off on them. Indulged their sick pleasure in watching children being sexually abused.

"There's no computer here," Burgess said. "Which is odd. Especially if the late Charlie Dornan was in the business of making and selling kiddie porn. So where would it have been? Is its absence another suggestion that Charlie's death is not a suicide? That someone else was here and took it away?"

"Or all these photos were taken somewhere else. Also, that if there are still photos like this, there's bound to be video as well," Kyle said. "Do you think they're stored here somewhere? Or on that missing computer?"

"Maybe his partner has them and this was Charlie's insurance policy?" Burgess asked.

"Didn't work very well, did it?"

"You think his partner is one of the men in these pictures?"

Kyle shrugged. "Could be."

"When we're done here, we'll take them back to 109. See if anything in the background looks familiar. If any of the…uh…" Burgess searched for a word.

Kyle supplied it. "Child rapists."

"Child rapists look familiar. If any of them might be the man DeSpain and Kit saw."

"I am so freaking glad I didn't have a chance to eat dinner tonight," Kyle said.

"I'm regretting mine. I can look at those two out on the couch, and it's a puzzle. It's sad that people are dead, but the crime scene becomes the challenge of learning everything it has to say. This stuff…" Burgess waved a hand at the photographs. "I have no words."

"We'd better check the rest of the drawers," Kyle said. "Every freaking drawer in this house. And we haven't looked in the basement yet."

"Did you want to be there when I photograph…" Dani said from the doorway. She was stopped by the pictures spread out on the desk and the bed. Speechless for a moment. These pictures were the kind of thing Wink always wanted to protect her from. But you can't protect an evidence tech from the ugliness of some evidence. "Oh dear, no. No. I guess. I mean I should have thought. Should have known, I suppose, because of those poor girls in that horrible cell. I just…"

She straightened her shoulders and turned so she couldn't see the pictures. "I'm ready to photograph that crumpled cloth under the bed. Do you want to be there?"

Burgess and Kyle put the photos back in the envelopes, then officially collected them as evidence and put them on the evidence log. Aucoin had finished securing the scene and was now keeping that log and taking the collected evidence to the crime scene van.

Burgess and Kyle followed Dani back to the bedroom. Kyle lifted the bedspread and she lay on her stomach to get her pictures of the object under the bed. When she was done, Kyle pulled it out. It was a very bloody bath towel with two holes in it. Dani photographed it again, then stored it, marked it as evidence, and gave it to Aucoin, who logged it in.

"She'll have injuries to her head where someone knocked her out, wrapped the towel around her head, and then shot her," Kyle said. "Or, if there were two people involved, bruises on her shoulders or arms where one of them held her down and put that towel over her face, while the other one shot her."

"You can tell that from a towel?" Dani said.

"We're speculating. Thinking out loud. The towel is information," Burgess said. "We put it together with what we've already observed in the living room, plus the signs of disturbance here. You'll want to bag her hands. She may have struggled with her killer. Bag his hands, too."

"You don't think her husband killed her?"

"That's just one possibility," Burgess said. "Your meticulous documentation, and collection of fingerprints and other evidence, is what will help us establish what did happen here."

"Back to work," she said with a faint smile. "Very meticulously." She began following, and photographing, the drag marks and dark dots that might have been blood, down the hall to the living room. She was almost back to the front door when there was a commotion—Gabe Delinsky's voice saying, "Sir, hold on, you can't go in without…" and a belligerent, "Let me pass!" Captain Cote, not wearing booties or looking where he was going, stepped through the door in all the vigor and indifference of his self-importance, and slammed right into her.

Burgess had held his temper a thousand times when Cote did stupid things at his crime scene, but those photographs had unlatched the hinge on his temper. He slid along the wall, stepped past Dani, who had dropped her camera and was rubbing her head, and stepped between her and Captain Cote, advancing on Cote and using his bulk to steer the man out the door.

"Get out!" he yelled. "You're not wearing protective footgear. You're stepping on drag marks, maybe footprints, and a blood trail. You're mucking up my crime scene. And you may have injured my evidence tech when we have two bodies and a long night ahead. What were you thinking, Paul?"

Burgess was thinking that Vince Melia should have been here by now to run interference for his detectives, so Cote couldn't have barged in like this. He stepped outside with Cote, blocking the man's access with his body so Cote couldn't push his way back in. He was carefully not touching Cote, but forcing him out onto the front walk and preventing him from entering the house.

"If you want an update, I'll give you an update. Just don't go stomping all over those drag marks and possible blood spots on the carpet, and contaminating my scene before Dani can finish her photographs and swab the spots."

He turned, grabbed protective booties from the box, and handed a pair to his boss's boss. "If you want to view the scene, you'll wear these. You'll follow right behind me. You'll step where I step. You won't cough or sneeze or touch anything. You won't ask my evidence techs questions that might distract them from the work they're doing. You used to do this, Paul. You know what a slow, methodical process it is. So don't be a chucklehead. Are we clear?"

Cote was clearly fuming, but miraculously kept his mouth shut.

"You want me to brief you first?" Burgess said.

Cote shook his head.

Before an audience of officers trying not to clap, and struggling to keep straight faces, Cote put on his booties and followed Burgess back into the house.

TWENTY-SEVEN

As they entered the living room, carefully following the path along the edge, Burgess narrated the events leading up to their discovery of the bodies. He was explaining how their knocks had failed to bring someone to the door, so he'd looked through the window, when Cote spotted the bodies on the sofa and made a beeline toward them.

"Dammit, Paul. No! You fucking stop right now."

He rarely yelled at a death scene. It was a subdued process, one where they spoke in lowered voices as they moved around the bodies and through the rooms, so Burgess's yell brought everything to a halt as he reached out, grabbed Cote's collar, and hauled him back to the wall. He'd tried his best not to touch the man, but if the captain was going to act like a willful toddler, he needed to be restrained.

Burgess didn't lower his voice, because he was speaking for the benefit of everyone who put in the long, slow, painstaking hours at scenes like this, not taking shortcuts however exhausted they got, and doing everything they could to avoid contamination or the destruction of evidence. Burgess said, "Don't you ever do something like that in one of my crime scenes again. You stay by the wall. You follow me and step where I step. You do not deviate from this line. You do not touch anything. You do not risk stepping on footprints, or evidence, or contaminating this scene like an impetuous eight-year-old boy. You do *not* approach the bodies until Wink and Rudy say they are ready. If you can't follow the rules, you'll have to leave. This is *my* crime scene and you are not going to screw it up. Are we clear?"

He had not released his grip on Cote's collar.

"Look, Burgess," Cote said. "I'm your boss. I'll do whatever I..."

"Are. We. Clear?" Burgess repeated.

"Let go of me, Burgess, or I swear, I'll have your badge for this."

Was that a cop show cliché or what? Burgess flicked a glance at the TV. CSI was just wrapping up. And where the heck was Vince Melia? The people here shouldn't be wasting their time arguing with Cote when there was work to do.

"You want my badge, Paul? Bulling your way through this scene is that important to you? Taking the risk that you'll step on evidence, destroy a footprint, or otherwise contaminate the scene, that's okay with you so long as you get a closer look at the bodies? Seriously? What are you, a child? Everyone else here is coming off an all-nighter at a related, horrific scene. Everyone here is exhausted, but we're still giving this the slow, painstaking examination it deserves. So tell me, Paul...why does being the boss give you the right to piss all over everyone else's work?"

Cote didn't reply.

Burgess didn't release his grip on the man's collar. "We've got a girl murdered and mutilated, Paul, a girl we believe was a foster child in this house. We've found suspected kiddie porn using young girls in this house. All this in the home of a woman who works with refugees and asylum seekers. Who may have had ready access to vulnerable children. We've got enough material here for a dozen press conferences, but we have to understand it first. Investigate. Link it up. Establish the connections. Right now, you are deliberately interfering with that, and I have no idea why."

He was still keeping his voice up, so everyone around them would know the score. "You want me to retire? Maybe I will. But not before I find who was responsible for killing that girl, and imprisoning those children we found the other night. Not before I understand the connections, if there are connections, between what happened here and those other events. Not before I do my job, which right now, you, for no good reason, are keeping me from doing."

He dropped his hand, releasing Cote. "Do you want to run this scene, Paul? Is that what this is about? Because if that's what you're here for, slamming into an evidence tech and carelessly contaminating a scene is not the best way to start."

From the doorway, Melia, who should have been here half an hour ago, said, quietly, "Burgess? A word."

It was softly spoken, but it was a command, and it put Burgess in a bind. Stay and disobey Melia or risk letting Cote wreak havoc here?

He reminded himself they'd gotten answers, and justice, before when idiots like Cote had pushed their way into scenes and mucked things up. Reminded himself that despite their cautious détente, Cote was still Cote and he would still be challenged to hang on to his temper whenever Cote appeared at a scene.

"Excuse me, Paul," he said. He stepped around Cote and followed Melia outside.

Before he could speak, Melia held up a hand. "Take some breaths and count to ten, Joe."

Burgess swallowed a mouthful of imprudent remarks, closed his eyes, and breathed in the sweet night air, gloriously free of the death smell that was already pervading the house. Fresh death has a smell of its own.

"When you're ready, bring me up on it," Melia said.

He took another minute. Then opened his eyes and gave Melia the story he'd tried to give Cote. The story that explained why everything in this scene was so important.

"You got enough people on it?"

"It's a small house, Vince. Too many bodies…uh, live bodies…and we'll be stepping all over each other."

"Okay." Melia eyed him, a cop's assessment. "You gonna be able to do this without losing it, Joe?"

"I hope so, Vince, if you can keep Cote from screwing things up. We're just getting started. Terry and I don't have enough to develop our theories yet. It's murky."

"Murky how?"

"Who killed whom, and whether there was a third party involved."

"You think that's likely?"

"Trying not to reach any conclusions yet. Trying to let the facts speak for themselves."

"Terry agree?"

"We haven't discussed it. Been busy. Still busy. Lots more to do in this house."

Melia took a moment. "Oh," he said. Meaning he understood their process. How they'd each reach a conclusion based on what they were seeing, and then debate if they didn't agree. Kyle and Burgess usually agreed, but not always.

"Terry and I need to finish searching the house. We'll do the basement next, the living room last, after the ME releases the bodies. Can you check on Dani, see if she's okay. Cote really knocked into her, and I'm pretty sure she hit her head."

"What else?"

"I've got Sage working on a warrant for the cars. The one the male was driving, the Prius, isn't his. I don't know about the other vehicle."

"And?"

"We need patrol to search the yard. No one has done that yet. And a canvass of the neighbors. Did they hear any gunshots. See anyone leaving the house. See any vehicles around the house or leaving the house this evening. The usual."

"It's late," Melia said.

"And their street is full of cops and flashing lights. Tomorrow they'll be back in their own bubbles, may have forgotten something they've seen."

"What else?"

"When Sage gets here with the warrants, we'll do the cars. Someone will need to do the trash. That's it for now. Lee is sending an assistant. Someone new. We're trying to get the scene processed—pictures and evidence collection—before anyone disturbs the bodies."

"So, not to let assumptions get ahead of the facts or anything…" Melia gave a faint smile as he used one of Burgess's favorite lines, "when you looked through the window, what did you think you were seeing?"

"You mean if I were just any old detective, seeing what I was supposed to see, instead of Burgess or Kyle, who question everything?"

"Yes."

"Murder suicide. Husband kills wife and then kills himself."

"And you're not buying that because?"

"Because I haven't finished my investigation. Haven't checked their hands for GSR. I haven't seen the autopsy results. I haven't done my victimology. I don't know enough about the people on that couch. I haven't even examined the bodies closely. I don't know if there are defensive wounds. If someone was unconscious before being shot. You know the drill, Vince. This is a classic case of assume making an ass of u and me."

Burgess told him about the photos he and Kyle had found. "Stomach turning, Vince. We need to finish searching, make sure there's not more in the house. That we're not missing something. So far, we haven't found a camera or a computer and no phones, though they may have phones on their bodies. In a pocket somewhere."

Melia nodded. "Where's Stan?"

"Hospital. Having a baby. Or Lily is. Actually, she just did. He called a few minutes ago to say they have a girl. Autumn Angela. I told him not to come in."

Melia shook his head. "I wonder if it will change him?"

"Temper him, maybe. Some of the time. We are who we are, and getting into trouble, larking off on his own, and pulling surprise rabbits out of hats, that's who Stan is. It's hard to picture him as a father."

"It was hard to picture you as a father, too, Joe, despite your compassion for the weak and helpless. But you and Chris seem to be doing okay."

"This week."

Burgess was eager to get back inside, but felt like there was something else Melia wanted to say, so he waited.

Melia didn't look at him. He stared off into the darkness. It was often easier to talk in the dark. "I think I'm changed, Joe. I've lost my edge, my passion for this. I look at my family, think what I've put them through, and wonder if I want to do this anymore."

He understood. Coming as close to death as Vince did had to have an impact. But Vince was a cop, through and through. Burgess thought maybe he just needed more time. Maybe a couple of good solves where justice was served. Maybe a good therapist.

"You talking to anyone? Getting help with this?"

Melia smiled. "You wouldn't."

"I have. Anyway, I'm a dinosaur. You're a modern man."

"Yes. I am seeing someone. But it goes so darned slowly."

Burgess put a hand on Melia's shoulder. "Just so you know. I didn't carry you out of that place and guard you at the hospital so I could lose you. I did it because we need to keep you. Because Terry and Stan and I can't do this without you. Without a buffer between us and those who get impatient with the fact that putting these cases together takes time. We need a touchstone, someone to act as our sounding board. Who can tell us when we're out of line and full of crap."

"Like now?" Melia said.

Burgess nodded.

"I'll be sure to tell my therapist that," Melia said. "And by the way. For the record. In there with Cote? You were out of line."

"Right," Burgess said. "I know. Getting back to the work thing. And your uncertainty. There's going to be fear, Vince. And hesitation. I'm sure the temptation to do something less intense is strong. Just also think about why you're doing this. What you get out of it. Maybe most important? How another job will meet those needs."

He tipped his head toward the house. "If you do step away from investigations, promise you won't become like him and forget what we all do." He considered. Said, "Like you ever would."

Melia went to check on Dani, then to organize a canvass of the neighborhood and a search of the yard. Depending on how they came down on the question of who died first, that towel under the bed could be very significant.

Burgess went to join Kyle in the bedroom, where Kyle was methodically checking the bottom of every single drawer. He left Captain Paul Cote to do whatever damned thing he wanted to do, knowing Wink or Rudy would let him know if Cote got seriously in the way. Or if it was time to do the man physical harm.

TWENTY-EIGHT

They found no more envelopes or other items taped to the bases of the bedroom drawers or the bottoms of either dresser. Nothing under the mattress. Then they checked the nightstands. There were condoms and ammunition in his, suggesting that there had also been a gun in there. That was something they'd have to check—whether the ammunition matched that used in the shootings. Whether it was his gun.

Her side had more colorful condoms, KY, and a burner cell phone. Together with all the lacy lingerie, it made Burgess wonder if she'd been involved with a man other than her husband. Maybe the records for the burner would answer that question. Maybe they'd find a best friend she gossiped to. A search of the bathroom wastebasket had revealed, among the usual detritus, a wrapper from one of her condoms.

As the night wore on, he wished, as he frequently did, that this were a CSI world, and he could get results in moments instead of however long it took the phone company to move its butt and give them records. Chris had once asked him if he was always this impatient, and he'd said he didn't think so. But he didn't have very clear memories of who he'd been as a child or a teenager. He knew concern for his mother and little sisters had played a big role and provided the impetus for doing small jobs and babysitting to supplement their income.

One thing he knew for sure was that he'd had a temper inherited from his father, who'd been a cruel and violent alcoholic. When Burgess was sixteen, the age Dylan was about to reach, he'd realized one night as his father was beating his mother that he was the bigger man. He'd made it very clear, physically clear, that if his father ever laid a hand on his mother again, it would be the last hand he laid on anyone.

The positive effect had been that his mother was never beaten again. The negative? That he'd found out how powerful his temper could be.

"Basement, Joe?" Kyle said.

He nodded. They'd do the living room last, after Wink and Rudy were done and after the ME had come and released the bodies and they'd been sent to Augusta. Then the TV armoire and the drawers in the end tables and the trunk that served as a coffee table would be searched like the rest of the house.

They returned to the kitchen, and opened the door that led to the stairs to the basement. Burgess flipped on the light with trepidation. Going into any basement was a risky business. After the horrors of the other basement associated with Charlie Dornan, they might find anything down here. As the bright overhead light came on, illuminating the room, it looked like they'd find nothing. No cells. No human heads. There were a washer and dryer on raised platforms. A shelf above with laundry products, all perfectly clean on a perfectly clean shelf. A long counter for folding laundry, with a rack above it for hanging clothes to dry. There was a metal rack with out-of-season clothing stored in large zippered bags, with a rack at the bottom for winter boots.

A door beside the washer led to a furnace room, another door opened with trepidation, which was empty except for a furnace and a hot water heater.

Kyle checked inside the washer and dryer. They were empty.

"Where are the garden tools? Lawnmower? Snow shovels? There must be a storage building of some sort," Kyle said.

"Let's look out back," Burgess said. He headed for the stairs.

"Wait," Kyle said, turning back to the platform the washer and dryer sat on. He bent and fiddled until he'd worked the nearly invisible drawer open.

Burgess bent to look. The drawer held neatly folded yellow towels. He lifted one out. Beneath the towels were six precise rows of CDs in plastic jewel cases. "Bingo," he said. "The merchandise."

"I say 'Oh fuck!' given the hours we'll now be spending staring at these things," Kyle said.

Burgess put on fresh gloves and bent to pluck a few, one from each of the six rows. He put on his glasses and studied the labels. "These all have different labels."

Beside him, he felt Kyle shudder.

Ignoring the protests from his knee, he knelt in front of the drawer and examined a few more. The same six labels, one title in each row. Like neatly stored merchandise. "Let's get Dani down here to get some pictures. Then let's send the whole drawer downtown for cataloging and fingerprints."

He stood, ignoring the protest from his knee. Kneeling was not its favorite activity. He looked at Kyle, who was staring at the contents of the drawer, realization dawning that he'd made a sexist assumption about the situation upstairs.

"You thinking what I'm thinking?" he asked.

Kyle nodded. "I believe I am. Which makes the porn aspect of it so much uglier."

"If she hadn't been so meticulous and precise…" Burgess began.

"It might have taken us a lot longer to figure this out," Kyle finished. "I'll get Dani."

When he came back, it wasn't with Dani but with Rudy Carr. "Wink has Dani sitting down in the van with ice on her head," Carr explained. "Even though she insists she's fine, and he's staring daggers at Cote, who is still in there watching. At least he's staying out of the way. Cote, I mean."

"For now," Burgess said.

"Dani and I think it's only a matter of time before Wink arranges for Captain Cote to join the other bodies in the room. Hate to say it, Joe, but we're all wondering what the hell you and Kyle were thinking when you saved that guy."

"Brotherhood. Camaraderie. Respect for the rank if not the man. The fact that we're all supposed to have each other's backs," Kyle said.

"Even if it's not a two-way street?"

"It's who we are,' Burgess said. "Not who he is. We were pretty deep into saving Portland cops at that point. Right now, saving the captain feels like a bad decision. But we're not supposed to pick and choose who we serve and protect."

"Maybe there should be exceptions to that rule," Carr said. "So, what do we have here?"

"One of those nifty storage drawers under the washing machine," Kyle said. "Obviously, we haven't looked at them yet, but we are speculating, based on our knowledge of the case, that these are collections of child pornography that the nice couple upstairs were in the business of making and selling. We're in the early stages of this thing, so I wouldn't share that speculation with anyone."

"Particularly not with a certain person upstairs?" Carr asked.

"Particularly," Burgess agreed. He didn't have time for recriminations or regret in the midst of this mess, but he admitted to himself that he'd hoped Cote's serious brush with death would have brought him back a better person.

Kyle, who was so good at reading minds, squeezed his shoulder. "*We* did the right thing," he said.

"Thanks, Ter. Now let's get upstairs and look at this with fresh eyes."

"From which the scales have dropped?"

"From which," Burgess agreed.

"You two are scary sometimes, you know that?" Carr said.

"We do," Kyle said. "Cool, isn't it?"

He and Kyle found Dr. Lee's new assistant in the living room, examining the bodies. Althea Chartener was young and serious, and unlike her boss, Dr. Lee, who skittered through the job like a waterbug on speed, she moved with the caution of a tortoise crossing a highway. Lee asserted that she was great. Burgess didn't know yet. This would be the first scene they'd worked together.

He looked at Wink, who gave a subtle nod. So far, Wink thought she was okay. Like him, Wink was an old timer, and one old timer was likely to know what another valued.

With Wink, Cote, the ME and two bodies, the small room was crowded even before he and Kyle came in. Crowded and hot and full of scents. Mostly of blood and death and one of death's final indignities, the foul smells of feces and urine. Over it, like lighter notes in a musical composition, were Cote's aftershave or some leathery man-scent, and the light, sweet scent of roses. Burgess figured the roses were from Dr. Chartener, not Wink.

She turned when they entered, and rose to her feet, sketching a wave with one gloved hand. "Sergeant Burgess? Detective Kyle? I'm Althea."

She had a pleasing, serious face framed by dark hair pulled back in a ponytail.

"Joe," Burgess said. "And this is Terry."

She studied them briefly, like they were more bodies in her scene, then turned back to the couple on the couch, pointing to the man. "Staged scene 101," she said. "We'll learn more at autopsy, but here's what I'm seeing. The gun is on the left, but the victim is right handed, which the shooter wasn't thinking about when he, or she, put the gun down. Also, the location of the exit wound and the pattern of blood and brain suggests his head was tipped up and back…" She demonstrated with her head. "Not a likely position for someone shooting himself. More like what would occur when someone was standing in front of him and slightly above, forcing the gun into his mouth."

"What we thought, too," Burgess said. "What else can you tell us?"

"She wasn't killed here."

They already knew that.

"Wink will be bagging her hands," the ME said. "She did not go without a fight. We'll check their pockets when we get them to our facility."

Burgess was glad to have his own conclusions confirmed. They *would* learn more at autopsy, of course. Things like blows to the head, bruises, injured hands, chipped teeth as well as the angle of the bullets. He realized they'd seen no purse anywhere in the house, which was odd even in a place like this, which made the term "sterile" seem flamboyant. For now, he thanked her and he and Kyle went outside. Melia had already done it, but Burgess wanted to check on Dani.

Prentiss had arrived with the search warrant, so Kyle went to search Marilyn Dornan's car while Prentiss, lucky fellow that he was, got the trash cans.

Dani declared that she was fine and wanted to go back to work.

"Promise you won't hurt Captain Cote?" he said.

Dani grinned, which was what really told him she was okay, not her words. "I'd say 'what were you and Terry thinking' but I bet everyone else already has."

"You've got that right. Okay. You can work, but don't overdo it, okay?"

"Okay." Another grin. She liked it that he was being protective.

They were protective of Dani, but not like she was their pet, unless that pet was a brilliant and amazing, highly trained lab or German Shepherd, smarter than most humans, and trained to find evidence most humans never would.

"Wink will look after me," she said.

He swung by the side of the house, where Sage Prentiss had found an outside light to illuminate the trash he had spread out on a tarp. The trash was as neat as the house, with everything inside the trash bag tied up in smaller plastic bags. It made the whole job less smelly. It also made it slower, as every individual package had to be opened.

"I went through the first can quickly, Sarge," Prentiss said. "Nothing but papers. This second one is like molasses."

"Papers like newspapers?"

Prentiss shook his head. "Like old printouts and things. Like someone had cleaned out a desk. And bills and things."

"You read through them before you moved on?"

Prentiss looked down at his shoes, which Burgess read as no, he had not. He had treated them like his own trash. Old papers were thrown out because they were no longer useful. Often not the case when the players were bad guys and cops.

Prentiss lifted his shoulders in a resigned gesture. "Sorry, Sarge. I'll look at them again," he said.

"Never know what might be important," Burgess said. "Finish that second can, then recheck the first one."

He headed toward the back of the house, where officers were searching the backyard. In the far corner, his light picked out a wooden shed. Likely where the tools and lawnmower were stored, since there wasn't a garage. He headed for it, a twinge in his gut warning him it might hold more than just tools.

Just don't let us find any more bodies, he thought. Three were more than enough for one case. His people would burn out.

He searched around the shed first. Nothing but grass that needed mowing. No strange mounds. No signs of recent digging. No flat cement pads that might hide an underground bunker. He'd seen all of those things. Underground bunkers gave him the creeps. Satisfied that there wasn't anything suspicious around the building, he pulled on gloves and reached for the latch. Unusual on a backyard storage shed, there was also a lock. Not a padlock, but a genuine lock. The door didn't open.

TWENTY-NINE

Remembering the keys he'd seen in a dish in the kitchen, Burgess returned to the house, slipped on some booties, and went to the kitchen to find them. If he got lucky, one of the keys would open the shed door.

He stepped carefully around Dani, who had gone back to photographing the drag marks and possible blood spots on the hall carpet, and snagged the keys. Then he let himself out through the back door and recrossed the yard.

Between the two sets, there were more than a dozen keys on the two rings. He got it on the fifth try, opening the door with trepidation and shining his flashlight around. No cells, no chains, no bodies. Everything looked normal. There were shovels and rakes and a lawnmower. All of the equipment was clean and rust-free. A neatly coiled garden hose. Bags of fertilizer and bug dust arranged on shelves in order of their size. A spare propane tank for a grill. A stack of folding plastic lawn chairs topped by a stack of cushions. The room was hot and smelled of dust, fertilizer, grass clippings, and a funk that might have been from mice.

He exhaled slowly, realizing he'd been holding his breath, fully expecting to find more bad stuff here. Cases like this, with multiple crime scenes, were rare, but sometimes shoes dropped like the perp was a centipede. Still, something here didn't feel right. He had the nagging sense that there was something here to find. That the order in this building, like the order in the house, was a deceptive neatness that hid horrible secrets.

Remembering his long-ago training officer's admonition to always look up, he checked the ceiling and the rafters. No blood stains. No photographic equipment for making pornography. No chains or handcuffs for restraining victims. No trunks or bins or boxes that might hold more of the Dornan's vile wares.

He paused, realizing that he hadn't seen any photographic equipment in the house, nor at Ida Mae Wilson's.

As he turned back toward the door, he saw a light switch he'd missed, and snapped it on. Nothing changed. It was still just an ordinary shed holding everyday garden tools. The only thing unusual was how neat and clean everything was.

He'd stepped out and was closing the door when he had a thought. Something about the dimensions seemed off. He paced the length of the building on the outside, then stepped inside and paced the length of the room. There was a five foot discrepancy. He went back inside and checked the end walls. The wall on the left had a window through which he could see flashlights leaving the yard and moving toward the house. The one on the right held sets of shelves and various racks for holding gardening tools. In the space between them was the stack of folding chairs and cushions. He focused his flashlight on the wall behind the chairs and could just see spaces around a flat plywood panel that suggested the chairs might be hiding a door. The devil on his shoulder, the devil that wanted to go home and sleep, whispered, "Leave it."

Burgess tried to listen to his angels and not his devils, though the devil sometimes won. This was not one of those times.

Setting his flashlight down, he shifted the chairs and cushions. Yes, there was a door. Not a proper door with a doorframe around it and a knob, just a hinged panel of plywood that opened with a leather thong threaded through a small hole. Just above the thong was a sliding bolt to hold the door shut.

Keep the door shut or keep someone in?

This all might be nothing, but people rarely went to the trouble of building a false wall and hiding a door if there was nothing worth hiding on the other side. He could hope that, given the excessive neatness of the house, this was Dornan's man cave, where he could escape to messiness and indulgence. Hope sprang eternal, right? But Burgess was used to his gut leading him to bad stuff, not a recliner and a TV or a stack of girly magazines.

Before he opened the door, he had to get all of this photographed. He wished he'd left the chairs and cushions in place so the effort to hide the door could be recorded, but it was too late now.

Once again, he crossed the lawn, went around the house, and entered through the front door. Dani was done with her photographs and was consulting with Wink.

They both looked at him warily when he came in.

"I need to borrow Dani for a minute," he said.

"No, you don't," Wink said. "I don't care if you've discovered a dungeon full of torture implements. We're tired. The ME's van will be here in a minute. Then we're going to call it a night and come back in the morning to process the rest of the house."

Burgess wasn't waiting until morning. "It's just a couple shots of a wall, Wink. It won't take long."

"Just a couple of shots of a wall," Wink mimicked. "And the wall has a door, and behind the door there will be another crime scene and then we'll be here for the rest of the night. Well, sorry but I don't care what you find out in that shed. I'm sending Dani home. See if Rudy can do it."

Rudy could do it, and was more than happy to get out of the hot, foul-smelling house. The two of them crossed the back yard, where moments before officers had been searching with their flashlights, looking from a distance like giant fireflies. No finds had been announced and now the yard was dark. If you turned your back on that small cape with the two bodies inside, on the street full of flashing red and blue lights, it looked like a peaceful summer night topped by a waning moon and a sky full of stars.

Burgess wanted to follow Wink's lead and call it a night. But if they'd called it a night instead of checking out Ida Mae Wilson's house, one or possibly two helpless girls would have died. It seemed unlikely that the Dornans would have held someone hostage here, instead of keeping all the girls at the Wilson house, but his message from the translator had been that another girl was still missing.

He lingered in the cool night air, reluctant to explore the possibility that there might be another victim on the other side of that wall. He literally ached for some sleep. His whole body ached, not just his whiny knee. Beside him, Rudy Carr waited patiently, perhaps no more eager than he to encounter another crime scene.

At last, Carr said, "Ready when you are, Sarge."

Burgess led him into the storage building, snapping on the light as they entered. Finding electricity in the building had made him wary. Most people didn't bother to put lights in their storage sheds. He pointed the blank wall. "I moved the cushions and chairs and found this. It looks like a door."

"It does look like a door," Carr agreed, starting to take his pictures.

After a few minutes, he lowered his camera. "You going to open it or shall we follow Wink's lead and come back tomorrow?"

Of course he was going to open it. He couldn't put it off any longer. Not when there was any chance he might find a missing girl. He just didn't want to find any more bodies. Maybe it would only be more storage, like that drawer under the dryer. His gut said that was not what they'd find. Sometimes, a cop's gut could be such a pain. Sometimes his gut was literally a physical pain, often a pain that lingered until a case was closed.

He slid back the latch, grabbed the leather thong that served as a handle, and pulled the door toward him.

Hot, foul air poured out, washing over them in a stomach-curdling wave. Air that reminded him way too much of the cell in the basement at Ida Mae Wilson's house.

Behind him, Carr said, "Oh fuck!"

Still avoiding the moment when he'd have to look inside the room and confront what was in there, he used his flashlight to examine the wall by the door, searching for another light switch. He found it and turned on the light, illuminating a barren cell with a mattress, a bucket, and a small naked girl curled on the mattress in a defensive ball. There was blood on the mattress. And on the child. Given the business the Dornans were in, his mind filled with ugly speculation.

Before he could stop himself, he said, "Oh, shit. Not another one."

The room was small, but Carr was able to stick his head in. "Holy fuck," he said. "Is she alive?"

He raised his camera and started taking shots.

"I'll check," Burgess said.

She didn't look alive. She was absolutely still and hadn't responded to the light or their voices in any way. Burgess stepped carefully along the space between the mattress and the wall until he was beside her, and knelt down. He reached out to check for a pulse, but before he could touch her, she wriggled frantically away from him and began to scream.

He looked up at Carr. "She's alive."

It was the camera, he thought. *Cameras meant she would be hurt again.* They needed to get the pictures, though.

"Make it as quick as you can, Rudy," he said. "The camera scares her. She thinks we're going to…"

Joe Burgess, tough guy extraordinaire, the man who didn't blink at the most horrific crimes, couldn't bring himself to say it. Luckily, he didn't need to.

"Got it, Sarge," Carr said. "Quick as I can."

They both knew it would take as long as it took to adequately document what they'd found. The child in the scene. The dirt, the blood, her terror. At least they could do the room after the child was gone. But Carr was good. Experienced. Quick.

Burgess stepped out of the room so Carr could take some pictures, pulling out his phone, thinking it was too bad you couldn't kill someone who was already dead. That foul couple on the sofa should have had to answer for this. They hadn't acted alone, though. He would find the other—or others—and they *would* answer for this brutality. All the brutality.

In the good old days, sometimes also the bad old days, cops might have made their negative feelings clear when they found the subjects who'd done things like this. Especially when the victims were children. Sometimes he wished he could bring the tender-hearted folks who were always screaming police brutality into rooms like this. It might help them understand how a cop could lose it.

Cops couldn't lose it because it would impact their cases and might let a criminal go free. But holding it in could eat them alive.

He called for an ambulance. He called Vince Melia, so Melia could add securing this building to his list. He called Wink, so Wink could add this to his dance card when they came back to finish in the morning. He hated to put it off. Burgess never liked to let time pass, the risks of "accidental events" that destroyed scenes and evidence was too great, but cops would be here guarding the scene, everyone was fried, and tomorrow would be here soon enough.

He was unbuttoning his shirt when Carr stepped out, his face pinched and sad, saying, "The poor little thing. Is there anything we could—" Like Wink, Carr was unflappable, but someone who wasn't affected by scenes like this wasn't human.

Carr saw the shirt and nodded. "Oh. Okay."

Burgess stepped back into the room, slowly and carefully approaching the terrified child. "Bella," he said. He pointed to himself. "Amiga."

The dark eyes stared at him as he wrapped her in his shirt and carried her out of the room, the child struggling in his arms.

"Amiga," he said again, struggling to remember the Spanish word for safe. "Seguro. I won't hurt you. Estas seguro, Bella."

"See if you can find someone who speaks Spanish, Rudy," he told Carr as he headed back across the lawn, the child a feather in his arms. She had buried her face in his chest. He didn't know, couldn't know, whether it was because she didn't want to see any more bad stuff, or because his words had reached her.

He flashed on carrying Neddy from the car to the house. On other children he'd carried out of crime scenes. Hadn't he vowed that he would not do cases with children anymore? Didn't the universe understand that his heart couldn't take it?

For years, until Chris begged him to take the pictures down so Nina and Neddy wouldn't see them, the inside of his closet door had been his bulletin board of brutalized children. Chief among them had been Kristin Marks, raped, suffocated with her own underpants, and thrown away in a landfill. Burgess had nearly killed himself trying to get her justice, until Cote screwed up the chain of evidence, lost key pieces that tied the killer to the crime, and her killer walked away with a slap on the wrist. Between Kristin and little Timmy Watts, Burgess wasn't sure there was enough left of him to take on this new batch of horrifically abused children. But now the child in his arms had raised her head and was staring up at him with huge, dark eyes. She needed everything the cops and the legal system could give her. How could he let her down?

"Seguro, Bella," he repeated. "Estas seguro."

Then, as the eyes continued their unwavering stare, he said, "Mi nombre es Joe."

He had now exhausted his Spanish.

He met Kyle halfway across the lawn, Kyle's eyes going from his face to the little bundle in his arms.

"Oh, fuck, no!" Kyle said. "Not another one."

"Another one. This is Sofia's little sister, Isabella."

Before he could continue, the small girl he believed was named Isabella said, "Sofia?" and launched into an explosion of Spanish, the only part of which he understood was "please."

"Si, Bella," he said, "we go to see Sofia."

The outburst seemed to have taken the last of her energy. She burrowed into his neck and her scared eyes closed.

"Sofia?" Kyle said. "Is she one of…"

"That's right. I had a message from the translator, asking if we had found Sofia and Maria's little sister."

Kyle muttered a string of expletives and jerked his chin toward the storage building. "She was in there?"

"Behind a hidden door."

"Pray God she is the last," Kyle said.

"Roger that," Burgess said. "By the time we put this one to bed, they're going to need a new A team."

Kyle nodded. "Stan's going to be sorry he missed this."

"Sorry? He should be glad. Tonight Stan is all about life, while we're all about death." He changed the subject. "You find anything in the cars?"

"Nothing like a note that says 'I shot my husband and then my lover shot me,' but I want to tow them both back to 109 and get Wink and Dani to go over them."

"Cote's going to love that."

"Cote is lucky he's alive, Joe. He ought to remember that."

"You think the shooter was her lover, Terry?"

"I think someone was. Maybe they were into threesomes. Given the other sordid stuff this couple was into, that wouldn't be much of a surprise."

"So you think she or she and someone else killed him and then that someone else killed her?"

"I think that's pretty obvious. Maybe with some exciting post-shooting sex in between? What's less obvious is why, if there was a struggle in the bedroom, and the towel the shooter put over her head was shoved under the bed, we didn't find more blood there."

Burgess shook his head. "Gonna take a real good detective to figure that one out."

Kyle did an elaborate yawn and stretch. "Ain't gonna be this one. At least, not tonight. This detective is signing off and going home to hug his family."

"One smart detective," Burgess said. "This detective wishes he could do that, too."

"He could," Kyle said, though they both knew Burgess wasn't done until this little girl was safely with her sisters.

In the distance, they could hear the approaching ambulance.

"You all set with the tows, Ter?"

"All set."

Kyle drooped with weariness, looking as tired as Burgess felt. He fumbled in his pocket for keys and held them out. "Take the truck, Ter. Leave it at 109. I'm going to ride to the hospital with Bella."

Kyle nodded and snagged the keys. "Thanks, Joe."

He turned away from the silent yard and back toward the house, still blazing with lights. "Doesn't do any good to say 'no more kids' does it, Joe."

"I keep saying it."

"And I'm right behind you."

Burgess handed off buttoning up the scene for the night to Melia, who was still standing in the yard, talking on his phone. Let Melia tell Wink that there was yet another scene to process. Wink was a steady as a rock, but he could get cranky when the work piled up. There were other officers who could process crime scenes, but on something big like this, they only wanted Wink and Dani and Rudy.

Then he carried Bella to the waiting ambulance, and climbed in with her for the ride to the hospital. She screamed when they tried to take her out of his arms, and clung to him, her eyes widening in panic.

"Guess it can wait a few more minutes," his favorite EMT said. "But Joe, you've got to stop bringing us these poor children."

"It's not on me," he said. "Tell it to the bad guys."

She patted his shoulder. "I know that." Then she poured some water into a cup and handed it to him. He took it with his freer arm and offered it to Bella. "Agua?" he said.

Now his Spanish was totally exhausted. But it worked. The little girl took the cup in two hands and gulped the water, holding out the cup to the EMT and saying, "Mas?"

"She's cute as a button, Joe," the woman said, "and I think she likes you. I wonder if Chris would like another daughter?"

"Don't even joke about it," he said. "She has two sisters." He hoped she still had two sisters.

The woman grinned as she refilled the cup and handed it to Bella. "Maybe five kids is too many."

"I used to think any kids was too many, and now look at me."

She just smiled.

He was too tired even to return her smile. He leaned against the wall, rocked by the swaying ambulance. If the girl's restless foot hadn't kept kicking him, he would have fallen asleep in an inappropriate place for the third time today.

THIRTY

Burgess stayed with the child until she was through her evaluation in the ER and finally settled in a room with her sister. He understood the phrase "bone weary" far more than he wanted to by the time he was ready to leave.

Dr. Cohen was in the ER, he didn't know whether it was still, or again, and she teased him gently as he delivered Bella into her care. "Haven't I told you to stay out of my ER?" she said.

He would have said that at this point in this day, nothing could make him smile, but she did. "I'm afraid I find you irresistible," he said.

She poked a finger into her chest. "Damage magnet," she said. "What have you brought me this time?"

"This is Bella. Isabella," he said. "We have two of her sisters upstairs."

"You catch the ones who did this?"

"Dead," he said. "Now we have to catch their killer."

She bent over the child, murmuring something, and once again, Burgess was impressed. It appeared this kind Indian doctor spoke Spanish. When she straightened, she said, "It appears that this brutalized little girl likes ice cream. Do you think—"

"I'm on it," Burgess said, happy to leave the desperate chaos of the ER behind. "Does she like chocolate?"

There was another exchange, and Dr. Cohen said, "Vanilla."

Burgess lumbered off in search of ice cream. He would need to know the girl's condition and what had been done to her, but the good doctor had rightly surmised that he'd rather have a report than see the damage inspected. She was right. His unspoken marching orders had been to get himself a coffee, take his time, and then return with ice cream. Burgess didn't always follow orders—Paul Cote could vouch for that—but in this case, he was glad to have them.

When he returned, the coffee having had no effect on his nearly somnolent state, Bella was clean and dressed in a small hospital johnny . She smiled at Burgess and held out her hands for the ice cream. Kids so often amazed him. Nina and Neddy had been through absolutely horrific experiences, and yet, while there was residual damage, mostly they went through life as normal kids. In reality, he supposed, few children got through childhood unscathed. But there were degrees. What Nina and Neddy and these girls had experienced was extreme.

"We're sending her upstairs," Dr. Cohen said. "Do you want to talk about it now?"

She gave him a head-to-toe assessment and shook her head. "I think we'll talk tomorrow. I'm off home soon, but I'll be back in the morning."

"Tomorrow's better," he agreed, feeling like he was wimping out. "I'll just lumber along and see her settled."

"Lumber's a good word, Joe," she said, "but don't sell yourself short. These kids would all be dead, now or sometime soon, without you and your team. You may feel like an old dog too weary to learn new tricks and too world-weary to want to, but you give the words "serve and protect" real meaning." She patted his shoulder—the same shoulder she'd mended for him not long ago. "Now get Bella settled and then go home and get some sleep. Otherwise, you're going to start hallucinating." She dropped her hand. "And I can imagine what those hallucinations will entail."

He called Patrol for a ride back to 109, grabbed the Explorer, and went home. If there were any more killings in his city tonight, someone else was going to have to deal with them.

There was a sandwich wrapped in plastic on a plate on the table, and two notes. One that said, "Eat me," another that said "Choklate Milk for my Joe."

He smiled at Neddy's spelling, though he supposed that as a parent, he should be concerned. Then, like a good soldier, he followed orders. Ate the sandwich and drank the surprisingly delicious glass of chocolate milk, then stripped off his clothes, showered, and got into bed. He was asleep before he could even finish wrapping himself around Chris.

Though tonight's events should have summoned bad dreams, he didn't dream. He didn't even stir.

When he woke, the house was empty and silent and it was almost nine-thirty. He couldn't remember when he'd last slept so late. Sleeping in was something other people did, people who didn't have helpless victims waiting for justice and cold-blooded killers trying to avoid it. His phone was beside the bed where he'd left it, but it was on vibrate. The number of messages he found when he checked it made him wonder how it hadn't spun itself right off the nightstand. Everyone in the world was looking for him.

He yawned, lay back down, and closed his eyes. He wasn't going back to sleep. He was mentally reviewing the case. He could do it just as well in a reclining position as when he was upright. The pillow was soft. The background hum from the fan Chris had set up by the window was soothing. Right in the middle of the to-do list he should right now be reviewing with his team, he fell asleep.

This time he woke because someone was banging on the door and calling his name. He yelled, "Hold on. I'm coming," threw on his robe, and went to answer the door.

Kyle, poised to knock again, was shifting nervously from foot to foot, his whippet-thin body trembling. "Where the hell have you been? I've called you six times. You never sleep in. You always answer your phone. I thought you were dead."

"Not dead but only sleeping."

Burgess checked his watch. Ten-thirty. No wonder Kyle was worried.

"Sorry, Ter. Let me get dressed. Anything happen while I was hibernating?"

"Nothing happens unless we make it happen," Kyle said.

Burgess surmised, from the sour tone, that Kyle was not in a good mood. Before he could cope with that, he needed coffee. Badly needed coffee. It felt like he was viewing the world through a haze of spider webs. "I need coffee, Ter. You want some?"

"Anything to delay going back to 109. Stan's still awol, going gaga over his new baby. Cote keeps stalking by, no doubt looking for you so he can harass you or snag some critical detail to share with the press. He thought he'd made Stanley his go-to guy, and then Young Stanley disappears. Dani looks like a bedraggled orphan and Wink is in the worst mood I've seen in all the time I've known him. Sage is keeping his head down, trying to help where he can while avoiding being noticed. The only person not out of sorts is Rocky."

He tapped his temple contemplatively. "What else have you missed? Wink has Rudy and Rocky out at Ida Mae Wilson's house, processing the rest of that—"

"Rudy and Rocky sounds like a kid's TV show," Burgess said.

"This could be a kid's TV show," Kyle agreed. "Only it would be—*it is*—a horror show."

Burgess massaged his forehead as though external pressure could wipe away those cobwebs. He was supposed to be in charge of this, and yet, as he slept, the world went right on turning.

Kyle, reading his mind, said, "No way, Joe. Just no way. They may be poking their way through this, but without you, it's chaos. And not organized chaos, either. You get dressed. I'll make the coffee."

In the bedroom, Burgess found a note on his bedside table that he'd missed before. Chris had written: Dear Sleeping Beauty, We held a meeting and the kids voted not to wake you. Hope you catch the bad guys soon. We miss family dinner. P.s. Alana Black wants you to call her. Here's her new phone number. P.p.s. Wear your knee brace.

Obediently, he put on the brace and got dressed. The brace was an amazing piece of equipment, but like most medical interventions, it had side effects. It supported his knee and kept him from screaming agony. It pinched his leg when he was in the car and made him feel old and pathetic. Pretty much a mixed bag.

He tied his shoes and went to the kitchen. The coffee smelled great and Kyle was rummaging through the refrigerator. He stepped back with a bag of bagels and some cream cheese. "Breakfast of champions," he said. "You want some jam on yours?"

"What am I, eight?" Burgess said.

"What you are is a grouchy bear emerging from hibernation. When bears come out of hibernation, they're hungry. It is wise not to cross them until they've eaten."

"Jam, then."

When the toaster popped, Kyle snagged the bagels and spread them with cream cheese and jam, then set the plate, not quite gently, in front of Burgess. "Where do we go from here?" he asked.

"Go back and take another look at that house and yard in daylight. Finish going over the cars. See what Sage found in those trashcans. There might be some interesting papers. We need to check in with our translator and find out when we can see the girls and see whether they can tell us anything about the other man who was working with Dornan. Follow up with the widow of the man whose plates are on the black town car. What else?"

"Someone has to attend a couple autopsies," Kyle reminded him.

"Right," Burgess agreed. "Dani and Wink need to finish processing those two houses and the shed. And Alana Black wants me to give her a call."

Kyle fanned himself. "Whoo hoo. I wonder what that's about?"

"Maybe she's still plugged in somehow?" Burgess said. "Has friends who are still in the game?"

"We have to interview Marilyn Dornan's employer and co-workers," Kyle said.

"Go over the results of last night's canvass and see who we need to interview or reinterview," Burgess said.

Kyle refilled his coffee. "We're gonna be a hundred years old before we put this one to bed."

"I was a hundred years old before we started this thing. I'm thinking of changing my name to Methuselah Burgess."

"Has a nice ring to it," Kyle agreed. "What's your nickname gonna be? Thuse or Meth?"

"Meth's probably not going to work in our business, Ter."

"Where's your sense of irony?"

"Rusted."

Burgess realized that his food was gone, his cup was empty, and the day was growing old. "Shall we lumber over to 109 and see what's shaking?"

"Not much shakes without you," Kyle said, "and please note that I am still a young fellow and do not lumber."

Burgess did his departure precheck. He had gun, badge, cuffs, wallet, everything except his American Express card. He could leave home without that. As he crossed the front yard to his car, he was smiling. He and Kyle were so busy these days they rarely had a chance to banter like this. But banter and black humor were what kept cops going when the cases were as dark as this one. As he started the Explorer and pulled out of the driveway, already beginning to prioritize the list he and Kyle had made, he wondered if there was any such thing as a light homicide?

THIRTY-ONE

On the way, he called the number Alana Black had left, but it went straight to voice mail. She was probably with a client. He hoped she was with a client. Burgess had a tangled history with Alana, a former prostitute he and his sister Sandy had struggled to set on a better path. Now she was working as a licensed masseuse. As far as he knew, she was doing well. But there had been some backsliding along the way, and like a parent, he never stopped worrying about her. He hoped she hadn't tangled with the law or otherwise gotten herself in trouble. He was the first person she'd call if she was in trouble.

He left a message that he was returning her call, and went back to list-making.

It was summer in Maine. The streets were clogged with tourists come to sample Maine's specialness. For tourists, that meant lobster and blueberry pie, boating and sailing, beaches and ponds, and visiting Freeport and LL Bean. For Mainers, summer meant working long hours, trying to earn enough money to make it through the winter. It meant hiding their secret dislike for those "people from away" with their resources and privilege. It meant the roads were crowded and it was difficult to get anywhere in a hurry. And of course it meant the usual crimes committed by those who preyed on tourists, more traffic issues, a new crop of high school graduates trying out adulthood in risky ways, along with the explosive potential of large drunken crowds in the Old Port.

He liked fall, when the air was crisp and clean and things had quieted down again. But right now, he didn't have time to pay much attention to which season it was, except that it seemed to be the killing and exploiting children season. He'd always hated that season.

Stan Perry was waiting for them back at 109, an unusual, smiling, elated Stan Perry, still high from the birth of his daughter. He eagerly showed off photos of Lily and Autumn before settling down to ask what his next assignment was.

"Give me five minutes," Burgess said, looking with dismay at his desk, nearly smothered in papers that hadn't been there yesterday. He was supposed to be keeping the paperwork orderly instead of sleeping in like a teenage slacker. He sorted it into piles. One pile for message slips. One for reports. There were a couple of manila folders from Rocky Jordan. He wished there was a file called "people who've called and confessed." Then realized he didn't. They sometimes had cases with those files, and it meant interviewing a boatload of crazies. There was the search warrant for the Dornan's trash, outbuilding, and cars.

He checked Rocky's folders quickly. Call records from the phone numbers Shelley Minor had given Kit and DeSpain. When Rocky was done helping to process Ida Mae Wilson's house, he could see what those phone numbers could tell him. They still didn't have phones for Marilyn and Charlie Dornan, except for the burner at the back of her drawer, but they'd called it a night before finishing the search of the living room. It was significant that they'd found no purse in the house.

A note from Sage Prentiss was clipped to a stack of papers. The note said, "Found these in the Dornan's trash. If you need me, I'm at the Dornan's, helping Wink."

There was the warrant for DHHS records. He reached for it. Then hesitated. He wanted to head out there right now, but Human Services—often such an ironic name—would be there whenever he was ready. First he had to get his case in order and identify the things that needed to be done soonest.

He started with the thick stack of pink. Alana had called him here, too, but left no message. There was a message from the ME's office, saying the autopsy was scheduled for tomorrow at nine. Unusual for Dr. Lee. Normally he'd scheduled the autopsies almost before the weary cops could shower off the crime scene sweat. Well, impatient as he usually was, this time, Burgess was grateful. He had too many things to take care of here to be heading off to Augusta.

Once again he had the thought that there were so many balls in the air he was bound to drop some. He gathered some papers into a pile and signaled for Kyle and Perry to meet him in the conference room. Then he stuck his head into Melia's office. "We're meeting on this, Vince. You want to join us?"

Melia was slumped in his chair, staring at a nearly empty desktop. He looked up blankly, said, "Wait. What?" then shrugged. "Be there in a minute, Joe."

Burgess headed back to his desk, briefly, to print out Patrol's report on the canvass. Then he went into the conference room.

Kyle and Perry looked at him expectantly as he set down his stack of papers.

"Rocky coming?" Kyle asked.

"He's out at Ida Mae Wilson's house."

"Oh yeah. I forgot."

"Vince?"

"On his way."

Burgess looked at Stan Perry. "You still getting married this weekend?"

"That's the plan, Boss. You still standing up with me?"

"That's the plan."

Rocky came in, moving very quietly for such a big man, and took his place at the table, looking please to be included. "Rudy and I started early. We just got done. You got the files I sent you, Joe?" he asked.

"I did. Thanks. Now I've got another phone for you to search." He described the phone they'd taken from Marilyn Dornan's nightstand. "We'll need a warrant." He gave the AAG's name." If she doesn't hate us now, she will soon enough. Also, Sage brought back a pile of records from the Dornan's trash, plus there's file drawers to be gone through. They were making and selling child porn. Their financial profile should be interesting. You want that job?"

"I want it."

Burgess gave him the stack of papers Sage had left on his desk and the Dornan's address. "We'll also need warrants for their banking records. The information is probably in those files."

"On it, sir," Rocky said. Then, "Oh. I haven't had a chance to write it up for you yet, but I got the info on those implants."

They no longer needed to identify their victim, but they were still very interested in who had paid for implants *and* convinced a surgeon to do the surgery on such a young girl. No way would anyone seeing her believe she was old enough for such surgery to be appropriate. He wanted that one, figured he'd take Kyle with him. "Great, Rocky. As soon as you can get it to me. And text me the doc's info before you head out."

Melia came in and closed the door. "What have we got?" he asked.

"Not what we've got, which is three crime scenes, three dead, including two suspects where the issue is who shot whom, and five raped and abused children. Right now the question is what we need to do, which is process those crime scenes, examine the evidence from them, figure out what the story on Michele Minor and those five girls is. Figure out who the Dornans were working with. Figure out how the Dornans and others got their hands on these poor children, which likely involves the Fed's Office of Refugee Resettlement. We'll see if there's any paperwork in the Dornan's house, and then maybe you can follow up with the Feds? How did this go on in nice neighborhoods and no one noticed?"

He thought Melia flinched, but it was the truth.

He passed over the pages he'd just printed out. "Stan, can you review the canvass reports from last night, and see what needs follow up, then grab Sage from the Dornan's house and start on that? Anything you can learn about people coming and going from that house. What cars they saw. Their observations about the Dornans. Any information they might have about the foster daughter, Shelley Minor."

Perry nodded.

"Vince, I know you're slammed with the press and everything else, but can you find someone who can help Wink and Dani process all the evidence. If he gets much crankier, we'll be looking for Wink 2.0, and there is no such thing."

"I'll take care of it, Joe. Other than that, have you got enough people?"

Burgess didn't, really, but the more people who held different pieces of information, the harder it got to put things together. And to stop leaks. Besides, what he needed were more evidence techs, and those were hard to come by. "For now," he said. "Thanks, Vince."

He was already at risk of losing pieces of it. Give more pieces to different people and it would spin out of control. He made a note to himself to remind Sage about following up with that hardware store about who bought the saw. Then he stood.

"Okay. Everyone has a job to do. Can we meet again at the end of the day, say, around seven-thirty, to touch base and determine our next steps?"

Stan Perry hesitated, but then he said, "Sure."

"Terry," Burgess said, "you're with me. Let's take another look at the

Dornan's house and then go visit a surgeon. Rocky, you'll text me that info?"

Jordan nodded, looking delighted to leave his desk and get out into a lovely summer day to help catch bad guys. Little did he know he was going to a hot, smelly house.

"Sounds like a plan," Kyle said.

Everyone trooped out.

He and Kyle drove back to the Dornan's house. The crime scene van was there, and the street was still full of Lookie Loos and a lone news truck, complete with a chic, made-up reporter who tried to grab his arm. He knew her. In the past, she'd done him harm and she'd done him good. She thought the good meant they now had a relationship. He thought it meant they were even and anyway, Burgess had no soft spots for the press. All they did was get in the way and misreport.

He brushed past her with brusque hello and headed up the walk. Today, now that the bodies were gone and the photographs taken, the door and windows were open, making it a slightly more palatable place to work.

Delinsky was gone and an officer he didn't know was at the door, taking names and handing out booties. He and Kyle dutifully gave their names and put on their booties. Then they entered the living room. Dusted with black power to bring up fingerprints, the surfaces looked like kids with dirty hands had been having a field day while mom and dad were out. Today, there were no children, and mom and dad were out for good.

He and Kyle searched under the cushions, under the couch, and in the various drawers in the room. No more caches of porn CDs, not even in the storage ottoman that served as a coffee table. No sign of Marilyn Dornan's purse. They found no phones. Unless they were in the victim's pockets, and could be collected from the Medical Examiner, they had been taken.

The word "victim" seemed so inappropriate here.

Abandoning the room as a lost cause, they went to the kitchen, where they found Dani wrestling with a drawer under the stove. The drawer was stuck. They'd missed it last night as they did the kitchen. Burgess wondered what else they might have missed in a small, hot house filled with too many people.

Finally, with a metallic clang, the drawer opened to reveal neat stacks of metal baking sheets and pans. Everything orderly except for the stack of square and rectangular pans. It looked odd, given her penchant for neatness, so Burgess lifted it out. Between two square eight by eight pans he found two cell phones. He and Dani exchanged triumphant glances. It would have been so easy to miss these. Two more burners. It looked like someone had taken Marilyn Dornan's purse and both of their cellphones. But these might be a gold mine, if they were used for the business.

Business was such an innocent word for what these two had been doing. At some point, they would have to sit down with the videos and see what they had. Burgess thought it might take an entire bottle of Jack Daniels to get through them.

"I'm going to look through every cupboard," Dani said. "Every jar. Every canister. Every bag of flour or sugar. Who knows what I may find."

"Flour and sugar," Kyle said. "I'll just bet."

"Don't let Joe rub off on you, Terry," she said. "One of him is enough."

"I couldn't agree more."

They left her doing her systematic examination of the cupboards and walked across the yard to the storage building, where Wink was busy making black fingerprints appear everywhere. Wink was a steady work-horse of a man. He loved to work. Loved to solve puzzles, to find evidence others would miss. Loved to play a part in their journey to catching bad guys and gals and securing their convictions. Like Burgess, though, he hated cases where children were hurt. This case was exponentially worse because so many children were involved. Wink would put more pressure on himself to find evidence and answers.

"I have a theory, Joe," he said. "Not one I want to have, but one the room may be telling me. We're going to have to take this damned mattress back to 109 where I can work on it."

"Chief's gonna have a fit, the way we're filling up the basement garage. Pretty soon, the brass is gonna have to park next door like the rest of us peons," Kyle said.

"Speak for yourself, Terry," Wink said. "I am not a peon."

"True," Kyle agreed. "You are a unique, talented, one-of-a-kind crime scene examiner, and we worship at your feet."

"As it should be," Wink grunted.

"And regardless of what Mrs. Wink says, you may never retire."

Wink Devlin turned his back on them and gave his attention to finger-print collection. Evidently Mrs. Wink was a subject to be avoided.

Burgess scanned the room again, wondering what Wink was getting from a barren room, barely five feet wide by twelve feet deep, furnished with only a bucket and a stained mattress. Then he saw it. The house, and the room where they'd stored tools was neat and clean. The floor in here was dusty, like the room hadn't been used in a while and hadn't been cleaned. In the dust, he could see the prints of several sets of shoes. Large prints. Likely men's shoes. Blood on the mattress. Blood on the child. The presence of more than one man. For the second time in less than twelve hours, he had the overwhelming urge to kill two people who were already dead. He would have used a method a lot slower than a gunshot.

Cops see so much bad stuff that they can get to the point where little can shock them. But he'd never been able to be easy with the kind of evil that allows someone to violate a child. At least the children weren't dead. Well, Shelley was still a child, and she was dead. A child that couple had taken into their home and raised as their daughter.

His stomach flipped, and he grabbed the doorframe for support.

"So you see it, too," Wink said. "I am going to find every fingerprint. Footprint. Every bit of trace evidence. Every hair. Every drop of sperm on this filthy mattress. And then you, Detective Sergeant Joseph Burgess, are going to find the men who were here and they are going to pay for this."

They'd worked together many years. He'd never seen Wink this angry.

Burgess remembered a Bible verse from Luke: *It were better for him that a millstone were hanged about his neck, and he cast into the sea, than that he should offend one of these little ones.* He'd like to attach a millstone to someone right about now. He knew Wink would gladly help.

THIRTY-TWO

Burgess and Kyle were silent as they walked back to the truck. As they climbed in and Burgess started the engine, Kyle said, "Where to?"

"I believe it's time to call on a surgeon, and to make that call unannounced."

"Fine with me," Kyle said. "I'm feeling just the right amount of mean."

"Me, too," Burgess agreed.

He checked his phone. In his nicely detailed way, Rocky Jordan had given them the name, address, and phone number of the surgeon who had done Shelley Minor's implants. He'd also included the serial numbers from the implants, and a note that he'd added a warrant for the doctor's records to his list, and put it right at the top. Those warrant requests had already gone to the AG's office.

Burgess wondered whether they should wait for the warrant before making their visit, but he wasn't in the mood to wait for anything. Patience was often a law officer's chief virtue. Today he must not be feeling virtuous.

The doctor's office was at the hospital, so he also called the translator and asked if she was available and could assist him in interviewing the girls. She said she could be there in an hour, and they made a date.

He parked in his favorite spot just outside the door, giving a nod to Charlie, the security guard on duty. Charlie gave him a cynical smile, and said, "Coming to grill some docs, Detective?"

"Why not, Charlie. Isn't this the grilling season?"

That got him a grin and a wave and he and Kyle headed for the elevators. "I wish this place didn't feel so much like my home away from home," he said.

"I believe you once put it beautifully as the place where, when you have go there, they have to take you in, and you're usually bleeding."

"Right. I did say that. I try to always tell the truth."

A smartly dressed redhead in the elevator with them was staring. Burgess wondered if she was coming to see the same surgeon. She looked like the type to grab every advantage, and someone who had the cash to pay for it. If he were a betting man, he'd bet she was here for breast enhancement. But Nina told him the new thing was butt enhancement. He couldn't wrap his mind around that.

Kyle gave her his almost imperceptible grin. "Detectives, ma'am."

She turned away and studied the wall. There was nothing to see there, unless scrapes and smudges were interesting. To cops, sure, but probably not to a woman in a white linen dress and black and white stiletto heels. Sure, she looked like a million dollars, but if she ever had to run anywhere, between the heels and the sheath dress, she'd be helpless as a babe. Oh. Right. Another expression given new meaning. Burgess grinned.

"What's that about?" Kyle asked.

"Tell you later."

They all got off together. All walked to the same suite of offices. All approached the counter to speak with the receptionist. The puzzled girl looked at the three of them, waiting for someone to speak.

"Detective Sergeant Burgess, Portland police," he said, showing his badge. "We need to speak with Dr. Morton."

When the girl hesitated, forming what he knew would be the excuse that Morton was a busy man and they should make an appointment, he added, "We're investigating three homicides, ma'am. Time is of the essence. It's important that we see him as soon as possible."

The woman from the elevator tried to shove Kyle aside. "Excuse me," she said, "but I have an appointment with Dr. Morton at one o'clock, and I am very busy today." She slipped past Kyle, who wasn't putting up much of a fight, and tried to eel her way in front of Burgess. Burgess stood his ground. When that didn't work, she leaned around his side, held out a tanned arm with an expensive watch, tapped the watch, and said, "Jessica Harmon? Appointment? Now?"

The receptionist looked at her, then up at Burgess, then at her phone. "I'll just check," she said.

She spoke hastily into the phone, explaining her dilemma to someone, most likely her supervisor and not the busy Dr. Morton. Then, still flustered, she set down the receiver and looked at Burgess. "Mrs. Stevens will be right out, Detective."

With a bright smile, she turned to her paying customer, and said, "I'll just check you in, Ms. Harmon."

Mrs. Stevens was just the kind of dragon who usually guarded the lairs of important people. She was tall, lean, impeccably suited and coiffed despite the hot summer day, and unsmiling as she gathered Burgess and Kyle together like absently discarded material, and shepherded them through a door and into her cubicle.

"How can I help you?" she said, waving a hand at a pair of chairs.

Neither of them sat.

"We're here to see Dr. Morton," Burgess said.

"I wish you'd made an appointment," she said. "Dr. Morton is very busy today."

"I wish we had, too," Burgess agreed, "but in my experience, people don't get themselves killed on any sort of schedule." He shrugged, inviting her to share his difficulty. "But when they do get killed, it becomes our job to investigate, investigation where the timing is urgent, and that's what we're here to do."

She flipped through a book on her desk, and then consulted her computer terminal. "I could squeeze you in for a few minutes at four."

Burgess gave her his best smile. The one often worn by a cat enjoying those moments of toying with a mouse. "Why don't you squeeze us in now, and he can run just a few minutes late for Ms. Harmon?"

"Oh, but Ms. Harmon is …" She stopped herself.

Burgess wondered whether she was going to declare Ms. Harmon a very important person or a regular paying customer. Neither would sway him, of course. Ms. Harmon could stand to wait a few minutes. It would be good for her character.

"A few minutes?" Burgess prompted.

"If you could tell me what this is about, perhaps I can help you?"

Burgess wanted to set eyes on the jerk who'd put artificial breasts in such a very young girl, but what he really wanted was information about who had brought the girl here, arranged the surgery, and paid for it.

"Maybe you can," he agreed. "We need some information about a patient of Dr. Morton's, a young woman who has been the victim of a vicious crime."

"Oh, I can't give you patient information," she said.

"The patient is dead," he said. "We're not looking for her medical records at this point. We're trying to identify the party who paid for the procedure. The person who arranged for the surgery and paid for it."

There was silence as the woman processed his request. He waited for her to tell him that billing information was also confidential. She didn't disappoint him.

"Does Dr. Morton have an office nurse who deals with his patients? Someone who might remember this girl and who brought her in?"

"He does. Of course he does. But I cannot condone your doing an end run around the issue of patient's privacy by speaking with her."

It was a hell of a sentence. Maybe if the police department had dragons like this to deal with the public, their lives would be easier. Burgess had been dealing with people like Mrs. Stevens for decades. People who loved to wrap their tongues around "No" and "I can't" instead of doing what they could to help.

"What we're looking for is information about whoever brought the girl for her surgery. That information is not covered by HIPA. It's simply a witness account," Burgess said. "It's just information."

Beside him, Kyle was beginning to vibrate. It was silent. It was subtle. It also had a kind of magnetic power, like he was emitting ozone into the atmosphere. Mrs. Steven's eyes shifted to Kyle and her look of smug certainty became one of unease.

This time, when she opened her mouth to deliver another helping of "I can't" Burgess interrupted her.

"I understand your dilemma," he said. "I hope you can understand mine." He was done playing nice guy or offering up reasonable explanations. He was also willing to tell a little lie just to shake her up. "So here's our problem. Our crime victim is difficult to identify because of the condition of her body…" He got out his phone and scrolled through until he found a photo of Shelley's body. "But we do have the serial numbers on her implants."

He passed her the phone and waited.

Her mouth opened and closed a few times, like a landed fish, before she handed the phone back, holding it between fingertips like it was hot.

"How dare you!" she gasped.

"How dare I what? Try to identify a homicide victim?"

"I would like you to leave now," she said, standing up to indicate the interview was over.

Neither Burgess nor Kyle moved.

"We came to see Dr. Morton," Burgess reminded her. "To ask him what he remembers about a particular patient and the person or persons who arranged her surgery. None of that involves her medical records except to confirm the serial numbers on her implants. Numbers we already have. No privacy is being violated, because she's already suffered the ultimate violation. We just have a few questions."

She remained standing. They remained standing. They were two tall men between her and the door. Finally she said, "I shall have to call Security."

"Really?" Kyle said. "You're going to call security to remove police officers who are here investigating a homicide? Who are only still here because you refuse to cooperate in any way with our investigation? That's how you want to handle this?"

"Excuse me," she said, and rushed past them before they could stop her.

Not that they would have stopped her. She didn't have to cooperate. Nobody did. If they didn't get answers now, they'd be back with a subpoena that would, they hoped, get them names, contact information, possibly credit card information that could be searched. It might get them a scrawled signature from someone purporting to be her guardian, giving permission for the operation. Information that would be helpful, but it wouldn't get them descriptions. It wouldn't get them the story. It wouldn't give the girl a presence or give them a sense of the man or men who had brought her to Dr. Morton and somehow convinced him to perform inappropriate surgery on such a young girl.

"We wait?" Kyle said.

"We wait a little while. Want to make bets on whether she returns with Dr. Morton?"

"Nah. Because we both think she will. Because she is accustomed to abusing people and having her power respected and she knows that won't work with us, and she doesn't know what else to do."

They waited. Waited too long. Probably waiting for Dr. Morton to finish with the peremptory Ms. Harmon. Burgess wondered how long it took to consult about getting bigger breasts. Did the doc have to take measurements? Did they look at videos together to pick the perfect size? Or perhaps, given her peevish face and pushy behavior, she was here to complain about breasts she'd already bought. In the great contest between enhancing breasts and finding a killer, he thought finding the killer should take priority. He was so self-centered, wasn't he?

About the time they'd given up and were heading for the door, a man in a white coat appeared from some mysterious place in the back. He called, "Detectives. Wait. Please."

He wasn't what Burgess had expected. His image of cosmetic surgeons—built from little experience—was that they were generally consumers of their own products, and were both handsome and vain. Morton was neither. He was a smallish man, slightly stooped, with a tired face and gold-rimmed glasses. His bow tie was slightly askew. His shoes needed polishing. *Not much of an advertisement for his profession,* Burgess thought.

Morton looked up at the tall detectives looming over him with so much trepidation in his manner that Burgess half-expected the doctor to say, "Please don't eat me." But they weren't the predators. They were knights in shining armor, even if that armor sometimes got kind of tarnished.

"I'm sorry to have kept you waiting," Morton said. "Mrs. Stevens should have explained. I was with a rather…uh…difficult patient."

"Jessica Harmon?" Kyle said.

The doctor nodded, though he looked surprised.

He led them back down the corridor past Mrs. Steven's office, where she now sat at her desk, staring very intently at her computer, her back to them.

When the doctor had closed his door behind them, he said, "Mrs. Stevens believes I am too tender-hearted. She does her best to protect me. But sometimes her judgment fails her and she simply reacts in the same rote manner no matter what the issue. I fear that's what she's done with you."

"You've got that right," Kyle said.

Morton waited until they were seated, then went behind his desk, sat, and tented his hands. "How can I help you?"

Burgess explained about Shelley Minor and her implants and how they were trying to track down the men involved in her killing and wanted information on her surgery, who had brought her, who had paid for the surgery, as well as what that person or persons looked like, and any interactions the doctor or his staff might have observed.

This time, he saw no need to show the pictures of her body. But something didn't feel right. Their interactions so far had been brief, but this quiet, unassuming man didn't seem like someone who would agree to perform breast enhancement surgery on a very young girl. He waited to see what Morton would say.

Morton didn't speak. He sighed. "I didn't perform that surgery. I would never agree to perform such an operation on a girl that young."

Before he could finish, Kyle said, "You are registered as the surgeon who inserted those implants."

They waited while the doctor fiddled with a pen on his desk. "This is embarrassing," he said. "I didn't do the surgery. Dr. Valentine did."

"Then we need to speak with Dr. Valentine."

"That will be difficult, I'm afraid. Valentine is no longer with the practice. He...I guess I should explain. I'm getting old. I'm tired of catering to the dreams of women who believe that cosmetic surgery is the solution to their problems. Much of my practice is doing reconstruction for women who've had cancer, or on children with deformities. I brought Valentine in to take over the cosmetic part of the practice. He was a real go getter. He had us advertising in magazines. He was scheduling procedures as tightly as he could. He was out to make money. He wanted to be named number one cosmetic surgeon in Maine."

Morton fell silent.

"And?" Burgess prompted.

"And bringing him in was a mistake. He was too greedy. Too willing to cut corners and ignore rules. No one should have performed that surgery. The girl was still developing. She was still a child. No one should have performed that surgery because it should have been evident that the child didn't want it." He ran a nervous hand through his thinning hair. "I blame myself because I wasn't here to stop him. While I was here, I could look over his shoulder and act as a brake on his ambitions. But part of the reason for taking on another surgeon was so I could slow down. I let my wife talk me into taking a fancy two-week cruise. It was January and she wanted to get out of Maine."

Another hand through the hair. Then the hand fell to the desk. "While I was away, he did three surgeries on girls like this who were inappropriately young, as well as other procedures we had agreed he would not do." He spread his hands. "And now it comes back to haunt me."

"Shouldn't it haunt Valentine?" Kyle asked.

"If he had a conscience. But he doesn't. He isn't treating patients, he's treating body parts attached to credit cards and checkbooks. The woman who was just here," he waved a vague hand toward the door, "is one of Valentine's patients. She was a poor risk to begin with. It was clear she'd never follow post-surgery instructions and that the implants she wanted were too big to look natural. He was careless. She was careless. She got an infection. Now we've had to remove them and instead of waiting to heal and making better choices going forward, she wants to do the same thing again. I told her she'd have to find another surgeon."

"Why not let Valentine clean up his mess?" Kyle said.

"Because Valentine, chafing under the sensible restrictions I imposed, has gone west to seek his fortune in pastures richer than Portland, Maine. And they are welcome to him, the ones who survive his tender ministrations."

Morton threw up his hands. "I'm sorry. You didn't come here to listen to my complaints. Let me grab the records and get my nurse in here, and we'll see what we can do to answer your questions."

He hurried from the room.

So much for dragons, Burgess thought. Stevens probably thought she was doing Dr. Morton a favor, protecting him from intrusive police inquiries. He wondered if it drove patients away or if the demand for corporeal alteration exceeded the supply of surgeons?

He smiled at the phrase "corporeal alteration." Then the smile faded. This case began with a corporeal alteration.

"What?" Kyle said.

"Corporeal alteration."

The faint smile came and went. "Not such a good thing in our business. I wonder if Dr. Valentine could have…" He stopped.

They sat in silence. Burgess was running his to-do list in his head, knowing Kyle was doing the same. The sensation of time passing was almost physical.

In a few minutes, which felt far longer, Dr. Morton reappeared, carrying a file and accompanied by a woman they assumed was his nurse.

Burgess's impressions of cosmetic surgery, mostly formed by scattered bits of TV, had led him to expect a glitzy office, big pictures of gorgeous men and women on the walls, and a staff that were walking advertisements for the product. The receptionist had been attractive, but the dragon, Dr. Morton, and now the woman with him, looked like everyday folks.

Morton introduced the woman as Carole Grover. "Carole has been with me a long time." The doctor hesitated. "Carole was not fond of Dr. Valentine."

"Which," the woman said after shaking their hands, "is partly because I was not receptive to his suggestions about liposuction, Botox and facial fillers, and 'just a small enhancement to make my body more balanced.' This isn't Hollywood, it's Portland, and much of our work is for those unfortunate women who've had mastectomies." She looked at Burgess and Kyle. "It helps to restore their self-esteem."

Burgess was sorry these people had gotten caught up in his case. He explained again why they were here and what they were looking for.

"I remember that girl," Carole said. "Such a sweet little thing. She tried to act like it was something she wanted but it was clear to me that she was being forced to get the surgery." She shot a glance at Dr. Morton. "Pete was on vacation, so I couldn't consult him, and Dr. Valentine was gung ho to do it. I did question him about it. About the appropriateness given the girl's age. He told me *he* was the doctor and that was that."

She shrugged. A rather sad shrug. "It wasn't my place to try and stop him. He was my boss and he was…" A quick glance at Morton. "He was such a bully. If I didn't want to experience abuse and lectures, I had to keep my head down and say, 'Yes, Doctor.' I said it a lot."

"We're interested in anything you can tell us, and anything the records show, about who arranged for her surgery. Who signed the permission forms, any billing or credit card information, what address or addresses were given. Physical descriptions, if possible."

Morton was thumbing through the files, looking increasingly irritated, as Carole told them what she could remember.

"She came in with an older man. I assumed he was her father, but he didn't act fatherly. That was when I started being suspicious. Well, I was suspicious from the start because the girl was too young. He was cold to her. Cold and cruel. It was clear she was afraid of him."

"Can you describe him?" Kyle asked.

"There wasn't anything distinctive about him," she said slowly, trying to remember. "In his fifties. A biggish man. Not heavy, just big. Graying dark hair. He was well dressed. Almost flashy, if you know what I mean. Like his jacket was conservative enough but his shirt and tie were too bright." She looked at Burgess and Kyle. "This might sound odd, but to me, he just looked mean."

Morton slapped the file down on his desk with a disgusted sound.

"What?" Burgess said.

"This is the sloppiest thing I've ever seen. There's almost no information about the patient. There's no permission form for performing this surgery on a person under eighteen."

"What information is there?" Burgess asked.

Morton passed him the form. The patient's name was Shelley Minor, and the address was the Dornan's. Her age was given as eighteen, no doubt to get around the requirements of a parental or guardian consent form. No prior health history. No height, weight, blood pressure. Nothing.

He looked at Morton. "What about the consent for billing? Any records pertaining to payment liability? Anything that shows how the procedure was paid for?"

"We shall have to ask Mrs. Stevens about that."

Instead of using the phone or intercom, Morton left to find Mrs. Stevens.

"He feels badly about this," Carole said. "He's a very nice man. If I may ask, why are you looking for information about this girl?"

Burgess was surprised she didn't know, but of course, Shelley's name hadn't been released to the press. "She's been murdered," he said.

"And you're using the serial numbers on her implants because—" She faltered. "Oh, dear me. No. That sweet girl is the one whose body was found out in Stroudwater Park?"

"I'm afraid so."

"And she was found without…" Carole didn't finish. She just sat staring at them, distress and shock making her pale. Then she said, "And you think this man, the man who brought her here, might have had something to do with it?"

"We do."

Burgess got out the photo of Charlie Dornan. "Was this the man?"

She studied the picture, then handed it back, shaking her head. "No. This man is too young and his hair is too light."

"We understand this was months ago, and you see a lot of patients and their families, but is there anything distinctive about him that you can remember?" Kyle asked. "Anything at all?"

"Only one thing. And it's such a small thing, I don't see how…"

"Tell us about it," Burgess said, already wondering if he knew what was coming.

"He had a pin on his lapel. Just a small pin, white enamel, with a red border and the number fifteen in red. I noticed it because he didn't seem like the pin-wearing type. And because, while I may be no fashion plate, a red and white pin didn't seem to go with his purple and yellow shirt and tie."

THIRTY-THREE

Burgess made a mental note to come back with a photo of the pin they'd found at the crime scene. Then Morton was back with the dragon, and the dragon didn't look happy. Indeed, if it was possible for a dragon to look abashed, this one did.

"Well, I don't see how any of this is going to help you," she said, "but what our records show is that the procedure was paid for by a check. We deposited the check but there's no further information in the file. No name. No address. No photocopy of the check."

She studied the file she'd brought with her. "These days, you know, we've started asking for license numbers when we take checks, and that information is supposed to be in this file. I've just skimmed through, and I can't find it anywhere."

"What about phone numbers?" Kyle said. "Do you have any phone numbers for the girl or her family?"

She looked through her papers again. "I do have a phone number," she said. She read it and Burgess wrote it down. It didn't sound like one of the numbers they'd gotten from Kit and DeSpain, so maybe it was a lead. But tracking down the second man, the mystery man, was not looking like an easy task.

They thanked Dr. Morton, Carole, and the Dragon, and handed out cards. Then they headed for the elevators.

Burgess had been hopeful, coming here. Hopeful, and ready to bully doctors willing to perform breast enhancement surgery on such a young girl. What he'd found was mostly a dead end. A decent doctor stuck with cleaning up a careless colleague's mess. Maybe the phone number or the pin would lead somewhere. He was feeling discouraged. So discouraged that when Kyle said, "Shall we check on the girls?" he almost said no. He was waiting for his get up and go, his enthusiasm for the chase, or at least his drive to secure justice for victims to arrive. It seemed to be stalled somewhere.

"Sure. We're already here, and the translator is available," he heard himself saying. "What I'd really like to know is how the Dornans got their hands on these girls."

"The Dornans or someone else," Kyle said. "We don't know that the Dornans somehow got custody, and we did hear about those mysterious vans arriving. Maybe there are people who shuttle bunches of these girls around."

"But they have to come from somewhere," Burgess said.

"Guatemala. Beyond that, I'd say it will call for some serious detective work. Searching their files, bank records, all that. Talking to neighbors. Interviewing their employers," Kyle said. "You have to wonder who hands five Guatemalan children over to anyone, where the girls came from, and who is supposed to be keeping track of them."

The elevator opened and they stepped in.

"Maybe the girls know," Burgess said.

"Now that is a radical idea."

They weren't alone in the elevator, so conversation ceased until they'd reached the lobby and headed for the wing where the girls were.

"Do you need some time, Joe?" Kyle said. "A day off. An afternoon off?"

"The rest of my life off?"

"I'm not listening to that 'I'm going to retire' crap, Joe. What on earth would you do with yourself? You don't have hobbies. You don't play golf."

"I could learn."

"It would be bad for your knee," Kyle said.

"Paddle boarding," Burgess said. "Fly fishing. Nature photography. I could sit on the beach and read novels."

Kyle made a face.

Burgess's phone buzzed in his pocket. He checked the number. Alana. "Gotta take this," he said, growling "Burgess" into the phone.

Instead of saying "hello" she laughed. "Hey, Copman. Someone's in a great mood today."

"You got that right. What's up? You got the solution to my case?"

"I have an idea. It's a long shot, but it might take you somewhere. Can we meet?"

That was Alana. She would never just give him information. It had to be face to face, on her terms. She'd always been that way. It was part of the games she played. They played. He had to show respect. Reassure her that he didn't look down on her because she'd once been a hooker. Prove he was willing to make time for her. She'd act all sexy and seductive, which, given that she was probably the sexiest woman he'd ever met, was something. He'd tell her to snap out of it. They'd get the dance out of the way and then they could talk. She did this even though she'd been to the house for dinner. Met Chris and the kids. Been treated like a fourth child. Chris said Alana was just looking for reassurance. Burgess thought she could be a pain in the ass.

"Can you do four?" he said, with no idea what he'd really be doing at four.

"Five," she said, and named a place.

"I'll try. You know how things can change in the middle of a case."

"I've been in the middle of your case," she said.

"Well, stay out of trouble, okay, and I'll see you at five."

"You bet, Copman."

There were four girls in the room now, making it very crowded. Although there were four beds in the room, only two of them were occupied. Isabella was tucked in beside her sister Sofia, clutching a large stuffed bear.

Gabriela was with Magaly and there were coloring books and crayons spread out on the bed. Someone was making an effort with these girls.

He and Kyle had entered carefully, not wanting to spook the girls, but the four welcomed them with smiles and a volley of Spanish. Even little Bella smiled. Cleaned and fed and reunited with her sister, she looked nothing like the terrified waif Burgess had carried out of that shed.

Someone had braided her hair and tied red ribbons on the ends. When she saw them come in, she ducked her head shyly into her sister's side, then picked it up to look at him and gave him a shy little wave. "Seguro," she said. Then, with a child's exuberant grin, she added, "Ice cream."

This, after what she'd been through? Burgess smiled and said, "Si, ice cream."

A moment later, the translator rushed in, apologizing for being late, even though she wasn't, and greeting the girls with hugs and smiles. The way she lingered with Bella made Burgess wonder if she, like Chris, loved children and longed for one. Maybe he was reading too much into it. Maybe she was simply a warm-hearted person and Bella a needy, and adorable, little girl.

Greetings over, she settled into a chair in the corner and said, "What do you need me to ask them?"

Burgess had lots of questions, but first he asked, "Can they all have ice cream?"

She nodded.

"There's at least one more man involved in this," Burgess said, "and we have no idea who he is. We're hoping the girls may have some information that will help us locate him. Before, you told us that all they would say about the man was that he wore colorful clothes. We're also interested in the woman's involvement. Marilyn Dornan."

Just as she had during their last visit, Clara Sanchez motioned them to join her outside in hall. She said something to the girls, probably reassuring them that she'd be back with ice cream, and led them to a small conference room. "I am sorry," she said, "but I didn't want to mention her name in front of the girls. They are reluctant to speak of her, but I can tell you that they are all terrified of her and say that she is very mean and beats them or has her husband beat them. She is also the one who uses the camera when they are…uh…assaulted."

Burgess looked at Kyle. Neither of them was surprised. He regretted that they hadn't gotten to her sooner and done an interview.

"I don't know if you want to tell them this, but Marilyn Dornan is dead. Someone shot her last night."

Sanchez nodded. "I see. The paper said it was a murder-suicide. Is that true?"

"We're still working on that," Kyle said quickly. They didn't want to go down that rabbit hole right now. "But about this second man. Have you learned anything more than colorful clothes?"

"He was mean to them. The blond man…is that Dornan?…he could be kind, but the other man was never kind."

"Again, a question you may not have asked or they may not know the answer to, but how did the girls come to be here?"

"It is complicated," she said. "They were sent by their parents to the border, to come to America and seek asylum because of the conditions at home. Magaly and Gabriela had an older brother who was killed because he would not join a gang, and that same gang said they would take revenge on his sisters also. There was a friend of the family who was coming north, and Magaly and Gabriela traveled with him until they reached the border. Then he told them they would have better luck on their own, and he left them. The U.S. government took them and they were in a shelter for immigrant children, but then one day, one of the workers there told them that a relative had been found in Maine, and they were being sent to live with that relative."

She looked at Burgess and shook her head in despair. "Without doing any checking or verification, the girls were sent here to live with a woman they didn't know. She had a Hispanic name, Ana Solano. She was no relation. She posed as a relative to obtain custody, but they have no relatives in Maine. They were only with her for a few days. Then a man with a white van came and took them to the house where…the house where they were found. And then the blond man and the woman named Marilyn put them in that cage and the men started coming." Her voice dropped. "They're just children! What kind of men would…"

She looked down at the floor. She was shaking.

Kyle put a hand on her arm. "We're sorry this happened to them and sorry that you get the hard job of telling their story."

"Our government," she said. "Our own government gave these helpless children to people who sold them for sex. It makes me sick, Detectives. Physically sick."

She stopped studying the floor. "I am angry on their behalf. I am angry that the Dornans are dead, because they should have to answer for this. They should have to face these children in court before being locked up forever. But it isn't just them. Others are responsible as well. The lazy bureaucrats who handed them over…"

She stopped. "I'm sorry. I know my outrage isn't helping."

"We don't blame you," Kyle said.

Kyle seemed to want to take the lead on this and Burgess was happy to let him. It looked like he and the translator were forming a bond, and that would be helpful here.

"What about the other three girls?" Kyle asked. "Did they come here in the same way?"

"They did. They came to a different woman. Her name was Inez

Lopez-Garcia. At least, that's the name she used on the paperwork. Also no relation, though she claimed to be their aunt. I think these women were being paid to pose as relatives so the Dornans could get their hands on these children."

She looked at them, anguish on her face. "Who knows how many other children have been tricked into sexual slavery like these sweet girls? Or what happens to them. Where they go when a new batch of girls arrive."

"We will do what we can," Kyle said, "but the federal government is not always very cooperative."

Burgess could hear the anger in his voice. Kyle was good at keeping emotion off his face, but someone who knew him could read it in his body and his voice. The rage that washed over Burgess from people willfully harming children could carry him when he was almost too weary to move. Kyle took it in a different way. As a father who had had to fight hard to get custody of his daughters, Kyle regarded parenting as a sacred trust. When people broke that trust, Kyle took it almost as a physical blow.

Burgess hoped that these poor girls would be adequately served by an investigative team that couldn't quite keep their emotions in check. But they were too far in to try and cobble together a B team now.

"The Dornans and their partner, or partners, must have had some inside contacts to help them find these children," he said.

"That's what I was thinking," Clara Sanchez said.

"Getting back to the second man," Kyle said. "Even the smallest detail might help. Can you see if there is anything they heard or observed that might help us identify him?"

"I will ask. As I said, I am approaching this very gently, because it makes them upset, and they've been subjected to so much already."

It looked like they'd reached a dead end, and they were on their feet and heading for the door when she said, "I will have to ask some questions to clarify, but I think that this other man may have had a dog. Or there was something about a dog. Someone brought a dog. I think it scared them."

So now they were looking for a flashy dresser with an ugly disposition and a dog. People who got their information about investigations from TV probably thought that was enough to let them find the man. Never mind that no one had a description or a photo, and he was driving a car with a license plate registered to a dead man.

Burgess was wondering whether they ought to revisit Cary McCann, the man who'd found the body when the translator shared one more piece of data. "Sofia says there was a conversation in which she heard one of the men say the word 'teacher' but she can't remember which of them it was."

He and Kyle exchanged glances. It was time to check out the faculty and staff at Shelley Minor's school. That task had gotten sidelined in the midst of their series of emergencies.

"Has there been an update about Maria's condition?" he asked. He could have checked with the ICU himself, but he didn't want her—or the girls—to think that they didn't care.

Clara Sanchez shook her head. "I do not think there has been much progress. Sofia is very worried but she tries to hide it so she won't upset Bella. She's a very brave girl. She thinks it is her job to look out for all of them, since she is the oldest. Only fifteen, and she thinks she is responsible for four other girls. When I was fifteen, I was worried about being too fat and whether my hair was too curly."

Burgess looked at Kyle, glad she couldn't read his mind. When he was fifteen, he'd just been excited by the idea of girls. He didn't notice too fat or too curly. He noticed they were these amazing and frustrating creatures who made his body do embarrassing things. He did not share this thought with Clara Sanchez.

They thanked the translator, got ice cream and delivered it to the four girls, and headed back to the Explorer.

THIRTY-FOUR

They stopped on the way out to see if Dr. Cohen was there. She was, and she was still smiling, at least until Burgess asked about Bella. Then the smile vanished.

"If I hadn't taken an oath to do no harm," she said. Then she stopped. "You'll see. It's in the report. I'll send you the reports on all the girls when they're ready. The ones who did this? They are the ones who died last night?"

"We believe some of the people who brutalized these children are dead," Burgess said. "We are trying to find out who else was involved."

"Please do," she said. "It is all sickening. There would not be this harm to children if there weren't men willing pay for it. Maybe you can catch some of them as well? And while you are doing that, promise me you'll take care of yourselves." She wasn't looking at Burgess, but at Kyle. "You wear it like a black cape, Joe, and in the waves of anger you give off. Terry carries it like a monster in his belly. If he isn't careful, it eats him inside."

"You can see all that from looking at us?" Kyle said.

"Physician and magician," she said, regaining her smile. She made flapping motions with her hands. "Get out of my emergency room, and don't you dare come back injured." She waved one hand at the controlled chaos around her. "I have enough to do."

They all had enough to do. He and Terry got in the truck and then just sat there. "What next?" Kyle said.

"We could go in so many directions," Burgess said, watching the flood of people coming toward the hospital. New fathers with jaunty steps surrounded by people hunched with worry and despair. "I'm thinking our first stop is lunch. Something to cushion the monster so it doesn't eat you alive."

"Good plan. Though I wonder how she missed the monster in *your* belly," Kyle said. "I think we all have them. The day we graduate from the academy each of us is given a monster to swallow. Some guys and gals manage to cough them up. Some try to drown the monster with alcohol. Most of us just become hosts who have to tend the monster."

"I'm fine when my monster is sleeping, which is most of the time. When it wakes, there's hell to pay. Where do you want to eat?" Burgess asked.

"Nowhere yet," Kyle said. "I'm hungry, but I'm hungrier for answers. Before we eat, let's swing around to the insurance company and check in on Cary McCann. I want to get a picture we can take back to the girls. See if they recognize him. We can ask what he was looking for out on the trail and whether he ever found it."

Burgess was just as eager to start moving this thing. "Let's go."

While Burgess drove, Kyle called up the information about the car so they could find it in the lot. These days, there was a Prius on every block. In a sea of blue Priuses, the plate number would be helpful.

"Something funny here," Kyle said, peering at the screen.

"Funny as in peculiar?"

"Yup. The guy in the license photo doesn't look a lot like the guy I interviewed at 109."

Burgess had been hoping to make some progress. Now he felt gloom descending. "Did anyone check his license at 109?"

"I don't know," Kyle said. "You and I were out at the scene. We'll have to ask the officer who drove him to 109. And maybe Vince. I'm guilty of assuming that that was already done, so I didn't ask him for ID myself. What if we all did that?"

There was silence in the car, both realizing that this was the kind of small carelessness that screwed up investigations and let bad guys walk. The chance for things to slip through cracks was why Burgess liked to keep things small and tight. They already knew that Charlie Dornan was using a fake ID. That should have made them more suspicious. But they'd seen Dornan's ID *after* McCann's interview. McCann's car had appeared the next day at McCann's employer's parking lot, though admittedly stripped of all the items that had been there when it was parked at the Stroudwater trailhead. The plates were registered to McCann at McCann's address. So, other than his behavior—slightly suspicious but mostly belligerent asshole—why would they check further?

Because their spidey senses had told them something about the man was off. The cop's sixth sense, or cop gut, was something to be listened to. They'd let themselves be too busy. Now, as they cruised the sprawling lot, looking for the right blue Prius, Burgess knew they were both hoping they'd get inside, ask for Cary McCann, and the person who appeared would be the man who had found Michele Minor's body. Not some puzzled fellow with a crazy story about how someone was using his identity or the assertion that he and his car had been together, or out of town, on the Fourth of July.

After driving around for what felt like miles, they found the car. Assured that McCann was at work, they pulled to the curb outside the door and parked. A slovenly guy in a security guard's uniform slouched over to tell them they couldn't park there. Despite the kind of neatness and authority the uniform called for, the man was unshaven and smelled like he was sweating out last night's booze.

"Hey," he called. "No way. You can't park there."

Burgess got out as Kyle threw the Police Business sign onto the dash. Maybe the guy couldn't read, because he came right up to the car, leaned over, scanned the sign, and repeated his words. "Nope. Don't care what business you're from. You can't park there."

"We're parking here," Burgess said, showing the man his badge. "You really want to argue about that?"

"I got my orders," the man said truculently.

"Me, too," Burgess said. He stepped past the man and headed for the door, Kyle right beside him.

"I told you," the man said. "Now I gotta call a tow truck."

"Good luck with that," Kyle called back as they pulled open the dark glass doors and stepped from summer sauna into air conditioning's icy blast.

A middle-aged woman with a pleasant face greeted them and asked how she could help. *Get someone to fire that oaf outside,* Burgess thought. He showed her his badge. "Detective Sergeant Burgess, Portland police. This is Detective Kyle. We'd like to speak with Cary McCann."

"Let me find him for you," she said, sliding her finger down a directory.

She picked up her phone and called a number, spoke quietly, and looked up at them. "He'll be right down." She indicated a seating area with comfortable looking black sofas and chairs, a table with magazines, and a few large trees in pots. "If you'd like to sit while you wait. Can I get you some water?"

Good old fashioned courtesy. It was a nice change from the tarted up, insolent airheads so many businesses employed these days. The ones who could barely pull their attention away from their phones long enough to answer a question. "That would be very kind," Burgess said.

They took some seats. The woman brought cold bottles of water. And they waited.

Even before he'd crossed the room to greet them, it was clear that Cary McCann was not the man they were looking for. He was an overweight twenty-something with longish mahogany hair and nerdy glasses. He had a friendly smile, seemed unfazed by a visit from the police, and initiated the conversation even before they'd introduced themselves. "Is this about my stolen wallet?" he said, setting a bottle of water down on the table next to Kyle's and shaking hands.

"It might be," Burgess said. "Do you have a few minutes to talk?"

"Sure." McCann plunked himself down on a sofa across from them and waited for their questions.

Kyle was pretending to check something on his screen. Burgess knew he was really taking McCann's picture. Then he put the phone away.

"On July fourth," Burgess said, "a man identifying himself as Cary McCann called the police, reporting that he had found a body in Stroudwater Park—"

"It wasn't me," McCann interrupted. "I wasn't around on the fourth. My wife and I took a few days down on the Cape. Her parents have a place there. We left on the first, came back early on the fifth because I had a special project to finish." He paused. Corrected himself. "That I'm still finishing."

"Did you take your car?"

McCann looked puzzled, but he answered the question. "No. We took hers. She just got a new car, a Mini convertible, and we thought it would be fun to make the drive in that. Which it was. So nope. The little blue Prius spent the holiday in my garage."

Burgess flipped through his notes and found the address they had for McCann. He read it and said, "Is this your address?"

"It is. But I'm getting concerned. Can you tell me what this is about?"

Burgess realized that Rocky Jordan, who'd collected the information about Cary McCann, never saw the man, and assuming they hadn't asked McCann for photo ID, Vince Melia, who had conveyed the results of Rocky's search to them, had never seen the license. That still left the mystery of why the man claiming to be Cary McCann was driving a car actually registered to the real Cary McCann. His head was starting to hurt, which might be the enormity of the case or simply that he needed to eat and get some coffee.

"Since you were going to be away, did you let anyone else use your car?"

McCann, looking puzzled, shook his head. "I know it sounds funny, but I'm pretty attached to that car. I don't loan it to my friends. Learned not to the hard way. See, Annie and I, we're not like a lot of our friends. We have our own condo, and decent cars and real jobs, when a lot of them are still camping out in their parents' basements and trying to get out of the gig economy. So it can get pretty old, friends asking to borrow the car, or if I can help them move their stuff. After I loaned it to one friend and he brought it back filthy and the seats covered with dog hair, I decided I wasn't doing that anymore."

He ducked his head and gave them an engaging grin. "TMI, huh?"

"It's fine," Kyle said. "So you didn't loan your car while you were away?"

McCann shook his head.

"Is there anyone you can think of who might have been able to access your car without permission?"

Another headshake. "We've tried to leave those friends behind."

"You didn't notice anything different about your car when you got back? No mess. No smells? Nothing out of the ordinary?"

McCann shook his head. "I keep it clean. It was just as I left it. You know, these are pretty strange questions, Detective. May I ask why you have all these questions about my car?"

Cops were not in the habit of answering questions but Burgess figured that McCann deserved an explanation, and anyway, he wanted to gauge McCann's reaction to the story. "On the Fourth, a man identifying himself as Cary McCann contacted the police and reported finding a body in Stroudwater Park. He was driving a blue Prius, and the plates, when we ran them, came back to a blue Prius registered to you."

McCann pulled off his glasses, got a cloth handkerchief from his pocket, and cleaned them thoughtfully. A classic stalling technique. "Seriously? Someone was driving my car and using my name? How do you explain that?"

"We can't," Kyle said. "That's why we were asking about someone who might have borrowed it."

"Maybe your computer made a mistake."

"It doesn't make that kind of mistakes," Kyle said. "If it wasn't one of your friends, could it have been a friend of your wife's?"

"Annie knows how I feel about people borrowing my car. She would never do that."

The man was either so ridiculously certain that he wasn't willing to entertain the possibility that someone had used his car without permission. Or the man knew exactly who had borrowed his car and was hiding behind a wall of outrage and obfuscation. Like they'd never seen that before.

But since their questions had gotten his back up, Burgess figured he'd move on.

"You mentioned your wallet was stolen. When and where was it taken?"

McCann cast a quick glance at the reception desk, then slid up the sleeve of a pristine white polo shirt, revealing a tattoo on his upper arm. A flowery, sinuous mermaid. They'd seen a similar one on a dead girl's arm. "They're pretty strict about tattoos around here," he said. "They want a professional look, even though I'm in IT and never meet with customers. So I always keep this covered at work. It was while I was getting this. I'd hung up my jacket with my wallet in the pocket and when I put it back on, the wallet was gone. Of course, you know those places. The people who run them and the people who hang around. No one had seen anything."

Burgess graciously decided not to point out that McCann had been one of those people. Everyone had their snobbish moments and their blind spots. His mother had been quick to point out that "let he who is without sin cast the first stone" meant few people could throw stones.

"Where was this?" Burgess asked, though he was sure he knew the answer.

"Sweety's."

"And you filed a police report?"

"Of course. I was pissed. Bad enough that it hurt like hell and the artist I wanted passed me along to his apprentice. Or assistant. Or whatever she was called."

"You remember her name?"

"Kit. She said it was short for kitten. Seemed like maybe she was flirting with me. When I'm wearing a wedding ring. But I guess that type doesn't take things like marriage vows seriously."

"And when was this?"

McCann shrugged. "January or February. I can't remember exactly." He checked his watch. "I should have known you weren't here to ask about my wallet, not after all this time."

They were losing him, Burgess thought. He had more questions, but didn't think he was going to get answers. McCann's affable geniality was fading fast. He wondered why. He said, "Does your wife also have tattoos?"

"She's a school teacher, so no. It would set a bad example for the kids. She didn't even like that I got one, but I told her we couldn't always be so straight arrow." He patted his arm. "This is my small rebellion."

"A teacher? That's great," Kyle said. "What grade does she teach?"

"High school. Freshman math. She's appalled at how badly prepared the kids are when they get to her."

They needed to track down the wife, Burgess thought. Maybe she had lent the car? And hadn't one of the girls reported overhearing something about a teacher? He did not want this plot to thicken, the net they had to spread to get wider, but they would cast it as far as necessary. He looked at Kyle, passing the conversational ball. McCann didn't yet seem irritated with Kyle.

"What school?" Kyle said. "My daughter's going to be a freshman this fall. Maybe she'll get lucky and have your wife for a math teacher. She loves math."

McCann named a school without much enthusiasm, then checked his watch again. "Sorry," he said. "As I mentioned, I'm in the middle of a big project. I really don't have any more time for…you. This. Talking. But I'd love to hear from you if you figure out who's been using my name. And, I guess, my license plates. Or my car. That is disturbing."

You're disturbing, Burgess thought. *Very disturbing.* McCann hadn't even blinked when hearing that his car was linked to the discovery of a crime victim's body and seemed only mildly upset that his license plates, and his name, had been used by someone he claimed not to know, and used in connection with a crime. He glanced at Kyle and got a faint nod.

"We won't keep you, then," he said, taking out a card and sliding it across the table. "But please do call us if you think of anything that might help us locate the person who is using your name. That's a very upsetting idea, I am sure."

He and Kyle rose and headed for the door, taking their bottles of water with them.

In the truck, Kyle tucked the bottle he was carrying into an evidence bag and labeled it.

"Sometimes," Kyle said, "people help us with our investigation even when they're trying not to."

"Especially when someone is as quick and clever as Detective Terry Kyle."

"I'm blushing," Kyle said.

"Wish I could read minds," Burgess said. "So I'd know what he's hiding. Is he in this, do you think, or just protecting someone. Maybe one of the more suitable friends he and his wife are acquiring?"

"We need to take a look at the wife," Kyle said. He got on the phone to Rocky Jordan, a man who, by the time this was done, was going to hate everyone on their team. He gave Jordan all the information they had about McCann's wife, like the make of her car and the school where she worked —or where McCann said she worked—and asked Jordan to see what he could find.

They headed back to 109, air conditioning blasting. Summer in Maine was short and intense, a season that flirted with the possibility of warmth all through June and sometimes into July. That was as likely to wrap you in cold fog as to bathe you in warmth. Today, anyone who could would be at the beach. Tomorrow the weather might do a 360.

He dropped Kyle off, Kyle looking almost smug as he carried the water bottle off to deliver it to Wink. Burgess headed back into the tourist-strewn streets to keep his appointment with Alana. Lunch had never happened. He was hoping this would be quick and he could make it home for dinner. He didn't have the stamina for the extensive game of verbal tennis with Alana that was shorthand for "prove that you respect me and care." He'd seen enough bad stuff today. He was ready for a few hours of sparring teens, Neddy's goofy cavorting, and Chris's smile before his team reassembled to assess what they'd learned and decided where to go next.

THIRTY-FIVE

He was on his way to their rendezvous, an oldies station blaring, when Alana called. He turned down the sound. "Dammit, Copman," she said, "I've got to cancel. Got a regular who absolutely has to have a massage today or he'll freak out. And you know, a girl's gotta make a living somehow."

He tried to keep his relief out of his voice. "Can you just tell me over the phone? Please. We've got three bodies and a quartet of brutalized children, I know there's another guy out there and I don't know where to look."

"It's just a hunch," she said. "Someone I met once who…" There was a woman's voice in the background, interrupting her, sounding bossy and peremptory. "I've gotta go," she said.

"Alana! Please. Just finish your sentence."

"Was trying to recruit young girls for his customers. He worked in one of the schools. That's all I know."

"Which school?"

"I don't know."

"Is this a rumor or did you actually meet him?"

"Met him."

Burgess felt explosive. "What did he look like?"

"Fifties. Big guy. Not good looking. Not bad looking. Hard looking, with short hair like military or a cop. He wore kinda flashy clothes for a school teacher. And even though he was trying to get girls to work for him, he was not a nice man."

It was something, but Burgess needed more. "Any distinguishing marks? Tats, scars, moles, a limp. Dammit, Alana, give me something."

The voice in the background got louder, demanding the Alana get off the phone and get to work. So much for creating a relaxing atmosphere.

"He was missing the tip of his left little finger. And his voice was funny, like it was too high and squeaky for such a big man. Sorry I don't have more. I gotta go. Give my love to Chris and the kids."

"Alana, what about…" But he was talking to an empty line.

He turned around, planning to head home, but realized he was in the neighborhood of the woman named Nancy Delude, widow of the man whose license plates were now traveling on the mysterious black town car. He flipped on his blinker and turned down Mrs. Delude's street, pulling to the curb to check his notes and find the house number.

Mrs. Delude lived in a tiny little Cape that remind him too much of the house he'd spent most of last night in, though this one had a garage. The garage was open and there was a blue VW bug parked inside. He went up the walk and knocked, holding his breath until the door was opened. From a dearth of information, he'd made assumptions. Like that the Widow Delude would be a helpless elderly lady who had simply failed to deal with her husband's plates and so somehow they had come into the possession of the man who drove the black town car. The woman who answered the door might have been a very fit seventy. She was dressed in tennis whites and appeared to have just come in.

He showed his badge and explained the reason for his visit. The man they were seeking, the car he drove, the plates on the car listed as belonging to her late husband and supposed to be on a Pathfinder.

Nancy Delude looked at him, puzzled, as she said, "The Pathfinder?" She wore a lot of eye-makeup for someone who'd just come from tennis. But it looked good with her tan and her tangled blonde-gray hair.

"Yes, ma'am."

"That's one thing I don't miss about John."

"Excuse me?" he said. "I'm not following you."

"Step in," she said. She opened a closet and tucked her tennis bag and racket away, then walked into the living room and plunked herself down in a chair. "Sit," she said. "I'll get a crick in my neck staring up at you, and anyway, Jeanne and I just beat the pants off Cheryl and Patti, and now I'm pooped."

When she was seated, she exhaled, like sitting was a luxury, and explained. "John was a lovely man. Absolutely lovely and so much fun. But a detail man he was not. So when he announced he was replacing the Pathfinder with that black behemoth that made him look like a chauffeur, I figured he had his reasons, and simply did the wifely thing of reminding him that he had to register the new car, not just attach the plates from the Pathfinder and keep on driving."

Burgess still wasn't sure he was following. "The dealer your husband bought the car from didn't take care of transferring the plates?"

"I know, right?" She shook her head, as though he understood her disbelief, and said, "John didn't buy the car. He won it at poker. He was an excellent poker player. So he comes home one night with that big black thing. Such a ridiculous car. Not that I liked his old car, either. It rode like a bucket of bolts. I told him he needed to wear a black suit if he was going to drive the black behemoth, but he was pleased as punch. Said it made him feel important. So he just slapped the plates from the old Pathfinder on it, and that was that."

She bounced to her feet, said, "I need a drink. Can I get you anything? I've got flavored seltzer if you'd like. I expect you don't drink when you're on duty. You look like that type of cop."

Like what type of cop? The kind who follows the rules? She could tell that from the few sentences he'd been able to utter? He wondered if John had crossed the rainbow bridge because he was exhausted from living with her energy. "Seltzer would be nice," he said.

He heard cupboard doors and the refrigerator door open and shut. The rattle of ice cubes, and then she was back, holding two tall drinks. "This one is yours. I think. Maybe you can sniff it and see if there's vodka in yours, but I tried to keep them straight." She put his glass down on a coaster, settled herself on the couch again, and took a long drink, like a wild animal at a watering hole, then tossed her head back, said, "Oh! Yes!" and grinned with great pleasure.

Burgess waited until she was settled, or at least as settled as a woman with her energy could be. "What happened to the car when John…when your husband died?"

"Good question. Well, I didn't know what to do with it. I hated it. I'm perfectly happy tootling around in my little blue bug. So John's cousin said maybe he could find someone to buy it, and I was all for that." She paused for a swig of her drink. "You know, when the guy came to pay me and pick it up, I never even thought about the plates. Well. I mean I asked him about the plates and he said he'd take care of it. And that was good enough for me."

"So your husband's cousin, he's the person who would know who bought the car?" Burgess asked.

"That's right. His cousin's name is Charlie. Charlie Dornan. Charlie's pretty much a useless human being. He's spent much of his life trying to butter up Aunt Ida Mae so she'll leave him her money. Trouble is, Charlie doesn't understand that for all that Ida Mae seems to favor him, and even lets him drive her car, Ida Mae is a practical woman. She'd never leave her money to Charlie, unless it was in trust, because Charlie would just piss it away, and Ida Mae is all about the preservation of capital. I think it's going to Charlie's sister Sharon, if there's anything left. That retirement place she's in is very expensive. If she really wanted to be smart, she'd leave it to Marilyn. Pretty, low-key Marilyn, who is actually a demon from hell. Marilyn can make a dollar bill beg for mercy. She'd steal your stuff and then try to sell it back to you."

She put a hand over her mouth. "Oops. That was way too much information, wasn't it?"

Burgess tried to smile, though he was feeling anything but cheerful. "Do you have any information about the man who bought your late husband's car? A bill of sale? A name and address or phone number? Anything?"

She drained her glass and shrugged. "I don't think so. Better to ask Charlie. I can give you his information."

"I'm sorry to be the bearer of bad news," Burgess said, "but Charlie and Marilyn Dornan were both found dead in their home last night."

Her merriment fell away like she'd shucked off a skin. She picked up her glass, looking for some cool alcoholic comfort, and found it empty. She stared at the naked ice cubes as she asked, "Dead? Did you really say dead? Last night? What happened?"

"Shot," he said.

"By whom?"

Burgess shrugged. Cops didn't speculate. At least, not with members of the public. "That's what we're trying to figure out."

"And you think the man who bought John's car might be involved?" The merry widow was gone. Her voice was breathless now, and strained.

"He and Charlie Dornan were engaged in a business enterprise together."

"Then his information will be in Charlie's records, won't it? I mean, John was a bit scattershot about record keeping, but most business people do keep records, don't they? And anyway, Marilyn is…was, I guess…about as anal as a human can be."

Not that they'd seen in the Dornan's files, but they hadn't finished. What if they got lucky and Marilyn Dornan kept records of every transaction regarding clients who used their girls, or every disk of pornography they sold?

He had another idea. "How did Charlie's friend pay for the car?" He was hoping it was by check, and that there might be an image of that check in her bank statements.

"Good old pleasantly pleasing cash," she said. "A whole big wad of it."

Another dead end. Dead end might be name of this whole case.

"Do you remember what the man looked like?"

She considered. "Biggish. Not attractive. Not in his person and not in his manner. It was like he wanted to hand me the cash and be gone. There were no pleasantries. There was no conversation. No questions about the car. Just 'here's your money, ma'am, goodbye.' Bossy and all business."

"So you didn't notice anything distinctive about him? Anything unusual?"

"I guess a lack of basic manners isn't unusual these days, is it?" She studied the ice cubes like they might give her some answers. "Flashy clothes. Yeah. But strangely flashy. A normal sports jacket but the shirt and tie were almost gaudy. And there was something else." She tapped her chin with a brightly manicured finger. "His hands. Something about his hands. Oh. Yes. He was missing part of his left little finger. I noticed it when he handed over the cash."

Burgess figured it was a lost cause, but he had one last question. "So, no identifying information. There was nothing in the transaction that might help locate this man?"

She shook her head. "I'm sorry, Detective. It wasn't important to me, so I didn't pay much attention. Excuse me." She headed for the kitchen. "I need another drink."

Burgess rose to go. It was time for family dinner and he needed a nice quiet ride in the car first to let some of the poison out of his system.

"Maybe Ida Mae knows something," she said. "The one thing I remember is the guy said to Charlie, 'Ida Mae might like a ride in this.' And Charlie said she would. Only he told the guy he ought to tone down his shirt and tie. Even Charlie, who had the fashion sense of a gnat, knew it wasn't right."

"Thank you for your time, Mrs. Delude."

"Nancy," she said. "Mrs. Delude makes me sound like your first grade teacher."

He let himself out, stumped through the late afternoon sauna, checking the sky for the possibility of rain, and got in the Explorer. When Maine did humid, it went all out. The still air smelled like seaweed and old fish. He fired up, turned the air conditioning to max, and headed home.

THIRTY-SIX

Home was chaotic, as usual. Dylan wanted to do some driving practice, so Burgess promised him half an hour after dinner. Nina was arguing with Chris about being allowed to stay out until after midnight on a babysitting gig. Neddy and two other ruffians were glued to a video game that looked more savage than most of the things Burgess dealt with. And Chris was looking tired. Usually she was bustling around making dinner at this hour, but there were no signs of dinner.

He put an arm around her shoulders and steered her out onto the back deck. A breeze had come up and in the shade it was cooling nicely out there.

"Tell Detective Burgess what's wrong," he said.

"Nothing's wrong."

Instead of pushing her for an answer, he kissed her. He was still kissing her when Nina stepped out, already in the middle of a complaint.

"I really don't see why I can't…oh. Eww. I can't look at this." She went back inside.

"Do you think it's child abuse to subject a child to the sight of two loving adults kissing?" he asked.

Chris shook her head. "Lately, the way she pushes my buttons, I find myself coming pretty close to child abuse. Sandy says that's the way it is between all moms and their teenage daughters and we'll get past it. But when I've had a hard day at work, like today, and come home to deal with this?" She sighed. "It makes me question whether I'm really cut out for this mothering business."

"No one ever said it would be easy." He took her shoulders and turned her to face him. "You're doing a great job. The kids love you, and they wouldn't have much of a life without you. Nina and Neddy would still be in foster care, and Dylan would be living with a stepfather who didn't like him much. Unless he was living with me, a guy who knows nothing about kids and is gone too much. Instead, they've got this. A home. A mom. Grandma Doro. Lots of love, and sometimes even a dad."

She stepped forward, bumping her soft chest against him, and buried her head in his shoulder. Her hair smelled like apples. He wrapped his arms around her and whispered, "Want me to make dinner?"

"Would you?" she murmured into his shoulder.

"It would be my pleasure," he said. "Stay here. Look at the summer sky. Watch the puffy white clouds. I'll bring you some wine."

Chris dropped into one of the white rocking chairs. "Thank you," she said.

Burgess went inside, poured a glass of white wine, and took it out to her. Then he opened the refrigerator, hoping he'd find something he could cook. He pulled out red, green, and orange peppers, a red onion, and two small zucchini and cut them into chunks, tossing them with some teriyaki marinade. He might have the normal man's aversion to vegetables, but Chris was gradually turning him around. He used the same marinade on thin-sliced chicken breasts. He lit the grill and filled a pot with water for pasta. It had been so long since he'd done much cooking in this kitchen it felt like an unfamiliar place, but he'd been a solitary bachelor for many years, and he hadn't dined solely at fast food places.

Forty minutes later, Chef Joseph presented his family with a heaped platter of pasta topped with grilled chicken and vegetables.

The moment was not arrived at without skirmishes. Nina complained that she couldn't eat pasta because it would make her fat. Neddy wanted his friends to stay for dinner, and Burgess hadn't made that much food. And Dylan hung around the kitchen, rocking impatiently from foot to foot, anxious to get in some driving time before Burgess headed back to work.

The friends were dispatched with the promise of another day. He told Nina she could pick out chicken and grilled vegetables, and Neddy and Dylan were sent to set the table. By the time they all sat down, the rest and wine had done its magic, and Chris was smiling again.

"You did this?" she said. "It's delicious."

"This is pretty much all I can cook," he said.

"Well, I am not complaining."

"Good," he said, "because now I have a favor to ask."

"What?" she said suspiciously.

"Can Dylan and I borrow your car for half an hour?"

She laughed and gave him the keys.

Dylan drove like he'd been doing it for years.

"Soon as you have your license," Burgess said, "I'll teach you to drive like a cop."

"I'd like that."

Dylan drove, and they talked, and Burgess was reminded how much easier it was to talk when you were both looking straight ahead. Dylan asked about his case, and Burgess told him about Michele Minor and the five girls. About the tattoo parlor that had helped them ID the girl and about last night's murdered couple. "Now we're trying to find a man we believe was their partner, but we don't have much to go on."

"What about what Cherry said? That she recognized that girl, Shelley, from school. Maybe someone at her school might have some ideas. Something someone saw, or something Shelley might have said. Teachers are good observers. Well. Some teachers."

Dylan hadn't been a cop's kid for most of his growing up years, but he'd settled into it like a natural. "Good thought," Burgess agreed. "That's on the agenda for tomorrow morning. Harder to do, though, because it's summer and most of the staff aren't around. Speaking of summer, how's your job going?"

"Bratty little kids who make Neddy look like an angel. Teenage boys trying to get girls to notice them. Girls doing the same." There was a hesitation, then his son said, "Girls always notice lifeguards. And this weird thing —moms of the little kids trying to get the life guard to notice them."

It didn't hurt that his son was tall, strong, athletic and very good looking. In a bathing suit and tee shirt, he was definitely eye candy. Burgess puzzled over the fact that they looked so much alike, yet he was a scarred old bear with a scary face and his son was a babe magnet. Looking at this version of his younger self made him feel very old.

"Dad?" Dylan said. "What am I supposed to do when a friend needs help and helping might involve doing something that could get me in trouble?"

"You could talk to your dad?"

"I am talking to my dad."

"About the specifics, I mean. It's hard when the person is a friend, but when someone asks you to do something illegal, or break the rules, you have to say no. Or ask for a grownup's help."

It was the right advice, and what he was supposed to say. But Burgess knew that loyalty to peers could skew a teenager's judgment. Even one as balanced as Dylan. "You want to tell me about it?" he said.

"Maybe later. Maybe it won't come to anything anyway," Dylan said.

Burgess didn't press him. Theirs was a cautious relationship. Slowly developing. He didn't like to push too hard. He could only hope that, having opened the door to a future conversation, Dylan would come to him before doing something impulsive or dangerous.

Their half hour flew past. It seemed like only minutes before Burgess was dropping Dylan at home and heading back in to work. Tonight, late or not, he was going to pay a call on Ida Mae Wilson.

Not far from the longest day of the year, there was still light as he drove to headquarters. It was summer in the city for sure. Swarms of girls in cutoffs and tank tops and guys who had to hold up their pants or shorts were on the sidewalks. Happy. Noisy. This early in the evening still relatively sober and not doing stupid things like wandering into traffic. Their music was different, but all summer nights seemed to have a driving beat. He could easily have just stayed in the truck, driving around with the window down, letting summer in. But people were waiting.

Kyle and Perry and Prentiss were there waiting for him. Ragging on each other, floating ideas. Waiting for him to bring some order to the investigation and tell them where to go next. There was a stack of folders on the table, courtesy of Rocky Jordan. A whiteboard waited.

"Okay, what have we got?" he said.

It was more of the same stuff they'd gotten from the neighbors near Ida Mae Wilson's house. People had seen the man in the black car. Had run-ins with the man in the black car. Described the man in the black car the same way Wilson's neighbors had. Belligerent. Disagreeable. Same physical description.

"We have a bolo out on that car, right?" Burgess said. He told them about Nancy Delude and the license plates. About the man who bought the car being a friend of her late husband's cousin. That her late husband's cousin had been Charlie Dornan. No name, and the car and plate were dead ends unless Ida Mae Wilson knew something.

"I feel like we're chasing our tails here. Everything we learn about this guy confirms what we already know, and nothing brings us any closer."

The whiteboard still waited.

"Is Vince going to liaise with the feds about whoever applied for custody of our girls?" Kyle asked.

"He's supposed to. He'll need the information we got from the translator today. The names of the women who claimed to be their relatives. The names of the girls. Tentative dates that they arrived here in Maine. Can you write that up, Ter?"

"Sure," Kyle said. "So that Captain Cote can share it all with the press. Then, in six months to a year, we'll get an answer back from the feds, unless the information has been lost or they can't locate it. These are helpless children and they literally gave them to sex traffickers. In my nearly twenty years, I have yet to see the feds man up and accept responsibility for anything. Why should this time be different?"

"You got a better idea about how we find the women who claimed to be relatives?" Perry asked.

Everyone was in a bad mood. It happened when the cases asked too much and the answers came too slowly. And nothing was helped when the weather got hot and stagnant and no one could sleep even if they had time to sleep.

"We could at least run their names. See if the girls can give us anything that might help us locate them," Kyle said.

"Anyone had a chance to check out who bought that saw yet?" Burgess asked.

He felt like he was losing it. He was supposed to be on top of things. Directing the investigation. Making sure questions got answered. Yet it seemed that the only question that got answered was about the mystery man in the black car. And the answer was always the same. A description but no name. No phone number. No address. And now the black car seemed to have disappeared.

"Wink and Dani have gone home," Prentiss said. "They were both toast. Rocky expects to get call lists from the three phones found at the scene last night and this morning some time tomorrow."

Burgess made a note. There had been a time when he could carry all this in his head. Unfair as it was, that was back before he also carried Chris, Dylan, Nina, and Neddy in his head. Maybe his head was too small for work and family. Maybe it was okay to use his notebook to help out. Maybe he was blaming family for what was really the product of getting older. Most cops his age were retired. Well, maybe that was many, not most.

He and Kyle filled everyone in on the visit to Dr. Morton. On their strange interview with the real Cary McCann.

"So who was using McCann's car?" Perry asked.

"And was the guy who said he was McCann the same man everyone is describing who scared the girls and drives the black town car?" Kyle said. "Do we have anything with his prints on it? And when are we going to interview McCann's wife? Did Rocky get a chance to look into her yet?"

The questions piled up, with everyone looking at Burgess for answers he didn't have.

He knew the way cases like this got solved. Shoulder to the wheel, and just keep pushing. Pile up the answers until they had enough. Wink and Dani and Rudy would be working on evidence. His team had to keep asking questions.

"Sage, you follow up on that saw, see if they have a name and a credit card for us yet. See if they have anything. Stan, you've got the real Cary McCann's wife." He gave Perry the folder on Annie McCann that Rocky had left on his desk. "Then you and Sage can hit the schools, see if the description of our mystery man rings any bells. That missing fingertip is pretty distinctive. Kyle and I will attend the autopsies. Then we'll all check in. Sound like a plan?"

There was a murmur of agreement.

"Before we call it a night," Kyle said, "let's take another look at the fake McCann's interview. I'd think if he was missing part of a digit I would have noticed, but just to be sure. Be pretty ironic if we'd had the guy here and let him go."

"And print a picture we can show to the girls," Perry said.

"And the neighbors," Prentiss said.

"And the real McCann," Burgess said.

Kyle found the video and queued it up, and they waited, expectantly, for a look at the man's left hand.

When they were done, Stan Perry spoke for all of them when he said, "Holy fuck! He kept that finger hidden the whole freaking time. Who does that? Doesn't this have to be our guy?"

In your face bad guys really push cops' buttons. But they still didn't know if their buttons were being pushed.

Kyle grabbed a good screenshot of the fake Cary McCann and made everyone copies. Then, because they'd put things in place for tomorrow and his team hadn't played Sleeping Beauty, lingering in bed like he had,

Burgess sent them home. He signaled for Kyle to stay behind. "I'm going to pay Ida Mae Wilson a visit. Want to join me?"

"Want to, but can't. I promised Michelle and the girls that we'd watch a movie when I got home. So unless there's an emergency…"

Burgess thought this whole freaking thing was an emergency, but he nodded. "See you in the morning. Want to ride up together?"

Kyle nodded, and they swam through the body temperature air to their vehicles. At Burgess's place, there had been a breeze. Here in the heart of the city, the still air felt thick enough to wring out.

Burgess paused before getting in the truck, listening to the city. Listening to his gut, which told him that a bad night lay ahead. He wished he could interrogate it. Make it tell what else was coming at them. But it was a feeling. A premonition of evil. That was all his gut would say.

He gave up and headed west to find Ida Mae Wilson.

THIRTY-SEVEN

There was heat lightning in the distance, dancing from cloud to cloud, while thunder rumbled far away. There would probably be rain before midnight. A nice cooling rain would be good. He just hoped that the warning from his gut didn't mean they'd all be out in the rain, looking for something or someone. Searches in the rain were the worst. No visibility. Sounds distorted. Impossible to keep track of people, which put everyone at risk.

Don't get ahead of yourself, the voice in his head reminded him. He was just on his way to interview an elderly lady. He put on the radio, found an oldies station, and tried to calm down.

He found Pine Tassel Estates by an elegant, well-illuminated sign and turned in between two massive stone pillars. The road wound up a hill, past a pond and some gardens, leading him at last to a brightly lit building that looked like the massive old summer houses wealthy people built all along the coast a hundred years ago. It had a wide pillared porch housing clusters of white wicker chairs, and big window boxes full of geraniums and dusty miller. He parked in a spot marked Visitors and climbed the steps. The double door was open, and through the screens he could hear the sounds of music and lively voices. He let himself in and went to the desk facing the door, where a neat young woman in a blue blazer and white blouse sat.

"Good evening," he said. "Detective Sergeant Joe Burgess. I'm looking for Ida Mae Wilson."

Instead of the greeting her pleasant face suggested, she only reached for his credentials and studied them like he was probably a fraud who just wanted to crash the party. At last she handed them back and said, "I believe she's gone back to her apartment. I'll have security take you there."

She had an accent. Middle European, maybe.

"That would be very kind," he said.

He waited. She watched him with an expression that suggested she wanted to say something but wasn't sure that she should. Finally she leaned toward him and said, confidentially, "She was a bit tipsy when she left. You should maybe keep this in mind?"

She said it like a question, and Burgess agreed he would keep it in mind. After a wait so long his knee began to complain, a burly man, also in a navy blazer, approached and held out his hand. "Douglas Ryder," he said. "I'll take you to Ida Mae."

Burgess shook the offered hand, noting that the man had not referred to her as Mrs. Wilson.

He followed Ryder to the back of the building, out a door, and along a path leading to a cluster of neat cottages. "She's in number ten," the man said. "It's this way."

They climbed a set of stairs onto a porch that was a mini-clone of the one on the main building, and Ryder knocked on the door. The door was open but the screen door was closed. "It's Doug Ryder, Mrs. Wilson," his escort called. "You have a visitor."

It's always interesting, in a case where multiple witnesses have referred to a particular person, to finally meet that person. He'd avoided forming an image of her, though he had to step on a prejudice against someone who would loan their house to a person like Charlie Dornan. But he'd seen plenty of people over the years who showed poor judgement in how they indulged their relatives. And he didn't actually know that Dornan had been using the house with her permission.

The woman who answered the door, after a slow progress of footsteps accompanied by the thump of a cane, was old and wrinkled and fighting it tooth and nail. Her hair was the color of rust, with a quarter inch of white roots. She wore a bright slash of red lipstick that didn't quite follow the contours of her mouth, and her nails were a garish pink that didn't match the lipstick. Neither lips nor nails matched her pearl pink twinset. Of course he disapproved, being such a fashionable guy himself.

"Ida Mae, this is Detective Burgess," Ryder said. "He'd like to ask you some questions."

"It is very late for a visit," she said. "I was just about to have my nightcap." She looked at Burgess. "Would you like to join me?"

His standard response was that he couldn't, he was working, but he sensed that he'd have better luck getting her to talk if he said yes, so he said, "What are we drinking, Mrs. Wilson?" as he stepped inside.

Ryder sketched a wave and disappeared, and Burgess followed her into a cozy living room.

"We're having Scotch," she said. "At least, I am. And since it's all I have in the house right now, I guess that's what you're having, too." She waved her cane at a tray on the coffee table. Two glasses. Some ice. And the Scotch.

"Were you expecting someone?" he asked.

"My nephew, but he's a very unreliable fellow. So now I guess I'm expecting you."

She poured two generous drinks, dropped in some ice cubes, and passed one glass to him. "To what do I owe the pleasure of this visit?" she said.

"We've been trying to track down the owner of a black town car that's been seen near the scene…uh…that may be involved in some illegal activities. Earlier today, I spoke with a woman named Nancy Delude. The car previously belonged to her husband John. She said that she sold the car to a friend of your nephew Charlie, and that you might know the man's name."

He knew what would she say—why don't you ask Charlie. Before she could, he took a sip of his drink and smiled. "This is very good Scotch."

She smiled, too. "When you get old, you start to wonder what you're saving it for. I've decided I was saving it for things that I enjoy."

"It's a good philosophy." He dug out his notebook, although he didn't really need it, and pretended to consult his notes. "Nancy says that the man who bought John's car took you for a ride in it. Is that right?"

She took another drink. Hers was disappearing fast. Doing the things that she enjoyed.

"It was one of those big black town cars, like important people get driven around in. John was foolishly in love with it. He won it at poker. Did Nancy tell you that?"

"She did."

"Nancy is my kind of girl. She knows how to have fun."

"About the car?" he prompted.

"Yes. I went for a ride in it. Charlie took me out to dinner at a nice restaurant, and his friend drove us and played chauffeur. It was fun. I got to wear real high heels, which, at my age, is a rare thing indeed."

"Do you know the man's name?"

"He introduced himself as Lawrence. Charlie called him Larry, but I could tell he didn't like that much. He made a good chauffeur. He was kind of a pompous man."

"You know his last name?"

She shook her head. "All I heard was Larry. Lawrence, actually. He seemed more like a Lawrence. The kind of man who'd be a bit precious about his name, so of course I called him Larry. He was a good driver, Detective. The only thing that wasn't quite right was his shirt and tie. They were ridiculous."

Inch by inch. They now had the possibility of a school connection. And a first name. If this were TV, he'd have it solved in the next five minutes. He'd type "school" and "Lawrence" and "colorful shirts" into a computer and the name, address, DOB, a high quality photo and other useful information would pop up on the screen.

"Charlie will know his last name, I'm sure. You should ask him."

Burgess got out the screen shot of the man who'd called himself Cary McCann. "Have you ever seen this man before?"

"Of course. I just told you about him. That's Lawrence. Charlie's friend. The man with the black town car."

Burgess changed the subject. "Can I confirm that Charlie has your permission to use your Prius?"

She studied her drink, like what he wasn't telling her was written there on the ice cubes. "He really doesn't, you know, but since I stopped driving, he's just come here and taken it, and he's kind of careless about bringing it back." She gave him a worried look. "He hasn't gone and had an accident in my car, has he?"

"No, ma'am."

He just wanted to keep the questions flowing, to put off the moment when he'd have to tell her about Charlie. "Were you close to your nephew Charlie?" Oops. He'd used the past tense. Cops were very alert to these missteps. He wondered if she would be.

She shrugged, then gave a kind of impish smile. Because her house, and her car, had been used by bad guys, he'd assumed he wouldn't like her, but he was starting to like her quite a lot.

"I think Charlie believes we're closer than we are. Perhaps it's unkind of me to say this, but Charlie is kind of an operator. He thinks I don't know it, of course. He thinks I'm a dotty old lady who dotes on him."

"An operator? In what way?"

"Well. There's the car, of course. And then there's my house. I know he was letting people stay there without asking me. I heard that from my old neighbors, that there were people coming and going. Rose Samson was quite concerned about it. In fact, she suggested he was using the place for prostitution. It's why I told him I was selling it, and arranged for the furniture to be moved out."

She gave him a wink. "Harder to let friends use the place when it's empty, you know. And yes. Charlie thinks I'm going to leave him my money. Silly boy. He's not very attuned to people, you see. Only to what pleases him or satisfies his desires." She waved a wrinkled and liver spotted hand toward the expensive Scotch. "The way I'm going, between what this place costs and the treats I like to indulge in, there won't be much left. Do you think I'm a mean old lady, Detective?"

He thought she was a wise old lady, but wondered if she was more attached to her nephew than she was letting on.

"Charlie and Marilyn have a foster daughter, Shelley. Have you met her?"

"Sweet as pie, that girl, which is kind of amazing, given that she's got Charlie and Marilyn for parents. Charlie can be feckless but kind, but Marilyn doesn't have a maternal bone in her body. Last time I saw Charlie, which was a few days ago, he said Shelley had run away."

She refilled her glass and gave him a knowing smile. "What's this really about, Detective?"

"It's really about trying to find the man with the black town car. Larry."

Burgess hesitated, deciding whether to give this feisty old lady the bad news.

Before he could speak, she said, "There's bad news, isn't there? Is it about Charlie?" She paused, drank, and said, "It is about Charlie."

"I'm afraid it is, Mrs. Wilson. Last night, I paid a visit to Charlie and Marilyn Dornan to ask them some questions about an on-going investigation, and…" He hesitated again. She put on a good front, but she was old. Very old. And very old people could have devastating reactions to shock.

"Spit it out," she said. "I may be old, but I'm one of those tough old birds."

"I'm afraid I have some very bad news, Mrs. Wilson. The Dornans have both been shot."

"Dead?"

He nodded.

"Murder/suicide?" she asked.

Before he could answer, she added, "Though he would have to have killed her, because Marilyn doesn't know the meaning of remorse and wouldn't have killed herself just because she shot him. And Charlie wouldn't have the guts to shoot Marilyn. She's got his manhood locked in a safe somewhere."

"We're still trying to figure that out."

This time, she nodded. "I'll miss Charlie. He was amusing. Even his greed was amusing, and it definitely worked for my benefit. When I wanted things done, he'd do them."

"You don't have a very good opinion of Marilyn Dornan."

"I'm not supposed to speak ill of the dead, am I, Detective?" There was a twinkle in her eye. Despite having just been informed of a favorite nephew's death, she was enjoying this visit. Maybe, despite the fancy digs and the country club atmosphere, she was lonely. Drinking alone was drinking alone, even when the drink was expensive Scotch.

Burgess shrugged. "Many of the people I interview speak ill of the dead. It's the nature of my business."

"I'll make a deal with you," she said.

Burgess waited.

"Drink your Scotch and I'll tell why I didn't like Marilyn."

"And if I don't?"

Ida Mae Wilson pantomimed an elaborate yawn. "Then it will be my bedtime."

"You drive a hard bargain, Ida Mae."

She grinned. "Always have, Detective. Always have."

He picked up his glass and took a drink. He was a bourbon man by choice, but this was very good.

"I don't like Marilyn because she's evil."

Mostly it was cops who knew people were evil. "How so?" he asked.

"Charlie doesn't…didn't…pretend to be anything he's not. He was lazy and greedy and would admit it to your face. Marilyn is sneaky. She's two-faced. She pretends to care about people. She pretends to embrace the values of her job. Pretends to care about the people who come here fleeing horrific conditions seeking asylum. But she doesn't care. She makes fun of them. She laughs at their pain. And she is always looking for ways to make a buck off people she's supposed to be helping."

So was Marilyn Dornan the engine behind the decision to prostitute children and sell their violation to the consumers of child pornography?

"Can you give me some examples?"

"She would help people get jobs and then make them give part of their salary to her, even though finding them work was part of her job. I know that she basically sold children to families eager to adopt. And Charlie and I began a parting of the ways—another incentive to sell that house—when they began prepping little Shelley to be part of their business."

"Excuse me," Burgess interrupted. "You knew they were planning on prostituting their own foster daughter?"

"I knew that's what Marilyn wanted to do. I told Charlie that if they went ahead with that ugly scheme, I was done with him."

"But you didn't call the police?"

"I called social services."

That was the third call. Who knew how many others there were? He now had a priority for tomorrow after the autopsy.

"When was this?"

"Maybe a month, six weeks ago. He had Shelley in the car when he stopped by and he didn't want to let me see her. That's when I made the call to the state and emptied the house and put it on the market. That's also when Marilyn, who never visits me, stopped by with a cake she'd made just for me."

"And?" he said, somehow knowing that she hadn't eaten it.

"And it's right here in my freezer. I was hoping for an opportunity to feed it to Charlie and Marilyn. That would have been fair play. And that's when I changed my will."

Even though the Dornans were dead, Burgess still wanted the cake tested. It would be part of building the case. "May I take the cake?"

"I think you often take the cake, Detective."

Kyle would love this woman.

"Only if you promise no one will eat it," she said.

"I promise."

"It's late and you're tired," she said. "Is there anything else you need to know?"

"I don't think so. May I come back if there is?"

"You can come back if there isn't. You're good company. Are you married?"

"Kinda," he said.

"What does that mean?"

"It means we've adopted two kids, plus I have my son, but she won't marry me."

'Why not?"

"Because she thinks my job is too dangerous. Because she doesn't want to marry me and then lose me."

"But she'll live with you?"

He nodded.

"So if anything happens, she'll still lose you. Well, it's been very nice having a drink with you, Detective. Go carefully on the drive out, because the deer think the road belongs to them, and so do the coyotes."

"I will. And thank you."

He waited while she got the cake from her freezer, and left her pouring a little more Scotch. He sat in the truck, not ready to drive, filing away all that he'd learned from Ida Mae Wilson and kicking himself because he hadn't made interviewing her a priority. Then he drove slowly down the long manicured drive.

It was good he was going slowly, because just as he approached the stone pillars a deer flew into his path. There was flash of brown and he stood on his brakes as the graceful creature landed once in the road and then disappeared into the darkness. A moment later three awfully healthy looking coyotes followed. It was most of the ride home before his heart stopped pounding.

THIRTY-EIGHT

He didn't go inside right away. He sat in the truck, going over things, considering whether what he'd learned from Ida Mae changed their agenda for the morning. It seemed like schools had moved to the top of the list, especially now that they had a photo they could show people. That photo also needed to be shown to Dr. Morton and his staff, and to Kit and DeSpain at Sweety's. He wanted this guy in custody. In particular because of the "in your face" game the man had played when he reported the body. No doubt his desire to get his phone back was so that he could warn the others. He must have been laughing up his sleeve when he walked out of 109.

Cops don't like to lose. Not only because of the competitive game of cops vs. bad guys, the battle of good vs. evil, but because of the pressure to get justice for victims. An unsolved case can haunt an investigator for his whole life. Here there were six victims that they knew of. No one involved was going to walk on this.

That assertion—that no one was going to walk on this—led him back to the interview earlier today with the "real" Cary McCann. What role did he play in all this? What was the connection that led the elusive Lawrence of the black town car to be driving McCann's Prius and using his name? Was it a connection through McCann's wife?

He wondered if the clue lay in fingerprints, and whether they would ultimately put McCann at one of their crime scenes. He also wondered—a sick kind of wondering—whether the real McCann was featured in any of the videos the Dornans had made.

He went upstairs, where the house was finally quiet, and into the bedroom. Chris turned sleepily and asked, "Coming to bed?"

"I wish. I just did an interview that opens some doors. I'm going to go back in. There's something I need to check out."

"Don't be too late," she said. "I miss you when you're not here."

"I shouldn't be long," he said, though he had no idea how long he'd be. He kissed her and headed out.

The city was quiet tonight. A weeknight. No cruise ships in town. The heat had cooled to a good sleeping temperature, and Portland's sensible citizens were grabbing sleep before the muggy heat forecast for the weekend made sleeping impossible. He liked to sit on Munjoy Hill and look out over the city, hoping all was well, and unable to avoid wondering what dark deeds were taking place. They'd hear about them soon enough.

Burgess didn't believe in psychic connections. He was too much of a cynic for that. He did believe in the cop's gut. Trying to sleep when a case was unsolved and new horrors kept breaking out could be impossible. When he turned into the garage and parked, he wasn't surprised to see Kyle's car. He wouldn't have been surprised to see Perry's as well, but Stan Perry was embarking on the complicated new balancing act of job and family. As he was punching in the door code, Perry appeared behind him.

"Couldn't sleep," he said. "Lily said to just go, I was making her nuts." As they headed up the stairs, he said, "Why are we here?"

"Did I call you?"

"On the psychic hot line."

"Right. We're here to look at the Dornan's videos."

"That's going to be ugly."

"Yeah. Couple years ago, we'd go to my place, get pizza and drink heavily. Now none of us has a place where we can watch that stuff. And we can't drink here."

"Which is too damned bad because I…"

"I know."

Stan Perry had been a father for less than two days, but it was already transforming him. He'd be as torn as the rest of them, seeing these videos. Viewing stuff like this—the sick, ugly things that people memorialized on video—took a cast iron stomach and forced the calmest and most detached investigator to contemplate breaking the rules and inflicting torture and death on the perpetrators. It could be challenging not to yield to that impulse.

The detective's bay was mostly empty, a few souls with the night shift on the phone, or sorting papers. Kyle was at his desk, working on reports. He looked up when they came and said, "It's about time."

"I was doing a very interesting interview with Ida Mae Wilson," Burgess said.

"I was walking a fussy baby. She seems really pissed off at being out here in the world. Lily says give her time. She'll adjust. I am envisioning a grim and sleepless future."

"Everything all set for Saturday?" Burgess asked.

"It is. I sure would like to have this wrapped before then."

"Optimist," Kyle said.

"And I wish the weather wasn't predicted to be so stinking hot," Perry said. "She wants me to wear my uniform."

"Me, too," Burgess said. He went to Evidence and got copies of each of the six different CDs they'd found in the Dornan's laundry room. How ironic to store such filthy stuff in a room devoted to making things clean. Then he reminded himself that they didn't yet know what was on these disks. They could be recordings of a church choir. But each disk had a name, and the names were pretty much a giveaway. Shelley, Sofia, Maria, Magaly, Gabriela and Isabella.

They took the disks into the conference room, and Burgess started the first one. Shelley Minor had been a sweet-face girl, very pretty. The enhanced breasts looked wrong on her child's body, but that didn't seem to stop the men who were taking advantage of her.

"How could they?" Kyle said. "She was their daughter."

"Ida Mae Wilson says that Marilyn Dornan had this in mind all along. That the woman was cold as ice and very greedy."

"Then why didn't she…"

"She did. She's the third person who called DHHS. Three chances to save the girl, and no one acted."

Sadly, it was not the first time and they all knew it wouldn't be the last time that an overworked, understaffed agency with a mission to keep families together let predators or incompetent parents destroy innocent children. It wasn't worth getting mad about, or they'd always be mad. Still, they were going to have an interview with Shelley Minor's social worker, and it was not going to be a pleasant one.

The videos were grueling to watch. Burgess was glad his dinner was long ago, or he might have lost it. Though many men cycled through the abuse of the girls, none of the three recognized any of them. Burgess wondered how the Dornans and their partner recruited their clients, and whether any of the client's fingerprints found in Ida Mae's house or the Dornan's shed would be somewhere in the system.

"This could take us months," Kyle said, reading Burgess's mind as he often did.

"I hope we catch some of these guys," Perry said. "I just wish we could put a few of these images on the front page of the paper and let the whole world see how foul and twisted these men are. These are fucking children!"

"These men are fucking children," Kyle corrected. "But sharing these pictures just feeds the type of creep who thrives on this stuff. It will be enough to charge them with child rape," Kyle said. "If we can. I hope we can. And by the way 'fucking children' is this case in a nutshell."

The talk was partly to dissipate the stomach turning effect of what they'd just seen. They knew these children. They'd seen them in that fetid cell, carried them in their arms, talked to them. And there was still number six. Isabella. Sweet, bright-eyed little Isabella. None of them were eager to watch that.

"I don't think I can…" Perry began.

"It's okay," Burgess said. "It doesn't take three of us."

"I'm just going to sit over here," Perry said, moving to a farther away chair and turning his back to the screen.

"You ready, Terry?" Burgess said.

"Just let me get my wastebasket over here, just in case."

It was as bad they'd feared, and confirmed the evidence of those shoeprints in the dust that Wink had focused on. Four men crowded into that small space, sharing it with Marilyn Dornan and a camera, waiting to take their turns with a small child. One of the men was the real Cary McCann.

"Sick," Kyle said. He used his wastebasket.

Kyle was gray and sweating. Perry wore the twisted face of a man who wants to kill the next thing that crossed his path. Burgess couldn't see his own face, but he felt gray and consumed by rage. He wished they had Ida Mae's Scotch. Or anesthesia. People who liked to imagine cops spent their whole days harassing the public and eating donuts couldn't imagine the impact of something like this.

Burgess ejected the disk, went to his desk, and wrote an arrest warrant for McCann and a search warrant for his condo, his car, his trash. They could have just arrested McCann, but they wanted to search the place before someone else—the mysterious Lawrence, or McCann's wife, cleaned house and got rid of evidence. "Now we understand why McCann let our mystery man Lawrence borrow his car."

"Can we do this now?" Kyle said.

"We're busy in the morning."

Warrants signed, the three musketeers, with some patrol officers for backup, climbed into their cars and headed out to McCann's condo, wearing their vests despite the heat and Stan Perry's complaints. The man's wife was a teacher, McCann had said. Burgess wondered if part of the attraction was access to children?

They all stopped a block away, and Kyle and Perry went to scope out the property. "Watch out for a dog," Burgess said. "The fake McCann said the dog was his, but maybe he borrowed the dog as well as the car."

Five minutes later, they were back. "Two entrances, front and back, and there may be an entrance to the garage as well," Kyle said. "Two cars in the garage. A blue Prius and a red Mini."

"No lights on inside," Perry added.

Finding two suspects dead last night had spooked them. What if the mysterious Lawrence had severed another connection in a very decisive way? It made any entry that much more difficult, because if they were entering a crime scene, they needed to think evidence preservation at every step. "Wink and Dani will kill us if we find more bodies in here," Kyle said.

"Don't even joke about it," Perry said. "I'm not feeling so left out that I need a crime scene so I can catch up."

The sky began spitting rain as they moved toward the house. Burgess sent two officers to the back, drove the Explorer across the front of the garage to block any possibility of vehicular escape, and the three of them went slowly up the steps behind an officer with a battering ram. If the McCanns were home, as their cars suggested, they were about to get a hell of a wake-up call.

Given the severity of the crime, they had a no-knock warrant. They weren't required to announce their presence or ask for permission to enter.

At Burgess's nod, the officer swung the heavy metal and the door burst open. The loud sound of the door shattering was echoed as the broken door bounced off the wall. Clenched with anticipation, the three of them stepped into the dark condo. Burgess found a light switch and flipped it on.

It was a pleasant, open kitchen-family room, painted pale yellow, with pretty furnishings. It probably was ordinarily neat. But not tonight. The place looked like someone had already searched it. Drawers were pulled open and their contents spilled everywhere.

They made their way through the two floors, clearing the rooms. Every room bore the same signs of a hasty search. The bed was unmade, with a man's pajamas and a woman's summer nightgown tossed on the floor beside it.

Although their cars were home, the McCanns were not. The condo was empty.

THIRTY-NINE

Since they were here, they might as well search. Perry took the upstairs. Burgess and Kyle the downstairs. Then they would check the garage and the trash. They let patrol go. No sense in tying anyone else up. It was too late for a neighborhood canvass.

The kitchen smelled faintly of cooking and there was a carefully wrapped, partially eaten chicken in the refrigerator. That suggested the McCanns had spent a quiet evening at home and gone to bed. Crumpled napkins and chicken bones in the trash seemed to confirm this. People didn't leave bones in their kitchen trash in this weather for long. The nightclothes on the bedroom floor suggested something had caused them to quickly dress and flee.

Burgess checked the dishwasher. Two water glasses. Two wine glasses. Two plates. Two sets of silverware. The TV was cold, the remotes neatly lined up on the coffee table. Aside from the disorder caused by a hasty search, the only thing out of place was a pair of small blue flats between the couch and the coffee table.

Did the hasty search and the fact that their cars were still there suggest coercion? Who leaves home in the middle of the night and leaves their car behind? Maybe the McCanns had lit out for the airport. They'd have to check with local taxi companies. And what did that hasty search mean? Were they trying to cleanse the place of any incriminating evidence? Had they been kidnapped? If so, how did that square with a messy search?

Had the kidnapper stashed them somewhere while he searched the condo?

Burgess was so tired of questions without answers. And yes, he knew it was his job to find those answers. Most investigations were like putting puzzles together. This was like working with a box where the pieces from several puzzles had been jumbled together. It was still their job to figure out how the pieces fit together.

The contents of drawers and cupboards had been spilled onto the floor, except in the kitchen. Maybe whatever the searcher had been looking for wasn't easy to hide among the silverware and cooking utensils and that was why those drawers hadn't been emptied. Kyle began going through the piles in the living room, while Burgess took the kitchen. But while Kyle was coming up empty in the living room, Burgess had a find in the kitchen. At the bottom of a stack of neatly folded dishtowels, he found two disks, wrapped in a faded holiday towel. Remembering the hidden phones at the Dornan's, he carefully checked the stacked pots and pans, but there was nothing there. Nothing in the flour or the sugar. But in a plastic bin that held gravy mixes and taco mixes and dried chilies and bags of nuts, he found two more disks. If the person who'd searched the house was looking for these, they hadn't done a very good job.

Unless there had been many more and these last few were overlooked? Did overlooking any disks suggest someone other than McCann was doing the searching? Unless one of the McCanns was hiding these from the other?

He wondered if McCann's wife, Annie, knew what her husband was into, and that the evidence was right here in their home? Could he have hidden these in their kitchen and not had them discovered? Maybe, if McCann did the cooking. Or was it possible that this was a shared deviance, and the couple got off on watching children being abused?

Leaving Kyle to finish the living room, he headed into the bedroom. On the dresser was the McCann's wedding picture. Annie was petite and pretty, and stared up at her new husband looking gloriously happy to be marrying the man of her dreams. If she didn't know about his sick predilections, what would it be like when she found out that the man she'd married liked to rape children, and collected videos of other men raping them? He couldn't imagine anyone going into a marriage knowing this about a spouse, or staying in a marriage to such a man.

McCann said she was a teacher. Most teachers he knew cared deeply about their students. How could she spend her day working with children, and come home to him? Was she innocently blind or willfully blind? They needed to find her and ask.

What had he told Kyle once? We're just the cotton pickers. Someone else has to spin it into cloth. Every time they got close to picking this cotton, a puff of ill wind blew it away.

He paused in his search as pain jacked through him. His stomach felt like he'd swallowed something hot and sharp. The monster was awake. Now it would clamor and gnaw until the case was over, and it would hurt. The only thing it wanted to be fed was solutions. Arrests. Justice.

He searched the bedroom drawers. The boxes on the shelf in the closet. The pockets of the hanging clothes. Nothing. He leafed through the books on the bedside table. Her bedside table. Neither of them had gotten to the McCann's small study when Kyle stuck his head in.

"I got a feeling, Joe. Gonna go check out the garage."

"Be careful."

"Always careful," Kyle said, which was pretty much the truth. When they said "Be careful" to each other, they meant especially careful. They meant they were dealing with a killer or killers who brutalized and murdered without compunction. Or hesitation.

The garage door opened, shut, then opened again. Kyle stuck his head in. "Come here," he said, and disappeared again.

Burgess abandoned his search of the bedroom and followed Kyle to the garage. Kyle had the lift gate of the Mini up, and was staring at something inside. Burgess's stomach flipped. *Please, no,* he thought. *Not another body.*

"Wink and Dani are not going to be pleased," Kyle said. "He distinctly said no more bodies."

"Oh, he always says that. I think he meant no more crime scenes until they catch up," Burgess said. "I guess we have another crime scene." He stared at the large duffle bag, unzipped to show the curled up form that was probably Annie McCann. "Is she dead?"

Kyle shook his head. "No. But she might have been if we hadn't come tonight. Some kind of drug overdose, I think. I've got Medcu on the way. Help me get her out."

They lifted the small woman whose wedding picture said she was Annie McCann out of the bag and turned her on her side. She wore shorts and a tank top. Her feet were bare. It was hot in the garage, but her skin was clammy.

"You check the other car yet? See if McCann is in there?" Burgess asked.

"Yes. And no, he's not there."

"I don't get it," Burgess said, hitting the button to raise the garage door. "I don't get any of it. If those are McCann's disks, he wouldn't have to tear the house apart, searching for them. So that must have been someone else. Most likely suspect is our mystery man Lawrence. But where's McCann?"

"Unless she hid them," Kyle said, "and her husband was looking for them. Maybe in a few hours Mrs. McCann can tell us what happened here tonight. She might even know Lawrence's last name, he being a good friend of her husband's and all."

Burgess went out to move the truck to make way for the ambulance. The rain was heavier now, and the night had the dusty smell of rain on hot pavement. It also felt heavy and ominous, like finding McCann missing and his wife drugged and left for dead was only the beginning of another long, awful night. He'd always liked nights, but this week was ruining that. He was going to start sleeping in the daytime. If he got a chance to sleep at all in a case Kyle had correctly called Whack a Mole.

They were standing in the shelter of the garage, watching the approaching lights of the ambulance, when Burgess's phone buzzed. Too late for anything but an emergency. He pulled it out and checked the number. His sister Sandy.

Puzzled, he raised the phone to his ear and mumbled "Burgess."

Without even a hello, Sandy's terror poured into his ear. "Cherry is missing, Joe. She didn't come home."

A gasp for breath, then she said, "She wanted to help you with your investigation. She said she had an idea about someone who might be involved. I told her to call you. Tell you what she knew and let you follow up. That if she was right, this man is dangerous. But dammit, Joe! She wants to be a cop like you, and insisted she had to investigate it herself. Like this was all a fun adventure. And now she hasn't come home. She always obeys her curfew or calls. But she didn't and she's not answering her phone. It's going straight to voice mail."

"Tell me everything she said."

Sandy's incoherent words filled his ears, a jumble of statements, worries, and speculation. Beside him, the ambulance was pulling up, its engine roar drowning out her voice. He moved back inside so he could hear.

"Slow down and take it step by step," he said.

"What's there to tell? Since she saw the photo that fell out of your briefcase, the one of the girl who was murdered, the girl she knew from school, she's been trying to figure out how she could help."

The words 'it's all your fault' were implied, if not spoken, and she was teetering on the edge of hysteria. He had to get her focused and answering his questions before she became totally incoherent. "She thinks the person who killed Shelley Minor may be connected with her school?" he asked.

"She didn't say that, but she did say 'It could be him.' Only when I asked her who he was, she said never mind and went in her room and shut the door. I think maybe she's talked to Dylan about this. About her suspicions."

Nothing that Dylan had mentioned to him. Unless this was what Dylan had been referring to when he asked about helping a friend. He wondered if Dylan was home, or off helping his cousin play detective. But if Cherry had a lead on the bad guy they were looking for, there was no playing about this.

He pushed away an image of holding Cherry when she was an infant. Her wise eyes and the little curious moons of her eyebrows. Her smooth, perfect forehead. The way her tiny hand curled around his finger. "When did you last talk to her?" he asked.

"Around nine. She said she was at her friend Eliza's house and they were going to watch a movie. I reminded her about curfew and she said not to worry. She'd be home."

"Did you call Eliza?"

"Of course I called Eliza. Dammit, Joe, do you think I'm an idiot?"

He thought she was the hysterical mother of a missing child. Sister of a cop or not, they were difficult people to get information from. "What did Eliza say?"

"That Cherry isn't there. That she was on and off the phone with someone all evening. It sounded like they were arguing. Then someone she referred to as a 'friend' picked her up around ten."

"You know the name of that friend?"

"I don't because Eliza didn't."

"Eliza wasn't surprised? Suspicious? She didn't wonder what Cherry was up to?"

"She was surprised. She said Cherry had been acting weird all evening, and then she'd called someone to come and get her and off they went."

"Does she know anything about who Cherry called? Male? Female? Anything?"

"She says she doesn't."

"Did she see the car?"

"Dammit, Joe! I am not a detective. You can call her yourself." She rattled off a number.

His sister sounded like she was at the end of her rope. He dealt with people in distress all the time. The fact that she was his sister didn't make it easier. Sandy wasn't good at answering his questions at the best of times, which this was not. She always wanted to turn things into an argument, even when it was the most unproductive thing she could do to help her daughter.

"Did you ask her if she saw the car?" he asked again.

"She didn't."

"Do you have a school yearbook there?"

"Somewhere," she said, sounding puzzled. He knew. She wanted him to get out there and move heaven and earth, not ask questions like a detective or proceed in a methodical way. She just wanted him to fix it. But he couldn't move heaven, or earth, without some idea what part of it needed moving.

"Go find it. I'll hold on."

Heart pounding with anxiety for his missing niece, he rocked from foot to foot while he waited for Sandy to come back to the phone.

"I've got it," she said.

He'd been going to direct her to look for the mysterious Lawrence, but it would be too hard to explain. He needed to do that himself. Look at the yearbook. Ask more questions. Take a look at Cherry's room. Her computer. "I'm on my way," he said.

Stan Perry appeared, looking excited. "I found his production studio," he said. "Cameras. Computers for editing. Machines for copying disks. Stacks of blank disks. He's even got a program for making cute little inserts for the jewel cases to hint at the contents. What's up down here?"

"Great job, Stan," he said. "Looks like we need patrol to sit on this."

"Patrol is going to hate us," Kyle said.

There was so much more to do here, but Burgess had a family emergency. He brought Kyle and Perry up to speed.

"We'll finish up here. Call us if you need us," Kyle said.

He headed out to his truck, cursing himself every step for the foolish enthusiasm he'd displayed when he told his niece about his work. He should have told her horror stories instead. Now, given what he'd learned about the people he was dealing with, a sweet sixteen-year-old girl he loved might have set herself up to become his next horror story.

FORTY

Acting on a hunch, he swung by his house on the way to Sandy's. Unfortunately, he was right. Chris's car was gone. His worry level, already amped up to the point where it was hard to breathe, went into the stratosphere. His foolishly chivalrous son had just broken both family rules and the law, and helped put himself, and Cherry, in grave danger. He could be pissed and disappointed later. Right now, he had to find them before something awful happened. If it wasn't already too late.

He drove to Sandy's house at speeds far in excess of what was safe in the city, even in the middle of the night.

His sister opened the door before he could knock, looking so much like their mother, in their mother's ratty old green bathrobe, that it took him a minute to focus. He followed her into the living room, where her husband and Maddie perched anxiously on the edge of the sofa.

"You'll find her, Joe, right?" his sister said.

He nodded. Part of the cop's job. Be reassuring, not matter how strong your doubts. "Do any of you have any idea what Cherry might be up to? Is there anything she's said or done that suggest where she's gone?"

"I heard her talking on the phone to someone," Maddie said. "I couldn't make most of it out, she was kind of whispering, but I did hear the words 'past Westbrook.' Does that help?"

"It may," he said. The child looked so terrified that he added, "It may help a lot."

He turned to Sandy. "Got that yearbook?" he said. "And did Cherry's school give you a staff directory?"

"I'll look," she said, thrusting the yearbook at him.

Trying to ignore their frightened faces, he sat down and opened the yearbook, turning the pages slowly, studying any pictures that had faculty or staff. He found the man he was looking for way in the back, in a group photo labeled "Counseling Staff." A big man, fifties, hard face, and there on the lapel, a tiny pin with the number fifteen.

He got out his phone. Called Dispatch and asked for a driver's license and address for Lawrence Cashman. In case they couldn't locate it, and because Cashman and his pal Dornan liked to play games with their identities, he also asked for contact information for the principal, a woman named Rosetta Pinette. While he waited, he asked if he could look around Cherry's room. Sandy hesitated a moment, and he watched the mother's protective instinct to guard her child's privacy war with the reality of the situation. The mother who wanted to say "I trust my child" recognizing that she couldn't.

At last she said, "Sure," and led him to Cherry's room. It was a pink extravaganza, a decorating choice he was sure was more Sandy compensating for the leanness of their childhood than Cherry, with a big desk made from a door on two sets of legs. The bed was piled with stuffed animals. The desk was more serious and adult, with neat piles of books, her drawing materials, and her music. He opened her laptop and looked at Sandy. "What's her password?"

His sister shrugged. This was where parents so often went wrong. In the interest of showing their kids that they were trusted, parents took a hands off approach, one that prevented them from checking their children's online activity and monitoring where their searches went. "I trust you" sounded good, but these were still children, with developing brains, and it was easy for them to get into conversations with the wrong people, visit the wrong websites, and get bullied, or be bullies, on social media without parental oversight.

Sandy read his disapproval and got defensive. "We trust her," she said, and then turned away at the ridiculous sound of her own words.

"Do you think Maddie knows?"

"Why would she—" Sandy began, then headed for the door. "I'll ask her."

She was back a moment later, just as his phone rang. He wrote down the address for Lawrence Cashman, and the contact information for Rosetta Pinette, then looked at her expectantly.

His sister gave him the password.

He logged in, then checked his niece's Facebook messages. A long back and forth with Dylan. He could almost picture the two of them, Cherry passionate and wheedling, Dylan cautious and protective. He knew why Dylan had agreed to do something so foolish. Cherry wouldn't back down, and his protective son wouldn't let her go alone. If Dylan hadn't agreed to drive, Cherry would have found someone else. Someone Dylan wouldn't trust to be careful or resourceful.

He then checked the school handbook that Sandy had placed on the desk. Astonishingly, in a time when everyone was extremely protective of their faculty and staff, Rosetta Pinette's phone number was listed.

He called her, identifying himself as a police officer to the man who answered. A moment later, she was on the phone, and he explained why he was disturbing her in the middle of the night.

"Larry is good with the kids," she said, "but he doesn't interact much with staff or faculty. His performance is on my list to review this summer. But I've never seen any signs of a threat to our girls. Or any kind of inappropriate interactions."

He didn't say anything, and she added, in a lower voice, "But then, we both know, don't we, Detective, that that is how predators work. How can I help?"

He explained about the false identities, the missing students, and their urgent need to locate Lawrence Cashman. He read her the address he'd gotten from dispatch, and asked if she knew whether it was correct.

"It's correct. That is, it's the address we have in our records, too. But I believe that Larry also has a camp somewhere on a lake. I think he takes his senior advisees there for a cookout during graduation week."

"I need an address," he said. "As soon as possible."

"I know you do," she said. "Let me make some calls and get back to you."

"I'll get back to you" was phrase cops heard far too often, usually without any further response. He could only hope that this time would be different. She sounded like she meant it.

While he waited for her to call him back, and his sister paced and stared daggers at him, he called Kyle and Perry to give them a head's up that he would need them soon. He wasn't about to go up against a man who had killed at least three people without some backup. Going into dangerous situations without backup or telling someone where you were going was stupid policing 101. Cops on TV did it all the time, which was one reason he couldn't watch cop shows. True, sometimes you just had to act, but in most situations, there was at least time to give dispatch your destination.

He got a laconic, "Terry Kyle" and an eager "Stan Perry," and told them to saddle up and he'd be back to them soon with a destination. Then he went back to waiting for Dr. Pinette's call, poking around on Cherry's desk as he waited. Nothing in her FB chat, and nothing on her desktop. But Burgess was a cop, so he also checked her wastebasket. He didn't find an address, but he did find the impression of a hand-drawn map, which he illuminated with light pencil. It wasn't much use if he didn't know where he was going, but it would be a big help once he got an address.

Sandy's pacing was driving him crazy. "Can you go pace in the living room, please? It's distracting," he said.

"Can you go find my daughter, instead of standing here like a big lump? I thought you were a detective."

"I am a detective. But I'm not psychic, Sandy. Maine's a big state with a lot of lakes. If I'm going to find the right camp, I need more to go on than that the guy has a camp on a lake. You know what would help?"

"What?"

"If you could make me some coffee. It's already been a long night, and it won't end anytime soon. Coffee would help,"

"You want me to bake a cake, too?"

"Just go make the fucking coffee, Sandy, okay?"

His sister stalked out of the room, slamming the door behind her.

He tried not to get sucked in, but Sandy had spent a lifetime pushing his buttons, and she was always worse when she was stressed.

His phone rang. Dr. Pinette.

"Detective Burgess, I think I've got an address for you. It's from a former student, and she was a little shaky on the details. But here's what she told me." She gave a series of directions, which he wrote down. "I left a message for another student, one who is a bit more reliable, but I don't know when she'll get it, if she's asleep. I didn't want to keep you waiting."

It was a sketchy set of directions, but he thought that, along with Cherry's map, he could find the place.

"This is great, Dr. Pinette. If you do learn more, please call me. Meanwhile, I'll work with this."

He called Kyle and Perry and set a meeting place. Then he headed out, stopping in the kitchen, where Sandy was standing in the middle of the room, staring at the coffee maker. No coffee making was in process.

"I've got an address. I'm going to check it out. Can you give me Cherry's cell number? I'm not sure I have it."

She gave him the number, then followed him into the living room. "Wait. I'm coming with you."

"No. You're not. This is a police operation. The person we're looking for has a gun and he may have other armed persons with him. I am not taking you into that. And I'm not taking you anywhere in that damned bathrobe."

She looked down at herself, surprised to find she wasn't dressed. Then she buried her head in her hands and sank onto the sofa. "Just find her, Joe. Please."

And Burgess went to find her.

FORTY-ONE

It was still raining, which had its pros and cons. Pros like being able to approach a cottage unheard because of the sound of the rain. Cons like someone could approach them unheard. And cons like how rain interfered with visibility and their ability to communicate with each other. It also made navigation on unmarked camp roads difficult. It seemed like half the camps in Maine were located on dirt tracks designated only by fire road numbers. He didn't know if that would be true here. He had imprecise directions, not route numbers or house numbers.

If time were on their side, and if it were daytime, they could confirm the address and camp location at the town office. But town offices weren't available to the midnight musketeers. They were flying mostly blind, and that did nothing to enhance their safety.

He met up with Kyle and Perry in the parking lot of a twenty-four hour convenience store and made a plan. They would ride together in the Explorer. They would park at a spot they estimated was maybe a quarter of a mile from the camp, and approach on foot from there. They had notified dispatch of their destination, and contacted the local police and explained their situation. Some available officers would be sent to monitor the road and provide back up if they needed it. Burgess and the shift commander on duty agreed that local officers would wait at the parking spot unless they were called on for assistance.

Police departments were usually glad to offer assistance, and it was courtesy to let a department know if you were conducting an operation on their turf. Burgess appreciated it. He just didn't want to put anyone at risk if it wasn't necessary. The local shift commander said he was sure that Cashman had a boat, and asked if they'd like him to contact the wardens to cover an escape by water. Burgess decided they'd try to disable any boats on their own, but thanked him for the offer.

With no way of knowing whether Cary McCann was their quarry's friend, or prisoner, they didn't know how many adversaries they might be facing or how difficult it would be to safely extricate two over-ambitious teenagers, if those teenagers were even at the site.

It was unnerving to face so many variables.

They drove without their usual banter. Everyone was so bone weary by this time that they just wanted to get in there, do the job, and get out with everyone in one piece. That seemed like a lot to hope for. The possibility of armed adversaries, injuries to themselves, or of finding Dylan and Cherry injured or dead, weighed heavily on all of them. Even the adventurous Stan Perry, famous for larking off on his own and taking crazy risks, was subdued. He was a father now, and about to be a husband.

"You don't have to do this, you know," Burgess told them. It was ridiculous, but he had to say it. This was his family's mess. Except of course that it wasn't. They were also here looking for a suspected killer and the man they suspected was his accomplice—a man who had, perhaps, stuffed his own wife in a duffle bag and left her to die in a hot garage. The unanswered questions, and the mysteries of this case, loomed over them like a black cloud, a cloud that would be there until the bad guys were caught.

"Hey, Joe," Kyle said suddenly, "how's your monster doing?"

"Kicking up a bitch of a storm. How's yours?"

"I fed mine a gallon of Pepto-Bismol," Kyle said, "and the little bugger went to sleep."

"What are you talking about?" Perry said. "Do I really have to do this with two old guys who've gone off their rockers?"

"Nope," Kyle said. "You've got to do this with two esteemed colleagues, because you want to be in on it when we rescue Joe's errant family members and catch the bad guys."

Perry grunted and the car went silent again until the GPS told them it was time to park and get out of the truck. As they were getting out and gathering their weapons, flashlights, and other useful stuff, a local police car slid in behind them and two officers got out.

They introduced themselves. Burgess introduced his team. Then the older of the officers, a seasoned guy with smart eyes, said, "What do you want us to do?"

"Block the road and stop anyone from leaving," Burgess said. "Hopefully, this will go down quietly, but we're not sure what we're dealing with."

"Okay. But don't be heroes, okay? Call us if you need us."

"We will," Burgess said. He hoped his heroic days were behind him.

They all exchanged phone numbers, then the three musketeers headed for what they hoped would be Lawrence Cashman's cottage. They walked quietly, Burgess in the lead. Their phones on vibrate. Guns in one hand, flashlights ready in the other. Eventually, the road forked, a driveway going right, the rest of the road going left. According to the map he'd found in Cherry's room, they wanted to go right. Down the gravel track, around a bend, and up ahead they could see three vehicles parked. One was the black town car. One was Chris's car. The third, a white van, was a mystery.

"I've got this," Perry said, creeping forward until he could read the plate, then stepping back around the bend to call dispatch. They stood still as statues, surrounded by the infuriating buzz of mosquitoes, while Perry made the call.

"It's registered to Annie McCann," he said.

Which didn't tell them much, since they knew Annie McCann wasn't inside and hadn't driven the vehicle here. But maybe her husband had. Had he drugged his wife, left her to die in that duffle bag, and then driven here? And why? To make an escape plan with Cashman?

"Okay," Burgess said. "Stan, you go around to the waterfront and see if you can disable any boats you find there. Disable or set adrift. Terry, you take the back. I'll slip up along the far side and see if I can see in the windows."

Quietly, their three black figures moved through the darkness. It was a foul night, but the lack of a moon or stars meant they were much harder to see in the darkness. There were no lights to the rear of the cottage, but they could see light spilling out the front rooms.

Burgess moved slowly along the side of the house until he reached a lighted window. He raised up and peered in. He was looking into a large open room with rustic pine paneling and a big stone fireplace flanked by two large picture windows looking toward the lake. There was a door beside the fireplace leading out, Burgess thought, to a deck or a porch. Two men were standing at the far end of the room, talking. One was Cary McCann. The other was Lawrence Cashman. Dylan lay on the floor in front of the fireplace, a pool of blood around his head. Cherry was on the couch facing the fireplace, bound with duct tape, tears running down her face, her eyes on the silent figure on the floor.

As he watched, he saw Dylan's eyes open, then close again. Alive! Stay still, he beamed the thought at his son. Play dead. Don't give them any reason to hit you again.

How many times had he observed scenes like this, with a bad guy or guys, and hostages? Willed the best result? Wished he could he transmit his thoughts into another head, calm a terrified victim? Ten? Twenty? Dozens? It was always tense. Always affected his breathing. But never like this. Parenthood with Dylan came to him slowly, in increments. He'd never had what Stan Perry was experiencing—the awesome responsibility of the birth of his baby.. The huge and magical moment of greeting a newborn. He hadn't known about Dylan—the child of a girlfriend who'd suddenly moved away and never told him why—for almost the first fifteen years of his son's life. But to his amazement, these attaching moments kept happening. And now this: Dylan the instinctive rescuer acting on impulse, without the knowledge or experience to handle the situation. Burgess had to somehow arrest Cashman and McCann without getting his niece or his son killed. Hopefully without getting anyone killed.

Seeing his son lying there, injured, possibly gravely, and Cherry so terrified, brought out a searing, protective rage. He wanted to burst through the window into the room and shoot both men. He stepped on his anger. He hadn't kept himself and others alive over the years by yielding to his impulses. Tension wrapped him so tight it hurt to breathe.

He didn't trust that Cashman and McCann were the only bad guys here. People had seen a Hispanic male driving the white van, so there might be a third man. He hoped that was all. For all he knew, Cashman and company had a small army to help them run their dirty business.

Through the rain, he heard faint sounds of splashing that were probably Perry taking care of the boats. Then, over the roar of the rain, he heard another sound, the soggy squash of footsteps coming his way. He melted back into the space by the bay window and turned his head to hide the white of his skin, watching from the corner of his eye. The footsteps got closer. And closer. Burgess stayed still, a skill he'd mastered in the jungle long ago.

He waited until the man was right beside him, then turned and grabbed him, one arm around his neck, the other across him mouth. He dragged the struggling man to the rear of the house and down past the bend in the driveway.

Kyle joined him there, producing a roll of duct tape and binding the man's arms and legs.

"How many of you are there?" Burgess whispered.

The man didn't answer.

Burgess shifted his arm just slightly, putting pressure on the man's shoulder. The man winced but stayed silent. He increased the pressure and the man's eyes opened wide, watering with the pain.

"How many?" Burgess repeated.

Still no answer. He increased the pressure until the man was almost whimpering. "Those men in there—McCann and Cashman—will be spending the rest of their lives in prison for the rape and murder of children," he said. "You're a part of this, so you go, too. And life means life. Things will go better for you if you cooperate. The choice is yours."

He waited, but evidently this man was more frightened of Cashman and McCann than of anything Burgess could say. They didn't have time for persuasion. Cherry and Dylan were in there with two armed and ruthless men.

They put duct tape over the man's mouth, dragged him into the woods, and duct taped him to a tree. A search of his pockets yielded a cell phone, a folding knife, and some cash, but no identification.

"Let's try to remember where we left him," Kyle whispered just loud enough for the man to hear. "Lotta hungry bear around here."

They were almost back to the house when they heard footsteps again. Could be Stan Perry. Could be another bad guy. They faded back into the bushes and waited. A moment later, a small man appeared, holding a gun out in front of him like he was waterskiing. Burgess stepped out to block the man's path, while Kyle grabbed him from behind. Burgess twisted the gun from the man's hands and they dragged him back around the bend. Once again, Burgess asked his question. Once again, he got no answer. They left bad guy number two on the opposite side of the driveway, fastened to another tree.

"Hope there aren't too many of them," Kyle whispered. "I'll run out of duct tape. What did you see inside?"

"The kids are there. Dylan's lying on the floor in a pool of blood. Cherry's tied up on the couch."

"Do you think…" Kyle began. Then stopped.

"He's alive."

"We should check on Stan. He should be done by now."

By unspoken agreement, Burgess took the right side of the house and

Kyle the left. They met no more patrolling men with guns. When they reached the front of the house, they stayed to the sides in the shadows, avoiding the center of the lawn where light spilled out from the house. They slipped down the lawn to the dock. They could see two boats drifting away. There was no sign of Stan Perry.

Then Kyle whispered, "Over there. By the tree."

Off to the side, where one wet black tree stood out from the rest, there was a crumpled black lump. Hunched and slow, they crossed the lawn to the lump. It wasn't Stan Perry. They used a bit of Kyle's duct tape to make sure the man caused no more trouble, then returned together to the window Burgess had looked in before.

McCann and Cashman had moved to the center of the room and were staring out the picture window. Cashman looked concerned. McCann looked like he was saying something reassuring. In the far corner, Stan Perry was slowly edging his way into the room.

FORTY-TWO

"Oh fuck!" Kyle whispered. "There goes Stan again. I thought having Autumn might have changed him."

"You take the back. I'll take the front," Burgess said. No time to do anything more. He took a moment to send a text to the officers out at the road, saying they needed backup and an ambulance. Kyle had already slithered away, quick and silent. Burgess moved to the front of the house and quietly mounted the steps to the porch, his voluble knee letting him know it was tired of all this stomping around and ready to quit for the day. He moved past the first window, and past the big brick chimney, gun up and ready.

Through the door, he could see McCann and Cashman turn away from the window toward the corner where Stan Perry had been standing. He couldn't see the corner. Couldn't tell if Perry was still there or if they were responding to a noise.

The inner door was open, only the screen door closed. Praying it wasn't locked, he pushed on it gently. Not locked. He opened it slowly, knowing how the springs on cottage doors like to screech and snap. Screen doors also like to slam, so he closed it carefully behind him. He stepped into the room, gun up, the thud and squish of his wet feet on the old fir boards causing McCann and Cashman to turn. Two big men and two big guns now facing him.

"Police," he said. "Drop your weapons."

Being on the business end of a gun never got easier.

He reminded himself to breathe.

"Police. Drop your weapons," he said again. More loudly this time. Sometimes it took volume and force to penetrate the tunnel vision of the person holding a gun. He knew he looked a lot less like a cop than a drowned rat. But this wasn't about appearances. It was about authority.

His niece gave a shuddering sob and began to scream. McCann, and his gun, started turning toward her and Burgess shot him. McCann went down on one knee, and took a shot at Burgess. He felt it thud into his vest and his chest exploded with spreading pain as he slammed back against the door. He managed to get off another shot. This time, McCann went down and stayed down.

He shifted his focus back to Cashman, who was moving toward Cherry and Dylan. Two potential hostages. There was a blur of movement as Stan Perry launched himself at Cashman, slamming him to the floor, his hand, and his gun, trapped under his body. Perry knelt on his back while Kyle wrestled one hand free, snapped a cuff on it, and began cautiously easing out the other hand with the gun. Burgess saw Perry sense Cashman's intent to rear up and use the gun, and he shifted one of his knees to the back of Cashman's neck.

Puddles formed where water dripped off their bodies and clothes, and Kyle's dark hair was slicked to his head, making him look like a sleek seal. A fierce-faced, blue-eyed seal.

"Give it up, Cashman," Kyle commanded. "You've lost. Now give us the gun."

"You will step away from that man," a new voice commanded. He had a slight Hispanic accent. Another small man with a gun. It seemed Cashman and McCann did have a small army.

"All right. All right, I'm moving," Stan Perry said, as Kyle stopped trying to wrestle Cashman's arm out and rocked back on his heels.

"Drop your guns," the man commanded. His eyes were on Kyle and Perry.

Burgess, fearing any sudden move might get one of them shot, yelled, "Watch out. Behind you. He's right behind you!" Oldest trick in the book. It stayed in the book because it worked.

The man turned and Perry launched himself, slamming the smaller man to the floor. Burgess covered Kyle as Cashman's gun hand came out and Kyle jerked the gun from his hand.

Cherry was still screaming.

Burgess helped Kyle capture and cuff Cashman's second hand. Despite his position working in a school, where presumably background checks had been conducted, Cashman's resistance suggested he'd been handcuffed before. Burgess tucked Cashman's gun into his belt. Then Kyle went to help Stan Perry subdue his man.

Burgess turned to his niece. "Shut up, Cherry," he said. "You're not helping."

She sucked in a shuddering breath and gave him a furious stare. "I found the bad guy," she said in a sobbing voice.

"And you damned near got a lot of people killed tonight. Including my son, yourself, and three fine cops." It wasn't kind, but he wasn't feeling kind. There would be time for kind later. He was feeling like if she really wanted to be a cop, she needed to work on her judgment. He was feeling like nearly getting herself and Dylan killed—never mind the rest of them—wasn't a good move and she didn't deserve coddling and a pat on the head. She needed to understand the enormity of what she'd done and the danger she'd caused.

Anyway, right now the issue was not people's feelings. It was getting the bad guys under control and making sure everyone was okay.

Holding his side, which hurt like he'd been kicked by a mule, he limped over to Dylan, pulling out one of the handkerchiefs he always carried and mopping blood off his son's face. Dylan had a nasty head wound, but Burgess males have hard heads. He thought Dylan would be okay, but seeing his son's still, white face shook him.

The boy's lids fluttered, then opened, and there were his dark brown eyes. Burgess eyes. Eyes that looked confused. Dylan's face twisted with pain.

"It's okay," Burgess said. "It's okay. We've got you. Cherry is okay. McCann and Cashman are in custody. And help is on the way."

Dylan's mouth moved between a wince and a smile. "Thought *you* were the help."

"I've noticed you all feel that way sometimes," Burgess said. "When I make dinner, maybe I am the help. Right now, I'm a cop rescuing a couple of reckless kids from the bad guys."

His son smiled and Burgess gripped his hand.

Dylan closed his eyes with a sigh. Burgess's son was not a happy camper. "My head feels broken," he said. Then, "I'm in pretty deep shit, aren't I?"

"You are. Not something to worry about right now."

He looked around the room. Kyle had Cashman on his stomach on the floor, hands cuffed behind him and was duct taping his ankles. Perry had the Hispanic man cuffed, also on his stomach, waiting for his turn with the duct tape. The man was swearing up a storm in Spanish and glaring daggers at everyone.

Burgess checked McCann's pulse. It wasn't strong, but the man was alive. If they'd had more handcuffs, he would have thrown some on McCann just to be safe. Many a cop has lost his life to someone deemed not to be a threat because he's injured. Duct tape would have to do.

He went to the kitchen to find some scissors so he could cut Cherry loose. It hurt to breathe. To move. He really wanted to lie down somewhere and die a quiet death away from prying eyes. Like so often in his world, his own issues would have to wait.

Cherry submitted to his ministrations without a word, but if his read was right, she wasn't sulking anymore. She was embarrassed. When she was finally freed, she murmured a quick "thanks" and threw herself down on the floor beside Dylan. Burgess assumed her quiet mutterings were apologies for nearly getting Dylan killed and getting him in trouble with his parents.

Burgess surveyed the room. There were more things he was supposed to be doing. This place needed to be searched. Vehicles needed to be towed. There were a zillion reports to write, twice as many because he'd fired his gun. But like a popped balloon, he was suddenly flattened. He didn't protest when Kyle took his arm, led him to the couch, and started unbuttoning his shirt.

"I'm okay, Ter. It's just a bruise."

"We both know about these bruises," Kyle said, fumbling at the wet buttons with tired fingers. "There's no 'just' about them."

At that moment, the cavalry arrived. The two officers from out on the road, followed by the wail of an ambulance, and then Melia was there with more Portland officers.

Kyle abandoned his effort to unbutton Burgess's shirt, uttered a curt "stay here" and led a contingent outside to collect the three men they'd already subdued. Melia used his cuffs on McCann and Stan Perry oversaw loading him into the ambulance while an EMT checked out Dylan's injuries, wrapping his head wound in gauze until it could get stitched.

"You want me to take Dylan to Maine Med, Joe?" Melia asked.

Burgess considered. He didn't want to let his son out of his sight, but there was also Cherry, who needed to be returned to her mom. And Chris's car. Cashman's car and the van to tow to 109 and search. The cottage to search.

His brain was running lists. His body was calling it a day.

"I'll take him. If you could take Cherry back to my sister's—"

"I'm staying with Dylan," Cherry said.

"Okay. But call your mother first." Burgess held his phone out to her.

"I don't want—"

"Pardon the language, beloved niece, but right now I don't give a flying fuck what you want. Your shenanigans put three police officers in grave danger. Not that you would have thought of this, but everything's a lot more complicated when there are hostages involved. You could have gotten yourselves and all of us killed because you wanted to play girl detective."

He shook the phone. "Make the damned call."

She took the phone and went into a corner where she crouched over the phone, her back to them. He heard her tentative, "Mom? It's me. I'm sorry. I'm so, so sorry. No. It's okay. I'm okay. Dylan's hurt, but I'm okay. Uncle Joe came to get us." Anything else she might have said was drowned by tears. After a while, he heard her say, "Yes. He's here. Hold on." She held the phone out to him.

The last thing on earth he wanted to do right now was listen to any more of Sandy's worries, criticisms, or complaints. Despite the warm night, he was wet and chilled and he hurt. He took the phone.

Sandy's words were an echo of her daughter's. "I'm sorry, Joe. I'm sorry I was such a bitch to you. Thank you for saving my daughter." Then she dissolved in sobs.

"It's okay, Sandy," he said, not sure what was okay, but always the protective big brother. "I'm going to take them to Maine Med to get Dylan checked out, then I'll bring her home."

"Checked out? Is Dylan okay?"

"Dylan's hurt."

"Is it bad? Is he? Will he be—"

Burgess cut her off. "I don't know, Sandy. We can talk about this later. I've got a crime scene to deal with right now."

Miraculously, his sister didn't argue. He disconnected.

He put his phone away and looked at Melia. "Can you take over here? I've got to get my kid stitched up…"

"Are you okay?" Melia looked at the hole in his shirt. Then studied his face. "You look like hell."

"Bruised. You know how it is."

Melia shook his head. "Joe? You know the protocol. You need to get checked out."

"I just want to go home. Can someone drive the little white car back to my house?"

"Thought I saw your Explorer. You came in two cars?"

"I'm good, but not that good."

Melia grinned.

Burgess jerked his chin toward his son. "A certain unlicensed driver 'borrowed' his mother's car to help his cousin do some detective work."

"I'll take care of it."

"Grateful," Burgess said. He was drifting, in danger of falling asleep in a room full of people again.

Then Kyle's hand was hauling him up. "Time to go. We can finish this mess tomorrow. Gotta get you and Dylan checked out."

"I'm fine."

"Melia's orders."

"We never leave—"

"Well, we're about to. A certain police detective I tend to look up to often reminds me that people come first. And like it or not, Joe, you are a person."

Burgess didn't feel much like a person. He felt like a semi-ambulatory ball of pain.

Kyle held out his hand. "Your keys."

He hated having to lean on Kyle, but he needed the help of that arm. Stan Perry came behind them, shepherding the kids, one arm around Dylan's shoulders, the other around Cherry's. Burgess's biological family and his work family. It had been a hell of a night.

As they passed the white van, he heard whimpering. "Stan, can you?"

Stan Perry opened the van, and a frantic, half-grown black dog tumbled out.

"Think this is Fideau?" Burgess asked.

At the sound of its name, the dog quieted and looked at Burgess with curious eyes, then approached and licked his hand. He didn't have the bandwidth to deal with anything more tonight, but had the vague feeling that the Burgess family was about to acquire a dog.

Melia, who'd come along behind them, said he'd take care of it.

"Fideau," Burgess said. "Treat him kindly. He's a witness."

As Kyle tucked him into the car, he thought of other times when Kyle had been there for him. Thought about how often Stan's impulsive antics helped them out of tight spots or secured a vital clue. He guessed that while he always thought he wanted Perry to grow up, there was value in the crazy way the kid could make things happen. If he didn't get himself—or them—shot in the process.

"Thanks, Stan," he said.

"Any time, Boss."

"I sure hope not," Kyle said.

The kids in the back were silent, except for the occasional sob from Cherry and some murmured comfort from Dylan. He and Perry and Kyle strategized about interviewing Cashman and McCann and who would cover the Dornan's autopsies.

Despite the pain from rocking on a bumpy road, comforted that the A Team, or The Crips, had things covered, he'd almost drifted off when his phone rang.

He pulled it out, gathering his wits. Chris.

"Hey," he said.

"Don't you 'hey' me," she said. "Your son and my car are both gone. You got any idea what's going on?"

FORTY-THREE

Burgess was trying to formulate an adequate response when Kyle took the phone.

"Hey, Chris," he said. "It's Terry." He listened, said, "Cherry talked Dylan into borrowing your car so she could track down a guidance counselor from her school that she thought might be involved in the homicide of a girl she knew. They ran into some trouble, but it's all taken care of now. We're going to run by the hospital and get some stitches in Dylan's head."

He listened. "No. We think he's okay, except for needing stitches. But they'll probably do a scan to be sure. And your car should be back in your driveway before you need it for work." He listened again.

Burgess felt like a piker, letting Kyle have the hard conversation he should have been having. Nor did he think Chris would let him off the hook that easily. She liked Terry Kyle, and she trusted him, but sooner or later, she'd ask the question he and Kyle were hoping to avoid.

"Just some stitches in Dylan's head, Terry? You aren't hiding anything from me? Like the possibility that Joe's been hurt, which is why I'm talking to you instead of him?"

"He was wearing a vest, Chris."

Kyle had the phone on speaker, so Burgess was hearing their conversation.

"And do you think I'm the sort of naïve person who believes that someone wearing a vest can't be hurt?"

"Someone who was wearing a vest is fine, Chris," Burgess said. "They just have to check me out. It's protocol."

"I'll see you there," she said, and ended the conversation.

"Uh oh," came from the back seat. Two voices in chorus.

"Betcha my mom will be there, too," Cherry said. "I am so grounded."

"Dad, is there any way to—"

"No," Burgess said. "I can't think of any good way to tell a woman whose car was stolen that she should stay home and not confront the thief."

There was silence in the back seat. Then Dylan said, "We are so screwed."

Burgess had no response to that. Likely all three of them were screwed, but that was not something to be shared with two errant kids.

They dropped Stan Perry off where they'd left the cars. He'd drive Kyle back to get his car later. They were all eager to get Cashman and McCann into interview rooms. McCann's interview would have to wait until his condition stabilized, but he'd lied to them, raped a child, and shot a cop, so he wouldn't get any slack. Kyle and Perry would take a run at Cashman as soon as Burgess was delivered to the hospital.

Burgess hated to miss that interview, but there was no way he could sneak back to 109 and join his team. Melia would be there.

"I could do it," Burgess said. "I'm fine."

"You're green," said Kyle. "You're moving like a thousand year old man. You need to be sure nothing's busted and your lungs are okay."

From the back seat, little Miss I Want To Be A Detective said, "I thought you were okay if you wore a vest."

"You're more okay than if you don't wear one," Kyle said. "But it's still a lot of blunt force trauma. Ribs can break and organs can be damaged. Now let's all be quiet boys and girls and let the poor man rest."

On quieter roads, in a quiet car, Burgess was just drifting off when Dylan moaned and said, "Oh. God. My head feels like it's exploding. I am so going to be sick."

It could be something. It could be nothing, but Kyle said, "Hold on if you can," and went for lights and sirens the rest of the way, rocking to a stop outside the ER. Dylan bolted out of the car and bent over, vomiting.

Burgess's philosophy about ERs was you got the fastest service if you arrived unconscious. Dylan was discovering the second best way—arrive with a bad head wound and uncontrolled vomiting.

Their reception committee—one woman over the top with anxiety and the other mad as hell—had to delay whatever they wanted to say while

Dylan was wheeled away on a stretcher. Burgess paused a moment with Chris before following, which let her get as far as, "Listen, you. I thought we were done with—" before Dr. Cohen appeared.

"Did you clone yourself, Detective?" she asked.

"Don't you ever go home?"

"Been home. Was home for hours. Don't *you* ever sleep?"

Burgess introduced Chris and gave them both the short version of the night's events. He didn't get to finish before Chris and Sarita Cohen, like twins, said, "You need to get checked out."

He was too tired to argue with two strong women. "As soon as I know Dylan's okay."

"Oh," Dr. Cohen said, "we are a big hospital. I think we can handle two patients at once," and somehow he found himself in a cubicle, on a bed, with a doctor and a nurse taking off his shirt. His vest. His undershirt. And staring at the huge purple bruise on his chest.

Then, it was if Chris and Sarita Cohen had been working together forever, tests were ordered and the official poking and prodding began.

"I'll go check on Dylan," Chris said. She put a warm hand on his naked shoulder, and kissed him before bustling off.

"I thought I told you to stay out of my ER," Dr. Cohen said.

"Believe me, I tried."

"But you found the men? The men who hurt those girls?"

"I did. We did."

"We are all lucky to have you." Correctly reading his desire to get up and go, she put a restraining hand on his chest, warm and comforting against his cold skin. "Rest now. We will make sure no ribs are broken and nothing internally is badly bruised." She gave him her impish smile. "Then you are free to go fight bad guys again. Chris is your wife?"

"She would be if she'd marry me. For now, just the love of my life."

"I heard that," Chris said, stepping through the curtains. "I remember another time, here in this hospital. Me a nurse, you on a gurney…"

"The beginning of something beautiful," he said. That got him a smile.

Switching gears, she said, "They've sent Dylan for a head CT."

He was awfully tired and wondering how long he could stay awake and be polite to these nice women when they did the twin thing again, both saying, "You should rest." And they left him alone.

He dozed through being wheeled here and there for tests, then fell into deeper sleep. He was having an unpleasant dream in which he was reliving those moments in the cottage—McCann turning toward the kids, the shot from McCann's gun, the breathtaking pain in his chest—when he heard someone giggle. It couldn't be coming from his dream. No one in Cashman's cottage had been giggling. Then he felt a hand on his arm. A small hand. He opened his eyes and found four sets of dark eyes staring at him. The moment his eyes were open, there was a barrage of Spanish. *Four voices*, he thought. He knew who his visitors were.

Behind the crowd of girls, Clara Sanchez said, "I am sorry for the intrusion, Detective Burgess. But the girls heard that you were hurt, and they insisted they needed to see you."

"Estas bien?" Bella asked, standing on tiptoe and peering anxiously into his face.

He looked at Sanchez. "How do I?"

"Estoy bien," she said. Then spoke to the girls, assuring them that he was okay.

Bella didn't look convinced. "Need ice cream?" she asked, touching his face with her small hand.

"What time it is?" he asked. "What are you doing here so early?"

They'd arrived in the dark hours. While he'd been dozing, the clock had crept toward nine-thirty.

She smiled. "It's not so early. And there was good news about Maria, so I came in to tell them." Then, ducking her head, "Against all rules, I am becoming attached."

He knew how that was.

"There's good news about Maria?" he asked.

Sanchez nodded. "She has turned the corner. It looks like she will recover."

He looked at the four small girls and found them amazing. After what had happened, they should fear—and hate—all men, yet here they were, concerned about him. It wouldn't be all roses, but Nina and Neddy had taught him how resilient children could be. He smiled at them, then looked at Sanchez. "Can you translate 'later we will have ice cream' for me?"

"With pleasure," she said. She relayed his message and shepherded the girls out.

They were almost instantly replaced by another small, dark-eyed woman. Dr. Cohen. "Was that your fan club?" she said.

"Looks like it. Am I done here?"

"Until the next time." That impish grin again. "You have a cracked rib, which means taking it easy. No vest. No heavy lifting. You know the drill. Please, try to set aside your macho nature and take it seriously."

He took a breath, ready to argue against her assertion. The breath hurt. "I'll try—"

"Try?" she said. "I told Chris. So don't mess up."

"I'm feeling outnumbered."

"By women who want you to take care of yourself? That doesn't seem like a bad thing," she said.

"And my son?"

"The Burgess clone? I'm torn between knowing you'll have a legacy of caretaking and anticipating another twenty years of patching up Burgesses."

"His head?" Burgess said.

"He has a mild concussion. Chris took him home."

Burgess could imagine how that was going to go.

She was watching his face. "She knows what to do."

Maybe she thought he was worried about Dylan's care. Or maybe she understood what Chris and Dylan had to settle between them.

"I'll repeat my admonition, Joe. Stay out of my emergency room, okay?" That fleeting grin again.

"I really did try."

Dr. Cohen left him.

He was ready to leave. He felt like he was marooned on an island. Couldn't stand the information void. He needed to get back to 109 and back into the loop as soon as possible. He had no idea where his car or his car keys were.

The clothes he found near his bed were not the clothes he'd been wearing when he arrived. Those had been wet and dirty and the shirt had a bullet hole in it. Chris must have brought clean ones. He figured someone had collected his shirt and vest. He struggled into his pants—not an easy process when every movement made him want to howl like a wounded animal.

He was buttoning his shirt when Kyle appeared, wearing an uncharacteristic smile.

"We got him. Once he realized what we knew, it all spilled out. He tried to put it all on the Dornans, of course. Like we didn't know he likely shot her. But he said plenty. I'm sorry you weren't there. It was fun!"

Kyle's idea of fun—fixing his cold blue eyes on someone until they squirmed like a bug on a pin. Getting into their face, their space. Calling "bullshit" on their lies in a deadly quiet voice once he'd pinned down those lies. It was Burgess's idea of fun, too. He felt gloom slide over him like he'd been licked by some giant tongue of despair.

"While I am being fussed over by women who want me to take it easy."

This time, Kyle gave the invisible smile. "Like Dr. Cohen?"

Burgess nodded.

"You can have McCann. Will that make you feel better?"

Burgess considered. "It will," he said, but he couldn't shake the gloom.

He thought about the last few days. No Cote at the crime scene last night. No Cote at the hospital. "Did Paul show up to get the scoop?"

Kyle shook his head. "Maybe you scared him out at the Dornans when you nearly took his head off."

"And Melia read me the riot act."

Kyle gave him a 'since when did Joe Burgess care about that?' look. "I don't care why he's not showing up. I'm just happy not to see him."

Not having Cote stick his nose in ought to have been disposition-improving news. He still couldn't shake the gloom. The feeling that he was a hopeless dinosaur that had to go off to the doctor while the other cops got to do police work.

"Something else that won't make your day, but you still want to know," Kyle said.

Burgess waited.

"Sage took the warrant over to Human Services bright and early this morning."

Something Burgess had wanted to do himself. Badly wanted to vent some of his rage over Shelley Minor's death to someone who could have prevented it. "And?"

"Turns out the social worker on the case has been on leave, being treated for cancer, and no one else picked up her caseload. They only assigned it to someone else last week. The poor girl is barely out of college, barely trained, and as soon as she read the file, she tried to get in touch with the foster family."

"Dammit," Burgess said. The agency was overworked, understaffed, and so kids fell through the cracks. The police couldn't be the safety net for all of society. At least they'd done their job.

He contemplated his shoes and socks. Getting into them would be only slightly less awful than being whacked with a baseball bat. Or shot in the chest. "What else?"

"Stan and Sage have gone up to Augusta for the autopsies." Kyle stopped. Gave him another assessing look.

If Kyle could read his mind, Burgess wondered what Kyle was reading.

"Why don't I catch you up over breakfast?" Kyle said.

"As long as it's not here."

Kyle was doing his impatient shift from foot to foot, which increased Burgess's sense of being past it. So past it he couldn't even put on his own goddamned shoes. He wasn't about to ask for help.

"Will you hurry it up, please? I'm starving." Then Kyle stopped vibrating and gave a slight duck of his head. "Sorry. I'm being stupid. But so, for the record, are you. Just let me help you put on your goddamned shoes, okay?"

Burgess let him help with the damned shoes. Then the two of them headed out. Kyle striding forward, rushing toward the promise of fuel, Burgess coming behind him, bent like an old man, glaring at everyone they passed.

FORTY-FOUR

"You need to look on the bright side," Kyle told him, as they sat before heaping platters of breakfast. "We did it. We got the bad guys. Even if McCann lawyers up and never says a word, we've got him. Sure, there's a ton of work ahead, but we've done it."

"I just can't get past the bad stuff," Burgess said.

"I know," Kyle agreed. "I know you always say we just pick the cotton and someone else has to make the cloth, but we do a hell of a lot more than pick cotton."

He picked up his fork and began demolishing eggs, pancakes, and fried potatoes. "Is it the paperwork?"

Burgess shook his head. Paperwork was just part of the job. He tried eating, knowing his body needed fuel to function and to heal. It all tasted like sawdust. He couldn't put his finger on what was bothering him. He wasn't a prima donna. He wasn't a depressive. At least, not often. He'd learned not to let the ugliness and inhumanity of cases get to him.

"Maybe I'm just tired," he said finally. "Getting old. I've fallen asleep twice this week during the day. Something about this case. It just seems to siphon off my energy." He started on a blueberry pancake. It tasted slightly better.

Kyle, whose plate was bare, watched him like a mother watches a fussy eater, a little anxious, a little encouraging. "You need a vacation," he said.

"Think that will fix things? Help me recapture my energy? My passion for the job?"

"Dr. Kyle thinks you're just tired. Burned out. Temporarily out of gas. A vacation can help with that."

"I've got five raped and exploited children and one child raped, exploited, and murdered. It would have to be a hell of a vacation."

"*We've* got five raped and exploited children and one raped and murdered," Kyle said quietly. "You're not in this alone. We've all got to wade through the filth, be baffled that someone can do these things, and then go home to our families."

Burgess looked at his plate, which, despite his lack of appetite, was empty. "I know that, Ter. Just thinking maybe you'd be better off without me. You and Stan could build a new team. I—"

"Stop right there," Kyle said. "Who would be better off without you? You think I want to learn to read someone else's mind? Mind reading is hard. You think I want to handle young Stanley's impulsivity alone? You think I want to work with cops so young they can't quote Shakespeare and don't feel their knuckles ache when they hear the word 'nun'?" Kyle gave it a beat, said, "You want to leave this to detectives who can't read crime scenes? Can't figure out how the bad guys work? You can't do that until you teach them your skills."

Burgess's eyes stayed on the empty plate. He didn't know what to say because he didn't understand his reaction himself. It was as though he'd gotten up on the wrong side of life this morning and couldn't get back.

Their waitress came by. Gave them coffee. Took away their empty plates. Came back with a plate of cinnamon rolls and blueberry muffins. She rested her hand briefly on each of their shoulders and said, "Thank you. I'm a mom, and just…thank you."

Burgess hadn't seen a paper yet. Wasn't sure what they were being thanked for. He'd never much liked being thanked for doing his job anyway.

He felt disconnected. Like Kyle and this waitress and the whole world were far away.

Kyle, who needed as many calories in a day as Burgess did in a week, grabbed a cinnamon roll and demolished it. He didn't say anything. Just sat. Patient and watchful. Waiting for something. Burgess had no idea what they were waiting for. But Kyle, impatient, jittery Terry Kyle, seemed to have all the time in the world this morning.

"Have you seen the paper?" Burgess asked. "Do you know what we're being thanked for?"

"Taking a bunch of child predators off the street."

Kyle took another roll.

"Not before they—"

"Dammit, Joe. Give yourself…give us…some credit, okay?"

Burgess closed his eyes. Saw McCann's gun swing toward Cherry and Dylan. Saw, as surely as if he was still there, his own gun come up. The bullet coming out and charging toward McCann. Striking him and driving him to his knees. He felt Bella's small warm hand on his face, her child's voice asking if he was okay.

He opened his eyes and looked at Kyle. "I said no more children. Please. No more battered, raped, murdered children."

Kyle nodded.

"I knew my soul couldn't take it."

Kyle waited.

"And then we got all these children."

Burgess was beginning to understand. His pain wasn't only about getting shot. It was about doing the hardest part of the job. Having to do it. Needing to do it. And needing to understand the toll it took. When you choose to play on the victim's team, you choose ugliness, pain, regret, rage. The dark side. Nobody made him do it. Except himself. In the aftermath, he could choose to walk away. Or he could choose to fortify and rebuild himself to fight another day.

The world was coming back.

To hell with controlling his weight. With healthy eating. He was a weary old detective with a bruise the size of a salad plate on his chest. He looked at Kyle and took the last cinnamon roll. "So I can live to fight another day."

A WORLD OF DECEIT

A JOE BURGESS MYSTERY, BOOK 7

Burgess was in a hammock under the pines. In a tee shirt and shorts, barefoot, his eyes closed. The summer breeze, warm and gentle, slid over his skin like a caress. Nearby, lake water lapped against the shore. Farther out, there was the muted roar of boat motors. Cedar waxwings bustled busily through the tree overhead. The book he'd been reading lay on his chest, ignored. Chris had taken the kids to the other side of the lake to rent paddle boats so he could have a quiet morning. He was on vacation. Absolutely alone. His phone inside and turned off. No matter what emergency the city of Portland might have, for these two weeks that would be someone else's problem.

His latest homicide put to bed, he was hoping this vacation might restore his energy. Lately, he'd been feeling too old and tired for the job—the word "dinosaur" was cropping up too often in his thoughts—and retirement had been on his mind. Then he'd gotten a call from his favorite ER doc, Sarita Cohen, a woman who had patched up his victims, and himself, many times. Her soft voice was tentative as she said, "Joe, I've taken a liberty here. I hope you won't be angry with me. But I was concerned that you were feeling so tired…" She'd given one of her gentle laughs. "Though with your job, it's no surprise. Anyway. I checked your thyroid function and I think, with medication, you can be more yourself again."

There was another laugh when he said, "The meanest, grouchiest cop in Portland?"

"That's the one. Anyway, stop by when you get a chance and I'll give you your prescription." A hesitation, because people who knew him didn't generally tell Detective Sergeant Joe Burgess what to do. "Do this. Get the script. Take the medication. It's going to help."

So he'd swung by the ER, gotten the prescription, and filled it. Now, while he waited for the miraculous return of his energy, he was practicing the mysterious art of being on vacation. Two days in, he was beginning to like it. He felt like his life had slowed down. There was no urgency. None of the daily pressure to track someone down, ask the right questions, and get results. He could walk across the yard and feel the softness of grass under his feet. Go down to the water and feel sand between his toes. Slide his body into the lake and feel refreshed as he floated on his back and watched the clouds.

It wouldn't last. Tomorrow his sisters and their kids would be here and family chaos would reign. Chris had insisted that he invite Stan Perry and Lily and baby Autumn, so they would be coming out one day, as would Terry Kyle and Michelle and Anna and Lexie. Soon peace and quiet and squabbling birds would be a thing of memory. But today he was going to lie here and vegetate and someone else could attend to the world of bad guys and the world of family and friends.

His only companion was a dog. An obedient, well-trained dog named Fideau. Part Lab, part who knew what? His crime scene dog. That was often how cops got pets. The bad guys got arrested and sent to jail and a sad cat or dog was left behind, destined for the shelter unless it was adopted. Fideau loved kids. Loved swimming in the lake. And for some inexplicable reason, the silly animal loved Joe Burgess. Today, while Burgess napped in the hammock, Fideau was curled up in a patch of sun a few feet away, on guard lest anyone approach his new master. The beast had already protected him from two squirrels and a curious chipmunk.

He was just drifting off to sleep when Fideau started barking and he felt a hand on his shoulder, gently shaking him. He said, "Fideau, quiet," and the dog obeyed. He opened his eyes and for a moment he thought he was seeing a ghost. A small apparition stood beside the hammock. A small, skinny apparition with white blonde braids, pale skin, white shirt, white shorts, and clean white sneakers. A small girl, one his mother would have called a "fairy child." He figured she was eight or nine.

"Excuse me, sir," she said in a small voice. "I didn't want to disturb you, but our phone isn't working and I need to call for help."

"My phone is inside," he said, tipping himself out of the hammock and standing. "What is your emergency?"

Damn. He sounded just like one of those operators in dispatch who sat in a darkened room and dealt with emergencies all day long, not like a father talking to a small, frightened child.

He tried again. "What do you need help with?"

"It's Papa," she said. "He won't wake up."

"What's your father's name, and where are you staying?" he asked, adding, "I'm Joe Burgess. I'm a policeman."

"We're over there." She pointed toward the next cottage. "I'm afraid I don't know our address. Papa's name is Theodore. Ted. Ted Gabbro."

"You don't have a phone?" he asked.

"Papa has a cell phone, but I can't find it." She was on the verge of tears.

"Wait here," he said, "I'll get my phone, and then I'll come back to the cottage with you."

So much for a quiet day. He hurried up the steps and crossed the deck to the cottage. Inside, he quickly put on shoes, grabbed his phone, and rejoined the girl. "Let's go," he said. "What's your name?"

"Arielle," she said. "Ari. I'm nine."

Accompanied by the ever vigilant Fideau, they covered the distance between the two cottages quickly and he followed her inside. Fideau slipped in before he could shut the door. She led him to a bedroom at the back where a man lay in bed. Probably in his fifties, Burgess thought. Burgess examined him quickly. Established that he was still breathing, though possibly in a coma, and made the call to summon EMTs and an ambulance, giving them the number of the fire road and which to turn to take when they got close to the lake.

He'd walked into too many crime scenes not to take note of the room. Perfectly neat. Nothing but a closed suitcase. Nothing on the nightstand. Not a phone. Pills. No watch or water. He wondered why the man's window was open, when it didn't have a screen. They were beside a lake, and Maine mosquitoes were often called the state bird. Then he led the girl back into the main room and settled her in a chair.

It was ten-thirty. Late in the morning for the father of a young child to still be sleeping, even on vacation. "How long did you try to wake him before you came and found me?" he asked.

"Not long. Maybe ten or fifteen minutes," she said. "But he didn't look right and I got scared."

"Does he often sleep so late?"

"Not usually. Just when we're on vacation," she said. "He's tired. He works very hard, so when he didn't get up this morning, I thought I should let him sleep. But then I remembered that he's supposed to meet with Mr. Fenton at eleven, so I tried to wake him." She stared at Burgess with frightened eyes. "And then he wouldn't wake up. Is he okay? Will he be okay? Will the doctors be able to wake him up?"

"I hope so. You were very smart to come and find me."

Burgess hated to be asking her questions an adult should be answering. She was only a child. This should not have to be her problem. But he had no one else to ask.

"What about your mother? Is she here with you?" In his brief walk through the cottage, he hadn't seen any signs of an adult female presence.

The girl shook her head. "They're separated. Getting a divorce. This was my time to be with my papa."

"So it's just the two of you?"

She nodded.

They should call her mother, he thought. *Get her here to care for her daughter until her father was better. If* he got better. What he'd seen in the bedroom didn't look good.

"Does your father have any medical conditions that you know about?"

She nodded. "He's diabetic. He takes shots. But he knows that and he is never careless about his medicine or what he eats." She shook her head solemnly. "Never. But I thought he might need a shot this morning and I couldn't find his medicine bag."

Burgess looked around. The cottage was almost obsessively neat. There were some art materials on the coffee table and two pairs of shoes, one large, one small, by the door. Otherwise, there were no signs of human habitation. He couldn't remember seeing any medical paraphernalia in the bedroom. Maybe it was in the bathroom? Or still in that suitcase?

The girl looked so small and fragile. Such a pale child shouldn't be dressed in white, but in bright colors. Or Fourth of July's red, white, and blue.

"Did you have your breakfast yet?" he asked.

She shook her head. "We don't have food yet. We only got here last night and we brought a pizza with us. We were going to go shopping this morning, when Papa went to meet Mr. Fenton. But it's okay. I'm not really hungry."

Burgess went and checked the refrigerator. The girl was right. Nothing there except a few slices of pizza. Not even milk or juice. So much for her papa being careful about what he ate, never mind taking care of a child. Once the ambulance had come and gotten her father, he would take her back to the cottage and give her breakfast, then drive her to the hospital.

Burgess found it a bit odd that a man with a serious medical condition would isolate himself and a small child in a cottage on a Maine lake, and not even provide food or a way to call for help if there was an emergency. He needed more information, but he didn't want to frighten the child more than she already was. "You said you couldn't find your father's phone. Is that unusual?"

She nodded. "Every night, when he tucks me in—when I'm with him and not my mom, I mean—he reminds me that in case I ever need it, his phone will be right beside his bed." Tears welled up. "He's never careless about that. But when I couldn't wake him, I looked for it, and it wasn't there. It wasn't anywhere in the room. It's not anywhere in the house."

Odd, Burgess thought.

Sirens signaled the arrival of the ambulance, and Burgess told Fideau to stay with Ari while he led the EMTs into the bedroom. He waited while they evaluated the man, told them their patient's name and that he was an insulin-dependent diabetic, and learned where they were taking him. When he followed the stretcher into the other room, Ari was cowering in a corner of the couch, stroking Fideau's head which was in her lap. The dog looked at him and lifted one ear in an inquisitive gesture Burgess read as, "Am I doing the right thing, Boss?"

Burgess said, "Good dog." Then, to Ari, he said, "We'll go over to my cottage, get you breakfast, and then I'll take you to the hospital to see your father."

She nodded. She didn't speak, but she took his hand when he offered it, and he started to lead her out of the cottage. Then he hesitated. Too many things here didn't seem quite right. "Is there a key to the cottage somewhere? I don't like to leave it wide open."

She pointed to a key hanging on a hook just inside the door, then watched him as he checked the windows, closed and locked the open ones, and locked the doors.

"You are very careful," she said. "Is that how policemen are?"

"Sometimes." He held out his hand again. She took it and followed him through the woods to his cottage.

"What does your father do?" he asked.

"He's a scientist."

There were many types of scientists, of course. "What kind of a scientist?"

She grinned, like she was very proud of this answer. "He's a geologist, Mr. Burgess. He's been up here in Maine looking for gold. That's why he is supposed to meet Mr. Fenton. Because he's found something. He says Mr. Fenton will be very excited. Papa says people think there isn't any gold left in Maine and that boy are they going to be surprised."

ALSO BY KATE FLORA

The Thea Kozak Mystery Series

Chosen for Death

Death in a Funhouse Mirror

Death at the Wheel

An Educated Death

Death in Paradise

Liberty or Death

Stalking Death

Death Warmed Over

Schooled in Death

Death Comes Knocking

The Joe Burgess Mystery Series

Playing God

The Angel of Knowlton Park

Redemption

And Grant You Peace

Led Astray

A Child Shall Lead Them

A World of Deceit

ABOUT THE AUTHOR

Kate Flora's fascination with people's criminal tendencies began in the Maine attorney general's office. Deadbeat dads, people who hurt their kids, and employers' discrimination aroused her curiosity about human behavior. That curiosity led her to the world of crime. The author of twenty books and more than twenty short stories, Flora's been a finalist for the Edgar, Agatha, Anthony, and Derringer awards. She won the Public Safety Writers Association award for nonfiction and twice won the Maine Literary Award for crime fiction. ***Death Warmed Over***, her 8th Thea Kozak mystery, was a finalist for the Maine Literary Award. Flora's nonfiction focuses on aspects of the public safety officers' experience. Her two true crimes, ***Finding Amy: A true story of murder in Maine*** and ***Death Dealer: How cops and cadaver dogs brought a killer to justice***, follow homicide investigations as the police conducted them. Her co-written memoir of retired Maine warden Roger Guay, ***A Good Man with a Dog: A Game Warden's 25 Years in the Maine Woods,*** explores policing in a world of guns, dogs, misadventure, and the great outdoors. Her latest nonfiction is ***Shots Fired: The Misconceptions, Misunderstandings, and Myths about police shootings*** with retired Portland Assistant Chief Joseph K. Loughlin. Her latest fiction is ***Schooled in Death,*** her ninth Thea Kozak mystery. Flora divides her time between Maine and Massachusetts.

www.kateclarkflora.com
www.mainecrimewriters.com

facebook.com/katecflora

twitter.com/kateflora

CPSIA information can be obtained
at www.ICGtesting.com
Printed in the USA
LVHW021759270619
622554LV00016B/787

9 781644 57044